ON DAVIS ROW

N.R. WALKER

BLURB

Nearing the end of a suspended jail sentence should unlock a brighter future for CJ Davis, only the chip on his shoulder is as hard to shift as his bad reputation. Born into a family of career criminals who live down Davis Road, an address the cops have dubbed Davis Row, his name alone is like a rap sheet that makes optimism impossible.

Brand-new parole officer Noah Huxley is determined to see the good in men like CJ. After all, he knows firsthand that bad things can happen to good people. His colleagues mock his doe-eyed optimism, but Noah soon sees CJ's bad attitude and bravado are weapons he uses to keep people at a distance.

Both men know one simple mistake can change a life forever. At first glance, they might seem to be polar opposites. Yet underneath, they're not that different at all.

COPYRIGHT

Cover Artist: Marianne Nowicki
Editor: Labyrinth Bound Edits
On Davis Row © 2017 N.R. Walker
Publisher: BlueHeart Press

Warning

Intended for an 18+ audience only. This book contains material that maybe
offensive to some and is intended for a mature, adult audience. It contains
graphic language, explicit sexual content, and adult situations.

Trigger warning

Minor character death. Reader discretion advised

Trademarks Acknowledgment

Glossary of Australian terms

Abattoir: Slaughterhouse, meat processing plant

Arvo: Slang for afternoon

Eftpos: Electronic Funds Transfer Point Of Sale (credit card machine at check out, for example)

Rort: Dishonest practice

Smelt: Past tense spelling of the verb to smell. Smelled.

Maccas: McDonalds

Thongs: Flip flops

Motorbike: Motorcycle

WHAT COULD AN EX-CON AND A PAROLE
OFFICER POSSIBLY HAVE IN COMMON?

On
DAVIS ROW

N.R. WALKER

CHAPTER ONE

NOAH HUXLEY

I WAS EARLY. Yet to be jaded by the system and endless files on society's forgotten and forlorn, I was keen to make an impression. I sat in my car, sipped my coffee and waited for the Hunter Correctional Services office to open. I'd moved from Newcastle to Maitland for this job. Not too far, geographically, but enough emotional distance between me and what I left behind. It also wasn't where I saw myself headed, but the salary was incentive enough. The desire to help those less fortunate still burned in me, and if that was admirable or naïve, only time would tell.

I was really hoping for admirable.

I was also possibly too young to be a parole officer. I'd interviewed well, even though the woman interviewer found my age and doe-eyed optimism amusing. She'd wished me well like it was funny, pursed her wrinkled lips, and mumbled something about the system eating me up and spitting me out. If she thought her words would deter me, then she was sorely mistaken. People like her, attitudes like hers, fuelled me. The fire to prove them wrong burned a little bit brighter.

I knew most other parole officers were older and probably wiser, but most of them were just biding their time
until they could claim a government pension.

I wanted to make a difference.

I was twenty-four years old, and today was my first day
as a government employee—a Community Corrections
Officer was the official title, though most people knew it as a
parole officer. With a quick glance in my rear-view mirror, a
flash of blue-eyed determination stared back at me, and at
five minutes to nine o'clock, I got out of my car and walked
into the office.

A middle-aged woman with a severe black bob haircut
was dumping her handbag on the reception desk with her
mobile phone pressed between her shoulder and her ear,
coffee in one hand, files in another. She wore a navy
cardigan and a frown as she spoke into her phone. It
sounded like she was having a conversation with a teenager
who'd left something on a school bus.

She mouthed an apology to me and continued her
lecture about responsibility and learning hard lessons. I
looked around the small waiting room just as a man down
the hall spotted me and started toward me.

"You must be Noah Huxley," he said, extending his
hand. He reminded me of the boss of the Daily Bugle from
Spiderman, minus the cigar and plus forty kilos. His handshake was soft but his smile was warm.

"I am," I replied, pleased someone was expecting me.

"Dave Baird," he introduced himself. "Come through
this way."

I followed him through the office. He showed me where
the break room was, told me to label any food I might put in
the fridge, and to wash and dry my own coffee cup. "Believe
me, you'd rather hear that coming from me than Sheryl. She

was the one on the phone out the front. She's got four kids and doesn't take any crap, runs this place with military precision. Makes a mean coconut slice, though."

I got the feeling Dave liked to chat.

"Here's your office," he said, opening a door off the hall. "But we'll make a cuppa first and do the rounds of introductions. Then Sheryl can get you set up with passwords and whatnot."

By the time we had coffees made, all the other staff had arrived and I'd been introduced to the other corrections officers and office staff. I soon learned my position was replacing a man named Wayne and that I was the youngest on the corrections officer's team by at least two decades.

Still, my enthusiasm couldn't be swayed.

For the rest of the morning, Sheryl sat with me in my office, showing me the government computer programs we used for reporting and accounting. I was given passwords and a security pass for the car park and my photo ID badge. I filled in work uniform request forms, sorted out employment forms, tax forms, and about another dozen different government forms for everything they did and didn't need to know.

After lunch, Terrell knocked on my open door. "I'm making some work-placement calls this afternoon. Dave thought you might wanna come."

I grinned. "Sure!"

Out of all the other officers, Terrell was probably the youngest. At a rough guess, he looked maybe forty, but it was hard to tell. Those forty years looked like they'd been hard, and whether his bent nose and the scar through his eyebrow were from football or fighting, I didn't know.

Keen to get out into the field, I grabbed my ID badge from my desk, and as soon as I got to the door, Terrell handed me a dozen manila folders. Okay, so 'some' work-placement calls looked more like twelve. I grinned at him and Terrell shook his head at me.

As we drove to the first job site, Terrell told me a bit about procedure and how all the in-house training didn't really prepare anyone for the real job. There was so much legislation and so many rules, boxes to be ticked and the paperwork . . . don't even get him started on the paperwork.

He explained how he also worked as the Indigenous Liaison Officer for some cases, and he'd smiled handsomely when he spoke of his accomplishments. I imagined twenty years ago he would have been hot, given dark hair and dark eyes were my type. And given the wedding band on his finger, I assumed he made someone very happy. I liked him, as far as first impressions went. And as the afternoon wore on, my opinion of him was reaffirmed.

We met case after case, parolee after parolee. Guys who were getting their lives back on track, working hard, honest jobs. One was a tyre-fitter, one worked the back dock of a wholesalers, two worked at the abattoir, two worked on road crews for the local council, one worked at the city library, and one worked at a nursing village helping the old folk manage their gardens.

They seemed like decent guys who just got dealt a shitty hand in life.

I knew firsthand how life could change on a dime. How sometimes all it took was getting laid off work and trying to make easy money to feed a family. Sometimes parents didn't give a shit and kids had to steal stuff to survive. Sometimes they got lost in the system, trampled on by life, blinded by the fact no one seemed to give a rat's arse. Sometimes they were forgotten; sometimes it was desperation or mental illness or addiction that kept company with bad decisions and unfortunate circumstances.

And sometimes good people did bad things. Sometimes they weren't good people at all. Sometimes evil lurked behind blank stares, and sometimes it screamed.

Terrell reminded me of that on my third day tagging along with him. The last case of the day was a home visit, and he said we weren't going to be well received, and he wasn't wrong.

Her name was Traci Coombs and she'd done three years at Delwynia, a women's correctional facility outside of Sydney. "Normally Teresa would handle the female cases." Teresa was another parole officer I'd met on my first day. I hadn't seen her since because she was in Sydney doing some compliance refresher course we were all expected to do at times. "But Ms Coombs is due for a visit," Terrell said. He looked out the windshield at the fibro-clad house in question. "She knows to expect us, but that don't mean she's gonna be happy about it."

And she really wasn't happy.

Terrell knocked on the rickety front door. It opened barely a crack and her warm welcome began with, "What the fuck do you want?"

"Department of Corrections Services," Terrell replied.

The door didn't open any wider. "Where's Teresa?"

"Stuck in a classroom in Sydney," Terrell answered. "You got us this time." The door remained still, a statement of unwelcome. Terrell stood back a little and sighed. "How you doin', Traci? Been okay? Heard you got a job stackin' shelves. They treatin' you okay?"

His tone was softer, gentle. But he never took his eyes off the slit of the open door.

I really did like Terrell. I liked his approach, his

demeanour. He wasn't jaded and apathetic like Dave seemed to be. Dave didn't seem to care one iota about the names in his case files. They were just numbers to him. But Terrell treated each and every case with respect. He even joked with some of them.

"You got a knife behind that door, Traci?" Terrell asked, same calm tone as before.

I took a quick step back from the door, no doubt looking as scared as I was wet behind the ears. *A knife? Jesus Christ!*

Terrell's disposition never changed; neither did his voice. "I sure hope not because then I'll have to write it up, and you don't wanna violate your parole, do ya, Traci?"

Silence.

"Can you step outside please, Traci?" Terrell asked. "We just need to ask the routine questions. You know how it is."

It was almost as if I could hear her weighing up her options. After a few heart-pounding seconds, the door opened some more and Traci stepped out onto the front stoop. She was tall and wiry, too thin, and a waft of cigarette stench billowed out from behind her. Her clothes hung off her, her hair was unwashed and oily, her pale face gaunt and pocked with sores. She looked me up and down, took a drag of her cigarette, and blew the smoke at me. "Who the fuck are you?"

"My name is Noah."

"He took Wayne's job," Terrell added.

Traci nodded. She answered his few questions with short grunts, her arms folded, her eyes wary. She said her job sucked but it was money, Terrell encouraged her to keep working, and reminded her if she needed help with anything to call.

Apparently that was the end of the meeting because she

went back inside and slammed the door behind her. Terrell nodded toward the car, and honestly, I was happy to leave. Feeling a sense of relief to be in the car with the doors shut, I couldn't take my eyes off Traci's house. "Do you think she really had a knife?"

"Probably," Terrell answered. He was writing something in the manila folder assigned to Traci's case. "It's her weapon of choice. She did three years for aggravated assault with a weapon. She stabbed her drug dealer."

I blinked and my stomach felt full of cold sludge.

"Lucky for her, he didn't die or she'd be still inside." Terrell sighed. "Looks like she's using again though. See her skin?"

"The sores?"

He nodded. "And her pupils were dilated. She was twitchy. Typical symptoms of ice."

I shook my head in disbelief, shock. "What happens now?"

"You tell me?" he said, handing me the folder. "What did your training tell you to do in this situation?"

I swallowed hard and tried to remember. "Document the meeting, report findings. Check her parole conditions, and if she's in violation, we notify the police. She'll be rearrested."

Terrell nodded slowly. "Yep. But drug use isn't cited on her parole conditions. She cooperated fully with questions and she's been working now for six months."

"So we make a note of her suspected drug use?"

"Yep. If she's fired from her job because she's high, then we can threaten her with violation codes."

"Because employment is a parole condition," I noted.

Terrell smiled. "You got this down pat already, kid. Soon you'll be out on your own."

I WENT home that night to my half-unpacked house. It was only tiny; just two bedrooms, but it was a detached house with a yard and a carport, and considering I was by myself, it was perfect for me. The house itself was probably a hundred years old, but the kitchen and bathroom got a revamp in the 90s, by the look of the cupboards and tiles. It was just a rental, but it was home for now.

I was too wired to be bothered with boxes of books and DVDs. I had all the essentials unpacked, and that was good enough for now. Plus, I had all weekend to get that shit done. It wasn't like I had friends here or a social life of any kind, or God forbid, a boyfriend . . .

I fell onto the sofa and took a swig of beer. Today had been a bit real. A violent offender could've pulled a knife. What would I do if I was on my own and that happened? Was I ready for this? Did I ever want to be?

I didn't get too much time to think about that because, on Friday morning of my very first week, Dave walked into my office at nine a.m. and dropped a tall stack of files on my desk. "Okay kid, you ready for your first solo cases?"

"Um . . ."

He nodded to the top folder. "Have fun with that one." He smiled at a joke only he knew the punchline to. "A good one to cut your teeth on," he said. "If you're sticking around, you'll need to get familiar with the folk on Davis Row."

CHAPTER TWO

CJ DAVIS

SOME PEOPLE HATED THEIR JOBS, but I loved mine. My boss, Mr Delfio Barese, was whistling in his office and occasionally cursing through an unending pile of paperwork, and I was busy working under the one and only car in the shop. It was a simple car service: change of oil and air filters, replace coolant, and in the older cars, we'd check the points and spark plugs, but in newer ones like this car, we'd check the on-board diagnostics.

Unlike the technology mechanics used today, Mr Barese was old school. He'd owned and run the only mechanic's in Ten Mile Creek for almost fifty years, and he still treated customers today the way he did in the seventies. He made sure each car he serviced was washed afterwards, the windscreen cleaned, the inside vacuumed. The water in the battery would be topped up, if it was an older car, along with the water in the windscreen wiper tank, no extra charge.

He would complain endlessly about how the art of customer service had all but disappeared. "The world just isn't what it used to be," he'd say sadly, waving his hands about as he spoke, in that Italian way he did. So the one rule he'd enforced since day one was that we treat our customers the way they used to be treated, "before the world went to hell" along with "that terrible fast food" and "those phones the kids stare at these days."

His work ethic was great, his attention to detail immaculate, and his penchant for old-school service was admirable. The problem was the customers. There just weren't enough of them.

Ten Mile Creek was a dying town. Ten miles, or sixteen kilometres, out from the ever-growing regional centre of Maitland, Ten Mile Creek was now down to one convenience store, a public school, a takeaway shop, and Barese Mechanical. Sometimes we didn't have a car in the shop for a week. Fuel was the only thing that kept us open, and that was only because Mr Barese said it was too expensive to have the fuel tanks removed.

The two hundred residents of Ten Mile Creek all worked in Maitland, if they worked at all. There was no money in this town. The majority of people who lived here were on dole payments of some kind—pensions, single parent, disability, unemployment. I'd spent my twenty-four years in it, hating every goddamn second. Wishing for better and brighter things but tied to it all the same.

Autumn rain kept the temperatures down and people off the streets, and like always, Ten Mile Creek was dead. Not even tourists stopped here. People out driving through the Hunter scenery preferred prettier towns: ones that catered to the old-world charm with pride and dignity. Ten Mile Creek's shops were rundown, neglected. A lack of funds and care summed up the feel of the place. The occasional Sunday driver'd pass through, but rarely did they stop.

I didn't blame 'em.

I cranked up the radio and wheeled myself up to the sump plug and proceeded to drain the oil from old Mrs Henderson's car. Del had dropped her home, just a block away, with a promise to bring back her car when it was done. All part of the service, he'd said.

He was one of a kind, Mr Barese. As the blackened oil sludged into the bucket, I tried to think of anyone I respected more than Del Barese.

There was no one.

I knew some days there wasn't enough work for the both of us, and I only did three days a week. But he was generous and kind, and for the last nine years, I'd kept my head down and my mouth shut and did the only thing I was ever good at: fixin' cars.

So I went about my business, makin' sure everything was as good as perfect and kinda lost track of time.

"CJ?" Del called out.

Thinkin' he just wanted me to watch the fuel bowsers for a minute, I turned down the volume on the small portable radio I had with me and slid out from under the car on the under-car creeper trolley, only to find he wasn't alone. Gettin' to my feet, I wiped my hands on my overalls and looked at the visitor. Del waved us off, going back to his office, leaving me alone with the stranger.

He weren't much older than me, but he was dressed in suit pants and a button-down shirt, neatly pressed. He'd come in from the rain, obviously, as he ran his hand through his wet hair. Then I noticed his ID badge clipped to his waistband . . . Wayne used to wear one just like it.

There was no way this guy was a PO.

He was too young, too good-looking. Blond hair, blue

eyes, and a jaw that could cut glass. The only parole officers I ever saw were old, worn down, and haggard.

He was sizing me up like they all did. Looking at me like they all did. I'd never seen this guy before in my life—believe me, I'd remember him—and he was already makin' his mind up about me.

Worthless. Trouble. Good for nothing.

I'd heard it all before. It was *all* I'd *ever* heard.

He cleared his throat. "Hi. My name is Noah Huxley. I'm your new parole officer."

Well, shit. *He* was *my* new parole officer? "What happened to Wayne? Finally burn out?"

"I uh, I don't know the reasons he no longer works for the Community Corrections Office. I'm his replacement."

I raised an eyebrow at him. I gave this guy a week before he resigned. No way, no how was he gonna last. I snorted. "Yeah, right." I ignored his pointed stare. "So, read my file? Or do we have to go through everything from the beginning?"

He never broke his stare. "I've read all I need to."

"So, tell me." I sneered at him in his fancy clothes and neatly ironed shirt, his clean-shaven face that looked as privileged as it was handsome. No scars, no bumps, just perfect lines and angles. "Just what did Wayne have to say about me in my file?"

He swallowed and looked around the shop. A droplet of rain ran from his hairline to his jaw, a fascinating path over perfect skin I couldn't help but watch.

He cleared his throat and my gaze shot to his. Had I been caught staring? Checking him out? Was *that* written in my file? He narrowed his eyes at me, and he frowned. "Is there somewhere we can talk privately?"

Oh, great. This'll end well.

I nodded toward the open garage doors that faced the creek at the back and followed him as he walked. He didn't speak for a while. He just looked over the creek and the weeping willow trees that lined it. "It's pretty here," he said.

"Pretty?" I scoffed. "Ain't no one called this town pretty in all my years here."

He—what was his name again? Norman? Nigel? Noah! Yeah, that was it—Noah smiled at the scenery. Ten Mile Creek was a small town on a creek that ran into the Hunter River, and lookin' at it and tryin' to see how Noah might see it, I guessed it could be pretty. The creek, barely a trickle really, was framed by long green grass and green willow trees. It was all green, that was for sure. The town's annual rainfall was almost as high as the unemployment rate and teen pregnancy statistics.

There was a rickety bridge that would probably be scenic, if not covered in graffiti, that led to the other side of the creek, the other side of town. The wrong side of town.

My side of town.

"Hmm," he hummed like he didn't really agree with me. Then looked upward to the sky. "I've never seen so much rain."

"Where you from?"

"Newcastle. So not too far."

"But far enough." God, I could only imagine living in a different town. Even moving from this shithole to Maitland, just fifteen minutes' drive away may as well be another freakin' planet some days.

"Yeah, far enough."

That was a weird answer, or maybe it was the way he said it that made me stop. Like he, some fancy-dressed government worker could understand what it was like.

"Anyway," I said, changing topics. "You takin' on all Wayne's cases?"

He nodded. "Yeah."

"Busy then?"

"Yeah, but I like it. I'm only new at it."

Totally called it. "I gathered."

He shot me a look that was part offence, part defiance. "New doesn't mean stupid."

I laughed at that, and seeing the rain had eased, I stood under the eave outside, took out a ciggie, and lit it. I took a long drag and blew the smoke out toward the creek. "So, what's with the work visit? Wayne never did 'em much. Used to make me come into town."

"Oh." Noah cleared his throat again and opened the manila folder he was holding. "I'm basically doing an introductory visit. And he should have. Wayne, I mean. It's part of your parole conditions."

I smiled at how naïve he was. "Will you speak to Mr Barese?" I took another drag of my cigarette and blew it out. "My boss?"

"Yes." He seemed to find some conviction. "Will he tell me anything you should tell me first?"

I stared at him and sucked back another draw of my cigarette. I knew it. He already had me written off. "I can guess what was in Wayne's file about me. I'm a Davis, right?" I didn't even bother hiding the disdain. "But I ain't done nothing wrong."

Noah kind of blushed. Embarrassed or reprimanded, I didn't know. I didn't care. He'd known me for all of two minutes and already had me pegged as a deadbeat because of my name.

Noah flipped through the papers in the file. "Actually,

Wayne's notes were pretty good. Never missed a meeting, attended all drugs and alcohol counselling—"

"Because I have to." I took one last drag of my cigarette and flicked the butt out onto the wet grass. "Because it's a condition of my parole. I ain't ever taken a drug in my life, yet I gotta go sit in a circle with all them losers and talk about problems I don't even have."

"You were caught—"

"I know what I was busted for. I know what the cops thought. I was there." I pushed off the wall and glared at him. "I did the crime, I'll do the time. What the fuck ever. You wanna speak to Del, then speak to him. If we're done here, I got work to do."

I didn't wait for an answer. I didn't need to. I was done talkin' to him, whether he was done talkin' to me or not. He wasn't gonna write me up for attitude. He was a greenhorn and wouldn't dare cite me because it'd make him look like he was shit at his job.

I got back onto my creeper trolley and slid back under Mrs Henderson's car. I pulled the small radio over and cranked up the volume so this new PO would know I was well and truly done talking. From under the car, I watched his feet. He didn't move for a while, and I knew I had him rattled. I smiled.

Then his feet walked around the car, past me, and to the office door. "Mr Barese?"

"Yes?"

"Do you have a minute?"

"Yes, yes," Mr Barese said. "Come in. Shut the door."

I watched the old office door close, and Noah's polished shoes disappear behind it. I stared at the closed door for a beat too long, then picked up my ratchet and went back to work.

CHAPTER THREE

NOAH

DEL BARESE WAS A SHORT, older Italian man. He was balding, wore glasses and blue overalls, and had thick, stubby fingers stained with oil and grease that he waved around when he spoke. He was loud; his accent still clung to the end of his words. He was seventy-one years old, he told me proudly, and had opened Barese Mechanical in 1963 when he first came to Australia. He'd worked every day of his life, except Sundays, when he'd take his wife to church in Maitland.

He clearly liked to chat, and when I asked about CJ— *Was he ever late? Did he ever not turn up? Has he ever turned up for work under the influence of drugs or alcohol?*—Mr Barese rolled his eyes and waved me off.

"No, no. Never. He's a good boy."

Then he proceeded to tell me everything he knew about his one and only employee.

"He was thirteen or fourteen when he started hanging around my shop," Mr Barese said. "His brothers were trouble, but this boy was different. His home life, it not much good." He shook his head. "See what I'm saying? No one there cared. No school, no food, nobody know, nobody care." He threw his hands up. "So he starts hanging around here during the day, curious at first. Didn't bother anyone, but I'd see him watching. At first I thought he be scoping out my shop for his brothers, yes? Seeing what he could steal or how much money I take that day. So I have two choices." He held up two fingers. "One, I could hunt him away, report him to the police or to the school for truancy. Or two, I could put him to work. If he was gonna be here all day, he might as well be useful, I told him."

"So he's been working here since he was fourteen?"

Del nodded. "Two or three days a week. I can't do what I used to. My mind is good but my body . . ." He waggled his hand in a so-so manner. Then he sighed, long and loud. "All it takes is for one person to care, you know? Just one person. To make all the difference. No one cared for that boy. No one. But I pay him. Maria, my wife, she feed him some-times. Maybe I changed his life, I dunno. But he's a good boy. If the police knew him instead of write him off, they would know he's a good boy. But they just think 'Oh, he lives on Davis Row, he's one of them.'" Del's tone, and the look on his face, was one of distaste. He looked at the file I was holding like it contained nothing but lies, systematic black-and-white lies. "Whatever happened to not judging a book by its cover? Innocent until proven guilty?" He sighed like he understood the weight of the world all too well.

Del was right. One person was all it took. One person to care, one person to smile, one person to say hello, to ask how they were, to take a minute. It really could save a life.

"It sounds like you did."

"Did what?"

"Changed his life."

Del smiled, a little teary. "He's a good boy. If it's quiet

here at the shop, he goes next door to my house and will mow my lawn, cut my trees. He knows I can't do it no more. I never ask him; he just do it. Tell me, what kind of criminal does that?"

I couldn't answer.

"No criminal, that's who. He made a mistake, is all. But he's a good boy."

I nodded slowly. "Thank you for your time, Mr Barese."

He smiled as he waved me off, probably knowing he'd given me a lot to think about. And he had.

I was due to go back to the office, even though it was the last thing I felt like doing. I drove to the T intersection on the highway where a sign declared Maitland was sixteen kilometres to the right or other smaller satellite towns that dotted the Hunter hinterlands were to the left. And for a long moment, I considered turning left and just driving until my mind cleared. But with a sigh and a sense of duty, I flicked the blinker on to turn right and headed back into town.

The rain had stopped, leaving the roads dark grey and puddled, and the countryside was lush and wet. I drove well under the speed limit, took my time to let things mull over in my mind, while I drove back to Maitland.

The clear picture I had painted in my head from the CJ Davis in that file was now abstract. How easy it was to read a case file and assume we knew the outlines of a character, the colours within, the brushstrokes that defined them. From meeting CJ himself, I'd assumed he was everything his case file said he was. He was all attitude and bravado, the chip on his shoulder a weapon he used to keep people distant and wary.

But speaking to Mr Barese, the picture changed completely. According to someone who'd known CJ for ten years, who spent a lot of time with him, CJ was thoughtful, honest and kind, hard-working, and well-meaning. *He made a mistake, is all*, Mr Barese had said.

God, hadn't we all.

I knew all too well how one stupid mistake could change a life forever. Could change a lot of lives. One stupid mistake and the path you're on changes direction, sets a new course. There are no maps or a compass for that, you just navigate the best you can.

Is that what CJ was doing? Navigating the best he could?

Mr Barese certainly thought so. His file said otherwise, but what did a skewed perception make when the previous parole officer never bothered to look beyond the cover?

What story did CJ Davis really tell?

What story did any of my file cases really tell?

I had a dozen cases just like CJ. What had I assumed of all of them? I'd tried to be open-minded, and I thought I had been. Each case was its own; each case was a person with a history and most likely a family or someone in their life who loved them.

I found myself back in my office going through each file, remembering their names, looking specifically at what their significant others had said about them when interviewed. I looked between the lines of the reports Wayne had done. By all accounts, Wayne had left this job burned out. He'd stopped caring years ago. Filling in forms and ticking boxes, doing the bare minimum to get his weekly wage.

I vowed to do better. I promised myself, right then and there, I'd do better. I'd ask different questions, better questions. I'd treat each case, each *person*, better.

And maybe it was the doe-eyed optimism I had; maybe

it was a Band-Aid over the gaping wound of my own past that made me want to fix the future.

It wasn't until Sheryl knocked on my door at ten past five and told me it was home time that I realised I'd had my head in paperwork for hours. So, I shut everything down and logged out, took my jacket, and drove home.

My house still wasn't unpacked. I had every intention of spending the weekend unpacking everything and making my house a home. I'd go shopping even and buy groceries and maybe a picture for the wall. Something to celebrate the end of my first week. Now that I'd been paid, I could. Nothing too fancy, but something.

Surprisingly, or not unsurprisingly, I finished unpacking on Friday night. I didn't have much, admittedly: just a few boxes of books and DVDs, some kitchen utensils, and some towels. Everything else I'd already unpacked during the week because I'd needed it. I didn't have much, the house itself wasn't much, but the lease was mine, for six months at least.

On Saturday, I spent the day getting groceries for the week, and I even found a new shirt for work, but I didn't find anything that caught my eye for my house. Not that I *had* to buy something. The pale yellow walls were okay, if a little old and scuffed. The colour scheme, the kitchen, the bathroom—hell, the whole interior—were products of the 90s renovators' boom. Yes, it was old, but it was clean and warm in the cooling autumn weather.

It certainly wasn't winning any *Fancy Living* awards, but it was better than some places I'd lived in.

On Sunday, I spent the day driving around. I wanted to get familiar with the area, so I drove out to Ten Mile Creek, past the turn-off I'd hesitated at the other day, and drove through all the tiny satellite towns. They were picturesque, quaint even. Though I had to wonder how much life they had left in them. Dairy towns, farming communities in the rolling green hills of the Hunter.

In one town, there was a small market stall set up aimed at the Sunday drivers. They sold homemade cakes and fresh-grown oranges and scented beeswax candles. The young woman behind the counter had sunshine and fresh hope in her smile, and it was hard not to feel her enthusiasm for her wares. I bought a bag of oranges, a carrot cake, and two lemon-and-eucalyptus scented candles. Not exactly what I was hoping to buy myself for a housewarming gift, but driving back into town, I was happy I'd bought them.

I turned off the main road and drove into Ten Mile Creek. I didn't know what made me do it. Curiosity, most likely.

The main street was dead, except for two younger kids walking from the corner store with what looked like some hot chips, and I thought that sounded like a good idea. I parked out the front and went inside and stepped back into the 1970s. Well, it felt like it. The old signs, the worn lino floor, the glass-cabinet counters. I would imagine when this business finally shut down, most of the fitout could go into a museum.

But the hot food smelt pretty good, and I could see why. It was straight out of the 70s too. Works burgers, rissole and gravy burgers, Chiko rolls, and corn jacks. Jesus. It was a menu for a coronary special.

The guy behind the counter looked like he slapped grease straight from the fryer into his hair. "What can I get ya, mate?" he asked.

Figuring I'd eat healthy all next week, I went big. "Works burger, please."

"Beetroot and pineapple?"

"Yes, please."

"Won't be long," he said and was soon sizzling a beef patty on the grill.

The store had three rows of shelves filled with sparse convenience items. I gathered that most residents of Ten Mile Creek did their shopping in Maitland and this place was a last resort for forgotten groceries. There was bread and toilet paper, tins of soup and beans. Weet-Bix and coffee and the usual array of chocolates, lollies, and packets of chips, and fridges of milk and Coke. I wasn't looking for anything in particular, and I certainly wasn't going to pay the ridiculous prices they were asking.

"Hey, CJ. The usual?"

"Yeah, thanks, Bart."

I turned the same time he did. I heard the name CJ and maybe he sensed someone else in the store, but we were soon staring at each other.

"Hey," I said, trying to be cheerful.

He, on the other hand, sneered. The man behind the counter handed over a packet of cigarettes and CJ handed him a fifty-dollar note. He took his cigarettes, pocketed his change, and walked out without so much as a word.

"Hey," I said again, following him out the door. "Hey, CJ!"

He stopped, standing halfway between me and a dirt bike. He turned on his heel and glared at me. "What?"

Well, I assumed he didn't like me too much, but the look on his face was closer to hate. I had to admit, I was kinda shocked to see it. "I was just, uh, I was just passing through . . ." *And what? Thought I'd say hi? God, what the hell was I doing?* "I was just driving around, getting to know the area. I went out to Bakersfield and Kirkton. Scenic but not exactly thriving."

CJ stared at me. I was babbling. Like an idiot.

"I thought I'd try a burger . . ."

He raised an eyebrow that questioned my sanity.

I was questioning my sanity.

"I'm trying to familiarise myself with things that might give me a better understanding of the people that live here."

"You think this town represents me?" He looked up and down the deserted street at the town that was forgotten, abandoned.

"No, that's not what I meant."

"Then what did you mean?"

"That it helps me get a better understanding of why people do what they do. I want to see the bad circumstances that produce bad decisions."

He squinted at me. "Not everyone who does bad things are bad people."

"I never said they were." I stared at him and he stared right back. "I don't believe that, not for one second."

He kept on staring.

"Sometimes bad things happen to good people."

God, why was I saying this?

CJ turned to stare at the peeling paint on the wall, like I'd plucked at a raw nerve. Then, like he was pissed at himself, he angrily tore at the wrapper on his cigarette packet and stabbed a cigarette into his mouth. His lighter wouldn't work, so he shook it and mumbled a curse at it, then tapped it against his hand.

"You shouldn't smoke," I said. "It's bad for your health."

He put the lighter back to his cigarette, glared at me, and lit it, first go. He drew back a breath then blew the smoke out at me. "You shouldn't tell a smoker to quit. It's bad for your health."

I smiled. "Anyway, what's there to do around here?"

"Around here?" He looked broadly around the street. "Absolutely nothing. Kids smoke weed down by the creek, if you're inclined. Or you can walk along the railway tracks. No trains anymore though, so if you're lookin' to do yourself in that way, you're shit outta luck."

I shook my head slowly but was still smiling. There was something about his fuck-you attitude I found funny. Or related to. I wasn't sure which. "Not inclined for either, but thanks. I meant in Maitland. What is there to do in Maitland?"

"Do I look like a tourist information guide?"

"Yep. Though your uniform could use some work."

He looked down at what he was wearing. His jeans were dirty, his white shirt not much better, his black denim jacket was now grey and frayed at the cuffs. He shot me another glare. "Fuck you."

I bit my lip to stop from smiling. Or from saying 'yes please.'

Jesus Christ, Noah. Get a grip on yourself.

He took a drag of his cigarette. "You know," he continued, blowing the smoke out into the street. "A few pubs and nightclubs in town go all right. HQ on Abbott Street's probably the pick of 'em."

"Okay, thanks. I haven't gone out yet. I might check it out." The truth was, I hadn't been out anywhere in a long time.

His lip twitched but he took another drag of his cigarette before he could smile. God forbid he be pleasant to anyone. "Suppose I can expect another visit this week?"

He knew damn well those appointments were to be impromptu, without warning. I smirked at his obvious attempt to trick me. "Probably."

He gave me nothing more than a 'whatever' roll of his

eyes before he turned and walked away. I watched him, his wary shoulders, his loping gait as he strode to his dirt bike and swung his leg over it. He took a last drag of his cigarette before flicking it into the gutter, knocked the bike stand back with his heel, kick-started his bike, and revved it, staring at me like a dare. Then he took off down the street, no helmet, not one care given.

"Mister? Your burger's ready," the man from the store called out.

Smiling at the direction CJ had gone, I turned and went inside.

CHAPTER FOUR

CJ

I KNEW my old man'd be calling on Thursday at four. He always did. It was his one allowed phone call a week, and I dreaded it every time. I mean, he was my father. I guess some part of me loved him, deep down, but on the surface, I was real glad he was doin' time.

Actually, in my entire life, I'd only ever known him to be on the outside six or seven times. And each time he was at home, he made my life miserable. It became very apparent, even from an early age, I was better off without him. We all were. Not that my brothers thought so. But I wasn't like my brothers. They adored him, idolised him, and were stoutly protective of him.

Where I, on the other hand, saw him for what he was.

I brought some more wood inside and stoked up the fire. Our house was old, and if the wind blew hard enough, there'd be drafts comin' up through the floorboards. The fibro cladding on the outside was old, faded, and did little to stop the cold seeping through. And this winter was supposed to be a cold one.

I looked at Pops, sitting in his old recliner. "You warm enough?"

"Yep," he said, giving me a smile. "No need to fuss."

I threw another log on the fire. There was plenty of reason to fuss. Pops was my one good thing. He basically raised me. Saved my hide plenty of times by stoppin' my older brothers from givin' me a flogging. And from my dad too. Pops was the one who kept me fed when I was real little, and he taught me how to cook. Not that I was any kind of fancy cook, but I could keep us both fed well enough now it was my turn to look after him.

"Want me to put your show on?" I asked, picking up the TV remote.

He looked at his watch. "Guess so. It's almost four."

Almost four.

My stomach twisted. I clicked on the TV and made sure it was on the right channel. Just as the theme music to *The Young and the Restless* started, the phone rang. I raced to the kitchen and snatched up the receiver. He didn't like it if I let it ring too many times. "Hello?"

"Hey, boy." The sound of his voice was familiar in an unpleasant way. Raspy and hoarse and always sounded like he knew the punch line to your joke.

"Hey, Dad. How's your week been?"

"Same old. Got good news but."

Oh no.

"Got parole. Comin' home, boy."

I swallowed down the lump in my throat and tried to act happy at the news. "That's great. When?"

"A week today."

A week?

"Make sure there's beer in the fridge waitin' for me,

won't ya, boy? And steak. Want some real meat, none of that prison shit."

I had no idea where I was supposed to get the money to pay for all that, not that he'd care. "Sure thing. Sounds good."

"Is Pops there?"

"Yeah, he's watching TV. Just stoked the fire up for him. 'S gettin' cold."

He grunted something I couldn't quite hear, then he barked down the phone. "You'll pick me up from the train station, wontcha, boy?"

Maybe I could borrow Mr Barese's car . . . "Yeah, of course."

"I'll need a ticket, too."

I bit back a sigh but leaned my forehead against the wall. "Sure. I'll let you know the details next week."

"Good lad."

And he hung up.

I slammed the receiver down. "Goddammit." With a heavy sigh, I fell onto the couch.

Pops took one look at me. "He coming home?"

I nodded. "Yep. Next week."

I could feel Pops' eyes on me, but I didn't look at him. I didn't need to. "Don't worry, CJ. He won't be out long. Give him a month. He ain't ever out much longer than that."

I was so pissed I couldn't speak. I couldn't even unclench my jaw. I stared at the TV, at Pops' silly show he watched, not seeing any of it. I didn't realise for how long until Pops stood up, his legs unstable. "Better start some grub."

"I'll do it," I said. "Lost track of time, sorry. You sit down and yell the answers out to me." *Family Feud* had started, his second favourite show. I went into the kitchen and took the last three potatoes out of the cupboard and started peeling 'em. "I'll have to get some more veggies tomorrow," I said loud enough for him to hear.

But he spoke behind me, "CJ," and I almost jumped out of my skin. He put his hand on my shoulder. "Sorry. Didn't mean to scare ya."

I turned back around, roughly peeling the potatoes in the sink. "'S okay. Didn't hear ya come in. Aren't ya watching your show?"

He waved his hand at the door, dismissing it. "It'll be all right, CJ. He won't be here long."

I sighed and let my shoulders fall. "We just had everything goin' good, didn't we?"

He nodded slowly. "And we'll have it just fine when he's gone again."

I looked at him then. He looked so much older than his sixty-three years. He was a full head shorter than me, silver hair, wrinkled skin, and his once-blue eyes were now grey. They'd been a hard-as-hell sixty-three years, and now, sober and clean for twenty-two years, only for emphysema to knock him on his arse. It wasn't fair.

A good man. The best there ever was.

And here he was again, looking after me. "I know. We'll be all right. I'll make sure of it." I went back to peeling the potatoes. "Bangers and mash okay?"

"Perfect."

"Go back and sit down. You know the cold air don't do your lungs any favours."

He waved me off as he shuffled back to his seat by the fire. I could hear him wheezing until I started frying the sausages. I made sure Pops had at least three veggies a night, and much to his disgust, I didn't cook with salt. He didn't need to add heart disease to his list of problems.

I served us up our dinner, then cleaned up afterwards. Pops was in bed early, like every night, and I made sure his room was warm enough. I watched some lame reality TV show in hopes of seeing some shirtless guys, or even naked ones.

It was pretty fucking sad when that was the extent of my sex life. I had to wait till my Pops was asleep in bed before I could perv on late night television. If I was lucky, there'd be an R-rated movie on SBS. And if I was real lucky, it'd be a gay movie.

But tonight I was shit outta luck. It was a double-header of some soccer series. Just my freakin' luck. I stabbed the Off button on the remote and took my sorry, frustrated self to bed.

I GOT up early to stoke the fire so the house was warm when Pops woke up. He normally shuffled out before seven, so I started his pot of porridge. He liked his oats every morning, and I liked him eating something hot and substantial. He needed more meat on his bones.

After we'd eaten and I'd cleaned up, I spent a few hours outside. I ran the mower over the front yard, hopefully for the last time before winter. I made a mental note to make sure Del's was done too. *Maybe I could go run the mower over his lawn this afternoon . . .*

I mean, our house wasn't anything flash. But it was still my home. I could still make it look the best it could look. I'd fixed the front garden as much as I could without spending any money. I'd weeded, pruned—hacked, probably, but whatever—and mostly tidied. It had never looked so good. The front fence was fallin' apart, and most of the palings were missing, so I fixed that up the best I could too. We weren't ever gonna win no 'best house' awards, but I didn't care.

The house needed new paint, a new roof, new plumbing, a new bathroom . . . hell, it needed bulldozing. But it was our house. It wasn't much, but it was Pops' and my home.

Around ten-ish, I went back inside, knowing Pops might want a cup of tea or maybe something to eat. I put the kettle on and remembered some washing that needed hangin' out, so I went and did that. The old washer just about shook the house off its stumps, and it didn't spin the clothes real dry anymore, but at least it still washed 'em clean.

"Dunno how much longer that washing machine's gonna last," I said as I came back inside and walked into the kitchen.

"It's been around since Jesus was a boy," Pops said, still watching his telly. The house was small enough that a conversation could be had no matter which room we were in.

I smiled. We'd had that washing machine all my life. I was surprised it still worked at all. "True." I poured the boiling water into his old teapot and fixed the lid. "Want a piece of toast with marmalade?"

"Nah, thanks anyway," he answered. "Maybe for lunch."

I took his teapot and favourite cup and sat it on the small table next to his seat just as a car pulled up out front. "Is someone here?" Pops asked.

I looked through the curtains. There was a white Commodore stopped right outside our front gate. "Yeah," I answered quietly. "Looks like a government car."

"They lost or something?" Pops asked, pouring himself a cuppa.

Normally I'd think yes. No one came down our road. Ever. Unless the coppers were bringing my old man home after a bender, but he was still in the clink. And this weren't the police.

Then the driver's door opened and I saw who got out. *Blond hair, blue eyes, and a jaw that could cut glass.*

Oh, hell no.

"What the hell does he think he's doing here?"

"Who is it?" Pops looked up at me from his seat and I saw a flicker of uncertainty, of fear, in his eyes. When he put his tea down, his hands shook more than normal. He started to get up, but I stopped him.

"Nothing to be worried about. You stay there. It's just my new PO."

"I thought you said he was all right?"

Is that what I'd said? He was all right, all right. Young and hot—for a government worker. Filled his work shirts out nicely, and his pants too. He had a crooked smile and his eyes would squint when he smiled. And he had a freckle above his right eyebrow that I wanted to touch. The edge of his jaw made him look a bit tougher than he was and I wanted to run my thumb across it. And he smelt nice, which'd always been my Achilles heel . . . Anyway, that was beside the point. That was stupid thinkin' and good for nothing but trouble. "Well, he *was* all right. But he ain't welcome here."

CHAPTER FIVE

DIRECTIONS TO CJ DAVIS' home address weren't exactly difficult to follow. Go over the railway lines, head out of town for half a kilometre, turn right onto Davis Road, and follow the dirt track a few hundred metres down past the overgrown trees and greenery to the one and only house at the end of the road.

According to rumour at the office, it had been named Davis Road after the only family who had lived on it for a hundred years. And for generations, the Davises were known for their lack of respect for the law, and if the rumours were to be believed, every single one of them had done time behind bars. All of the Davises, except for CJ, that is.

No, he never did time. He got a suspended sentence instead.

And looking at the state of the house, it was the original home. It was old. Neither weather nor time had been kind to it. Gravity, either. It had a bit of a lean, the roof was more rust than tin, and the cladding on the outside walls hadn't seen paint since before WWII by the look of it. It was now a damp grey colour, despite the sunshine. But the lawn was mowed, the garden tidy, and someone had made an effort with the front fence. There was a glimmer of house-pride there, underneath the beaten exterior.

I walked up the narrow concrete path with CJ's case file in my hand and nervous butterflies in my belly. I don't know what it was about him, but something about him stuck with me. Like a pulled thread on a woollen blanket, holding its own at the moment, but it could unravel if I wasn't careful.

The front door opened before I could knock, and CJ stood in the doorway. His arms were crossed; his jaw was set. "What do you want?"

"Hello to you too."

He didn't reply. He didn't move.

His bravado didn't fool me. "I was hoping our scheduled meetings could be done in a less official capacity. I'm just here to have a quick chat, and I'll be on my way."

He stared.

"Or I could be an arsehole and make you come into the office, and if you miss one appointment, the police can give you a ride to prison for the remainder of your sentence. Your choice."

His nostrils flared, and someone inside—a frail voice—said, "Let him in, CJ."

CJ took another moment to glare at me before he stepped back, holding the door for me, allowing me to pass.

The first thing I noticed was the small living room. Old cream walls, probably once white, carpet that had survived the seventies, an old potbelly stove in one far corner, a square box TV in the other. Close to the fire, an old man sat on a single recliner that looked almost as old as him, and a mismatched two-seater couch sat near the front window. Nothing else would have fit. I could see a small kitchen through one door and a hall. It was old, but it was clean and it was warm.

I headed for the couch but smiled at the old man and offered him a handshake before I sat down. "My name's Noah Huxley."

"Nice to meet ya," he said with a wheeze and a smile. "Name's Ronnie, but you can call me Pops. Everyone does."

I learned two things immediately. Pops was a nice old guy. And he was sick. I was no doctor, but by his constant wheezing and struggle for breath, my guess was emphysema. He was very thin, frail even. He had grey wispy hair, was a little unshaven, but there was a sharp light in his eyes. His body might be failing, but his mind was still there.

"You come all this way to see CJ?" Pops asked.

"Yeah, thought I'd take a drive."

"Well, that's mighty nice of ya." He looked at the folder I was holding. "Whatcha got there?"

"This is CJ's file," I said. I held the file out towards CJ, who still stood by the door. "Can take a look if you like. There's not much in there."

CJ didn't look at me. "Pops, you warm enough?"

Pops nodded. "Yeah, of course."

And with that, CJ was gone out the front door. Pops gave me a smile. "Boy worries over me too much. He's a good boy. Keeps me warm and fed." He nodded toward the door CJ had walked out of, then started to cough.

"Can I get you a glass of water?"

He shook his head and waved me off as he kept coughing. And he just kept coughing, so I went into the kitchen, found a glass on the sink, filled it with tap water, and took it back to him. He sipped it and settled enough, though he still wheezed and spluttered. "Thanks."

"That's okay."

He nodded toward the door. "If you came to speak to CJ . . ." He wheezed some more. "Can you tell him I'm just going to lie down for a bit?"

"Yeah, of course."

I helped him get to his feet and watched as he gingerly made his way to the hall, then I took my file and walked out the way I'd come.

I found CJ around the side of the house at the old shed that was once probably the garage. It was too small for a car now, barely big enough to house his dirt bike and an old lawnmower. He was pretending to be busy with a spanner and a spark plug, and he was very deliberately pretending I wasn't there.

"Uh, Pops has just gone for a lie-down. He wanted me to tell you. He was coughing pretty bad, so I got him a glass of water."

The spanner slid off the spark plug and he took a measured breath. "I can look after him."

"And you do quite well," I said. "He said you do everything for him."

CJ knelt beside his bike, knees spread, and refitted the spark plug and worked the ratchet to tighten it in. The muscles in his forearms bunched, his hips flexed a little, and his dirty white shirt rode up so I could see the skin above his low-slung jeans.

God, he was . . . a fucking client who I should not be checking out.

He jumped to his feet and I snapped out of my own head. "Whaddya want?" he asked, brushing past me as he walked back out. He put a cigarette between his lips and I was transfixed. Smoking was a filthy habit, but I'd never wanted to be a cigarette so much in my life.

"Oh, that reminds me," I said, ignoring his question. "Thanks for the bar recommendation. Had a great time."

The lighter stopped just shy of his cigarette.

Oh, what's that? A chink in the armour of CJ Davis?

He lit the cigarette and blew out the smoke. "You went there?"

"Last Sunday night. They have a happy hour at eight."

He stared at the line of trees to our right and remained utterly silent.

"Did you send me to the only gay bar in Maitland for a laugh? Thinking I'd be horribly offended? Because the back room was just what I needed, if you know what I mean . . ."

His nostrils flared and I bit back a smile. The truth was, I had two drinks, chatted to a few guys, nothing more, and left very much alone. But I sure as hell wasn't telling him that. He told me to go there as a joke. Maybe he thought *I* was a joke. Maybe he thought all gay people were. He had no idea I was gay, so maybe he thought sending me there was an insult?

"You got a problem with gay people, CJ?"

His gaze shot to mine, a hard, cold stare. He bit on his cigarette and drew back hard. "Fuck you."

Maybe there was something underlying in his anger, it was hard to tell. Maybe the nerve I'd hit was a little too raw? "Have you been there?" I asked. "To HQ?"

I didn't miss the way his eyes flickered back to the house, like the walls or the old man inside might hear. But then he glared at me, took one last drag of his cigarette, and flicked it away. "You done?"

"Yeah, I'm done." I took two long steps and stopped in front of him. "Next week's appointment is at the office. You know the drill. If you can't make it, you need to check in with me first, okay?"

His jaw bulged. "Whatever."

"You have a drugs and alcohol meeting next Thursday. Why don't you make it after that, to save you a second trip into town."

He folded his arms, making his jacket stretch across his shoulders, defining his biceps. It also made his shirt ride up at the front, revealing a dusting of dark hair below his navel.

God, this was so inappropriate. I didn't know what it was about this guy that sang to me. Maybe it was his stunning rough looks or how he had no idea how good-looking he was. Maybe it was his bad-boy image that I was drawn to. Wouldn't be the first time.

Even if there was any remote chance he was into guys, and then by some remote chance he was single, nothing could happen between us. We had a professional relationship that could not be violated, in any shape or form. Was that what attracted me to him? Wanting what I simply couldn't have?

"You all right there?" he asked, catching me checking him out. He had a look of indignation on his face, but there was also a spark of daring in his eyes. The tips of his ears were a red that matched the colour of his lips. He stood with his feet spread and his arms crossed. It was purely defensive, confrontational even, but he wasn't threatening to me. He was a challenge, a puzzle I wanted to solve.

I met his gaze and smiled. "Nah. Not *all* right. Only down one side."

He rolled his eyes but I got a small smile.

"See you next week." I walked back to my car, not waiting for a reply. I wasn't expecting one. I smiled the whole drive back to Maitland.

I had no clue what I was doing. I was new to this job and probably in way over my head. I knew I couldn't pursue anything personal with any case, but that still didn't mean I couldn't help. And there was truth in the saying 'you catch more flies with honey than vinegar.' Meaning I would help the likes of CJ more if he saw me as a friend rather than an authority figure who represented everything that reminded him of his mistakes.

The same went with all my case files. I didn't want to see any of them go back to jail. I wanted them to get their lives on track and be active members of a functioning society.

It was that optimism that made the rest of the day fly. I saw all my cases and left them all with smiles and a handshake. I felt positive and energised, and whereas my colleagues in the office were heading home for the weekend, dragging themselves out the door, I was pumped.

I got home, decided on pizza and a six-pack for dinner, and not even a night by myself in front of the footy on TV could dampen my mood. I was used to my own company. I rather enjoyed it, if I was being truthful. Sure, I had moments of loneliness and there were times I wished I had someone to share things with, but ultimately, I was alone.

I had been for years.

When the footy was over and some lame movie had started, I was lying on the couch with my phone. I scrolled through Facebook, looking at what people I used to know were doing now. People I used to call friends.

Family.

No one mentioned me; no one tagged me. No one missed me.

I checked my messages. There were none.

I sighed, not sure how I felt about that.

Hurt. Regret. Guilt.

But not surprised.

I considered going out, finding some random hook-up at HQ but couldn't have been bothered. I had a pretty decent buzz from the beer and I knew any more and I'd regret it tomorrow.

I also couldn't be bothered with the whole hook-up scene. Finding some random guy, making small talk, asking awkward questions . . . it didn't have to be so complicated. I grabbed my old laptop and, doing something I hadn't been able to afford before now, found a famous porn subscription site and bought myself a membership. I'd only ever scoured free porn sites before. I'd seen short clips of these longer videos with famous stars in them, but I'd never had the money to pay for the full subscription.

And good Lord. One movie in and I doubted I'd ever need to leave the house again.

I made a mental note to buy more self-care products and added lube and tissues to my grocery list.

ON SATURDAY, I went for a run, did my laundry, cleaned my already tidy house, and got my groceries. All before lunch.

In the afternoon, I took a walk down to the local park, which backed onto the sport fields. There were a few teams of men training for soccer, and it occurred to me that if this was my new start, I needed new hobbies and new friends.

Not that I'd played soccer since I was a kid, but I was reasonably fit and I was sure it was nothing I couldn't handle. So, feeling like a new kid at school, I walked over and watched the game, and when it was done, I introduced myself.

I told them I was new in town and keen to play, and as it

turned out, this was their signing-up day, and thankfully, they were looking for players. Training was Tuesday nights at six; first game was on Saturday. The team captain was a guy named Zach, and he seemed friendly enough. All the other guys were, at a guess, between twenty and thirty years old, with varying degrees of fitness, and I could see myself being friends with them. There were a bunch of names I'd probably never remember: Davo, Chris, Gibbo, Foxy, Kamahl, and one guy with a particularly nice smile, Gallan. If that was his first name, his last name, or a nickname, I had no clue. But he was cute and his gaze lingered a little longer than necessary.

Yes, making new friends was a great idea.

By the time I got home, I was feeling pretty damn good. Fresh air, exercise, conversation, and even a laugh was a bloody good way to spend an afternoon. I made myself a stir-fry for dinner, settled in bed with my laptop, my new self-care supplies, and my new gay porn subscription.

By the time I fell asleep, I almost had myself convinced that I wasn't utterly alone.

I CARRIED my optimism with me into next week. Even the mountains of paperwork didn't bother me too much. Without any bitching or the long-suffering sighs I could hear from the other offices, I just trudged along, report after report, file after file, one at a time until the pile was done.

Tuesday night, I put on my new soccer boots and was ridiculously excited to go to training. The evening was cool, and I tried not to let it bother me too much that my team-mates were mostly already friends with each other and I was the new kid. We started with a jog around the soccer fields, then some simple ball exercises. It was pretty apparent I was rusty, given it had been over a decade since I'd played. But the guys were forgiving and encouraging, and by the end of our first training session, I was glad I'd signed up. Exhausted, but glad.

When we were packing up our gear, Gallan chose the spot next to me to stand while he stuffed his shin pads into his backpack. He was taller than me, with floppy brown hair, and wore an ever-present smile. "Have fun?"

"Yeah, it was great," I answered. "Though I think a jog every day's in order. I didn't realise I was so unfit."

He nodded sympathetically. "Yeah, it can get away from ya."

"I think I should be goalie until I can get through training without wanting to hurl."

He laughed at that, but then he shrugged. "We normally grab a beer after the game on Saturday arvos. You up for that?"

If it was an invitation to be a teammate, a friend, or something more, I didn't care. I was up for any or all. "Sounds good."

"You're new to town, yeah?"

I nodded. "Yep. Been here for a few weeks."

"Where from?"

"Newcastle."

"Oh, that's not too far," he said, like it couldn't possibly be a life-changing move.

"No, not too far at all," I lied. The truth was, it wasn't far in kilometres, but the emotional mileage was huge.

The team was dispersing, saying goodbyes, so we had no reason to stay and chat. Gallan started walking to his car, but he gave me a parting glance and smile. "See ya Saturday."

I wasn't blind or stupid. There was definitely interest there. A swoop of exhilaration tightened in my belly. "Sure thing."

I went home, almost giddy. It was ridiculous, but I think I was actually happy. Though I couldn't get something out of my head. When I'd told CJ I'd moved from Newcastle, he immediately understood the significance of even the smallest distance. Gallan simply brushed it aside.

I didn't know what it meant, but it was something that gnawed at my periphery for the next few days.

CJ was due to come into the office on Thursday. I knew he had the compulsory drugs and alcohol meeting to attend first, but with every minute ticking down to five o'clock—the cut-off time—his absence made me nervous.

Out of all my cases, I wanted him to succeed the most.

I tried to keep them all equal. They each had potential, and I had equal hopes for each and every one of them. But CJ was different. If it was because I wanted him to walk through those doors to prove to me that he was worthy or to prove it to himself, I wasn't sure. And I hadn't yet figured out why I'd put myself in that equation at all.

"You almost done?" Terrell asked.

I stared at the door. It was raining outside; maybe that's why he was late. "Yeah, almost."

Terrell nodded slowly. "Who're ya missing?"

"CJ Davis."

"A no- show?"

I looked at my watch and sighed. He had five minutes. "Maybe."

Terrell hummed. "Sometimes it doesn't matter how much we wish they'd do the right thing. No matter what we do for 'em, the responsibility comes down to them. We can't physically make 'em walk through that door."

Disappointment soaked in my chest like a sodden sponge. "I was sure he'd be here."

Just then, the front door pushed open and a very wet CJ barrelled inside. He shook his head, spraying a halo of water around him. His leather jacket was slicked wet, his jeans much the same. Water pooled at his feet.

He looked like a puppy that had fallen in its water dish. A very cute puppy that huffed and glared at the rain outside. Terrell clapped my shoulder as he walked away, and I stood up. "Raining much?" I asked, unable to stop my smile.

"Fuck you," CJ said.

I could feel the other officers turn our way at his slur, but all I could do was laugh. That cute puppy's bite was playful at best. I pulled a chair out for him. "Take a seat."

He squelched in the seat as he sat. He really was soaked through. "Man, it's pissing down out there."

"I can tell."

He ignored me. "Can't be here long. Five thirty's the last bus and I gotta be on it. Plus the only bus stop to Ten Mile Creek is from High Street, so I've got like five minutes, tops. The drugs and alcohol meeting was fine, if not a complete waste of my time. I went to work three days this week. Mr Barese'll tell ya the same thing if you gotta call him. Is that everything? 'Cause I really do gotta go." His knee bounced and he looked around the room. "What's the time?"

I really did understand his need to leave, but there was a procedure to go through and he knew that. "I just have some papers I need you to fill out. It won't take a minute." I slid the two-page form across the desk toward him.

He stared at it, then his dark eyes met mine. "Can I take

it home and bring it back in? I really gotta go. I can't miss that bus."

"CJ," I started.

"If I miss the bus, I can't get home. Pops needs the house warm. If it gets too cold, he starts coughing worse than normal. And I gotta cook him dinner, otherwise he don't eat."

I couldn't deny the desperation in his voice. His need to leave wasn't for himself, it was for someone else. I gave the papers a pointed nod. "Sure. Take them."

He quickly took the form, folded it in half, and stuffed it into the inside of his jacket. He stood up and started for the door. But before I could stop myself, before I could ask myself what the hell I was doing, I called out to him. "CJ, wait!"

He stopped and half-turned to face me.

"Gimme two minutes and I'll drive you."

His surprise quickly became suspicious and I regretted my offer, but I couldn't very well take it back. "It's pouring rain, and it's getting dark already," I added to justify it to him or myself, or possibly the both of us. I had no clue at this point.

He was obviously stunned into silence because he just stood there. "Just wait here," I said. I dashed into my office, plucked my jacket off the back of my seat, packed my files away, and collected my phone and keys from my top drawer. I was sure he'd be gone already by the time I came back out, but much to my surprise, he was still there. Arms crossed and suspicion unmasked on his face.

"Oh, quit acting like it's the first time someone's ever done something nice for ya," I said, trying to make a joke of it. "Car's out the back." I nodded toward the hall I'd come from, the opposite direction from the door he'd used.

He stood there like a rabbit in headlights. Caught between fight or flight. It was an internal battle I knew well. "Come on, this way. I don't bite."

I didn't have to turn around to know he was following me. I could hear his boots squelch with each step. If any of my co-workers wondered what the hell I was doing, none of them said anything. Hell, I don't even think any of them even noticed. I got to the back door and held it open for him. "After you."

I smiled at him as he walked past, but he kept his head down, not looking at me. The back of the building and the car park were covered, so we didn't have to worry about getting wet. I pressed the unlock button on my key to save me telling him which car was mine, and we both walked toward it.

"Thought you drove a Commodore," he said, obviously meaning the one he'd seen me drive to his house last week.

I opened my door and got in and waited for him to do the same before I answered. "That's a company vehicle. This one's mine." My car was an older model blue Corolla. Nothing flash, but I owned it outright. "Got her secondhand a few years ago. She's not too pretty, but she's cheap to run."

"She?"

"I haven't named my car," I replied, "if that's what you mean. She's just a she." I reversed out of the park and headed down the drive toward the exit. I wound down my window and fed my card to the scanner, making the boom gate rise.

"I meant why a she?"

I pulled the car up to the street and waited for a bus to pass before joining the other traffic in the rain. "Because no girl has broken my heart. Figured it was a good omen because she hasn't broken down on me yet."

His lips twitched like he was trying not to smile, but then he looked the opposite way I was driving and he frowned. "Uh, you're going the wrong way. High Street's that way." He pointed toward the rear window.

"High Street?"

"The bus stop?"

"Oh." Well, shit. "I was driving you home, yeah?"

"I thought you meant you'd drive me to the bus stop."

I instinctively checked my watch. "If I head back in that direction now, I don't think you'll make it. It really is fine. I'll drive you and you'll be home quicker."

He huffed and sank back in his seat. "Thanks," he said quietly. "Though I'm making your seat all wet."

I shrugged. "It'll dry."

It was normally a fifteen-minute drive, but with the rain and peak-hour traffic, it was slower going. The windscreen wipers made a lonely sound and seemed to get louder with each swipe, and the static in the car increased in tempo with the damn windscreen wipers until I couldn't stand it. I stabbed the radio button before something combusted.

CJ seemed completely unaffected. "I think you should name her."

"You what?"

"Your car. You can't just call it a she. That's . . . disrespectful or something."

I almost laughed at the absurdity. "Got any suggestions?"

"Nuh. I said you should name her. Not me."

"Well, I dunno . . . What about Coroline? Like Corolla but not."

He squinted at me. "No."

"You can't criticise unless you come up with a suggestion."

He scowled at me until I turned onto the road that would take us out of town. Or maybe he didn't like me smiling at him. He turned to look out the window, and when I thought he had no intention of answering, he said, "Roller Girl. As in Corolla Girl."

I laughed. "That's pretty good. I like it."

And then we fell back into silence. It wasn't awkward, but it wasn't exactly comfortable either. I kept trying to get a look at him without being too obvious, which wasn't easy. I could smell the cigarette smoke on him and his wet clothes. It wasn't terrible. It was kind of earthy in an ashtray kind of way; a thought that made me smile. I hated smoking, so why didn't I hate the smell on him?

I bumped up the heater. "You warm enough?"

"Yeah. Fine, thanks." He chewed on the inside of his lip. "Thanks again for drivin' me home. You didn't need to do that."

"I'm doing it for Pops. Can't have him getting cold."

One corner of his mouth curled upwards. And God, his smile really was something else.

I let a moment of silence pass between us. "I'm really glad you turned up today."

He shot me a surprised look. "You thought I wasn't gonna show?"

"You only had eight hours to come in and you left it seven hours and fifty-five minutes."

"I had that stupid meeting. Across town. And I had to walk. In the rain." He scowled at me again. "I wouldn't ever miss a meeting. I can't go to jail. I can't be leavin' Pops on his own."

I nodded slowly. "That's why I'm glad you made it. I don't want you to fail."

He gave me a look that was curious and disbelieving.

"You're not like the other POs."

"Well, I hope not. I'm trying to make a difference."

He frowned at his rain-splattered window, and I could almost see him close down on me, which was not what I wanted at all. I wanted him to like me. I had no idea why, but I did.

"I joined a soccer team," I announced, steering the conversation into safer waters. "I haven't played in years and I'm unfit as hell and we've only had one training session, but it's been fun."

Now he looked at me like I was shit on his shoe. "Soccer? Are you actually trying to win citizen of the year?"

I snorted. "I totally am."

"It'd be easier if you just went and bought yourself a trophy."

I laughed at that, happy he at least felt comfortable enough with me to joke, even if he was taking the piss. "I'm trying to make new friends," I admitted. "It's not easy being new in town and not knowing anyone."

CJ's brow furrowed. After a long beat of silence, he said, "Yeah, I get it."

"Being new in town?" I thought his file said he'd lived in Ten Mile Creek all his life.

"No, the part about friends. There ain't many people my age in Ten Mile Creek. Not that any of 'em give me the time of day. To them, I'm nothin' but a Davis."

I looked from the road ahead to him. "And that's a bad thing?"

Now he snorted. "You have no idea."

"Well, I'm sorry they judged you without getting to know you." And I was. God knew I'd worn the brunt of judgement in my life. I knew firsthand how it stung. "If you want to join the soccer team . . ."

CJ barked out a laugh. Like, a loud, harsh laugh. "Soccer? Me?"

"Yeah."

His eyes were almost bugging out of his head. "Sport? Of any kind?" He laughed again. "Jesus. Fuck no."

I chuckled at his response. "Fair enough."

I flipped the blinker on and slowed to turn into Ten Mile Creek. The rain had lifted a little, though the clouds were low and set in, and it was almost dark. It was gloomy, and I was a little disappointed that our time together was coming to an end.

As I drove over the railway lines, CJ cleared his throat. "So, my visit next week will be a home one, yeah?"

"I'm not supposed to tell you." I frowned at him. I was pretty sure he knew that. "Why? Something up?"

He made a face. "I'd rather you didn't come round my house no more."

"Oh yeah? Why's that?"

He chewed on his lip again. "It unsettles Pops. He gets upset."

I didn't want to call bullshit outright, but I didn't buy that one bit. I hated to leap to conclusions, but my first instinct was to believe he was hiding something. It didn't make sense though. I'd been in his house and it was clean and smelt fresh. Now that I recalled, it didn't even smell of cigarettes, which meant CJ only smoked outside—probably due to Pops' emphysema—but if he wouldn't smoke in the house, it was highly unlikely he'd have any other kind of drugs in there. I'd seen his shed, the neatly kept yard. If I were a betting man, I'd say no to CJ having any drugs in the house.

Then again, for all I knew, maybe he and Pops ran the

state's largest drug manufacturing ring. Or not. Maybe CJ was telling me the truth. Maybe Pops did get upset.

"Well, I can't promise anything."

"Wayne never came around home," CJ said, like telling me my predecessor was incompetent was going to make me the same.

"I get the feeling Wayne didn't do much of anything."

His brow furrowed like he wanted to say something else, but movement at his house made us both turn. The front door opened and Pops' small frame barely filled the doorway. "Gotta go," CJ said, getting out of the car and running, slightly hunched against the rain. It sounded like he called, "Thanks for the lift," but I couldn't be sure.

It wasn't until I got home that I remembered the forms I'd given him. Dammit. I could have waited while he filled them out . . .

WHEN I GOT to work the next morning, Sheryl was already behind the reception desk. She gave me a bright and cheery 'good morning' and handed me some familiar papers. "These were slid under the front door when I got in," she explained.

It was CJ's question form. He must have been up early to get them here before we opened, and I wondered if he came into town on his dirt bike and needed the cover of darkness. It didn't look registered, and I had to wonder if he even had a licence.

Should I report him for that? What would happen to him if I did? What would happen to me if I didn't?

I fell into my office chair with a sigh and flipped the page to see what he'd written. The writing was messy. Not in a poor-handwriting kind of way, but in a shaky-hand kind of way. Like CJ hadn't written it at all. It looked more like Pops had. Except the signature on the bottom was pretty obviously written by a different hand. Like CJ's hand.

I pulled out CJ's file, then logged into my computer and pulled up his digital file as well. I was looking for anything else that might have been handwritten . . . But that wasn't what I found.

There, in CJ's history, was a child welfare report. I read through it with a twist in my gut and an ache in my heart.

At the time, CJ was nine years old and had been taken to hospital for a broken arm. The child claimed he fell out of a tree; the child's grandfather claimed the same. Healed, but obvious, cigarette burns on the boy's arm said otherwise and DoCS was called. The boy's father, parolee Dwayne Davis, was arrested, charged awaiting sentencing, and sent back to jail. The child was released into the care of the grandfather. Regular check-ups declared the child healthy and happy with his grandfather.

But it was a later notation that caught my eye.

Attends school sporadically.

Numeracy and literacy skills: nil.

I closed down the screen and pushed his file away. I had no clue, not one iota of what it was like to walk in CJ's shoes. What he'd been through, the life he'd lived, the shitty childhood he'd endured. I really didn't know much about him at all. Other than he was, at his very heart, a good man. He cared for his ageing grandfather; he helped his boss out with yard work he could no longer do himself.

He wouldn't read the forms I put in front of him. He wouldn't fill them out or sign them in front of me.

And I was also pretty sure CJ Davis couldn't read or write.

CHAPTER SIX

CJ

WAITING at the train station was like waiting for my court hearing all over again. I was nervous to the point of almost being physically sick.

Mr Barese had very generously loaned me his car. His face when I'd asked, when I'd told him why I'd needed it, was enough to break my heart. He'd frowned and nodded without so much as a word.

He knew how I felt about my old man.

He knew how much I never wanted him to come home.

But the thing was, it was his home. He'd said Pops'd be able to claim a better pension if the house wasn't in his name, and so in good faith, Pops'd signed the deeds over to him. As it turned out, he did get a better pension, my father didn't lie about that. It just meant Dad held all the cards.

He owned the house, which in his sick and twisted way of thinkin' meant he owned us. And if I was bein' honest, I guess he did.

I wasn't like my brothers, though. Where they'd all jumped when he said how high, they did it out of respect.

They idolised him. Thought his words were gospel, thought his way of living was the only way.

The reason I obeyed every order wasn't out of respect. It was fear. As much as I tried to pretend otherwise, I was shit scared of my old man.

Him being out on parole put a stop to everything I was trying to do. All I wanted to do was keep my head down and stay outta trouble. I wanted normal. Not that 'normal' was a mould I'd ever fit into, given the fact I wasn't ever gonna find myself a girl and settle down. A guy, maybe . . .

And that was the root of my problem with my old man. Not that he knew I was into guys, not that he could ever know—no one could ever know—but with him being home again, I was back to being someone else. I'd always had to pretend around him. Pretend to be tough like him, pretend not to care like him. I just had to pretend to *be* like him. Jesus, if he ever found out that the only bar I went to was HQ . . . well, let's just say it wouldn't end well for me. It'd be a beating I doubt I'd survive.

So, with my father out of jail, I was forced back into the Davis frame of mind. To act like, to be like everyone expected a Davis to be like. That fucking name followed me around like a cursed shadow.

I just hoped he wouldn't be out long. It was, after all, only inevitable that he'd get tossed back in jail at some point. The question was, how miserable would he make our lives in the meantime? And for how long?

The train pulled into the station and my stomach curdled. There was no putting this off. I strode over to where other people were waiting, and a few people got off the train first. Happy, normally dressed, clean and tidy, greeted by smiling family and friends with hugs and warm hellos.

I watched them and wondered what it was like to be normal. To have a happy family. None of these people seemed to be dreading their family or friends' arrival. I watched them as they laughed, linked arms, and walked off to a life of happiness.

A life so very different to mine.

A thud at my feet made me turn. And there he stood. My father. God, he looked old. It'd been four years since I'd seen him, but those four years had not been kind. His hair was now more grey than black, his face was drawn and hardened. His eyes were still the dull black they'd always been, and his smile was more menacing than kind. He had even less teeth now, and his dirty white singlet did little to hide his prison tattoos.

"Hey boy," he said, punching me on the arm. He kicked the small bag he'd dropped at my feet. "Pick that up, will ya?"

I grabbed his bag and turned toward the car park. "This way."

"Man, it's so fucking good to be out," he said, way too loudly. A woman close-by with a small kid shot me a dirty look, and I cringed. I swore every now then, but never in front of kids or ladies.

"Keep your voice down," I said.

Now, four years ago, I'd have never questioned him or spoke out of turn. Ever. But I wasn't that kid anymore. Sure, I was scared of him, of the meanness he was capable of, but I was older now. Things were different now.

He clearly didn't like it. He slowed his strut and tried to bore holes into the side of my head with his eyes. "I can say whatever the fuck I want."

"You want the cops to come?"

He grumbled something I couldn't make out and then, "Fuck the cops."

Just great. This was going to be bad. On the bright side, with this fuck-everyone attitude, he wouldn't be out long.

I stopped at Mr Barese's car. "Del loaned me his car to come get you," I said, throwing his bag into the backseat. "On the condition that no one smoke in it."

My father looked at me like I'd told him he had to donate a kidney. "Don't see no bars on the windows," he said, tapping the passenger window. "It's not a fucking jail, is it?"

I sighed. "If you want a cigarette, have it now before we get in. It's no big deal." What I wanted to say was 'show some goddamn respect,' but I kept that to myself. My father respected nobody and nothing.

He held his hand out over the bonnet of the car. "Gimme your smokes. If you won't let me smoke in the car, the least you can do is gimme a fucking cigarette."

I fished out my ciggies and considered throwing him the whole pack, but I knew I wouldn't get them back. So I walked around to his side and offered him a single cigarette, and needing one myself, I leaned against the car and had a cigarette with my dad.

Nothing like quality family-bonding time.

"How is Barese going anyway?" he asked, looking at the cigarette like it wasn't good enough for him. "The fat old fuck."

"He's going good. Business is a bit slow though."

He took a harsh drag and blew it out his nose. "How many days you doin' there now?"

"Three." I don't know why it bothered me to tell him that. Probably because his first thought would be how much money that worked out to be, which to my old man, equalled cigarettes and alcohol. Before he could ask me to buy him either, I quickly changed the subject. "Pops isn't doin' so great. His lungs are shit." Not that he'd even asked about him.

"Ah, the old bastard's too miserable to die."

Nice. Really fucking nice.

I took a final drag of my cigarette, dropped it to the road, and trod on it. "You good to go?"

"Yeah," he said brightly. "Can't wait to get home."

I walked back around to the driver's side thinking home was the very last place I wanted to take him.

He spoke nearly the whole way home, telling stories of his time inside, making out like he was some kind of hero. I didn't believe a word of it. When I didn't laugh at something that wasn't funny, he whacked my shoulder. "What crawled up your arse and died?" he asked.

"What?"

"I'da thought you'd be glad your old man was home, but you ain't even tryin' to smile."

"Nah, it's all good. Course I'm glad you're home," I lied.

Easily pleased, he smiled out the window. "Jesus, this town hasn't changed."

Well, the town hadn't. But I had. At least I was trying to. "Some things are different," I hedged.

He shot me a look. "Yeah? What's that?"

"You can't smoke in the house."

He stared, that cold, hard glare.

"It's no good for Pops. His lungs can't handle the smoke."

My father stared at me all the way from the railway lines to the house. I could feel his stare burning into the side of my head. But I wasn't turning to look at him. No way. So I shouldn't have been surprised when we'd been inside the house long enough for him to grunt a hello at Pops when he took out a cigarette and put it between his lips, stared at me like 'whatcha gonna do about it?' then lit it.

"I asked you not to do that," I said.

He snatched the cigarette from his mouth and smirked. "It's my house. Don't tell me what I can and can't do in m' own house, boy."

Anger bubbled in my chest, but just before I could speak, Pops put his hand on my arm. "It's fine, CJ. Not worth fightin' over."

"It's not worth you gettin' sick over either."

Pops waved his hand like it didn't matter. When really, it mattered a whole lot.

"I gotta get Mr Barese's car back to him," I said, walking out. Goddammit. He'd been home less than a minute, and I already didn't want to be there.

"Bring me back something t' eat," my old man called out.

I pretended not to hear. It was better than telling him to fuck off. Safer, anyway.

MR BARESE TOOK one look at me and sighed. "I take it he's home."

I nodded. "Yeah. And he hasn't changed. If anything, he's even more of an arsehole now than he ever was."

"You come and stay with me," he said, concern on his face.

"I can't leave Pops."

Mr Barese sighed heavily. "I figured you'd say as much."

"Anyway, thanks again for the loan of the car." I handed him his keys. "I really appreciate it."

"I know you do." He looked around the shop. "Hey, can you help me for a minute? I got some paperwork to finish up and the floor in here needs a sweep and the tools could use a clean . . ." He was already walking into his office, not waiting for a reply. I knew what he was doing, keeping me away from the house for as long as he could.

I picked up the broom and swept the already clean floor, then started wiping down all the wrenches, ratchets, and sockets, and when that was done, I tidied the few spare parts we kept. I didn't realise it had gotten late until Mr Barese lowered the old metal roller door at the front. "You right to work tomorrow?" he asked, sliding the lock into place. "We got the O'Malleys' Cruiser in for a check-over tomorrow."

"Oh, for sure." I wasn't rostered on but I would always come in if we had a car in the shop.

He nodded his head toward his car. "Come on, I'll give you a lift."

The sun was getting low and I knew the house'd be getting cool, so with a reluctant sigh, I nodded. "Yeah, thanks." I left the 'can't put it off forever' unsaid.

The house looked as it always did. Silent and peaceful, though I knew that would change the second I walked through the door. Mr Barese gave me a kind smile. "See you in the morning."

"Thanks again," I said.

"Hey," he said before I could get out. "If you need somewhere to stay . . ."

I nodded. "Thank you."

But I got out and he waited for a long second before he drove off, and by the time I got to the front door, he was gone. Taking a deep breath, I went inside.

My old man was sitting in the comfy recliner—Pops'

seat—watching some shit on TV with a stubby of beer in one hand, cigarette in the other. God fucking dammit. "Where's Pops?"

He shrugged and Pops' answered from the kitchen. "In here, CJ."

I headed straight for the kitchen and Pops was sitting on one of the old, hard wooden chairs at the table. He hated sitting there, even just to eat. The chairs were too hard on his bony frame. I pointed to the lounge room and whispered, "He's in your seat and he's smoking inside!"

Pops waved his hand. "It's all right." But he was wheezing, and I wondered if they'd argued.

"He treatin' you okay?"

Pops nodded but couldn't lie for shit.

And the rage bubbled a little bit more.

"I'll start dinner in a sec," I said, louder this time so Dad didn't think we were talking about him and come in. I looked at Pops again. "Stay here. You can keep me company while I get some veggies started."

I went into his room and pulled his pillow and blanket off his bed. I put the pillow in his seat for him, then wrapped the blanket around his shoulders. Once he was settled, I went into the lounge room and opened the fire door. It had almost gone out, but with a few bits of kindling and some old cardboard, it soon took. I put a bigger piece on, opened the air vent, and shut the door.

"You could have kept the fire going," I said, talking to my father but not looking at him. "And that's Pops' chair. He needs to stay warm and he watches his soaps at this time."

I didn't give him the satisfaction of eye contact. I just stood up and walked back into the kitchen. I thought he might follow me in and give me a touch up for telling him what to do, but he didn't.

He never said a word. And that was kinda worse.

At least when he was yellin' and throwin' things and punchin' people, you knew what was coming. But him being quiet was like not knowing. And not knowing was walking on eggshells.

Fear. The bastard thrived on it.

Once I was pretty sure he wasn't gonna follow me into the kitchen and give me a shove for speaking to him like that, I stood at the sink peeling veggies, telling Pops how Mr Barese needed me to work for a bit, which was why I was late. I told him I had to work again tomorrow and he asked a few questions, and when I looked over at him, he smiled at me.

He was my fucking saviour.

When dinner was cooked, I plated it up. "Dinner's ready."

My father appeared in the doorway. "What am I eating?"

"You're having steak. Pops and me are having rissoles."

I'm pretty sure most people would feel bad that they were eating expensive food while everyone else wasn't, but he just grinned. He tapped the side of my face. "Good lad." Then he grabbed my ear and pulled it, which I'm sure was the payback for the way I'd spoken to him earlier. I pulled my head back out of his grasp and pulled my chair out. I didn't want to fight with him, but I was done with being touched up by him. I wasn't a kid no more. If he really wanted a fight, he'd get one.

But I sat down and said nothing, for Pops' sake, not mine.

Dad ate his steak, though I didn't know how he

managed to chew it given his lack of teeth. He clanked his plate with his knife and fork, shovelled food in, chewed with his mouth open, and breathed through his nose while he ate. His manners were fit for a cell-block mess hall. It was disgusting.

Pops gave me a smile. "Tastes good, CJ."

"Thanks, Pops."

Dad grunted, in appreciation or disgust, I couldn't tell.

We finished our dinner in silence, then to my surprise, my father took our empty plates to the sink. "S'pose it's the least I could do," he said, then proceeded to wash up.

I stared at Pops, he stared at me, and I shrugged. But I surely wasn't going to argue. "Come on, Pops. I'll get you into your chair."

He nodded and I took his blanket and pillow while he walked into the lounge room. When he was seated, I fell into the old sofa and watched some crap on TV. Soon afterwards, Dad came back with a beer in his hand and sat beside me. "Thanks for cleanin' up," I said.

He grunted in reply and took a swig of his beer.

It was awkward, and I kept waiting for him to say something horrible or to punch my arm and order me off the couch. He did neither, which was unsettling.

"So, how 'bout we head into town tomorrow night," he said after a while. "Have a few drinks, find some women . . ."

Oh God. "Uh, how will we get there?" We didn't have a car and I certainly wasn't doubling him in on my dirt bike.

"When's the last bus leave?"

"Four."

"That'll do."

"I work till five."

"Leave early."

He truly had no concept of what a job was. "I can't."

"Sure ya can. Just tell Barese you're goin' out with your old man."

"He needs me there till five, Dad. I can't just leave him."

He gave me a filthy look. "You prefer to make him happy? Or me?"

"I prefer not to piss off the guy who pays me money. You know, for food and bills. That kind of shit."

He glared at the TV like he was two seconds away from gettin' up and puttin' his foot through it, so I quickly tried to smooth it over. "If you catch the bus in, I can meet you later. I'll ride my bike when it's dark so the cops won't see me." *And just pray they don't catch me.*

"How'll we get home again?"

I shrugged. "Dunno. We can figure that out later."

Finally he smiled. "All right."

I let out a slow, relieved breath. "Okay then, well I'm going to bed. Gotta get up early." It didn't matter it wasn't even seven o'clock, I just needed to get out of the room.

I almost made it to the hall when Dad said, "Gonna need some cash, boy. Just how much is old Barese payin' ya?"

And there it was. There was no way he could ever know about the money I was saving. If he found it, he'd bleed me dry. "He pays okay, given I ain't qualified for nothin'." I figured that said enough without sayin' too much. I pulled my wallet out and gave him the two tenners I had in there. "That'll get you into town and a few beers till I get there."

He snatched the two ten-dollar notes from me and took an obvious look in my wallet to make sure there was nothing else in it. "Gonna need more than twenty bucks," he said, "but it's a start."

I bit my tongue and patted Pops on the shoulder. "You right, Pops?"

"Yep. See ya in the morning."

"Night," I said as I left the room. I stripped down to my briefs and undershirt and climbed into bed. I stared at the ceiling with a heavy ache in my belly for what must have been hours. I never heard a word between Dad and Pops, and I doubted they spoke at all. Pops went to bed a little while after me and I fell asleep before I heard the TV turn off. Whether Dad passed out on the couch or not, I didn't know.

I didn't care.

When I woke up, it was still dark. I opened my door as quietly as I could and went to the bathroom. The sound of loud snoring from Dad's bedroom was as much a relief as it was annoying. It meant he was out cold. So, knowing I had some time, I went back into my room. Keeping an ear out for his snoring, I quietly lifted my wardrobe away from the wall far enough to reveal the hole that'd been punched through the gyprock.

Who was responsible for the hole, I didn't know. One of my brothers, or more than likely my dad, probably during a fight with one of my brothers. I don't remember it specifically, so I must have been young when it happened. But it left a perfect fist-sized hole, which I'd made big enough so I could hide stuff in there. Not that I expected Pops to ever go snooping or to steal from me, but old habits died hard. And now my old man was back home, I was glad I did.

A small Weet-Bix box fit just perfect and sat on the wall stud below the hole. I pulled it out as quietly as I could, stopped, and listened . . . He was still snoring. Inside the box I had money stashed. Two hundred and forty dollars. It wasn't much, but it was my entire savings. I'd squirrelled away every spare dollar I could, not knowing what emergency might crop up. Or maybe to start life over somewhere; me and Pops could disappear and Dad would never find us.

I knew I was due to get paid tomorrow—Mr Barese always paid on Fridays—so I didn't need to take any from my stash. But I would sometimes just take it out and look at it, like it was some kind of security blanket. In many ways, it was.

Dad was still snoring, so I quietly put the box back and silently lifted the wardrobe back against the wall. I pulled on my jeans and a flannelette shirt and threw a small log into the fire. There were enough embers to salvage it, so I closed the door and set about making Pops some breakfast.

The sound of the kettle whistling and the smell of toast cooking usually brought Pops out of his room. "Morning, CJ."

"Hey, Pops. Sleep okay?"

"Yep. You?"

I let the sound of the snoring be my answer and added a shrug. Pops got it. He knew all too well. "You're a good kid, CJ."

"'Cause I had you lookin' after me," I said and handed him his cup of tea. "I'd hate to think what would've happened otherwise."

"You'd have been just fine," he answered.

We both knew that wasn't true.

The toast popped and I buttered it and spread some marmalade on it. "Here ya go. I gotta get to work early, so at least I'll know you've had something to eat today."

"I ain't completely useless," he said, but he took the plate of toast with a grateful smile.

"I know. Just like to look after ya."

"I know you do."

I sipped my tea and waited for my toast to cook; all the while the snoring never stopped. Thank God. I was hoping to get out of the house before he woke up.

"You gonna make yourself scarce every day he's home?" Pops asked.

The toast popped up and I took my time buttering it before I sat across from him at the small table. "I don't wanna leave you here with him . . ."

Pops waved his hand. "Don't you worry about me. I figure he'll start spending more and more time in town. Nothing happens here and it'll drive him crazy soon enough."

"I hope so." I bit into my toast. "What do ya make of him washing up last night?"

Pops let out a wheezy-chuckle. "Didn't know he knew how. Must have taught him something in jail."

I laughed just as the snoring from the bedroom became a snore-choke-snort that was followed by silence, which meant he'd be waking up soon. I shoved my toast in my mouth and washed it down with my tea. In a quick trip to the bathroom, I scrubbed my face, shaved way too quickly, sprayed some deodorant, and brushed my teeth. Then back in my room, I pulled on socks and grabbed my jacket and put on my boots.

I was going to make a dash for the front door but decided to put some more wood on the fire, and no sooner had I opened the fire door, when I heard the toilet flush.

Great.

I stoked the fire up and closed the vent, just as Dad walked in. "You're off early," he said grumpily.

"Yeah, busy day." I stood up from the fire and dusted off

my hands. "Uh, if you could bring in some firewood today from the pile out the back, that'd be great."

He glared.

I tried to smile. "There's bread for toast and the kettle's not long boiled. Enjoy your first full day of freedom." I was going for enthusiastic but I didn't think he bought it. "See ya, Pops," I called out and headed for the door.

"Leave your bike," Dad said.

I stopped and turned back to face him. "What for?"

"I ain't fucking walking to the bus stop. I'll ride it to your work in time for the bus. Then you can ride it into town." He didn't wait for a reply. He just walked into the kitchen like his word was final.

Just great.

I wanted to scream but settled for slamming the door behind me instead.

And so I walked to work, marching to the beat of 'fuck him' with every step. I'd burned off my anger as I walked, and by the time I got to the shop and with the help of a few cigarettes, I'd calmed right down.

Mr Barese left me alone most of the day. I guess he knew when I needed space, and he gave it. I worked on O'Malleys' Cruiser, finding the problem was the alternator. The belt was almost frayed through, so I replaced that too, added some oil, coolant, and topped up the windscreen wiper fluid.

Mr Barese made me stop for lunch. Like every day, his wife Maria brought in some beef sandwiches and an apple for both of us. I knew he was going to ask about my old man, and I was grateful he'd left it till our lunch was done. "How's things at home?" he hedged.

I shrugged. "Yeah, all right. Dad's gonna drop my bike off before he catches the bus. Can you do me a favour?"

"Sure."

"Can you not pay me till after he's been in?"

He nodded, knowingly. "Of course."

And sure enough, a few hours later, my old man didn't surprise me. I heard my bike coming down the road before I saw it, and that nervous dread churned the food in my stomach. He pulled up on the bike, kicked the stand down, and swung his leg over. He wore a smile that was supposed to be friendly, but it only chilled me to my core.

"Nice ride," he said.

"Thanks."

"Who'd ya flog it from?"

"I didn't steal it. I paid for it." I'd saved so hard for it too, not that he'd care.

He laughed like something was funny. "Headin' into town early. Gotta register at the dole office. Fuckers better pay me some money."

I looked around quickly, hoping Mr Barese—or worse, a customer—didn't hear him swear. Thankfully it didn't look like it.

Dad held out his hand "Gimme your wallet."

God, he would never change.

I fished my wallet out of my pocket and handed it over. He was checking that I wasn't holding out on him, hiding anything from him. He could look all he liked; my wallet was empty. For this very reason.

He slapped it to my chest and sneered at me. "Ain't been paid yet."

I took my wallet. "Not yet." I nodded to the Cruiser I'd been working on. "I better get back to work or I'll be late to meet you in town."

He lifted his chin in some kind of nod of defiance. "Meet me at the Federal."

"Sure thing."

Jesus. The Federal Hotel was a dump. Full of no-hopers, losers, and druggos. I guess on the bright side, if he was gonna slot back in with that crowd, he wouldn't be out of jail for long.

Thank God he did come in early, because not long after, a familiar government car pulled up. I stayed on the creeper trolley underneath the car I was working on and watched Noah get out of his car. I could only see his shoes and his pants from the knees down, but it was definitely him. He walked up to the Cruiser I was under, his feet just a metre from me, then bent over to look at me. He gave me an upside-down smile. "It'd help if you were trying to hide from me not to have your legs sticking out the side."

Grabbing the undercarriage of the Cruiser, I wheeled myself out. "I wasn't hiding."

"Oh, really?"

"Avoiding, maybe."

He laughed, and it was weird . . . I liked how it sounded. I dunno what it was about him, but there was something I didn't want to examine too closely, scared of what I might find. I looked down at his empty hands. "No folder today?"

"Nah. Thought I'd give it a miss."

Figurin' I could use a smoke, I took out my ciggies and nodded to the back roller door. He followed and waited for me to light one up. "Nice day anyway," he said, lookin' upward.

I took a long drag. "Really? We're gonna talk about the weather?"

He chuckled and his eyes did some weird crinklin' thing that made my stomach clench in an unfamiliar way. In a good way. "Small talk. I suck at it."

"Yeah, you do." I took another drag of my cigarette. "Can't you just say what needs sayin'?"

"Conversation never killed anyone."

"Unless they died of boredom."

"Am I boring you to death?"

I had to shove my cigarette in between my lips to stop from smiling. "Dunno. How long you plan on talking?"

He laughed and leaned against the back wall of the shop. He didn't look like a parole officer. He looked nothin' of the sort. He seemed kinda stuck for words for a while, then he turned to me. One eye was squinting from the sun. "How's your week been?"

I took another long drag of my smoke. Jesus, that was a loaded question. "My week's been kinda shit actually, thanks for asking."

He frowned. "Anything I can help you with?"

I snorted out a laugh. "Uh, no. Thanks."

He stared out over the creek for a bit, chewin' on his lip and thinking. My cigarette was almost down to the butt before he spoke. "So, I uh . . . read your case file."

I took a final drag and flicked the butt toward the creek. "And?"

"Can I ask you something?"

We both knew damn well he was gonna ask me anyway. "No."

"Your school records show no graduation date."

"Because I didn't finish." Hell, I barely even started. I didn't want to have this conversation. Not with anyone, but especially not with him. I didn't know why it mattered, but I didn't want him to think I was a loser.

A Davis.

"CJ, there's nothing wrong with not being able to read."

I stared at him. "Fuck you."

He ignored that. "I can help you learn, to read, that is. It's nothing to be ashamed about."

What the fuck would he know? I pointed my finger at him, right in his face. "Fuck. You."

He batted my hand away. "Stop with the attitude."

Then it happened. I made the mistake of pushing his hand, then he grabbed mine. I never started a fight in my life, but I sure as hell knew how to give as good as I got. I shoved him, and he shoved me back. He was taller than me by a few inches, but I grabbed his arm and he grabbed my overalls, and in a push and shove, he rammed me against the outside wall. He held me with his body, rough and strong. He wasn't a pen-pushing desk jockey. He was a brawler, he knew how to handle himself, and goddammit, he knew how to handle me. His strength, his heat, and his smell— deodorant or aftershave—and he pinned me against the wall. I couldn't help it. I looked at the fire in his eyes, the pink of his lips, and I was one second away from grabbing the back of his head and kissing him.

But in that split second, I saw it, in his eyes, on his face. Recognition. His eyes went wide, he let go of my shirt, and he smiled.

Fuck! A warning bell went off in my head. Too late. Too fucking late. He knew. He knew already, and the look on his face made me want to run. The opposite of my father; his instinct was to fight. Mine was flight. I took off, running alongside the outside of the shop. I needed to escape, to get away from him and the fact that he *knew*.

I ran, but he was fast. Faster than me. "Hey, CJ, stop!" He grabbed my arm and pulled me to a stop. My back was at the wall and he stood in front of me, not caging me in, but not lettin' me move either.

"Don't run from me."

Fight kicked in again and I grabbed his jacket, but there was no resistance this time. He let me grab him. "Fuck you."

"CJ, it's okay."

No, it's not. It's so very far from it. "Fuck. You."

"CJ. It's okay."

I shook my head and let go of his jacket. "You don't know me."

He took a step back and let out a nervous breath. "Maybe not. CJ, I won't tell anyone."

I played stupid. "Won't tell anyone what?"

"Anything." He let out an almighty sigh and ran one hand through his hair. "I just want to talk."

"Well, I'm busy. I got work to do. You've seen me at work. You don't need nothin' else." I pushed off the wall and walked back to the roller door, my heart hammering.

"CJ, stop!"

I didn't stop.

"I'll need to speak to Mr Barese."

I kept on walking and said, "You do what you gotta do." When I got back inside, I cranked up the volume on the small radio, slid back under the Cruiser, and did my very best to try and calm the hell down. After a while, I watched as Noah's feet walked to Mr Barese's office door. I couldn't hear anything—the music was too loud—but he spoke to Mr Barese for about five minutes before he came back out. He stood at the end of the Cruiser, as though he wanted to speak to me but didn't know what to say.

My heart hammered for every second he stood there, and I couldn't breathe. But then he turned and walked away, back to his car. I didn't know if I was glad or disappointed.

I had to get him out of my head.

I had four weeks of my parole sentence left. That was it.

I had just four weeks to avoid Noah Huxley at all costs. The fact he was my parole officer made that damn near impossible. The fact I didn't know what I wanted more just five minutes ago—to punch him or for him to kiss me—didn't help.

God, he smelt so damn good.

Four weeks. I just had to get through the next four weeks without Noah Huxley ruining my life.

CHAPTER SEVEN

NOAH

I WASN'T EXPECTING him to retaliate with force. He pushed me. A citable offence in itself. But I'd retaliated too. Old habits were hard to break, I guess. But when confronted with a hard shove and a push, I shoved and pushed right back.

I always had.

Call it self-defence. Call it stupid. But things with CJ escalated to out of hand in half a second. And when he'd shoved me and I shoved him back, he backed into the wall and I pushed myself against him, everything changed.

He changed.

He looked at my mouth, his eyes darkened and his nostrils flared. He licked his bottom lip like he wanted to kiss me.

Like he wanted me to kiss him.

So, CJ was hiding more than one secret. Not only did he have illiteracy issues, he was also gay. Or bi, or curious.

Or interested.

He was complex, that was for sure. Another layer I wanted to peel back, unravel, undress.

CJ Davis was a puzzle I wanted to solve. I wanted to see how his pieces fit, how they interlocked, to see what bigger picture they made. And that's where the problem was. I *wanted*. And wanting anything with a case I was working on was not only forbidden, but incredibly unwise and unethical.

But my time working with CJ was running out. Which meant if I wanted to help him—which I did—I needed to hurry.

I knocked on Mr Barese's door. "Can I have a moment?"

He greeted me warmly. "Of course. Come in."

I walked into his small office and waved at the loud radio blaring behind us. "I think I overstayed my welcome with CJ."

Mr Barese laughed. "What can I help you with?"

"Well, it's about CJ. Can I ask when he got qualified to do mechanic work?"

His expression told me all I needed to know. But he answered anyway, "Well, he doesn't have a ticket. But I check everything he does. He's very good, and he knows it all."

I put my hand up and gave him a smile. "I'm not going to report anything. But I figured he didn't go through an apprenticeship."

He shook his head slowly, then studied me for a while like he wasn't sure he should say what he was about to. "I don't think he reads too well."

I nodded. "I know." I bit my lip. "Look, this is probably way out of line for me, but if I could convince him to get qualified, would you consider, as his employer, to put him on as an apprentice?"

Mr Barese stared at me, then laughed. "You think you can convince him to do that?"

"I can try." I shrugged. "You'd be subsidised through the government if he was your apprentice. There are benefits and incentives. I haven't looked into it too much. I thought I'd ask you first."

He grinned. "Of course I would. He's a good boy."

I shook his hand and couldn't help but smile. "Now I just need to convince him."

He barked out a laugh. "Good luck with that. You'll need it."

I almost snorted. "I think I'll need more than luck."

He smiled but eyed me cautiously. "You really are trying to make a difference, yes?"

"Yeah. I'm trying to, anyway."

Mr Barese shook my hand again, and on my way out, I stopped by the car CJ was working on. But from the volume of the radio, it was pretty obvious he didn't want to speak to me. I could take a hint. Plus, as was evident from our altercation earlier, the more I pushed him, he'd either push back harder or run. And I wanted him to do neither.

SATURDAY AFTERNOON WAS our first soccer game, and I was really pumped for it. And nervous. Gallan went through a few ball skills with me before the match. "What are you nervous for?"

"Because I haven't played in ages." I kicked the ball back to him. "I'm sure I'll get smashed out there today."

Gallan laughed. "You'll be fine."

There were a few lingering looks and smiles and I was interested to see if it would lead anywhere. It had been a while since I'd been with anyone, and the prospect of hooking up made me forget about my pre-match nerves.

We lost 2-1 but it was fun and I didn't play anywhere near as bad as I thought I would. I was more interested in the after-game drinks and we headed straight to the pub afterwards. Being social and having a laugh was a huge step for me. It felt good and positive, and if I were being honest with myself, the prospect of spending more time with Gallan felt kinda nice too. We joined a few tables together in the beer garden and he chose the seat next to mine.

"So, what do you do for work?" I asked him once we were all sitting down.

He looked me right in the eye and smiled. "I'm a lube fitter."

I choked on my beer, and a few of the guys laughed. "Always gets a laugh," one of them said.

I composed myself, thankful I didn't spit out my drink. "Seriously?"

"Dead serious," he said, sipping his beer. His smile made it hard to tell if he was being honest. "No, honestly. I work for one of the mining companies in the Hunter. Lubrication fitter is the actual title, but it just means I work with high-pressure grease and lubrication, hydraulic systems and fluid coupling."

I hid my smile behind my beer. "Sounds interesting."

His eyes creased at the sides, his stare knowing, because really, straight men didn't often get lube jokes. "It has its rewards." He shifted in his seat and cleared his throat. "So, what do you do? You've just moved here, right?"

"Yeah. I'm a corrections officer."

"A what?"

"A parole officer."

Both his eyebrows shot up. "Really?"

"Yes, really." I shrugged. "At least there's no lube jokes."

Gallan laughed, as did a few others, and the conversation moved on, but Gallan stared at me, his head tilted, and we spoke amongst ourselves. "A parole officer. Wow. I wasn't expecting that."

"I wasn't expecting the lube fitter either."

"Lubrication," he clarified. "Lube is for something else entirely."

I took a swig of my beer. "Noted."

He picked at the label on his beer. "So tell me, what's it like working with . . ." He gestured broadly with his hand. "I don't know what the politically correct term is. Released offenders, ex-criminals . . ."

"Parolees?"

He nodded. "Yeah. Do you have to carry a gun?"

I snorted. "Uh, no. And actually, it's pretty good. Rewarding, I guess. I want to help these people integrate back into the community. They're not all bad people." An instant replay of my meeting with CJ Davis ran through my mind—his face, the way he licked his lip, the heat in his eyes followed by fear—and I did my best to shut it down.

Gallan seemed to think about my not-all-bad-people comment for a while. "I guess not. So you're one of the good guys then?"

"I'd like to think so. I think the politically correct term for that is doe-eyed naïvety. Well, at least I'm pretty sure that's what some of my colleagues think of me."

"Are you naïve, or are they jaded and cynical?"

I smiled. "A bit of both."

"So, been doing it long?" he asked.

"Nope. Only since I moved here."

"Wow." He drained his beer bottle. "Are you liking Maitland?"

"I do. It's a nice change."

"Been back to Newcastle yet?"

"No, not yet." Not ever was on the tip of my tongue, but we were interrupted by someone asking if we wanted refills, and thankfully our private conversation was over. Another beer later and a lot of laughs about how we played and I was feeling pretty damn good. Not drunk, or even buzzed, just happy.

But when Tony asked me if I wanted another beer, I shook my head. "Nah thanks, mate, I'm driving."

Tony shot Gallan a look. "Beer?"

"No, I promised Nina I'd take her to the movies. I better get going soon."

Nina? Had I read this all wrong? Was there a girlfriend?

Someone else was leaving as well, and it seemed a good time to pull the plug. "Yeah, I better get home too," I said, getting to my feet.

Gallan stood up as well and we said our goodbyes and a few of us walked out together. When we got to the car park, the others split off, but Gallan kind of stopped walking, so I did too. "So," I hedged. "Nina . . . ?"

He smiled at me. "Sister."

I nodded slowly. "So not a girlfriend then."

"No." He smiled like my reaction pleased him. "She uh, she just broke up with her boyfriend so I said I'd take her out for dinner and to the movies. Being a good, dutiful big brother."

A good, dutiful big brother.

Jesus. Who would have thought words alone could feel like a sledgehammer? I took a step back. "Um, I . . . that's wow . . . That sounds fun. I better get going . . ."

If my reaction confused him or disappointed him, he didn't let on. "Okay."

I took another step back. "See you at training on Tuesday, right?"

"No, actually I work nights this week. Rotating roster. But I'll see you at the game next Saturday, yeah?" He sounded hopeful.

"Sure thing. See you then." I gave a wave and walked quickly to my car, trying to get a hold of myself. I took a few deep breaths, started the engine, and drove home, refusing to let my memories drag me under.

———————————

AT WORK ON MONDAY MORNING, I checked emails, went through my to-do list, and was researching apprentice-ships when Terrell knocked on my door. "Got a minute?"

"Sure."

He had a folder in his hand and he put it in front of me before he sat down in the chair across from me. "Thought you might wanna take a look at this."

Frowning, I opened the file.

Dwayne John Davis.

I saw the surname, then checked the address. Davis Road, Ten Mile Creek.

His date of birth made him—

"CJ's father," Terrell added, clearly watching me trying to join mental dots. "Got parole last Thursday.

Oh no.

"Yeah, he's a real piece of work." Terrell sighed. "CJ's one of yours, yeah?"

I nodded. "And he's a good guy. He works hard, looks after his sick grandfather, and does yard work for his boss. Doesn't get paid to do it. Just does it because his boss can't."

Terrell made a face. "The Davises have been through this office forever. All of them. Long before I started."

"All of them?"

"The brothers. CJ's older brothers."

I'd read CJ's file, but there was nothing about siblings. I think I remembered CJ mentioning them . . . "How many are there?"

"CJ's got four brothers."

"Four?"

"All of them are in jail. I highly doubt they'll ever get out. Two had their sentences added to for violent crimes inside." Terrell shrugged. "Victims of the system. They never redeemed themselves or learned from their mistakes. They went from bad to worse. The other one was already doing fifteen years for aggravated assault; got into a bar fight and the guy he punched the shit out of died from his head injuries." Terrell visibly shuddered.

Fuck.

I scrubbed my hand over my face. "I saw CJ on Friday. He never mentioned his father." Then again, why would he? It wasn't like I knew him. We weren't friends . . . Then I remembered. "Actually, the meeting before last, he said he'd prefer it if I just did work calls. No home visits. He told me it upsets his Pops, but I wonder if it's because he knew his father would be there."

Terrell sat back in his chair. "Dwayne is on my books. Dave thought it'd be better if I handled him, given you haven't been here long."

"Yeah, fair enough."

"I gotta go up and see him later this arvo. Did you want to reschedule your appointment with CJ this week? We could go up together; kill two birds with one stone."

"Sure." I swivelled my computer screen around to show him. "I was just researching apprenticeships for CJ, actually. Thought I'd see if I can convince him to get qualified."

A slow smile spread across Terrell's face.

"What?" I asked, pretending to look in my breast pocket, then under my desk. "Is my newbie status showing?"

Terrell laughed. "It is. But don't ever lose it. I wish everyone still had it."

I sighed again. "They've all got potential, ya know? I hate that they feel forgotten or cast aside. They're still people."

Terrell's smile took on a sad edge, but he nodded. "Do me a favour. Don't lose sight of that."

"I don't plan to."

"So? After lunch okay to head up to see the Davises?"

"Sure thing."

TERRELL DROVE, and as we turned off the main road into Ten Mile Creek, he said, "Let me lead this one, yeah?"

I gave him an odd look. "Okay."

"You can still talk to CJ, of course. But Dwayne ain't gonna be too happy to see me, just so you know."

"You expect him to fight?"

"No, nothing like that. But don't expect a warm welcome."

I held up the folder in my hand. "Yeah, I don't think I'll be popular either."

Terrell chuckled, and we drove in silence until we pulled up in front of their house. He sighed deeply and unbuckled his seatbelt. "Well, no putting this off, I guess."

I got out of the car and saw CJ in the shed at the side of the house. He must have been working on his bike or mower because he came out wiping his hands on a rag. He looked a mix of curious as to what two of us were doing there and angry that we were.

"Hey CJ," I said with a smile. I didn't want him to assume we were here for bad news.

He lifted his chin in that nod or acknowledgement way he did. He looked at Terrell, then spoke to me. "What's this for?"

Terrell answered. "Your father in?"

CJ's eyes narrowed. "Yeah."

"He's not in any trouble," I said quietly. "Just a routine check. Your dad's first check since his release."

CJ's face was hard to read. "Right."

I gave Terrell a nod. "Should we do this inside?" Which was really just me asking if he wanted me inside with him when he met Dwayne.

"Sure," he said.

I turned to CJ. "It won't take long." I held my hand out, gesturing for him to lead the way and go inside first.

He sighed heavily and reefed the front door open and walked inside. "POs are here."

Terrell and I followed him in. Pops was in his recliner chair, and a man who I assumed to be CJ's father stood in the kitchen doorway, stubby of beer in hand.

He was a stocky man with short greying hair and a hard, lined face. He wore tracksuit pants and a dirty white singlet, which showed poorly done tattoos on his arms and hands. He had a tear tattooed below his left eye.

Terrell smiled and stuck out his hand. "Mr Dwayne Davis? Terrell Craigie. I'm your corrections officer."

Dwayne reluctantly shook Terrell's hand and grunted in response.

I offered my hand to him. "Noah Huxley. I'm here to see CJ."

He shook my hand and his grip was hard and rough. "Well, ain't this cosy," Dwayne said.

His teeth looked like the keys on a piano. There were more gaps than there were teeth. Terrell didn't seem to notice. "Yeah, well, we thought we'd kill two birds with one stone, then we can leave ya's alone for the rest of the week." He gestured to the two-seater. "Can we take a seat?"

Dwayne took a step back into the kitchen. "In here'd be better."

"Oh sure," Terrell said and walked into the kitchen. I hadn't noticed a small table in there before, but they both pulled out a chair each and I stood in the small lounge room like a sore thumb.

"Come in, take a seat," Pops said.

I gave him a smile. "Thanks."

I sat on the sofa. "How've you been?"

"Yeah, all right." He still wheezed when he breathed, but he didn't sound any worse. And he certainly didn't appear to be upset, like CJ had implied when he said he'd prefer I didn't come around again. "You know," Pops continued with a smile, "you look comfortable here."

What an odd thing to say. "Comfortable?"

"Like you don't mind it." Pops wheezed some more and I waited for him to continue. "We've had all sorts here, parole officers, home nurses, doctors. None of them like it too much. Sit where you're sittin' and look like they're too good for it, know what I mean?"

"Your house?" I clarified. I looked at CJ, who was still standing at the front door, then back to Pops. "Reminds me of the house I grew up in. I ain't too good for anything, Pops. We're not that different."

I didn't know why I said that. Why I admitted that much. Giving that much of myself away wasn't in any plan of mine. I could feel CJ's eyes burning into me but I couldn't bring myself to look at him just yet, so I concentrated on Pops. "Weather not too cold for you yet?"

"Nah. CJ looks after me. Makes sure I'm warm."

My gaze shot to CJ and I gave him a smile. "That's good. I'm glad to hear that." I could hear Terrell and Dwayne going through their questions and answers and I knew they'd be a little while yet. "CJ, maybe you and I should talk outside?" He didn't speak, just turned on his heel and walked out the front door. I stood up, patted Pops on the shoulder. "You take care."

He smiled up at me. "You're a good lad."

I went outside with the manila folder still in my hand and found CJ back at the shed. It was his bike he'd been working on. It was up on an old drum can so both wheels were off the ground. He stared at me, put a cigarette between his lips, and lit it.

"Should you be smoking near that?" I nodded toward the bike. "Fuel or whatever."

He blew smoke upwards. "What do you want?"

Well, here went nothing. He hadn't told me to fuck off yet, so I figured now was my chance. "I've been doing some research into apprenticeships."

His eyes narrowed.

"And I reckon you'd be a good candidate for a mechanic—"

"No."

"They have these programs these days that help—"

"No."

"You could be qualified—"

"What part of no don't you under-fucking-stand?"

I sighed. "CJ, I can help you."

"I don't want your help."

"Why not?"

"Because I don't."

"If it's because of the paperwork involved, I can help you with that."

He clenched his teeth so hard his jaw bulged. "I said I don't want your help."

"But you didn't give me a good enough reason."

"Because fuck you, that's why."

I tried not to smile and stayed silent for a while. I needed to change the subject. "What's it like to have your dad home?"

Something flashed in his eyes, just for a second, before it was gone. He shoved the cigarette back to his lips and drew hard on it. "'S all right. Why?"

I shrugged. "Dunno. Just thought you and Pops had a good thing going, that's all. It's not easy when things change." I figured I'd hit the nail on the head with that because he stayed silent and didn't tell me to fuck off.

"Did you mean what you said before?" he asked, flicking his cigarette butt away. "About growing up in a house like this?"

"Yep. I grew up in community housing."

CJ chewed on his lip. He didn't say anything for a long time but there was something different. A tiny part of his defensive wall was down. "How'd ya soccer match go?"

I was surprised he'd remembered, but I was glad that he had. "Good. We lost, but it was fun."

"It was fun to lose?"

I snorted. "Yeah. Felt good to be part of something."

He made a face and laughed me off. "Whatever."

"You should come watch one time," I offered, knowing damn well he never would. "Or play, even."

He squinted at me. "Did you hit your head or something?"

I laughed, and as much as I wanted to stay and talk to him, I felt it was time to go. I waved my hand toward the house. "I should probably go see how Terrell's getting on."

CJ's only response was a slight nod.

I took a step toward the house and stopped. I turned and stared at him and thought *fuck it*. I held up the manila folder. "Just hear me out on this apprenticeship deal. Listen to everything, and if you still want to tell me to fuck off, then you can. But just hear me out."

I thought for a second that he would fly off the handle and hurl a bunch of profanities, but he didn't. He shook his head and smiled. "You don't know when to quit, do ya?"

I tried not to look too hopeful. "Nope." Figuring this was my one and only chance, I opened the folder. "They have avenues now where you can get what's called recognised prior learning, which means if Mr Barese'll sign off on what you do every day, you'll get passes on most of the subjects."

"Mr Barese don't have time—"

"I've already asked him and he said yes."

CJ raised an eyebrow that was as scary as it was perfect. "You did, huh?"

"Yep. Anyway," I kept on going, "hopefully we can get it down to maybe sitting the final exam."

And just like that, the mask was back. Cold, detached, defensive.

"But you can have what they call a 'writer.' So the test is verbal, and someone, this 'writer' writes down everything you say. You don't have to read or write anything."

He crossed his arms. "I ain't fucking stupid."

"Far from it. In fact, the reason you made it this far, I'd reckon, is because you're smarter than most."

His jaw bulged. "Made it this far?"

"Yes." I wasn't backing down on this. "You got this far through life dodging the need to read or write very well, and that takes a different kind of smarts. Not many people can do that."

He was half a second away from telling me to fuck off.

"But you don't have to anymore. I can help you. First, I'll get you qualified. You'll have a full mechanic qualification by the end of the year. Then," I hedged, "we can start on the reading and writing."

He stared, silent, angry.

"It's nothing to be ashamed of, CJ."

"Noah?" Terrell called out from the driveway. I hadn't heard him come out.

"One sec," I replied. I turned back to CJ. "You should know that you didn't fail anything. You didn't fail school. The education system failed you."

His nostrils flared. "Fuck you."

"No. Fuck them. Fuck them for not giving a shit. Fuck the world for dealing good people shitty hands." I pointed my finger at his chest. "You deserve better. You deserve better than a fucked-up father who broke your arm when you were nine and fucking teachers who didn't care if you turned up or not." I'd said far too much, but he hadn't punched me in the mouth yet, so I took it as a win. I looked him right in the eye. "You deserve better."

With that, I turned and walked back to the car, adrenaline warring with resignation. I opened the door and took my seat and Terrell started the car. "How was the old man?" I asked, doing up my seatbelt.

"All right. Reckons he's turned a new leaf, but the attitude hasn't changed much." He sighed. "I dunno. He's got a real mean-bastard look in his eyes. What about CJ? Looked pretty intense between you two."

I resisted the urge to groan. "I suggested the apprenticeship and pathways to recognised prior learning."

"And?"

"And I'm pretty sure it's a no."

"Pretty sure?"

"Well, the words 'fuck you' don't exactly say yes."

Terrell stopped the car at the intersection to give way, right in front of the old, weathered, broken street sign that said 'Davis Road.' He stared at it for a long second. "What the hell does it take to break the cycle of Davis Row?"

I frowned and sighed, resigned. "I wish I knew."

I TRIED HARD NOT to think about CJ or to wish he'd call, but every so often a slither of dark eyes or a waft of cigarette smoke would assault my memory and he'd be in the forefront of my mind yet again.

He never phoned, not that I expected him to. But I hoped. And whether I hoped he'd call me for his benefit or mine was something I didn't want to examine too closely.

By the time Saturday came around, I was keen to put on my soccer boots and really keen for a night out. I needed to de-stress, and sweating it out on the soccer field and having a few beers afterwards was the perfect fix.

We lost the match by one goal, but we held our defence well and passed the ball around pretty good. For a team of mismatched newbies, we did all right. It was good for a laugh anyway and the constant running pushed my legs and burned my lungs in a feels-good way. By the time we were back at the pub I couldn't even remember the stressful week I'd had.

I sipped my beer. "Man, that tastes good."

"Yeah, you up for a session?" Gallan slid in beside me.

"Could be. Had a pretty shit week. A few drinks sounds pretty bloody great."

He nodded and sipped his beer. "I know what you mean." He launched into his description of shift work and a hard boss, which didn't sound all too pleasant either. "Though it ain't really my boss' fault. He's got his bosses breathing down his neck."

"My boss is okay," I said. "Actually, they're all okay. Some of the people I work with are a bit jaded but most are in it for the right reasons. And most of the cases I have are fine, but then there's some that just don't want help. It's really frustrating."

And just like that, I was thinking about CJ again.

"Yeah, I can't imagine doing what you do." Gallan nudged his knee with mine under the table where no one else could see. "But a few beers tonight sounds like a real good plan."

Okay, so things with him were definitely headed in a personal, possibly physical direction. And maybe I needed that more than the beers. Maybe I needed to hook up with Gallan to get CJ out of my head. Which was ridiculous, because there was nothing between me and CJ, there couldn't ever be something between me and CJ, but damned if my short-sighted brain could tell my heart that.

And Gallan was a good-looking guy. Not my usual type, but he was kinda cute and he was looking at me every so often like he wanted to undress me. I paced the beers and ordered some food for our table to share. Most of the guys had gone home by the time the sun had set and our conversations were getting louder and funnier and I had a heady buzz. I didn't think I'd stopped smiling and it had been so long since I'd been out and had a laugh.

But then Tony stood up. "Better get home or I'll be in the doghouse. You guys wanna share a cab?" Tony asked.

"I will," Davo said, then downed the rest of his beer and got to his feet.

"Nah, I'm right," I replied.

"Yeah, I'm good," Gallan added.

Then it was just me and him.

He looked around the pub, at all the average fellas just having a drink and a chat. It certainly wasn't the kind of place where we could do anything . . . Then he leaned in and asked, "Wanna go down to the HQ?"

I smiled. Yep, something was definitely gonna happen tonight. "Yes, I do."

We finished the last of our beers and walked the few blocks down to the HQ. Maitland's only gay bar wasn't exactly pumping at seven on a Saturday night, but it wasn't dead. We ordered a Jim and Coke each and took a tall table near the back.

"Soooo," he hedged. "Gay? Bi? Curious?"

"Gay. You?"

"Same."

"So, are you out?" he asked point blank.

I sipped my bourbon. "Yeah. You?"

He nodded. "Mostly. I don't make a point of bringing it up in conversation, but if someone asks, I don't hide it."

I didn't want to get into the whole family thing. "No one at work's asked me yet," I said with a smile. "But yeah, I have no problem with telling them either."

He leaned in closer. "Can I ask . . . top or bottom?"

I almost choked on my drink. "Jeez. You just jump right in, don't you?"

He laughed. "Figure there ain't no point in beating around the bush. I've been trying to figure out which way you'd go, but I can't get a read on you."

Maybe it was the alcohol in me, but all I could do was laugh. In the end, I told him, "I'm vers. I do prefer to top, but if a guy knows what he's doing, then I'll ride cock for days."

Gallan busted up laughing. Like, so loud that others stopped and stared. "Oh, I like you."

It was weird, and as much as I liked him too, there were no sparks. No hint of anticipation, no nerves, no physical attraction, no . . . anything. I felt like I was out having drinks with an old friend. Which was nice, but it fell far short from hook-up material.

I drained my drink. "Want another one?" I asked.

His eyes were smiling or swimming, with alcohol, I wasn't sure. "Why not."

I bought that round, then two songs later, he bought the next. More people were filing in, but I was a bit too drunk to notice, apart from the jostling of bodies and the noise. But I was feeling pretty damn good. "'S my shout," I said. "Want another one?"

Gallan, who was a smiley drunk, shrugged then grabbed my hand and led me toward the backroom. I went willingly. More than willingly. His hand was warm and strong and I wanted that human contact. Needed it. It had been far too long.

The backroom was lined with bench seats, hidden nooks for privacy, and lit with blue lights. He crowded me against a wall, his eyes intense, and he licked his lips. I waited for the thrill, the expectancy, the pre-kiss butterflies. My lips parted, he kissed me, and . . .

Nothing.

Gallan pulled away with a look on his face like he couldn't remember if he left the stove on. It made me laugh.

A slow, somewhat confused smile spread across his face. "You felt nothing, right?"

"Absolutely zilch. Nada."

"Oh, thank God. Or that could be awkward because that was like kissing my cousin."

I snorted. "Kiss your cousin often?"

He scrubbed his hand over his face. "Never. But we're good, right?"

I pushed off the wall. I wasn't even disappointed. "We are good."

"Thank God, because it's your shout."

I laughed and pushed his shoulder toward the door, just as it swung open and someone came barrelling in, almost collecting me. And I found myself staring into dark brown eyes and the subtle smell of cigarettes.

And every response that had been missing with Gallan bombarded me. My blood ran hot, my nerves zinged with desire, and butterflies exploded in my belly. He was right there, almost touching me. My breath caught and I licked my bottom lip.

"Noah," he said, his voice low and laden with warning.

I fisted his shirt and pushed him against the wall. "CJ."

CHAPTER EIGHT

CJ

I'D MADE sure Pops had dinner, the fire was stoked, and my old man had a six-pack of beer and a game of football on TV. I got changed into something clean, took forty dollars from my secret stash as quietly as I could, grabbed my jacket, and was out the door before my father could ask me where I was goin'.

There was no way I was telling him the truth. If he knew I was headed into town to HQ in hopes of runnin' into my parole officer, I didn't know whether he'd laugh at me or punch me.

I was more inclined to go with the latter.

I had no clue what it was about Noah Huxley that got under my skin, but I couldn't stop thinkin' about him.

About his offer. About what he said.

I had to wait till dark so I could ride my bike into town, and I pulled up around the corner from HQ and took off my helmet. My old leather jacket was good protection, but the night air was getting cold.

God, I hated winter.

I pulled up my collar to stay warm and ducked inside

the bar. It was dark inside; it usually was. I hadn't been to HQ in a while, but it was familiar enough. I bought a Coke from the bar and hid in a corner so I could get a scope on the guys. I wasn't one for dancing, but I liked to watch guys dancing with other guys. Especially when they got all sweaty, grinding and kissing. It was hot as hell.

I wondered if Noah would even turn up. I had no proof that he would, I just hoped, which was a scary-as-hell feeling.

I scanned the crowd and saw him. The rush of seeing him was doused pretty quick when I realised he was here with someone. A tall guy, solid build, good-looking, and funny, it would seem. Noah was laughing. They both were. Something was funny, and they chatted easily. Both of them were drunk. I had the sinking feeling I'd read him wrong. I didn't know why on earth I thought for one foolish second that he'd be interested in me. He was way outta my league. He was smart and wore fancy clothes; he worked a government job. And what was I? Nothing but a fucking Davis.

Anger, at myself mostly, made my drink taste bitter. I was just about to leave when the tall guy grabbed up Noah's hand and took him to the backroom.

And I knew what happened in there.

I had to put my glass down before I crushed it. Or threw it. I ran my hand through my hair and looked at the exit door. Leaving was the sensible thing to do. But the door to the backroom was like a beacon. I couldn't take my eyes off it.

Fuck it, and fuck him for turning everything upside down. For making me think of him, for making me fantasise . . . For making me hope.

I was through the backroom door before I really knew what I was doing. I didn't really have a plan. Just to stop them, interrupt them . . . I didn't have a clue. If I found Noah with his fly undone and that guy on his knees . . .

But he wasn't. Noah and Tall Guy were laughing and I literally ran into Noah as they were walking back out. God, he was gorgeous, and why did he have to smell so damn good? Did he somehow know what it did to me? His smile became something else, his gaze fell to my lips, and he licked his. Jesus. God, he was trying to kill me. "Noah."

He grabbed my shirt and shoved me against the wall. "CJ."

Fucking hell.

He pushed his body against mine, in all the right places. I almost melted. My knees nearly buckled. I gripped his face, ready to crush my mouth to his, when Tall Guy barked out a laugh beside us. "Well, shit. That's what was missing," he said and laughed again.

Noah seemed to snap out of whatever spell he was under and he took a step back. He let go of my shirt and patted my chest. "Sorry. I don't know . . . shit. I'm sorry."

I still couldn't catch my breath.

Tall Guy said, "He's not sorry. Are you . . . ?" He looked at me and held his hand out to shake.

"CJ," I managed to say.

"Right," Tall Guy said. "I'm Gallan."

I shook his hand, and Noah cleared his throat. "Um. Yeah."

Just then, a short, pretty blond guy walked into the backroom. He stopped, looked at Gallan from his shoes to his hair, and gave a raised eyebrow in invitation. Gallan stared right back for all of two seconds before he mumbled, "Hell yes," and Noah and I watched as Gallan lifted the tiny guy up against the wall, his skinny legs wrapped around Gallan's huge frame, and they were going for it, right in front of us.

It literally took all of five seconds.

"That's what was missing," Noah mumbled. I didn't know what that meant, but he turned back to me. "What are you doing here?"

I ignored that and nodded to where Gallan and Tiny Guy were basically dry humping against the wall. "Uh, if he's your boyfriend . . . ?"

"He's not." Noah looked at the two of them, then back to me. "Come on, let's leave 'em to it." He didn't wait for a response. He just took my hand, pulled the door open, and dragged me toward the bar. It was a decent crowd by now, and when he stopped at the bar, he turned and I basically pressed right against him in the push and shove of people.

"Sorry," I mumbled.

He smiled. "I'm not." He was obviously pretty drunk, but from the way he looked at my mouth then into my eyes, the desire was clear in his gaze. "Want a drink?"

I shook my head. "No."

Just then, I got pushed from behind hard enough to press right into Noah, making him groan.

Fuck. "Sorry," I said, not really meaning it. The only thing I was sorry about was that I couldn't take it further.

He put his hand on my hip. "I'm not." Then he seemed to remember himself. He dropped his hand and tensed, his face now unreadable. "Shit."

He squirmed away from me, like it just occurred to him how much better he was than me. Well, fuck that. *What the hell did you expect, CJ?* Needing this to be over, I turned on my heel and stalked back through the crowd toward the exit. I didn't need that shit in my life, and I was stupid to come here.

I was stupid to think he was different.

"CJ!" I heard him call out.

But I was done. I just wanted to go home, back to where I belonged.

"CJ, wait!"

I got to the front door and stepped outside, only to see blue and red flashing lights down the street. I stopped cold. *Goddammit*. There were three marked cars, one highway patrol, and a bunch of uniforms standing around talking. They were just setting up a random breath test station by the looks of it.

Then Noah all but fell out the door and followed me to my bike. I didn't know if it was the cold air or if he was drunker than I first thought, but he swayed on his feet and almost came unstuck. "Whoa," he mumbled with his hands out, trying to balance himself.

I grabbed his arm to steady him. "How much did you drink?"

"Too much. Don't normally drink bourbon." Noah only then noticed the blue and red flashing lights. "Wha's going on?"

"Looks like an RBT," I replied. "Looks like I'll be waitin' a while till they're gone."

"Your bike?" he asked, looking at me, then my bike with one eye shut.

"Yep."

Noah swayed again. "But you didn't drink."

"No. I also don't have a licence."

Noah frowned. He looked to the cops and back again. "You can't ride it then."

I poked my finger into his chest. "How 'bout you don't tell me what I can and can't do."

"You get arrested for riding unlicensed and you go to jail."

"You know what? Fuck you."

"You're 'mpossible." He pointed his finger at me again. "How about you drop the bullshit and lemme help you. Why won't you lemme help you?"

"Because I ain't no charity case."

"No one said you were."

I rolled my eyes at him. "I ain't having this conversation with you right now." I stood at my bike, but there was no way I could ride out without going past the cops. Fuck, fuck, fuckity fuck.

"CJ," Noah said.

I did up my jacket, but before I could swing a leg over my bike, a uniformed officer walked over. "Everything all right here, gentlemen? Sounded like you were arguing."

Fuck.

"Yeah, no. We're all good," I managed. Noah was right. If they found me riding unlicensed while on parole, I was going to jail.

"Evening officer," Noah said slowly. "Everything's just fine." It wasn't really. He could barely stand up or string a sentence together, and I was considering turning and making a run for it.

But then Noah said the strangest thing. "Was gonna ride m' bike home but he won't lemme."

The policeman eyed Noah. "Sounds like he knows what he's talking about."

"Just live up the road," Noah said, waving his hand up the street. "If he won't lemme ride it, he can push it."

Oh, can I?

The cop then looked at me. "Are you right to push it?"

Hell no. "Yeah. I haven't been drinking."

The cop studied us both for a long second. "Right then. Push only. Don't even sit on it. If I hear the bike start, we'll have to chase you, and believe me, you don't want that."

No, no I didn't. "Thanks."

Noah grinned. "Come on then, *Clinton*, start pushing."

Clinton. *Clinton?*

He called me Clinton?

I clenched my jaw so I wouldn't swear in front of the cop. But I glared so hard at Noah, if looks could kill, he'd have dropped dead. All he did was laugh. He pointed up the street. "Bike won't push itself." And he started to walk. Or stagger was probably more like it.

I considered tackling him to the ground and smacking him in the mouth but decided my energy was better spent pushing my damn bike. He was, after all, doing me a favour. He'd just given me an excuse to push it away from the cops instead of riding it. I should have been thankful, but I swear everything he did just rubbed me the wrong way.

And then, as if his smug smile wasn't enough, halfway up the block he started to sing.

"Shut up," I hissed at him. He was on the footpath; I was on the street, pushing the bike as close to the gutter as I could. "Or the cops'll come and arrest you for disturbing the peace. Or butchering Cold Chisel. That's a federal offence in this country."

He laughed. "And you're welcome, by the way." He looked back to where the cops were now pulling cars over doing random breath testing. "For getting you outta that." And then, because he couldn't help himself, he chuckled. "Clinton."

"Don't fucking call me that."

"Why not? I like it."

"No one calls me that."

"Well, they should. It's a nice name."

Jesus Christ. "Are you takin' the piss? Because with a name like Noah, you probably shouldn't."

"What's wrong with Noah? Apart from the whole biblical thing." Then, because God didn't hate me enough, he started to sing, "The animals came in two by two," and doing what I thought was some kind of hopscotch up the footpath.

It would have been funny if I wasn't supposed to be pissed at him.

"Where the hell am I supposed to be pushin' my bike to?" I asked.

Noah stopped and looked up the street. "Just up there. 'S my place."

His place? "I ain't going to your place."

"Why not?"

"Because."

"Because why?"

"Because I ain't. That's why."

"Well, you can leave your bike at my house 'n walk home."

I stared at him. "I am not walking to Ten Mile Creek."

"Then you can sleep at my place."

I looked at him like he was crazy.

He pointed back toward the RBT. "If you'd prefer to spend th' night in a holding cell . . ."

"Oh shut up."

He started walking again, so I did too. "Whasso bad 'bout staying with me anyway?"

"Ah, you're my parole officer?"

"Yes, Clinton, I am. For three more weeks." He held up three fingers.

I ignored how he used my full name. It seemed the more

I scowled at him, the wider he smiled. "Are you counting down till you're rid of me?"

"I'm countin' down so I know how long I got t'change your life." I stopped pushing the bike and he stopped walking too. He stared at me. "What?"

"You want to change my life?"

"If you'll lemme." He pointed to a house across the street. "This is me."

He jumped off the gutter and I pulled him back before he got hit by a passing car. And then the bike almost fell over. "Goddammit. Will you watch where you're going?"

He stepped in real close, so close I could feel his body warmth. He stared at my mouth, then he grinned. "I *am* watching."

"You're drunk."

"And you're really fucking hot."

Stunned, I stepped back and he managed to cross the road without getting run over. I followed, wheeling the bike into his driveway.

"We can put it roun' the back. My carport's fine for m' car, but the bike'll be safer out the back," Noah said, walking down the side of the darkened house. He fumbled with a gate, then held it open. "What're you waiting for?"

I pushed the bike through the gate and around the back of the house. As much as I didn't want to agree with him, I didn't want someone to steal my bike either. I lined the bike up along the back fence, out of the way and out of sight in the dark. Then it was just me and him. I had no reason to be there. Not one. But a cold breeze blew in and I shivered. Or maybe it was the way he was looking at me.

"Come on," he said, pulling out his keys. Of course he couldn't get the key in the door, and the more he fumbled, the more he giggled.

"Here," I said, taking his keys. "Are you sure it's even the right one?"

He snorted out a laugh. "I'm very familiar with th' back-door option, yes."

I stopped trying to get the key in and stared at him. "That was the worst joke ever."

"No it wasn't. I'm really funny."

"You're really drunk." I couldn't see a damn thing. "Got your phone on ya? Shine a light on the door handle."

Then it took him two long minutes to fumble with his phone. Jesus Christ. "You're a pain in my arse," I grumbled, finally sliding the right key in once he'd got the light to work.

"I'd like to be," he slurred. "If you'd lemme." Then he laughed at himself. "Get it? A pain in your arse? Told you I's funny."

I pushed the door open, and Noah stepped in and swiped blindly for a light switch and the room lit up to reveal a laundry. He waved his arm around the room. "Can you believe the real estate tried t' call this a mudroom?" He barked out a laugh. "Ah, no, morons, it's a laundry."

"Most houses built a hundred years ago had the back door through the laundry," I said lamely. I dunno why. God, talk about awkward.

"Th' house is okay," he went on to say, walking through a door and flipping on another switch. "Small, old. Middle o' town. But the rent's cheap. And with the hideous lino, I'm not surprised."

I followed him into what was the kitchen. He was staring at the floor, or more importantly, the patterned lino floor. He looked up and put a hand to his forehead. "Jesus. Remind me to never look at this lino when I'm drunk."

I tried not to smile. And I really tried not to look at that damn freckle above his right eyebrow. "You're gonna feel like shit tomorrow."

"Nah. Water, Panadol. She'll be right."

"You should eat something."

"Probably. Oh my God, I could totally go a toasted cheese sandwich right now." He staggered to one cupboard and somehow managed to pull out a sandwich press without falling over.

God, he was going to hurt himself in a minute. "How about I make it?"

"I'm not that drunk."

"You ain't real sober, either."

He put the sandwich press on the counter and had to take a few steps to balance.

"Jesus. Sit down and I'll make it."

He turned unsteadily and squinted at me. "I'll go turn the heater on. 'S cold. You cold?"

"A bit."

He walked out of the kitchen and I heard him mumbling to himself about the heater, and I figured as long as I could hear him talking, he was fine. I found the bread in the pantry, sliced cheese and butter in the fridge. I wasn't familiar with the toaster, so I found a frying pan next to the stove and switched the hotplate on. Then I thought of something. "Is that heater gas?" I yelled out. Jesus, if it was, he could kill us all.

"'S electric," he replied.

Thank God.

I turned to find him leaning against the kitchen doorway, looking at me. "What?"

He didn't even try to hide the fact he was staring at me. "Like seeing you in m' kitchen."

I swallowed hard and turned back to the pan. "I dunno

how the toaster press thing works so I'm cooking 'em in the frypan. Taste better, anyway."

I fixed two sandwiches and put them in the frypan together.

Then he was beside me, peering into the pan. "Tha's how my mum used to make 'em when I was a kid."

I wasn't sure what to say to that or to the fact he was basically leaning on me, so I just concentrated on the sizzling pan instead. I flipped them when they were done and by then, Noah was leaning against the cabinet staring at me.

It made my stomach do crazy things, and made the room feel too small. I had no clue what I was doing. I was standing in my parole officer's kitchen, for fuck's sake. He was drunk, and I was makin' him toasted cheese sandwiches. I was starting to think I'd lost my mind. I turned the stove off. "Can you grab some plates?"

He managed to put two plates on the countertop, then did some three-step dance at the fridge and managed to find two bottles of water without falling over. Once he was leaning against the kitchen counter again and looked like he wasn't going to face plant, I handed him a plate. "Eat that."

He only took one bite and made a groaning sound that was low and filthy. "Tha's so good."

Jesus. If that's how he sounded when he ate food, I could only imagine what he sounded like in bed. It sent my mind to places it had no right to go. "Uh. Thanks."

We ate in silence. Well, he kept making obscene sounds that made my heart thump funny, but I never made a sound. When I was done, I took a mouthful of water. "I uh, I wonder when the cops will be done down the road . . ."

Noah put his empty plate on the bench. "You can stay here. I got a spare room. Or the couch."

"I'm not sure that's a good idea."

"Better than getting busted." He downed half his bottle of water in one gulp. His Adam's apple bobbed up and down with every swallow. God, I wanted to lick it. I quickly looked away and gripped the countertop behind me so I wouldn't move. "An' anyway, now I've got two things to help you with." He held up two fingers. "Getting you qualified as a mechanic, and getting your rider's license."

"You're gonna do all that in three weeks?"

"Well, it'll take longer than three weeks. But I'm in it for the long haul." He pushed himself off the counter to stand right in front of me. "If you are."

He was so close. Too close, yet not close enough. I wanted to pull him against me. I wanted to feel his body against mine. His warmth, his strength, his smell. God, he smelt so good. He was staring at my mouth again, his eyes fixated and dark.

"Wanna kiss you," he mumbled. He pulled his bottom lip in between his teeth in a way that made my knees weak. If he noticed the rapid rise and fall of my chest or my shortness of breath, he never said. He leaned right in, our lips not quite touching. God Jesus fucking help me, I wanted it. I could almost taste him. So close, so very close . . . and then he pulled away. "But not for three weeks."

I had to shake my head to get my thoughts in order. "What?"

"Three weeks till I can kiss you." He slow blinked and I remembered that he was drunk. "When you won't be one of m' cases. Can't be messin' around with anyone on my job list."

"What makes you think I'll let you kiss me?" It was a lame response but all I was capable of right then.

He smiled. "I seen the way you look at me. And you make a really good toasted cheese sammich."

I laughed because it was safer than talking.

Then he put his hand on my chest. The heat of it burned in the very best way. "I wanna help you. So you should lemme. And I wanna kiss you. In three weeks. So you should lemme."

"Is that right?"

He nodded. "I meant what I said at your place. You deserve better."

"And you think you're better?"

"Nope. Not at all." He shook his head and frowned. *God, why did I believe him when he said that?* "But I know what you're doing."

I could barely speak. "What am I doing?"

"You get through life trying to be invisible. You think no one'll notice you don' read or write too well if you just hide in th' background. Disappear. You think if they don' notice you, they won't ever know. Well guess what?" He slid his hand up to my neck and ran his thumb over my jaw. I couldn't breathe. "I see you, Clinton Davis. I see you."

I tried to speak. I tried to swallow. I couldn't do either.

"I need to go to bed," he said, slow-blinking. "You can sleep in the spare bed or on th' couch." Then he grabbed the front of my jacket and led me into the living room. He let go of me and smiled. "If you get into my bed by mistake, I won't tell no one."

"I uh, I don't think I should."

"Don't go." He said it like he was stone-cold sober. "Don't risk it. Please." And with that, he walked down a short hall and disappeared into what I assumed was his bedroom.

I sat on the sofa with every intention of waiting an hour

or two, then riding home. The cops'd be gone by then and I could sneak out of town. It was a nice living room. He had one of those flat-screen TVs and a fancy bowl on a cabinet along with some nice family photos; mum, dad, sister, and Noah. I mean, it was literally picture perfect. He was so much more put-together than me. I could only dream of living in a place like his or having what he had.

Noah fucking Huxley was well and truly under my skin. I should have left right then and there. I should have never gone home with him. There was something about him I couldn't get enough of.

I lay back on his surprisingly comfy couch and tried really hard not to think about what he'd said. How he'd touched me, almost kissed me. Admitted to wanting to kiss me. About how much I wanted him to.

God, I'm in so much trouble.

The next thing I knew it was morning, and something smelt a lot like bacon and eggs.

I sat up, remembering I was at Noah's place, wondering how the hell I could get out the door without it being awkward. I had to walk through the kitchen to get out the back where my bike was, so there was no way I could not see him. *Shit.* I rubbed the back of my neck and scrubbed my face, trying to think of something to say.

"Hey, Sleeping Beauty's awake." Noah's voice was a little rough. "How're your coffee-making skills?"

I got up and walked into the kitchen. He was standing at the stove wearing nothing but a pair of grey tracksuit pants that kind of hung a little low and looked real soft. His shoulders were broad; his back had muscles in all the right places. He wasn't built; he wasn't skinny either. He was decidedly normal in an extraordinary way. Then he turned around. His chest had a spattering of blond hair with a trail from his navel that disappeared under the waistband of his sweats.

God damn.

Noah held an egg flip in one hand, a smug smile and curious eyes. I'd just blatantly checked him out and he saw the whole thing. "Hungry?"

I cleared my throat. "I didn't mean to fall asleep."

"Lucky I left the heater on." He turned back to the stove but waved his hand toward the kettle. "Can you make some coffee?"

Okay, so this was weird. He didn't think this was awkward at all? "Do, uh, you have strange guys sleep on your couch often?"

He snorted. "No. Just you."

Just you.

I tried real hard not to like that.

I filled the kettle and flicked it on. "How's your head?" I asked. "You were pretty cut last night."

"I feel like absolute shit." He was oddly cheerful about that. "I'm hoping a greasy breakfast fixes me. I was gonna make coffee earlier but didn't want the kettle to wake you."

"I don't think I moved all night. Your couch is comfortable."

He laughed and started dishing up bacon and eggs. "Yeah, I've lost count how many times I've fallen asleep on it."

I opened overhead cupboards until I found coffee cups, and thankfully he had a jar of coffee and a bowl of sugar left out on the bench so I didn't have to go looking for it. "How do you like your coffee?"

"White with one sugar. Kinda strong."

I could do that easily enough, but then I went to his fridge for the milk. Of course he used a different kind of milk than I was used to. But there was a box in the door shelf that had a jug of white stuff on the front of it. I knew what the word 'milk' looked like but it wasn't written on it. I could either look like an idiot and get the wrong one or I could ask. Neither was preferable, but I took the lesser evil. I took it and held it out to him. "This one good?" It was always better asking if it was the right one to use, like it might have been out of date or something, rather than ask a stupid question like, 'Is this milk?'.

He took a quick glance before putting the frypan in the sink. "Yep. It just says Barista's Own instead of milk. Dunno why. But I buy the UHT milk from the shelf, not cartons of cold milk. It's cheaper."

I quickly turned back to the now-boiling kettle. Did he just explain why the word 'milk' wasn't visible? I mean, he knew I couldn't read too well, but he didn't treat me like I was stupid or spell it out to me. I didn't know what to make of that. I was waiting for him to make a point of it, but he just acted like it was normal.

I poured the water, then the milk. "Yeah, me too."

It was true. I always bought the cheapest groceries I could. Usually home-brands or packaging I was familiar with. Walking into a grocery store was hard enough when I couldn't read the fucking labels. Having pictures on the front helped so much, but what kind of milk company made a carton of milk without the word milk on it?

Noah put the two plates on his dining table, then got the cutlery. I put his coffee on the table and sipped mine, not sure where he wanted me to sit. I wasn't expecting breakfast, that was for damn sure. He took another plate of toast out of the oven and sat it in between the plates and fell into a chair. He sipped his coffee and hummed. "Oh my God.

That is good." He nodded toward the other plate. "Take a seat. Dig in."

We ate in silence. Him, trying to fix his hangover. Me, just savouring the taste of bacon. I hadn't had it in a while. I really should buy some for Pops . . .

"So, about last night." Noah sipped his coffee again. "First, I should apologise. I was drunk and made a bit of an arse of myself. I really don't drink very often. As you could probably tell."

I put my knife and fork down on my empty plate. "You remember last night?"

He frowned, and his cheeks tinted pink. "Uh, yeah. I remember all of it."

So he remembered the 'three weeks till I can kiss you' conversation . . .

"And I meant it," he added. He shifted in his seat a bit and chewed on his bottom lip. "I do want to help you. If you'll let me." Then he stared right into my eyes. "And I meant what I said about the waiting three weeks." He blushed some more but didn't look away. Jesus. He was braver than me.

I had to look at my plate. Anywhere but at him. The air in the room suddenly felt like it could catch fire. "Um, yeah, right."

He chuckled. "You don't have to answer that part yet. You have three weeks to decide."

"Now you're letting me decide?" I shot him a look. "Last night you kinda implied it was a done deal."

He snorted. "Well, I know you want it as much as I do."

"Is that right?"

"Yep."

"How can you be so sure?"

"Because you're still here."

"I fell asleep."

He shrugged. "And you haven't told me no." He sat there, staring at me, waiting for me to tell him no. All I had to do was say the word no . . .

Fuck. I couldn't. Not even close.

He grinned. "That's what I thought." He took my plate and set the dirty dishes in the sink. "I need to shower, but then I was thinking we could load your bike into the boot of my car and I'll drive you back to Ten Mile Creek."

"I can ride from here."

"I don't want you getting busted. It'll take me twenty minutes, tops. No big deal."

I frowned at that. It was a big deal, to me at least. No one really ever went out of their way to help me.

"I can drop you off at the corner if you don't want your old man to see me," he added.

God, I hadn't even thought of that. "Yeah, probably a good idea."

"Does he know? That you're . . . that you go to HQ?"

I smirked. "That I'm gay? Hell no. He'd belt the ever-loving piss outta me if he found out."

Noah's jaw clenched, but he nodded. "Then we better make sure he doesn't find out."

I shrugged one shoulder. "Don't matter none. He won't be out for long."

"You sound pretty sure of that."

I snorted. "I know my old man."

Noah seemed to think that over for a bit, and if he wanted to say something about my father, he chose not to. "I'm just gonna grab a quick shower. Please still be here when I get out. Make yourself another cuppa if you like. And maybe make me another one to be ready in about ten minutes." He walked past and put his hand on my shoulder. Just a simple touch that made me crave more.

More human contact. More warmth, more anything . . .

"Noah?"

He stopped at the hall. "Yeah?"

"Thank you."

"What for?"

For not making fun of me when I didn't know what carton the milk was. For understanding about my father. For being nice to me. "For breakfast."

He smiled like he knew what I didn't say. "Anytime."

TWENTY MINUTES LATER, we had my bike secured in the boot of Noah's car and the boot lid strapped down. "I don't have to take you back straight away," Noah said while I had a cigarette. He sounded hopeful and I liked that more than I should.

"Nah, I better get home. Make sure Pops is okay."

I was kinda nervous about the drive home with him. I didn't want a twenty-minute lecture on gettin' qualified or riding my bike without a licence. But he never mentioned any of it. He talked about random shit like the song on the radio and how he was finding Maitland. He told me about his soccer game and how he had to get groceries later and do more laundry, all the boring shit no one really talked about.

I didn't know whether he was talking so much to keep it from gettin' awkward between us or if it was so I wouldn't ask him any questions. I really didn't know much about him, and I wanted to know more but was kinda too scared to ask. Maybe he knew that too.

Just before the turn-off to Ten Mile Creek, he pointed

to a huge 'Sold' banner pasted over a 'For Sale' sign. "That wasn't there the other day."

"Must've been cheap, because who the hell'd wanna buy land out here?" I wondered out loud. "It's a hole."

"It's fifteen minutes from town. The mines are pushing up rentals and house prices. It'd be cheaper out here than in town, that's for sure." He turned off the main road into Ten Mile Creek. "You know, this town ain't so bad."

"You didn't grow up here."

"True."

"It's dying. There's no money here."

We passed Mr Barese's garage. Noah nodded at it. "How many years do you reckon Mr Barese'll keep the shop open for? He's getting on, isn't he?"

"Dunno. I haven't really thought of that." Jesus. Why hadn't I thought of that? That'd leave me with no money, no income. Nothing. Ain't no one else'd give me a job . . .

"That's why we need to get you qualified. And licenced." He smiled at me like he'd won first prize in something.

I didn't reply, just frowned at the countryside out the window until Noah pulled over at Davis Road. He did a U-turn and cut the engine. "You good?" he asked.

"Yeah." I got out of the car and went to the back and started undoing the straps. Together, we lifted my bike out and Noah closed the boot.

"Well then," he started. "Have you got a mobile? I could give you my number . . ."

I shook my head. "Nope. Never had a need for one."

He nodded slowly and shoved his hands in his back pockets. "Well, I don't have home visits this week so it'll be up to you to come into the office."

I nodded. "Yeah, I know."

"What days do you work?"

"This week? Monday, Wednesday, and Friday."

"I think you're due in on Thursday, yeah?"

I nodded again. He knew damn well when I was due in. "Yeah."

"Okay then." He walked back to the driver's door and opened it. "If you need to . . . not be here"—he pointed his thumb down the road to my house—"you know where I live."

Before I could reply, he got in, started his car, and drove away. I threw a leg over my bike and kick-started it. The loud roar made me smile, and I was still smiling when I walked into my house.

Until my father took one look at me. "Where the fuck've you been?"

And just like that, gone were the happy thoughts of Noah and the happy time I'd spent with him, and my reality came crashing back to earth with a resounding thud.

CHAPTER NINE

NOAH

I SPENT TOO many hours thinking about CJ Davis. I thought about him when I cleaned my house. I thought of him when I was in my car. I thought of him when I was in the shower, when I was in my bed at night.

I'd laid my cards on the table with him. I'd told him outright I wanted to wait until we were no longer in a professional relationship so we could possibly find ourselves in a personal one . . . a physical one.

And holy hell, I wanted him in a very physical way.

It was easy enough to tell him with a belly full of bourbon bravado. I'd put my hand to his neck, feeling the strength of his jaw, and it had taken every cell of self-control not to kiss him. Even sober, I admitted to remembering what I'd said. I wouldn't deny it.

I couldn't deny it.

There was something about him that picked at my subconscious, that tugged at my heart. And he didn't say no.

So three weeks . . . we just had to wait three weeks.

I meant what I said about wanting to help him. And I would put that above everything else. I wanted to help him make a better life for himself, and he needed to know that was a priority over my wanting to kiss him. If I had to choose one over the other, it'd kill me, but I'd help him before I ruined a chance at a better life for him.

So many people had turned their backs on him—teachers, welfare, his family—and I needed him to know I wouldn't do that. Even if we did start something personal and it didn't work out, I still wouldn't give up on him.

I gave myself until Thursday, when he was due to come into my office, to work out what the hell I was going to say to him.

But I didn't get until Thursday. Because first thing Tuesday morning, I'd just sat down at my desk and took my first sip of coffee when Sheryl knocked on my door. "You got an appointment with a CJ Davis first thing?" As the office manager, she would have had him down for a Thursday visit . . .

My heart galloped and I tried not to give anything away. "Ah, yeah. It was a late change, sorry. Is he here?"

She nodded. "Yep. You can finish your coffee if you want. I'm sure he can wait five minutes."

"No, it's okay." I stood up and met her at the door. We had meeting rooms and interview rooms for clients, but I wanted to keep this as private as I could. "I'll bring him into my office. I have some apprenticeship stuff online I want to show him."

"Okay," she said, obviously not really caring either way.

I followed her out to the reception area, and there he was. Sitting in a chair, his long legs spread wide in front of him. He wore work boots, black jeans, a grey shirt, and a black coat. My God, he could be the poster child for gorgeous bad boys. I fought a smile as we made eye contact, and he smirked as he stood up.

I cleared my throat. "Ah, we'll meet in my office today," I said for Sheryl's benefit.

CJ shrugged and followed me down the hall to my office. I stood aside and closed the door behind him. He took a seat across from my desk and smiled at me as I sat down.

"You're in early this week. Everything okay?" I asked.

He nodded. "I've been thinking about what you said."

"Which part?"

He let out a slow breath, and with a courage I couldn't begin to fathom, he said, "I wanna get my mechanics ticket. And I wanna get my licence." He swallowed hard. "And I want to learn to read."

Well, holy shit.

After a moment of shock, I grinned at him. "Absolutely." But then I wondered why the change of heart. "Did something happen?"

His eyebrows knitted together. "Not really. Well, when you dropped me home . . . I walked inside and my dad started yelling cuz he was outta cigarettes, like it was my fault. And I kinda realised that if nothing changes, nothing changes. Know what I mean? Like if I want things to be different, I need to make 'em different."

I had to grip the arms of my desk chair so I didn't get up and hug him. "I know exactly what you mean." I couldn't stop the grin that spread across my face. "I'm really excited for this, so thank you. It can't have been easy."

He shrugged. "Well, what you said about how long Mr Barese'll have the shop for kinda hit home too. If he were to shut up shop tomorrow, I'd have nothin'."

I nodded slowly. I was glad my words had some impact on him, but I hated that he was doing this out of a sense of helplessness. I picked up a pen and started making a list. "Okay, so we need a plan. A list of priorities and what we need to get started. I'll start contacting the local community college and see what I can do about the recognised prior learning. We'll need to get you enrolled, so there'll be some paperwork but I can help you with that."

He shifted in his seat. "I have some money saved. I was keepin' it in case Pops needed something medical, but I can use that."

I paused. "Let me see what grants I can find. There are initiative-based or incentive grants for people like you."

He stared at me. "People like me?"

God, he was always on the defensive. "Yes. People who are trying to make changes in their lives. People who want better for themselves and their families. I might be able to get the enrolment fees covered, that's what I'm saying."

He seemed to relax a little once he realised I wasn't having a shot at him. "Oh, okay."

"Look CJ, I have to tell you something." Here went nothing. "I need you to know this won't be easy. There'll be times you'll wanna quit, and there'll be times you'll wanna pull your hair out. But it *will* be worth it. There is a goal at the end, and there is a finishing line. It's not forever. But everyone involved will want to help. It's their job to help."

He flinched. Just barely, but I saw it. "Like it's your job to help."

"Well, yes, but I meant the teachers and program administrators. Those people. But that brings me to the next part . . ." I took a breath and a whopping leap of faith. "No matter what happens between us, it doesn't affect or change what happens with you, okay?"

"What do you mean?"

"Well, I meant what I said about the three-week thing." I gave him a second to catch on. He did. "Three weeks and you're no longer on my books, and then if I happen to run into you in a bar one time and we start up a conversation that leads to . . . other things, then we're not breaking any rules, right?"

His lips twitched. "Right."

I grinned at him. "I'm glad we're on the same page with that. Anyway, if for whatever reason you decide I'm too sexy or too good in bed and you think you'd rather part ways, then our work agreement—getting you qualified and licenced—that doesn't change. Or stop, or whatever. You don't lose that if you'd rather we just be friends, okay?"

"Too good in bed?" He pursed his lips together like he might bust up laughing at any second.

I chuckled and nodded. "Stranger things have happened."

"I bet they have."

We sat there and stared at each other, both of us smiling for a moment. "How long are you in town for?"

"Just a bit. Gotta grab a few things. Mr Barese loaned me his car."

I picked up my pen and added 'Roads and Maritime Services and car licence' to the list. "RMS for your car licence too then."

CJ sighed. "I ain't drivin' around with no stupid L plates."

"Yes you will. I'll help you get your hours up. You can learn in my car."

"In Roller Girl?"

"What's wrong with her? She's a good car!"

He rolled his eyes, but he fought a smile.

"How's Pops going?" I asked.

"Yeah, good. It's a bit harder for him to stay outta my old man's way, but he's okay."

"Do you think your dad might find work? That'll get him out of the house a bit."

CJ snorted. "He ain't ever worked a day in his life."

Oh.

"Well, hopefully the dust'll settle soon and things'll be easier."

He raised one eyebrow but didn't reply to that. He let out a sigh. "He doesn't know I'm doing this."

"Getting qualified?"

He nodded. "Yeah."

"Why not? What will he do when he finds out?"

"Probably laugh at me. Tell me to stop thinkin' I'm better than I am."

My stomach tightened. "CJ, no matter what he says, you know that's not true. You are better than you think you are. And you deserve a shot at this."

He looked down at his lap and eventually gave me a nod. "I want to be."

Bloody hell. I wanted to hug him again. "You'll nail this. You watch. You'll pass everything and the only thing you'll be left wondering about is why you didn't do it sooner."

When he looked up, his dark eyes were vulnerable, like the true CJ Davis was exposed within them. "Because ain't no one believed in me before now."

All of a sudden I had a lump in my throat and my eyes burned. Fuck. "They must have been blind."

He shrugged and it seemed that our talking time was done. "So, what do I do now?"

"Can you come back today? In about an hour or so? Whenever you're finished doing whatever it is you came to town for. I should have our full list done by then."

"Yeah, okay." He stood up and walked to the door.

"CJ?"

He stopped, turned, and waited for me to speak.

"Thank you."

He gave a nod and opened the door.

"And don't get busted by the cops."

He smiled and disappeared down the hall.

I threw my pen down and leaned back in my chair. Sheryl appeared a moment later. "Everything okay?"

I was grinning. "He's agreed to an apprenticeship." I left out the part where he didn't have a licence in case she saw him driving away. "And to getting help with reading and writing."

Her smile matched mine. "A good start to the day!"

"The best."

BY THE TIME CJ came back into my office, I had a complete list of things we needed to get done. And it was a long list.

He sat at my desk again, smelling of mint and cigarettes. A mixture I was getting to like. "Did you have lunch yet?"

"Nah. I'll grab something when I get home."

"Okay, so I made some progress," I started, tapping the notepad in front of me. "It looks a little daunting, but I promise it's not that bad."

He didn't look at the list. He looked at me and offered a sarcastic, "Great."

"Do you have a birth certificate?"

He scratched his head. "Yeah, I think so. Somewhere. I think Pops has it stashed some place."

"Well, we're gonna need that to get a photo ID card at the RMS. It'll help when getting your licences. Oh, and we'll need a utility bill, like power or phone. With your name and address."

"Okay."

"I'll take you into the RMS and we can get that done anytime. No worries. You'll need to sign your own name, but that's it."

"I can sign my own fucking name."

I ignored his tone. "Then we can apply to sit the motor-bike rider licence. There are two three-and-a-half hour sessions with an instructor, here in town. It's pretty much just to see if you can ride and obey road rules. You'll pass that, no problem."

He nodded.

"Then there's a test. It'll be in the RMS office, on a computer where you answer random questions. You're allowed to have a helper or a translator, someone from their office who will read you the question and answer only what you tell them. They don't answer for you, they just read the questions and you tell them the answer."

He let out a deep breath.

"You'll have your L's for three months, but you're allowed to ride on public streets by yourself. Then you can sit for the provisional test. It's another six-hour skills test, then another computer test where you can have the assistant again."

He blinked.

"Now, for the driver licence for a car, it's a bit different. It's your birthday in four months, right?" His date of birth was in his files, so I knew it was in October.

"Ah, yeah? So?"

"If you sit for a driver licence over the age of twenty-five, you don't have to do the 120 hours and twelve months on your learners. The test is a bit different but I can help you study for that, and in four months, you'll nail it."

He puffed out his cheeks and exhaled slowly.

"I know it's a lot to take in, and it's kinda daunting straight up. But we'll tackle them all one at a time, and you'll be fine."

He swallowed hard. "And the apprenticeship?"

"Well, I spoke to the boss of the automotive department at the local TAFE. The year has already started; they're about halfway through. But, if you enrol part-time, you can join anytime of the year. And, because I reckon you'll qualify for recognised prior learning, you'll have it done by the end of the year."

He was starting to look a little overwhelmed.

"The downside is the fees are the full amount, whether it takes you the full three years or six months. And it's 2,900 bucks."

The colour drained from his face.

"But—" I held up my hand. "There's an office in town called the Support for Adult Australian Apprentices, and I've requested a meeting with them because they run subsidies and they're gonna call me back. I can't guarantee a full waiver of fees, but I'll do my best."

CJ licked his lips and leaned back in his seat. He looked defeated already. "I can't afford that kind of money."

"I know. We'll work something out. Each TAFE has a payment program as well, so we have options. Let's just see what the Support office says. I want to meet with them personally so I can push your case rather than just a phone call."

He was quiet for a minute. "It's a lot to take in."

"It is. But like I said, one thing at a time. Isn't there a

saying about how even Everest was conquered by taking one step at a time?"

He snorted. "How the fuck would I know?"

I laughed at that. "But you're still keen, yeah? We're gonna do this?"

"We?" He tilted his head. "You mean me?"

"Well, yes. But I'll help you."

He let out an almighty sigh and his head fell back. "God, I dunno."

"One thing at a time, CJ. You don't have to agree to everything right now. Just say you'll get your rider licence first. Then I know you won't get picked up for that."

He gave me a bit of a growl before he sighed. "And the reading?"

"There are a few options. The best one, I think, is to have a tutor once a week. You can meet them here, not at home, for like an hour a week."

He made a face.

"Or you can go sit in a classroom with ten other people. Or you can do it all online."

His frown deepened. "All those options suck."

"I know. But I think a private tutor lesson would suit you better. It's one-on-one, and no one has to know. They'll probably give you some homework to do, but—"

"Homework?"

"Well, yeah."

CJ sighed. "Jesus Christ."

"If you sign up for it while you're still on parole, it's free. If you wait three weeks, you'll have to pay."

He looked at me like it was all my fault and like he was about to say it was all just too damn hard. I pushed my seat out from my desk. "You hungry? I'm starving. Let's grab some lunch." I didn't really give him a choice. I just held my door open and waited for him to join me. There was a café on the next block, and I figured the fresh air and walking time would be a good buffer.

The walk was short and I didn't mind the silence between us. I'd given him a lot to think about. He crammed his hands in his pockets and kind of hunched over as we walked, keeping his head down. I guessed it was him making himself as invisible as possible and it really bothered me that this was his default. I'd have rather he held his head up high so the world could see what a great guy he was. That he'd overcome the kind of adversity and shit people rarely survived. That, against everything life had thrown at him, he was still striving to be better.

Not many people could admit to that.

I held the door open for him. "After you." He rolled his eyes but almost smiled, though when we got to the counter, he hung back. "It's my shout. Pick whatever you want."

Then it occurred to me, he couldn't read the menu. God, I was such an idiot.

The display fridge had a range of pre-made sandwiches though, so I tried to cover my faux pas. "These look all right. Is there anything you don't eat? Not allergic to anything?"

"Um . . . nah, not allergic to anything. I'm not that hungry . . ."

He said he hadn't had lunch, so I didn't believe him. "Let me buy you lunch. It's just a sandwich. Then we can talk about where you want to start on that list." I pointed back to the sandwiches. "There's ham, cheese, and tomato? Or chicken, mustard, and cheese?"

His answer was quiet. "Ham. Thanks."

I ordered one ham and one chicken sandwich and two coffees, and we sat at a table. He was quiet as we ate, and I wondered if I'd pushed him too hard. I knew it was a lot to take in, and he was probably so overwhelmed right now.

I tapped his foot with mine, making him look up at me. "Sorry if I threw you in the deep end earlier. I know you're probably thinking it's too much, but I promise you, you'll be fine."

"How do you know?" He shook his head. "What if you set up all these things for me and I fail?"

"You won't fail. It won't be easy, but you'll get through it. You're smart, CJ. Don't let anyone tell you otherwise."

He rolled his eyes and mumbled, "I didn't even finish the seventh grade. They wanted to put me in some special learning class because I didn't read too good, so I bailed. Pops tried to help me a bit, though, but it was just easier to work with my hands. Fixin' cars is easy. I don't need to read much, and when I do, Mr Barese helps me with it."

"There are a lot of people who can't read or write too well, CJ. A lot. It's nothing to be ashamed of. The fact you've got where you are is a testament to how smart you are. And brave."

"Brave?" He laughed at that. "Yeah, right."

"Hell yes, brave. I can't even imagine walking into a store or a supermarket and not being able to tell the difference between toothpaste and haemorrhoid cream."

He finally broke with a genuine eye-crinkling smile. "Can't say I ever had that problem."

"I'm glad. Because it'd be bad enough tasting butt-cream, but applying toothpaste to an already sore arse would be hell."

He chuckled again, then leaned in and whispered, "I did get some studded condoms by mistake once. That were interesting."

I almost choked on my coffee. "I bet it was."

He lifted his coffee to his lips. "The second time I got them wasn't by mistake."

I laughed so loud people looked at me. But I noticed his cup was already empty, so I finished my coffee and stood up. "Come on, I better get back to work."

As soon as we stepped outside, he stopped to light a cigarette. I was gonna have a shot at him but figured we'd made good ground and I didn't want to end on a sour note.

He took a long drag and blew it out skyward. "No anti-smoking comment today?"

"Figured I'd save it. Let you enjoy your cancer-causing, artery-clogging cigarette in peace."

One corner of his lip curled into a smile; his silence was a happy one. We started the walk back to my office, but slower this time. Less hurried, like neither of us wanted our time together to end.

"So, you're not working Thursday, right?"

"Yeah. Why?"

"Well, how about I pick you up and we make a start on that list. First things first, a photo ID card and some rider licence application forms, we can grab the road rules book-let, and book you in for the next rider course."

He blew smoke out his nose and stared at me. "Hmm."

"I can pick you up from Mr Barese's shop if you don't want your old man knowing."

He squinted one eye as he took another drag of his cigarette.

I almost had him.

"Just bring your birth certificate, if you can find it. And a power or phone bill. Say, ten o'clock?"

We stopped at the front door to my work. "You ain't gonna let me get out of it, are ya?"

"Well, it's your choice . . ."

He rolled his eyes and started walking toward Mr Barese's car. He opened the door and just before he got in, he called out, "Ten o'clock."

My heart did some stupid skipping thing and I grinned like a fool. And, though I couldn't be one hundred per cent sure, as CJ drove away, it looked like he was smiling too.

CHAPTER TEN

CJ

WHEN I PULLED Mr Barese's car up front of the house, I considered telling my old man what I was signin' up for. Maybe it was my excitement, or maybe it was wishful thinking, but I thought for one minute that he might be happy for me. Or even proud.

I should have known better.

I put the three grocery bags on the kitchen table and he snatched them away, rifling through them. "Fuckin' took ya long enough." He found his cigarettes and walked back into the living room, sat his worthless arse in the chair, and lit up a smoke.

No thank you, no nothing.

Pops came into the kitchen and put his hand on my arm. "You're a good lad," he said quietly. He seemed a little more breathless than usual.

"You okay?" I asked as I pulled out tins of beans and tomatoes.

"Yeah, I'm fine." He was wheezing more, so he weren't fine at all.

I sighed and let my head fall heavy. "Dad," I called out.

"Can you not smoke in the house? I told ya, it makes Pops worse."

His reply was a short and angry. "You tellin' me what to do again, boy?"

Pops shook his head, silently telling me not to answer. I gritted my teeth and bit my tongue. "It's okay," Pops whispered.

"It's not okay," I replied just as quietly. There was no point in arguing, we both knew it wasn't okay, but we both also knew what my old man was like. I'd have better luck trying to get a brick wall to listen. I put the few groceries away and filled the kettle with water. "I'll make you some tea," I said, assuming he hadn't eaten lunch. "Want some beans on toast?"

Pops sat down at the table and gave me a smile. "Thanks, CJ."

I fixed him his lunch, and when I sat it in front of him, he covered my hand with his. His skin felt papery and cool to the touch. "I appreciate everything you do for me," he said.

His acknowledgement made me smile. "I know you do." I shoved Mr Barese's keys in my pocket. "I'll stoke the fire up and take Mr Barese's car back. I'll be walkin' home, so it might take a while."

"Okay."

He started eating his lunch, so I leaned in and whispered, "When he's not here, I'll tell you about what I'm signing up for."

He never spoke, but his eyes asked all the questions.

"It's all good, I promise. Gonna make a better life for you and me. Just you watch."

His eyes brimmed with tears and pride, and he nodded. I clapped him gently on the shoulder, loaded some more wood into the fire, and without a word to my father, I walked out.

——————

MR BARESE WAS in his office when I arrived. "Thanks again for the loan of your car."

He gave me his usual warm smile. "No problem."

"So," I started as casually as I could. "I was speaking to Noah, uh, my parole officer, about getting qualified."

Mr Barese's eyes lit up. "What do you reckon? A good idea, yeah?"

I nodded and broke out in a grin. "Yeah."

Mr Barese clapped his hands together. "Excellent!"

"He's gonna see if I can pass earlier because I've been doing it for years, but he said he will help me."

"He's different than the last one, isn't he? The last guy didn't care, but this new one is a good guy, yeah?"

"Yeah, I think so." I could feel my cheeks heat up, but Mr Barese didn't seem to notice. Thank God. "He's also gonna help me get my licence and with my reading."

Mr Barese put his hand to his cheek, and for a second, I thought he was going to cry. "I am so proud of you," he said, all emotional. Then he gave me one of his Italian hugs.

It made me feel so damn good to make him proud of me, and Pops too. Both of them were better fathers to me than my own old man ever could be, and it stung a little knowing, if I told my dad what I was doing, he would either laugh or make me quit.

"But my dad can't know," I said. "It ain't worth the hassle."

Mr Barese's face fell and he nodded. He understood. "He won't hear it from me. You just let me know if you need anything signed or help with any papers." He pointed to his own chest. "I fix them for you."

"Thank you."

"See you bright and early tomorrow, yeah?

I nodded. "I can open up for you, if you like?"

"Yeah, okay, thanks."

"Have we got anything booked in?"

"Nah."

"Then take Mrs Barese out for morning tea. I'm sure she'll like that. I can handle it here."

He brightened. "Oh, she would like that."

"And if it gets quiet in the afternoon, you can mind the shop and I can see if your lawn needs mowing. Any tree-trimming you need done before heavy frosts, just let me know."

"You're a good boy."

I gave him a smile and a salute as I walked out and headed toward the railway tracks for the walk home. I stopped to light a cigarette and enjoyed the peace and quiet before I got back to face what other shit-fight my father could throw at me.

ON THURSDAY, I was more excited than I probably should have been. And nervous. And I was sweating on my old man sleeping in. I got home pretty late from work the night before, cooked dinner while he sat his lazy arse in the chair, and waited for it to be put in front of him. He'd had a few beers, so I was hoping he wouldn't be up too early. I needed to speak to Pops without dad being around.

I boiled the kettle for Pops' tea and started making his

porridge, and I could hear him before I saw him. His wheezing breaths gave him away. "Mornin'."

"You're up early," he said. "Can I help you with something?"

Every morning he asked and every morning I told him no, but not today. "Actually, there is something."

He leaned on the table and waited.

"I need my birth certificate."

"What for?"

"I'm going into town today, and I need it so I can get some paperwork in order." I could still hear my father was snoring so I didn't need to speak too quietly. "I need the certificate so I can get a photo ID. I'm gonna sit for my bike licence, and I'm gonna see about getting qualified as a mechanic."

His whole face lit up. "You are?"

"Yep." I stirred the oats on the stove. "Noah reckons I can get qualified early because of some prior knowledge thing. He's gonna help me. But I can't do it without photo ID."

It went without saying that my father wouldn't be told. "I can grab it for you real quick." Pops shuffled out the door.

If the last few weeks were anything to go by, my dad wouldn't be out of bed for another hour or two yet, but I didn't want to risk it. "Thanks."

By the time I plated up two bowls of porridge, Pops came back in with an old, blue, faded piece of paper. It had been folded for what looked like years. Pops opened it, gave it a quick once-over, then handed it to me. Not that there was much point. There was an Australian government emblem, and I could read my name, but not much else. I quickly folded it again and shoved it in my jacket pocket. "Thanks."

Once we'd had breakfast and Dad got up, I showered and made myself busy outside before telling him Mr Barese needed me to help out for a bit. I added that I might need to go into town if he needed me to, but without any more details than that, I left.

Noah had said ten o'clock and I got there a bit early, but he was already there. He and Mr Barese were chatting and smiling and they both grinned when they saw me. "Sorry, I thought you said ten o'clock."

Noah checked his watch. "Yeah, I did. I've been here for like two minutes." Then he looked me up and down in a way that made me warm all over. "Get everything?"

"Yeah."

"Well, we'll be off," he said and shook Mr Barese's hand.

Then I told him, "I uh, I told my dad I was helping you out today. Said I might need to go into town, so if he calls in, which I doubt he will, just tell him I'm picking something up for you."

He waved me off. "No worries."

I hated involving him but didn't really have a choice.

As soon as we got into the car, Noah clicked up his seatbelt and started the engine. "You look really good today."

I froze. "What?"

He smiled and drove us out of town. "I said you look really good today. Love the jacket."

It was my usual black leather one that I'd scored from a charity shop in town. And I was wearing black jeans and my work boots. It wasn't anything he hadn't already seen me wear. And it was hardly as nice as his clothes. "I wear this all the time."

He grinned. "I know. You look good every day."

I ignored him and the way my face felt all hot. "You done takin' the piss?"

"I'm being honest." He shrugged but seemed genuine enough. "Did you bring the papers I asked you to bring?"

"Yeah." I pulled out the two folded papers from my jacket pocket. "Phone bill and birth certificate."

"Excellent."

"Where are we going first?"

"RMS. Photo ID and rider licence application all in one."

I let out a nervous breath. "Right then."

He gave me a smile. "You'll be fine. The photo ID will be easy. And we're just grabbing the application forms and booking in for the rider licence. You don't have to actually do anything today."

"Oh." The knot in my stomach let up a bit.

"Don't stress about any of it. I'll be with you the whole time."

"Can you just take a day off to do this shit?"

"This shit, as you put it, is my job. It's part of my job to help you." Then he must have realised how that sounded. "I'm not just doing this *because* it's my job. I want to help you. And like I said, even if we don't . . . happen . . . then I'm still helping you."

"I knew what you meant." I didn't want to smile around him so much, but I couldn't seem to help myself. "Three more weeks, huh?"

"Technically, it's now two and a half."

I rolled my eyes, but yeah, that damn smile I fought against just wouldn't quit.

When he arrived at the RMS, there were machine kiosks that spat out tickets for the right department. Noah pressed some buttons and took our ticket with a number on it. There were a lot of people sitting and waiting, but Noah went around and took some pamphlets and brochures and papers and stuff.

There was a counter with pens, and Noah nodded toward it. "Come over here." He pulled out a form first. "Okay, this is the photo ID form. So, full name . . ." He went and filled in the whole form for me. I just answered what I had to and handed over the phone bill and my birth certificate.

Funnily enough, I was okay with numbers. I sucked at maths, but I could identify numbers easily enough like phone numbers and dates. I'd learned how to use the eftpos machine at the shop because Mr Barese taught me. I could punch in dollar amounts and press the green button for yes or the red for cancel. I wasn't scared to try new things, but words were different. They had different shapes and the same word meant different things and sometimes the same word was spelt different. I could identify letters individually, like *a*, *b*, and *c*, but putting them all together on a page full of words and it was too much to process.

Like the form Noah filled out.

He never made me feel stupid. He just asked each question and wrote the answers down without any fuss. When he was done, he slid it in front of me. "Sign here," he pointed to the box at the bottom.

I took the pen and signed my name. It wasn't perfect, and Noah pretended not to notice how my hand shook a little. When I was done, he held up one of the booklets he'd collected. "Rider licence book."

I could tell that from the picture of the guy on a motorbike on the front but didn't say that. I took it and flipped through the pages. Lots of pages, lots of writing. "Great."

Noah nudged my elbow with his. "I told you I'd help you," he whispered.

"With the whole book?"

"Yep."

"How?"

He grinned. "What are you doing this weekend?"

I snorted. "Learning road rules for motorbikes, apparently."

Our number flashed up on the screen with which counter to go to, and Noah led the way. The lady behind the screen looked blankly at us. "We need a photo ID," Noah said, sliding the form over.

She asked some questions, scribbled something on the form, and ticked a few things. She asked for my birth certificate, so I handed it over. Then for proof of address, so I gave her the phone bill. I had to sign my name again, then stand in front of a screen. She took my photo and two minutes later, I had legal photo identification.

And the woman had no clue I couldn't read or write too well. Not that I needed to be literate to get ID, but it still felt pretty good. Like it was an accomplishment. And I hadn't had many of those.

We needed to get a new ticket to make a booking for the riders' licence, so we sat in the waiting chairs and, well, waited. I studied the small plastic card in my hand. The photo was crap, but it was me, with my name, address, and date of birth.

Clinton James Davis.

Davis Road.

Ten Mile Creek."

There was writing across the top in blue writing and I tried spelling it out in my head.

NSW.

Well, that's easy. It stood for New South Wales. I knew that much.

The next word started with a *p*, then *r*, *oo*, and an *f*. P-rrrr-oooo-ff. Proof! The rest came easier, not just because the words were smaller but I'd heard Noah say it before. Proof of Age. NSW Proof of Age card.

I looked at Noah to find him smiling at me. "Proof of Age card," I said.

His smile became a grin. "Sure is."

"This is gonna make me sound lame, but I've never had anything like this. It feels . . . I dunno . . ." I finished with a shrug.

"Validating?" he offered.

"Yes. I feel validated." That was exactly how I felt.

His eyebrows furrowed. "Have you got a bank account?"

"Nope. Mr Barese gives me cash. I ain't ever had a bank account. Never needed one."

He sat back in his seat. "I'll add it to the list."

"I don't want no bank chargin' me fees and shit."

"How do you get government allowances?"

"What?"

"Government allowances? Like welfare payments or carer's payments?"

"I don't get none of those."

Noah blinked. "You're Pops' full-time carer. You should be getting allowances for that. For you and for his medications."

I shook my head. "I don't need the government's help."

He frowned at me and was just about to say something else when our number flashed on screen. It was a guy this time, and Noah gave him a cheery smile. "I'd like to book in for the rider course."

"Your name?"

"Oh, it's not for me," Noah said, standing aside.

I stepped forward. "It's for me."

If the guy looked any more disinterested, he'd be dead. "Can't speak for yourself?"

I glared at him. "Yeah, and ya wanna know what else I can—"

Noah bumped me with his knee and interrupted. "He just needs to book in for the next rider licence course. Please." He smiled sweetly at the arsehole behind the counter, then shot me a look.

The guy glared at me while he tapped on his keyboard, then glared at me when he charged sixty-five bucks. He glared at me when I paid him cash, and he glared at me when he handed me the printout.

"No, thank *you*," I said when he didn't.

The arsehole looked at Noah. "Two weekend course, first session next Saturday at the high school car park. Nine a.m."

"Thank you," Noah said and pushed me toward the door.

As soon as we were outside, I took out my cigarettes. "What the fuck was his problem?" I didn't wait for an answer. I lit a smoke and breathed in deep. "How does a jerk like that even get a job? Did you see how he looked at me?"

Noah apparently found something funny. "He's in customer service. What do you expect?"

"Uh, customer service? Some manners. maybe."

"Don't let people like that bother you."

I took a drag and pointed back to the door. "If I treated Mr Barese's customers like that, I wouldn't have a job."

"Well, you probably would. Mr Barese loves you."

That stopped me, like a brick fucking wall. I blinked a few times and shook it off.

"What?" he asked. "You act like it's a first."

I swallowed hard and stared at the lit end of my ciggie for a long second. "It is a first."

I couldn't look at him, but I could feel his eyes burning into the side of my head. I could hear him breathing and he seemed to be standing closer. "CJ," he whispered.

I shoved the cigarette between my lips. "No big deal."

"It's a huge deal. I'm sorry."

I looked at him then. "What're you sorry for?"

"Someone should have said that to you before now. Everyone in your life should have told you that."

I shrugged. "Yeah, well. We didn't all grow up with the Brady Bunch."

"No, we didn't," he mumbled. "Sorry."

Wanting to drop the subject, I took a long drag of my cigarette and asked, "So, you drivin' me back yet?"

He shot me a surprised look. "No, I wasn't gonna. When did you need to be back by?"

"By three or four at the latest, I guess."

He checked his watch. "Plenty of time."

"For what?"

"Finish your cigarette and I'll show you."

Normally shit like that would piss me off, but with his half a smile and squinting one eye in the sunshine, I couldn't help but smile. He headed for his car, and I followed, flicking my cigarette into the gutter.

He stopped to stare at me. "If you get done for littering, I can't help you." I snarled at him, and he laughed. "What? No, 'fuck you' today?"

"I was saving it up for when you told me to quit smoking."

He snorted out a laugh. "Just get in the car."

We drove for a bit and then I realised I had no clue

where we were going. "Ah, you gonna tell me where you're taking me?"

"I have to print a few things off at work, then we can grab some lunch. How does that sound?"

"While you're on the clock?"

"I'm allowed to eat. And I'm helping you."

"Oh, that's right. I'm work to you." I fought a grin. "For another two and a half weeks."

He smiled at that. "Nice to know you're counting down too."

"I wasn't. You told me what it was. And anyway," I said, giving him a raised eyebrow, "what exactly do you plan on doing in two and a half weeks."

He pulled the car into the driveway at his work. He scanned his card thing to make the boom-gate go up. "I'm going to kiss you first."

"Are you?"

He looked me right in the eye. Didn't even flinch. "Yep."

My stomach tied itself up in knots. "Well, we'll have to see about that. Who says I'm gonna let ya?"

He just stared right at me. "You'll let me. In two and a half weeks, I'm pretty sure you'll be begging me to."

It was suddenly way too fucking hot in the car.

"You all right there?" He was all smug and sexy as he pulled into his parking spot. He gave me a once-over again. "Looking a bit flushed."

"Fuck you."

"There it is! And I didn't even have to tell you to quit smoking." I growled at him, and he just grinned. "And CJ?"

"Yeah."

"You shouldn't smoke. It's bad for your health."

"Fuck you."

He laughed. "You coming in or you gonna wait in the car?"

I considered my options. Get eyeballed by every government employee in the building or stay in the car. "I'll stay here."

"Okay, won't be long."

He got out and left me alone. In a government car with the keys still in it. I wondered idly if he could lose his job for that. I was a parolee, after all.

I took out my new photo ID and looked at it again. I tucked it into my wallet, in the slots for cards, which I didn't ever have any cards to put in before now. I double-checked how much cash I had left, taking the time alone to count it. I didn't like counting money in front of people. I wasn't particularly fast at it, but I liked to keep it in order and to make sure people didn't rip me off. From the money Mr Barese paid me, I bought some smokes for me and Dad, beer for Dad, bought some groceries, and I took some money from my stash to pay for today. So this morning, I started with one hundred, I paid the RMS asshole sixty-five bucks. I pulled out the money I had left. One five, one tenner, and a twenty.

Twenty, thirty, thirty-five.

I folded the notes in half and put them back in my wallet. I was going to take out my birth certificate, but Noah's door opened and he climbed in. He had a manila folder with him and reached back to slip it on the backseat. He kinda leaned closer to me as he did and I got a waft of his scent. His deodorant or aftershave or something that smelt really good.

"Get everything you need?" I asked, trying to distract myself.

"Yep. So, lunch? I was thinking drive-thru. What do you prefer? Maccas or KFC?"

"Neither. I don't eat 'em."

"Oh. Well, you pick something. It's my shout."

"I can pay for my own lunch."

He backed the car out and drove up to the boom-gate. "I know you can. But it's a work lunch, so I can charge it back."

"The government pays you to take lunches? Jesus. No wonder the country's economy is shit."

He rolled his eyes, swiped his card, and drove out to the street.

"And anyway," I continued, "the government's payin' and all you're gonna offer is McDonalds or KFC? You cheap bastard."

He laughed. "No, I was thinking drive-thru so we could go straight back to my place."

I stared at him. "Jesus. You're smooth."

He chuckled again. "I don't mean it like that. I just figured we could talk easier without worrying about who's watching. There's a nice café near the park. We can go there if you want. Your choice. Public park or my place."

Now it was me who rolled my eyes. "Shut up."

He decided on KFC but he paid, so I didn't complain about spending fifteen bucks on a meal for one person. But we did go to his place, and after we'd eaten and cleaned up, he didn't seem to be in any hurry to show me the papers or booklets he'd got for me and I certainly didn't push it.

I wanted to know something, and it wasn't something I was comfortable asking Pops, and I certainly would never ask my old man. I trusted Noah to tell me the truth, but I wasn't sure how to ask. Asking someone for help wasn't something I was used to.

I put my rubbish in the bin and stood at the sink for what must have been too long because Noah noticed. "Something wrong?"

"Um . . . no. Nothing's wrong exactly. I just . . ."

He stood up and came closer. "You can talk to me. You know, as a friend. Because that's what we are, right? Even before the next two and a half weeks?"

I tried to smile but couldn't quite pull it off. "Could you, um, could you do me a favour?" I asked.

He was serious now, and closer. "Sure. Just ask me, CJ."

I took my folded birth certificate out and handed it to him. "Can you read that to me."

CHAPTER ELEVEN

NOAH

CJ HELD out his birth certificate and I took it. It wasn't what I was expecting him to ask me. We'd been joking and even flirting with each other, getting comfortable, so his serious questions threw me for a six.

He shoved his hands in his pockets and hunched over a little, doing that 'trying to make himself smaller' thing.

I hated that he felt bad and alone. Being illiterate must be so isolating, I couldn't even imagine. So I stood beside him, leaning against the counter, just like him. We touched from shoulder to thigh and I gave him a bump with my hip. "Of course I can."

I unfolded the piece of paper and held it out between us both so he could see it. I read it out loud, word for word.

"Name: Clinton James Davis. Mother's name: Lindy Mears. Her age when you were born was nineteen. She was unemployed." I'd never seen anything in his file about a mother. "Did you know her?"

He shook his head. "Nope. She bailed when I was one. Apparently she was hardly around before then anyway.

Dad said the drugs got her in the end. His words were 'he met her in a crack house, left her in one.'"

Jesus. "Sorry."

He shrugged like it was no big deal. "After that I was looked after by whoever was in the house. My brothers or my dad. Sometimes no one. Then when I was two, some bible-bashing door knocker found me at home by myself. I was a mess, apparently, and they don't know how long I'd been alone or when I ate last. Dad was on some booze-bender. In town. DOCs were gonna take me until Pops said he'd move in. He stopped drinking right then and he's been looking after me ever since."

"He's a good man."

"He's the best."

I gave him a smile and went back to reading the certificate. "Your father is Dwayne Davis. He was thirty-one when you were born. Unemployed."

CJ made a low hum. It sounded like distaste, but he said nothing.

"It says they weren't married, and there were no previous children to their union."

"My brothers aren't on it?"

I shook my head. "No. The notice of birth was filed two days after you were born."

He frowned and stared at the floor. I wanted to tell him he wasn't alone, despite what his birth certificate said. But instead, I said, "Your brothers. Tell me about them."

"I'm the youngest of five boys to four different mothers. Richard's the eldest. Then there's Kenny, Stephen, and John's ten years older than me. They're um, they're all in jail. Like father like sons." He sighed. "They haven't seen the outside of a jail since they turned eighteen, and they did juvie before that. They weren't around much when I was a kid, so it's not like I know them. Richard got done for armed robbery. Kenny did theft, break and enter, but had time added for stabbing an inmate. Stephen and John got done together for break and enter, unlawful imprisonment, assault. They broke into a pub, thinking it was empty, but it wasn't. They tied up the barman and held him there but couldn't open the safe."

Jesus Christ.

"That's why they call it Davis Row," he mumbled. "It's not just the cops or community services workers who call it that, but the locals in town too. And it's not just my brothers or my dad. My uncles weren't much better. All of 'em were in trouble for something."

"Not you and Pops."

He shot me a sceptical look. "Uh, you're my parole officer. That kinda means I found some trouble."

"But you've stayed out of jail."

"Because of Pops. Well, I'm pretty sure I'd be dead if it weren't for him."

I folded the birth certificate and handed it back to him. "You're lucky to have him. And he's lucky to have you. He looked after you and now you look after him. I never knew my grandfather."

He slid the paper into his pocket. "Pops isn't my grandfather."

What? But . . . "What?"

"He's my dad's uncle."

"Your great-uncle?"

He shrugged. "If that's what you call it, I guess. But I was little and called him Pops and it stuck. And we just told the doctors he was my grandfather and no one ever questioned it. He wanted better things, ya know. He was different to the rest of 'em, but he got lumped with me when

I was two, and by the time I was old enough for school and he could work full-time, he got sick." He shook his head and scowled. "It's not fair. Emphysema is so cruel. Why do the good people suffer? Why can't people like my old man suffer instead? Pops is a good man. He raised me when my own father didn't. He never complained. Not once. He never got asked to look after me, he just stepped up when no one else would."

God, I wanted to hug him. And then I thought, *fuck it. That's exactly what I'll do.* I pushed off the kitchen counter and stood in front of him. I slowly put my hand to his neck and his eyes went wide, but I didn't stop, and he didn't stop me. So I leaned in slowly, giving him plenty of time to react, and gently pulled him against me.

He was rigid, uneasy, but he didn't recoil, and he didn't tell me to fuck off.

"You can hug me back, you know."

Then I realised that maybe no one had ever bloody hugged him before either. Pops was a great guy but none of the Davis clan seemed overly affectionate. Without pulling away, I said, "I've wanted to hug you for a while."

Still, with his arms by his sides, he asked, "Why?"

"Because sometimes people hug as a way of saying things are gonna be okay."

I could feel his chest rise and fall, then slowly, unsurely, he raised his hands to my sides, and after a few rapid heart-beats, he slid his arms around me. Then he held on tight and fisted my shirt and he breathed in real deep. I felt it, the moment something in him gave way. He gave in and let himself be held.

And there, in my small kitchen with the hideous linoleum floor, I broke down a small part of the wall around CJ Davis' heart.

Only when he let go did I pull back, but not very far. With my face close to his, I cupped his cheek and ran my thumb along the edge of his bottom lip. His eyes were dark; his breaths were short and sharp. God, I wanted to kiss him so bad. I wanted to feel his lips and taste his tongue. I wanted to hold his face and thread my fingers in his hair and kiss him for all I was worth . . .

But I couldn't.

I took a step back and let out a rush of air. "Holy shit," I said breathlessly.

He looked dazed, a little confused. "Right."

I held up two fingers. "Two and a half weeks."

He rolled his eyes but he smiled. "I still haven't said I'll let you."

"Let me what?"

"Kiss me."

I knew what he meant. I just wanted to hear him say it. "You won't 'let me.' You'll beg me."

He rolled his eyes and pushed my shoulder. "Fuck off."

I snorted out a laugh, thankful the tension between us had simmered. "How about I show you what printouts I did and the information booklets I got?" Not waiting for him to answer, I took the folder from the bench and went into the lounge room. I fell into my couch arse first and opened the folder. He sat beside me and I took out the first sheet of paper.

"When we were at the RMS, I saw this and it got me thinking," I explained. It was the standard eye test everyone had to do when getting a licence, with a big letter at the top and the letters getting smaller each line down. I handed it to him. "The one I saw at the licensing desk had an *E* on top, so I Googled it and printed it, but the one you have to read from might not look like this. I'm pretty sure they change them around a bit. I thought we should practise the letters so they don't think you need glasses or something and refuse your first attempt."

He frowned at the paper. "What if I get it wrong?"

"You won't. That's why I printed it. So we can practise."

"Isn't that cheating?"

I made a face. "No. Think of it more like practising and being prepared."

"So, it's cheating?"

"Not at all." I cleared my throat, because I had no clue if it was technically cheating or not. "So, what are you like with letters like this?"

He shrugged one shoulder. "*E . . . F . . . P?*"

I nodded and gave him an encouraging smile. "Keep going."

"*T . . . O . . . Z?*"

He was slow, unsure, and he said each letter like it was a question, but he got them right. I nudged him with my elbow. "Perfect."

He blushed. "Yeah, well, Pops helped me a bit when I was growin' up, and letters by 'emselves I can do okay. Put them all together in words and then add a whole lotta words on a page and I come unstuck."

"Well, for this eye test, you only need to read letters one at a time." I took the piece of paper, stood up, and crossed the room. I pointed to the fifth line down. "Can you read this line from there?" I was about two metres away, but he did fine.

"*P . . . E . . . C . . . F . . . D?*"

"Now cover your right eye and read the line above it." He did that and then again with his left eye covered, and he managed just fine. "Excellent. Your eyesight's perfect. But we can keep practicing it though, just to make sure we nail it."

He took the booklet for the rider licence and turned to page one. "This'll take me forever."

"No it won't. I'm gonna help you. We'll get through it in no time at all."

He shook his head. "When're you gonna help me? The course thing is in two weeks. I can't be reading this whole thing and learning all those rules and shit."

I sat back down beside him and took his hand, and I don't know if I shocked him or me the most but I never let it go. "CJ, listen to me. You can do this. I know you can." He looked about ready to argue, so I kept going. "How long have you been riding a motorbike for?"

He shrugged a bit. "Since I was ten, probably."

"And you can fix one when something goes wrong?"

"Well, yeah."

"And you've never been pulled over by the cops yet?"

"Nuh."

"So, you already know most of the rules. Stop signs, give way signs, roundabouts, intersections, pedestrian crossings . . ."

He squinted at me. "Yeah. I ain't stupid."

"Exactly. So what are you worried for?"

"I ain't ever sat a test before."

Of course he hadn't. "Well, I'm sure they have mock tests, like trial ones, online. We can do those this weekend. You know the answers. You just need to get used to how they're gonna ask you the questions."

"This weekend?"

"Yeah. Are you free?"

"I, um, I guess so."

"I can pick you up after soccer if you want. You can

make sure Pops is good and I can drive you home after dinner. How does that sound?"

He made a face. "Sounds like you've got it all worked out."

I grinned at him. "Well, I don't want to push you, but . . ."

"We've only got two and a half weeks?"

I chuckled. "Yep. Come on, I've gotta get back to work. I'll drive you home."

"What do I do with all these?" he asked, looking at the folder full of papers.

"Well, you can take them home or you can leave them here. Whatever you want."

His eyebrows knitted together. "I don't want my dad to know."

"Then leave them here." I gave him a smile, stood up, and went into the kitchen and grabbed my keys and wallet. CJ followed with his hands shoved back into his jean pockets.

He was kinda quiet again as we got into the car and headed out of town. Eventually, he said, "Thanks for what you're doing for me."

"It's no problem. Thanks for agreeing." I wanted to keep the conversation going, so I asked, "What are you doing tonight and tomorrow?"

"Uh, tonight'll just be the usual. Pops watches his soaps on TV and then the quiz shows. He likes 'em. Sometimes I'll watch with him, sometimes I'll be fixin' stuff outside. Then I cook dinner and make sure there's enough wood inside for the fire. Not very exciting."

"Sounds nice though."

"Yeah, it is. Well, it was. Until my old man got home and bitches through it all. Does nothing to help. He washed up a few times, but the novelty of that wore off pretty quick."

"That's gotta be rough."

"Well, it was easier when he wasn't there, that's for sure."

"Do you think your brothers will come home when they get out?" I asked. God, I couldn't imagine what that would be like.

"Nah. They'll stay around Sydney. But they're never out for long anyway; a few months, tops. Two are in Silverwater, one's in Goulburn, and one's in Long Bay."

"Jesus."

"Yeah. Tell me about it. Richard, he's the one in Long Bay. He won't ever come out."

"Do you go to see them?"

"Nope. I don't even really remember Richard. He was in juvie when I was born and pretty much went from there to one jail or another. Don't really remember Kenny either. I remember Stephen and John, but not much. They were out of juvie when I was like five or six but went back to jail after their stupid robbery went wrong. When they were out, all they did was beat on me."

"Bloody hell."

He sighed, long and loud. "What about you? You know all about me and my fucked-up family. What's yours like? Perfect? Like the Forrester family from Pops' soaps?"

"The Forrester family?"

"Yeah, from *The Bold and the Beautiful*. It's his favourite show."

I barked out a laugh. "Do me a favour. If you wanna keep your bad boy reputation, don't go telling people you watch *The Bold and the Beautiful*."

"Oh, fuck off." He rolled his eyes. "You didn't answer my question. About your family."

My stomach sank and my heart squeezed. My mouth was dry and I had to swallow. "My, um, my mum and dad, and my sister . . ." God, I couldn't even bring myself to say it.

"Your mum and dad and sister what?"

"They died."

He stared and I let out a steady breath, looking at the road—anywhere but at him.

"Shit. I'm sorry."

"It was a car accident. Kind of. Three years ago. It's a long story."

"Fuck."

"Yep."

"Man, I'm sorry. Were they your only family?"

My chest felt all tight and there didn't seem to be enough air in the car. Fuck. I pressed the button to roll down my window. I needed fresh air. "Can we not talk about it?" I said. "Sorry."

"Don't be sorry. Shit, man. I'm the one who's sorry."

I took some deep breaths and we drove in silence the rest of the way. When I pulled up at Mr Barese's shop, CJ turned in his seat to face me.

"I'm sorry. I didn't mean to upset you."

I scrubbed my hands over my face. I had better control of myself now. "It's okay. I'm fine."

He made a face. "So, this Saturday . . . ?"

"Yeah. I can, um, I can pick you up after soccer."

"You sure you're okay?"

"Yeah, I'm good. If you had a mobile phone I could text you."

"Nah. I never had a need for one."

"Well, you have my office and mobile number if you need to call me. If any plans change or whatever."

"Yeah. It's on some papers at home, I think."

I pulled out one of my cards. "Here. Just in case."

He took the card and slid it into his wallet. "Thanks."

"Have fun at work tomorrow."

He snorted. "Yeah, thanks."

"If your dad gives you a hard time about not being at home . . ." I wasn't sure what I was offering.

"Don't worry about him. See ya Saturday."

He got out of the car and Mr Barese greeted him with a smile. I waved them off and drove back to town. I had work to catch up on after spending the entire morning with CJ, and I needed the distraction.

I hadn't thought of my family in a while. I didn't know if that was a blessing or a curse. Or both. And it didn't matter how much time passed. I didn't think it would ever matter. Those wounds ripped open, as fresh as the night the police came to my door . . .

I SPENT the rest of the afternoon doing house calls, and it was the perfect distraction. I took work home with me to keep myself busy, and I spent all day Friday doing work placement calls—anything to keep myself occupied.

I spent all Saturday morning getting shit done around the house, but I was excited to get to the soccer fields. Gallan gave me a grin and a fist bump. "We good?"

I grinned right back at him. "Yeah, of course. You seemed to be getting on okay with that guy when I left."

He laughed. "Meeting him again tonight too."

That was a pleasant surprise. More often than not,

random hook-ups were only that. "Awesome. So, you gonna buy the guy dinner, or are you meeting him up against the wall in the backroom of HQ again?"

He laughed and shoved my shoulder. "Dinner, for sure. Then up against the wall in the backroom of HQ."

"I'm really happy for you. That's good news."

"What about you? You and bad-boy hottie certainly had eyes for each other."

"Ah well, not yet." I couldn't exactly divulge the work/caseworker situation. "It's kinda complicated."

Gallan's reaction was surprised. "Man, I thought for sure you were hooking up."

Tony kicked the ball to us and told us to quit chatting and get training. We only had half an hour before the game. So we started with some ball skill exercises and went for a bit of a warm-up jog before we ran out onto the field.

We were getting better as a team and were holding our own but they'd edged us out with an early goal. We were down 1-0 with ten minutes still left in the first half when Gallan called out to me and nodded toward the sideline. "Doesn't look too complicated to me."

I followed his line of sight and my heart skidded to a stop. CJ was there, leaning against his motorbike, in his black jeans and boots and his old leather jacket. He put a lit cigarette to his mouth to hide his smile when our eyes met.

Then someone yelled at me to get the ball and I remembered I was actually playing a game of soccer. An opponent was coming toward me and I ran at him, tackling the ball from him. I edged it from around his feet and tapped it out of his hold, breaking away with it. I dribbled it a few metres away, then booted it to Davo, who was free from his opponent in the centre of the field. He raced up toward the goal, and with a sharp kick to the right of the net, the goalie dove left, and we tied the game 1-all just before the half-time buzzer went.

We ran off the field to our side and grabbed our water bottles, happy with our game. I copped a few claps on the back for my efforts and a few 'good job' and 'well done' comments, and it felt kind of amazing.

But I couldn't stop looking over to CJ.

"Be back in a sec," I said to my team before running over to where CJ still sat against his dirt bike. "Hey," I said in greeting.

"Hey yourself."

"I thought I was coming to pick you up?"

"I thought I'd save you the trip." He fought a smile. "You did good out there. Gettin' the ball off that other guy."

"Thanks."

"Though your legs could use some sun."

I looked down at my legs . . . my very white legs. "Shut up."

He laughed. "Better get back to your team. Your boyfriend keeps looking over here."

I shot a look at the guys to find Gallan was watching us. "He's not my boyfriend."

"You went into the backroom of HQ with him."

I raised one eyebrow. "Are you jealous?"

He answered with a laugh.

"Because I can take you into the backroom any time you like," I added.

His eyes flashed with something like a challenge. "Not for two weeks, you can't."

Dammit. Why did I have to go and make such a stupid rule? "Professional ethics really suck."

"Is that so?"

I think he was going to say something about my choice of words but decided not to. *Thank God.* The mental image of him sucking anything didn't bode well for flimsy soccer shorts. The grin he gave me, and the quick glance at my crotch, told me that was his plan all along. I had to readjust my protector. "Fucker."

He barked out a laugh and I ran back to my team. Gallan gave me a grin. "There ain't nothing complicated about that."

"Oh, shut up."

He laughed and we ran back out onto the field with our team. We played well and the game ended in a 1-all draw. There wouldn't be overtime until the finals, so while some were pissed that it wasn't a result either way, I was just happy it wasn't a loss.

I guess that summed up my optimistic nature.

"Coming to the pub for a few drinks?" Tony asked.

"Nah. Can't today. Already have plans." I wiped my face with my towel. "And I can't after next week's game either." CJ was doing the first week of his rider licence course next weekend; I wanted to be there when he finished.

Gallan shoved his gear into his bag and winked at me. "Not complicated at all."

I rolled my eyes and a few of the others gave us a weird look. I waved them off in a 'never mind' kind of way and when everyone was leaving, I told Gallan to have fun tonight. "So did you even get a name of your date?"

"Yep, and a phone number." He waggled his eyebrows tauntingly. "Who knows? Maybe one day he might come watch me play soccer." He gave a pointed glance to where CJ was still waiting. "Good luck."

I nodded them off and made my way over to CJ. He lit

up a cigarette just as I got there. I dropped my bag at my feet. "Wasn't too boring for you?" I asked.

"Nope. It was good to watch. Rather you than me though. Too much running."

"It feels good actually. I like my lungs to burn in a good way," I said with a smile and a nod to his cigarette.

He grinned, looked right at me, and took a long drag. "Me too."

I was smiling right back at him. I liked this playful side of him: banter, easy going, and a spark of mischief in his eyes. Just then, a drop of sweat ran from my hairline down my temple, so I pulled my shirt up and wiped my face, giving him an eyeful of my stomach. I wasn't ripped but I was in okay shape.

He totally checked me out, and it was like he took another drag of his cigarette for the distraction. "But on the bright side," he waved his hand from my head to foot, "at least I won't be the only one who stinks."

I chuckled. "You smell of cigarettes. I was gonna go home and have a shower before I came to pick you up. Now you'll have to put up with me being all sweaty."

He smirked and took another drag of his cigarette. "I won't mind."

Jesus. Did everything he say have an innuendo, or was it just my wishful thinking?

"So? You want to load your bike into the boot of my car or you gonna risk riding it to my place?"

"I'll risk it."

"Then drive in front of me. I'll follow, and if you get pulled over by the cops, I'll tell them I'm chaperoning you to get your bike to the workshop. Or something."

He blew his smoke skyward then looked at me. "Lying

to law enforcement is kinda frowned upon. Especially someone in your job."

"It isn't a lie. Kind of." I picked up my bag. "Just don't do anything the cops'll want to pull you over for."

Now he grinned, like it was a dare or a challenge.

"I'm being serious."

He rolled his eyes. "Whatever."

I walked to my car, opened the door, and sat with my legs out. I pulled off my soccer boots; the cleats weren't much good for driving. By the time I had my slides out of my bag and on my feet, CJ had put on his helmet—which he only seemed to wear when he came into town, so I was grateful for that at least—and he'd slowly ridden over and waited for me to close the door and start the car. He lifted up the visor of his helmet in an impatient 'are you ready yet' kinda way. After I gave him a nod, I watched as he flipped the gears with his foot and took off slowly. It was only a few blocks, but there were a few intersections and he slowed down and had to give way. He lowered one boot to the ground, and from my view behind him, his posture, his thighs, his arse on that seat, and his shoulders in that jacket . . .

Yeah, I was in trouble.

He pulled up out the front of my house, and when I drove into my driveway, CJ wheeled his bike up beside my car. He took his helmet off, and as I got out of my car, he looked down at my feet. "Now, I ain't one for fashion, but socks and thongs . . ." He squinted at my slides. "What the hell are those?"

"They're slides. Fifty bucks Adidas slides."

"They're like old man toeless slippers."

My mouth fell open. "I am duly offended."

He laughed and tucked his helmet under his arm. "No,

seriously. I think the green and white knee-high soccer socks just make the whole look complete."

I probably would have been a little pissed if he wasn't smiling and being so damn cute. I pulled my gym bag out of the car. "Shut up. And there I was thinking you were sexy AF, but then you go and open your mouth."

He stopped. "You think I'm sexy as fuck?"

I growled at him and pushed through the back gate. I unlocked the back door, dropped my gym bag at the washing machine and kicked off my slides so I could pull off my socks. Then, because he was being a dick, I pulled off my shirt too. When I turned back around, he was staring at me. "What? Nothing smart to say?"

He licked his bottom lip. "I, uh, I just, um . . ."

Now I laughed. "Have you eaten? How about I go have a shower so only one of us stinks while you make toasted cheese sandwiches. In the frypan like you did the other night."

"Maybe I would, if you didn't just tell me I stink."

"You said I stink before."

"Because you just played soccer. You're all sweaty."

"You said you liked me sweaty."

"No I didn't."

"I'm pretty sure you did. You said you like it when I'm hot and sweaty, particularly shirtless." I made a show of running my hand over my chest. "And you think my socks and slides are sexy as hell, and you really wanted to make me a toasted cheese sandwich."

He rolled his eyes. "Shut up and go have your bloody shower."

I tapped his flat stomach as I walked past. "Won't be long. Make yourself at home." I left him to it, happy at the banter between us. I figured he'd feel more at ease if I treated him like he was part of the furniture; if I let my nerves show at having him here alone, then he'd be nervous too.

I had no issue with leaving him in my house while I showered. I trusted him. I don't know why. He was a parolee. A convicted criminal. But he was hardly the type to run off with my flat-screen strapped to his bike.

I scrubbed myself quickly, rinsed, dried off, and threw on some jeans and an old shirt. I could smell the toasted sandwiches before I walked into the living room, and I found myself smiling.

He was holding two plates. "Made one for me too, if that's okay," he said, and held a plate out to me.

"Yeah, of course."

And so, for the next three hours, sitting side by side on the couch, we went through questions and answers for his rider licence. I read the booklet with him, letting him sound out each word, and when he got frustrated and cranky and wanted to throw the booklet out the window, I read it to him. Then we went through the mock test online, and when he passed it twice in a row, we were done for the day. My mind was fried; I imagined his was worse.

"Want a drink?" I asked, standing up. "Coffee, Coke, water?"

"A Coke'd be great, thanks."

I went to the kitchen, wondering how I might ask him to stay for dinner, and came back out with two cans of Coke. And I stopped.

He was standing next to the cabinet with the photo frames on it. He stared at the picture of me with my parents and sister, then he frowned and looked almost apologetic, but it didn't stop him from asking.

"Is that your family?"

CHAPTER TWELVE

CJ

SHIT, shit, shit. Shit. I didn't want to hurt him, but I wanted to know him, and more than that, I wanted to trust him. And I wanted him to see that I was trying. I liked him. In a way that I'd never let myself like anyone. He knew everything about me. He'd read it all in those files and I never had to tell him nothin'. But I needed something from him in return. Like it would somehow prove that he was . . . I don't know . . . real. That I was more to him than just a case file number.

He talked about wanting to kiss me, about being physical, about things moving between us to a personal level. And despite everything I'd ever told myself about avoiding that kind of complication, I wanted it with him. I was risking so much, so I needed to know if he was being real with me.

But the look on his face made me wish I'd kept my damn mouth shut.

"Sorry, I just . . ." I just, what? Knew it would hurt him but asked anyway? "Sorry."

He swallowed hard. "No, it's okay." He put the cans of

drink on the cabinet and almost touched the photo frame but stopped himself. And God, he smelt even better, all clean and soap and deodorant and Noah. I almost forgot what I was waiting for him to say when he answered, "That's my mum and dad and my sister, Karly."

I wanted to ask what happened to them, but the sadness on his face, the quietness of his voice, stopped me. I wanted to tell him I was sorry. I wanted to pull him in for a hug. Like he did to me the other day. He said a hug was a silent way of saying that things would be okay, and I swear it was true. When he'd hugged me, I could feel the weight of my troubles get that little bit lighter. And I wanted to do the same for him, but I couldn't move. I was too damn scared.

"Can we not talk about it," he mumbled. "I don't do too good talking about it."

"Of course. I'm sorry." My hand burned with the need to touch him, but I still couldn't bring myself to do it. "I shouldn't have asked. I just wanted to . . ."

He waited for me to finish, but I couldn't. "You just wanted to what?"

I shrugged and didn't know how to answer. "I just wanted to get to know you, I guess." God, I could feel my face burn.

He picked up the cans of Coke and handed me one. I took it this time. "Do you really want to know what happened?" he asked quietly.

I looked him right in the eye. "I want to know you better."

He took a deep breath and opened up his heart to me. "My Mum and Dad died in a car accident. They were passengers in the car my sister was driving. She'd been to a party the night before and had her learner's permit. Mum insisted she drive home to get her hours up, but she and her friends had popped some pills the night before. She couldn't exactly tell Mum and Dad that."

Oh, God.

"My sister freaked out and ran a red light, and they got T-boned by a truck. Mum and Dad both died. My sister walked away."

Dear God. I couldn't even imagine it.

He looked at the photo, took another deep breath, and let it out slowly. "It's funny how accidents can be like that. Some people die on impact, some walk away without a scratch."

"Oh, Noah . . ."

"Well, physically, she was okay. But because she failed the drug and alcohol test, she was found guilty. She was sentenced to three years."

My eyes went wide. "Jailed?"

He replied sadly. "Yeah."

Then it all made sense. "Is that why you became a parole officer?"

He gave me a sad smile. "Yep. Four months after she went in, she committed suicide. She had a cell to herself, and one morning they found her, and they found a knife."

My mouth fell open. I couldn't believe it . . . "Oh, my God." I put my hand on his arm, needing him to know that I might not have known what to say but I was listening.

"I studied to become a parole officer after her funeral. I met some corrections officers during her stint, and some of them were trying to make a difference. I thought, you know, bad things happen to good people. Karly was a good person who just made a bad judgement call. She'd just finished high school and had applied for all kinds of jobs. She didn't want to go to uni; she wanted to work in retail. She never did anything wrong. She'd never even said swear words in front of my parents before the accident. Her friends said she'd never taken drugs before that night and it probably explained how wired she was."

Jesus, it was all so horrible, and yet I was still glad he told me. "Oh, God. I'm sorry."

"Yeah, I am too." He sighed long and loud. "My parents didn't own a house or anything, and we never had much money. I had to sell most of their stuff to pay for their funerals."

My heart ached just hearing this. "I'm so sorry, Noah."

He sighed again. "It's not easy to talk about. Just knowing who to tell is the hard part."

"Well, I'm glad you told me."

"I am too." He let out a long, slow breath, though the pain was still etched on his face. "It's funny that most of the people my parents used to know stopped coming around or calling. I guess they never knew what to say. Even my old friends back at home, I think it was too hard for them, ya know? It was hard enough after my parents died, but especially after Karly died. Being around me was too hard, and eventually they just all stopped."

"That doesn't make them very good friends."

He made a face. "Well, it probably didn't help that I dived into studying to be a parole officer. It wasn't a direction they thought I should go in."

"For what it's worth, Noah, I'm glad you did."

He almost smiled. "Me too."

"You like helping people."

"I do. It's good to know I'm making a difference. If I can just help one person, then it's a good thing."

"You help me."

He took in a sharp breath and something in his eyes sparked. I think telling him that helped him more than I realised. "Thank you. But you're the one doing all the hard work, I'm just helping."

"No one ever really gave a shit before." *God, I dunno why I'm telling him this.* "You're the first person to see the real me."

"Pops and Mr Barese see the real you."

"Yeah, but I mean . . . you know what I mean. The first guy . . ."

"Oh."

I made a face. "Yeah. Okay, now I'm not embarrassed at all."

He chuckled. "Don't be. I like that I am."

A few seconds of comfortable silence passed while we took in the gravity of what we'd just shared. Whatever this thing was between us had changed, or grown. He'd shared a part of his soul with me and he knew the dark parts of my life as well.

"Tell me more about you," I said quietly. "I want to know more."

He walked over to the sofa and sat down, looking at me to follow, so I did. He seemed to have shaken off his solemn thoughts about his family. "Do you want to know about my childhood, when I first realised I was gay, my first kiss, my first time? Or are you asking if I'm honestly interested in you?"

Jesus. "Yes."

Noah smiled at my eagerness and the corners of his eyes creased in a way that made my belly flip. "I grew up in Stockton. My dad worked at the steel factory, my mum worked as a cleaner in the caravan park. We were working class, then my dad got laid off when the plant downsized, and we had even less money. We lived in community housing. We never had much of anything, but we got by. At school, I never had any cool surfer clothes, any labels or shit like that. I went to school with kids who got a car for their sixteenth birthday. Mum gave me fifty bucks and told me I could buy whatever I wanted with it. So I paid for takeaway Chinese food and we had a family dinner." He smiled at some memory in his head. "Mum cried and Dad drove me down to pick it up for us. We sat around the table and laughed. It was one of the best nights of my life."

It said so much about what kind of person he was. Not many sixteen-year-olds would do that. "That was a nice thing to do."

He stared at me and gave me a slow smile. "We're not that different, you and me."

"How so? 'Cause from where I'm sitting, you're a mile in front of me."

He took a drink of his Coke. "You'd do the same thing for Pops."

I guess I would.

He smiled like he knew he was right. "I first realised I liked guys and not girls at soccer. The other guys'd wanna watch the girls play." He shook his head and grinned. "But I could watch the guys all day long. My first kiss was with Daniel Corner; we were in the ninth grade. It was awkward and probably terrible but kinda perfect and reaffirmed that I was into guys. Like, it was a confusing time so it was good to have it validated, if that makes sense?"

I nodded. "Yeah."

"And my first time was awkward and over embarrassingly fast. His name was David, I think. I don't really remember. I was eighteen and drunk and just kinda wanted it over and done with. Second time was much better." He winked. "What about you?"

I didn't mean to groan out loud. "Well, you know about

where I grew up and how that story goes." I scrubbed my hand over my face. "My first kiss was with some kid from Cessnock High. I went to visit my old man in jail and he was there seeing his cousin or brother. His name was Jamie, and we met on visiting day a few times. Then he stopped coming. Dunno what happened to him. Maybe his brother got out of jail. Maybe he went to juvie." I shrugged. "First time was with some guy from HQ. Never got his name. Never asked for it. But yeah, I just wanted it over with too. It got easier after that." I was sure my face was bright red. "I don't got no Internet at home, so my knowledge back then was pretty limited. Guess it still is." I flicked at the metal tab thing on top of the can to avoid looking at him. "I ain't ever had a boyfriend or nothing like that. Just casual hook-ups."

He reached over and slid his hand over mine. Whether to stop me from making that annoying tinging sound with the metal tab on the can or as some kind of comfort, I didn't know.

I didn't much mind either. If he wanted to touch me or hold my hand, I certainly wasn't gonna stop him.

When he threaded his fingers with mine and brought our hands to his knee, I looked at him. His eyes were intense and I couldn't look away, even when I tried. And that goddamned freckle above his eye . . . "Are you opposed to having a boyfriend?" he asked. "I mean, I know it's not easy with your dad and all, and maybe boyfriends is a bit fast, but friends with benefits to me is just another name for casual fuck and I'd prefer something more permanent. More exclusive . . ."

Jesus. "Are you asking if I'll go out with you?"

"Not necessarily. I'm asking if you're opposed to the idea." He bit his lip and shrugged. "In the future."

"To having a boyfriend in the long-term future?" My

heart was trying to gallop out of my chest. "Or in two weeks' time?"

He smiled again and looked down at our joined hands. "Either. Both."

I tried to speak as calmly as I could, though my voice was barely a whisper. "I don't think I'd be much good at it."

"Why?"

"Well, I ain't ever done it before. You know, whatever it is boyfriends do."

"Cook dinner? Watch movies? Hang out? Make out?"

"I'm not out."

"I don't expect you to be. I would never make someone do something they didn't want to do or something they're not ready to do."

"Um." I had to swallow because my mouth was suddenly dry. I took a drink of my Coke. "Is there a right or wrong answer?"

He barked out a laugh. "God no. Like I said, regardless of what happens between us, I'm still gonna help you. If you'll let me. I'm not putting any pressure on you. Please don't think that." He wasn't smiling now.

"No, I don't. That's not what I meant." I hadn't even thought of that. "I just think that I'm . . . that you're . . ."

"What?"

God, how could I explain this? "That if we were engines, you'd be a twin-turbocharged three-litre inline, six cylinder, 360 horsepower. And I'd be one-point-six litre, four cylinder, 100 horsepower . . ."

"If we were engines?"

"Well yeah. You'd be a European sports car, and I'd be a shit box that sounds like a lawnmower."

He laughed. "No way. I'm more of a Holden Commodore. Just an average engine. You'd be a Ducati."

Now it was me who laughed. "A Ducati? Are you drunk?"

He squeezed my hand. "You have sexy bad boy written all over you."

That sounded like a compliment. I pulled my hand away and let out a deep breath. "Yeah well, I dunno about that."

"But it's to just keep people away, right?" Noah took another drink and shot me a look to dare and argue. "You figure if you look like you're gonna bite, people will stay away. But that's not really who you are. You're a diamond in the rough, CJ Davis."

"I thought I was a Ducati."

He laughed. "You wanna stay for dinner?"

"No, I better get goin' home. Pops'll be lookin' for dinner soon."

His pout became a smile. "Okay. When will I see you again?"

I sighed. "Well, I've got a stupid drugs and alcohol meeting on Tuesday. It finishes at five."

He brightened. "What a coincidence! I happen to finish at five also."

I rolled my eyes. "And I'm pretty sure my parole officer'll be doing a"—I used quote marks in the air—"random, unscheduled work placement call on Thursday."

He laughed and bumped my shoulder. "Hopefully I'll have some forms for Mr Barese to fill out for your apprenticeship. It doesn't start yet, but we'll still need to get the enrolment forms in."

"And my first motorbike licence thing on Saturday," I said. "Which is gonna suck, I have to say. It'll probably be some old know-it-all arsehole who'll hate me on sight."

"No he won't," he countered. "Just give him that

dazzling smile of yours and nod every now and then when he talks and you'll be golden. Did you want to go back over the road rule booklet? In case he asks you any on-the-spot questions?"

I frowned. "Do you think he will?"

He shrugged. "Maybe. I don't know. Probably. It's not the test for your licence, but he will either pass or fail you."

"Oh."

He took my hand again and gave it a squeeze. It felt better than I was expecting. "Hey. You will nail it."

I ran my thumb across the back of his hand, marvelling at how nice it felt.

"What?" he asked, smiling at our joined hands.

"Nothing. I just wondered why people held hands. It feels nice."

He blinked. "You've never held hands before?"

"Uh, no. I told you I ain't ever had a boyfriend before. And random hook-up guys in the backroom of HQ aren't there to hold hands."

"Oh, of course. Sorry." He threaded our fingers and used both hands to hold my one. "Do you like it?"

I nodded. "Yeah. But my hands are stained. The oil and grease at work just gets ingrained."

He held up my hand and took a closer look at the blackened fingernail beds and in the creases, the callouses. "I like it," he said, turning my hand over and looking at each side. Then he grinned at me. "Tells me you're good with your hands."

I didn't want to laugh at the corny line but couldn't help it. "I've never had any complaints."

"I should think not," he said, still smiling. "You know, maybe we should start a list of firsts. First hand-holding, first boyfriend . . . anything else we should add?"

I ignored his pry for more information. "What is it with you and lists?"

He grinned. "What can I say? I like to see my own progress."

We both sat there holding hands and smiling at each other like giddy schoolboys. This was getting absurd. "I should probably go."

"I'm adding first sleepover to the list."

I snorted and stood up, reluctantly pulling my hand from his. "Thanks for lunch, and the drink. And helping me with the reading and stuff. And thank you for telling me about you."

"Thank you for listening." He stood up, getting to his full height with just an inch between us. He looked at my mouth, then leaned in slowly and almost kissed me. My heart damn near stopped. But he pressed himself against me, with his cheek to mine and his warm breath at my ear. I gasped as a shiver ran through me. "What are you doing?" I whispered.

"Counting down the days," he replied, a soft murmur in my ear.

I took a step back, dizzy. "Whoa."

His grin made his eyes do that crinkling thing, which didn't help at all. "Still think you won't beg me to kiss you in two weeks?"

"You don't play fair."

"Never said I did. But for what it's worth, I'm playing for real. To answer your question earlier. If I'm being serious, the answer is yes."

I couldn't form words to speak, so I blushed instead. God help me. If this is what having a relationship did to people, I didn't think I'd survive it.

He just smiled like it was nothing. "Come on. I'll drive you."

"I brought my bike."

"We'll put it in the boot like we did before." He walked into the kitchen and grabbed his keys, like I had no choice. He sighed. "You have two weeks to go before your parole ends, CJ. It's not worth it."

"I managed just fine before you came along." That came out harsher than I'd meant. "I mean, I ain't ever been caught yet."

"And you're not about to be. Help me put your bike in the boot of my car."

I wanted to argue, but he was right. And it wasn't all bad. I got to spend another twenty minutes with him.

And the boot of his car wasn't real big, but with the front tyre lifted up, we could each grab one of the back shocks and lift the bike in easily enough. He had some ratchet straps to tie the boot down, and a minute later, we were on our way.

As soon as he pulled out onto his street, he started with the licence questions. "What's that road sign mean?"

"What does the broken middle line mean?"

"What does a flashing traffic light mean?"

"How many metres from a bus stop can you park?"

I answered each one and so I asked him a few back, which he answered, and it was funny, in a weird kinda way, that we could talk non-stop about nothing and everything, and it felt so . . . normal.

I considered telling him he could go ahead and add 'real friend' to that list of firsts, but then he'd really know I was a loser and that he was well and truly out of my league.

"You okay?" he asked. "You look like I kicked your puppy."

I snorted. "Yeah, I'm fine. Just thinkin', that's all."

Just then, before the turn-off into Ten Mile Creek, he pointed to where all that land had been for sale. There were now bulldozers and earthmovers and a huge sign with some kind of fancy writing that was all swirls and not much else.

"I saw that sign the other day," I admitted. "But I couldn't make out that kind of writing."

"Yeah, it's a bad cursive font. It says Eagle Estate. Looks like a new subdivision going in. It'll be good for your town."

I raised an eyebrow. "You reckon?"

"Yep. And good for Mr Barese's business."

Oh. Well, I didn't think of that, and I kinda felt a bit foolish for not thinking of it first. "True. Hopefully."

Noah turned off the main road and drove slowly into Ten Mile Creek. Mr Barese's shop was closed, as it should be on a Saturday afternoon, but Noah pulled up out the front of it. We unloaded my bike, and holding my helmet, I wasn't sure what to say. I wished I could have stayed with him. I wished I could take his face, right here in the street, and kiss him. Instead, I took a deep breath and said, "I had a really good day today. Thank you."

"I did too." He smiled so damn perfectly. "And I'm glad I didn't go to the pub after soccer today with the fellas. Saved myself a fortune, and no hangover."

"Were you supposed to be going out with them?" I asked. "If you needed me to leave earlier . . ."

He laughed. "No. I told them I wasn't going. And I'm not going for the next two either. You have your rider course the next two Saturdays. I'm not missing them."

I kinda felt a bit kid-like, that he was almost babysitting me, but dammit if it didn't feel nice that someone cared. "Yeah, thanks. Hopefully it won't suck too much."

"Not for another two weeks, you know the rules." He

said it so deadpan, it took me a second to get what he meant. I think my eyes almost fell out of my head, because he laughed. "Sorry, was that too rude? Too forward? Too much?" he asked with that damn grin. "Because I'm thinking kissing won't be the only thing you're begging me for in two weeks' time."

I was too shocked to reply. Sure, I'd had guys say shit like that to me. But not sober, not in broad daylight, and not with a promise in their smile. He laughed and got back into his car, waved me off, and drove away.

I swung my leg over my bike, willing my now-interested dick to calm down. God, the next two weeks were gonna kill me. I rode home, still buzzing, unable to stop smiling. Until I walked inside. Pops was coughing in the kitchen, and Dad was slouched in the recliner—Pops' chair—with a beer in one hand and cigarette in the other. "Where the fuck've you been?"

I ignored him and went straight to Pops. "You okay?"

He waved me off, wheezing as he tried to catch his breath. "Yeah, yeah." He sipped his water and did seem to settle down a bit. He gave me a smile. "You had a good day?"

I nodded, just as my dad yelled. "Hey boy, I asked you a question."

"I've been in town," I yelled back. Then I patted Pops' arm. "I'll just go check on the fire, then I'll start some dinner, hey?"

He nodded. "I'll help." He'd opened the fridge door as I walked back into the living room. The fire was almost out, so I threw on some kindling.

"Whatchu grumblin' about?" Dad asked. He was in a foul mood. I could see it by the set of his jaw and the dead gleam in his eye.

"The fire. Would it have killed you to throw a log on it?"

He glared at me. Last time he was out of jail, I would have never spoken back to him, but I wasn't that kid anymore. I was a grown man now, and I'd run a good house with him gone. I stood up and stared right back at him. "And I told ya not to smoke in the fucking house. Can you hear him coughing? Or do you just not give a shit?"

His jaw ticked, and his fist around the beer bottle knuckled white. That dead gleam in his eye went cold. He was either gonna point his finger and yell and cuss me out for an hour and probably punch a hole through a door in a rage. Or he was gonna leap out of that chair and punch the piss outta me.

He did both.

NEEDLESS TO SAY, dinner was forgotten. I made Pops some toast and sat with him at the kitchen table after my old man had fucked off to his room. Pops looked over my banged-up eye and split lip, and he was on the verge of tears. "Sorry, CJ. I can't do nothing to stop him when he gets like that."

"Don't be sorry. Ain't your fault." God, if Pops tried to stop my dad when he was in a rage . . . "Just stay outta his way. I can look after myself." And I did, all things consider-ing. I'd shoved him back. I hadn't closed my fist at him or punched him. But I'd pushed him off me and told him to fuck off back to jail. He'd stormed out, swearing and yelling, while Pops put some frozen peas on my eye. "I'm not putting up with his shit no more, Pops. No way."

"Don't go pickin' fights with him. Please, CJ." Pops looked so sad it broke my heart. "Promise me."

"I won't start 'em," I promised. "But I won't let him treat us like crap no more."

We both sat in silence for a while, then I made Pops another cup of tea and had one myself. My lip stung a bit and my eyebrow throbbed, but I'd had worse. If it weren't my brothers picking on me, it was my father. But Pops had always, always been on my side. "You and me," I said, giving him a nod. "We'll stick together."

"Is your eye okay?"

"Yeah, it'll be fine." I sighed. "And I had a good day today. Noah, he's been helping me with my bike licence and stuff and helping me read. And he's super patient, ya know? He doesn't treat me like I'm stupid or nothin'."

"When's your course thing on again?" he asked. I'd told him before, but I reminded him. "Next weekend?"

I nodded. "Yeah. Saturday, for three hours."

"What'll ya tell your dad?"

"Nothin'. I don't care if he finds out anymore. He can't stop me from going. He might make life more miserable for me, but"—I waved my hand to my banged-up face—"can't get much worse, huh?"

Pops smiled sadly. "With a bit of luck, he'll be gone again soon."

God, I wished so. "We can only hope."

AS SOON AS I walked into work on Monday, Mr Barese took one look at me and his shoulders fell. "You okay?" he asked sadly.

My bruises had more colour and my shiner was a beauty; the eye was almost closed yesterday but I could still see out of it. It hurt, but I'd survive. "Yeah, I'm fine."

"I know he's your father," Mr Barese whispered angrily.

"But he's a piece of shit," I finished for him.

Mr Barese nodded. "He doesn't deserve you. I've told you before. You can come stay at my house. Mrs Barese won't mind. In fact, she'd love to have someone else to fuss over."

I smiled at him, stretching the split on my lip. I licked it, tasting blood. "Thanks anyway. But we'll be okay. Me and Pops are a team."

He sighed heavily. "I worry, that's all."

"I know. Thank you." Then I remembered what Noah said. "Hey, did you see the new housing estate just before the turn-off into town?"

"Yes," he said, brightening. "There was a write-up in the weekend paper. Some big developer, twenty blocks in the first stage, another twenty in stage two."

Wow. I didn't realise it was that big. "That's good for the town, yeah? That'll help your business?"

He gave me a beaming smile. "I hope so."

I looked around the quiet workshop. "Me too."

I REALLY DIDN'T WANT to go to the drugs and alcohol meeting. I mean, I never wanted to go, but today I *really* didn't want to go. I told them every freakin' time I never did drugs, that I very rarely drank alcohol, but they all looked at me like I was in denial. And now with a black eye and split lip, I looked like a loser even more.

They all assumed the worst. Because I didn't have much money, because I weren't book-smart, because I had to go to drugs and alcohol meetings as part of my parole, and now because I come in all banged up, I could see it on their faces.

Stereotypical bullshit, that's what this was. But I had one more session left and then it was all over.

For two years, I'd attended these stupid fucking meetings and never missed one. When Maryanne, the group leader, asked if I'd like to contribute anything, just like always, I shook my head. "I ain't ever taken drugs," I'd say, each and every time. All I needed from her was to sign off on my attendance and participation for my parole conditions. But I sure as hell wasn't gonna lie.

For the first year, Maryanne had tried to get me to talk or to admit some deep dark secret of addiction. But now she just nodded and smiled. The rest of the group looked at me like 'sure you haven't buddy,' but I didn't care what they thought of me.

One more meeting to go.

Just one more meeting to go.

Knowing I was seein' Noah afterward helped, and I was counting down the minutes to the end. When Maryanne closed the meeting, I was quick to stand up, just wanting to leave. But then Maryanne put her hand out in my direction. "CJ, can I see you for a moment?"

I resisted the urge to groan, barely. "I have a bus to catch," I lied.

"It won't take a second," she said.

Everyone dispersed and I waited for her to speak. She scanned my face. "You've been in some trouble?"

What? Oh, my face. "No, it's not what you think. I wasn't fighting."

She raised a judgemental eyebrow. "It looks like you have been."

I was so sick of this bullshit. "I said I wasn't fighting. Do you see someone with a black eye and just assume they got it in a bar fight?"

"No," she started quickly, but clearly she did.

"Well, you certainly didn't believe me when I said it just now." I looked around and there was some guy standing off just watching us like he didn't trust me either. I was so fucking done with this shit. "You wanna know what happened? My old man belted me. So instead of blaming me, maybe you could try a little sympathy."

I turned and walked out. She tried calling out to me but I didn't give a shit. And then because the world fucking hated me, as soon as I got outside, it started to rain.

Fuck it all to hell.

I pulled up the collar on my coat and trudged the four blocks to Noah's office. The walk did little to help my mood, and to make the whole fucking thing worse, the door was locked when I got there.

I considered kickin' the shit out of it. I wanted to.

But with a deep breath instead, and a whole lot of disappointment, I turned around and wondered what the fuck I was supposed to do now. If I ran, I could make the bus. Or maybe I could walk to Noah's place . . .

"Hey."

I spun around, and there was Noah's car stopped in the drive beside the building, the passenger window down. I could make out his smiling face in the darkened car, and it was like a tightness eased up around my chest. The relief was like oxygen to starving lungs.

I ran over to his car, opened the passenger door, and jumped in. I was soaked and probably making a helluva mess in his car, but damn, I was happy to see him. Like I had no idea how much I needed to see him. "Sorry I'm late. The meeting went a little longer than I was expecting, and then, of course, it had to fucking rain."

He was staring at me, not smiling.

"I didn't miss my appointment on purpose. Fuck, does this mean . . . ?"

He scanned my face. Oh. My face.

"CJ," he whispered.

"It's nothing." My high of seeing him deflated like a balloon from the look of pity on his face. I'd been so looking forward to seeing him, and now he looked at me like that . . . I grabbed the door handle, ready to get out and run, but he snatched up my hand.

"Don't go," he said quickly.

Before I could get out, he drove out into the street, never letting go of my hand. The ride to his house took just ten minutes, but neither one of us spoke.

God, I hated this.

I hated my old man for ruining the one very good thing in my life.

Noah pulled the car into his drive, and without a word, he got out and opened the gate. By the time I'd followed him, the back door was unlocked and left open, and with a heavy heart, I went inside. He was in the kitchen, leaning against the cabinets and gripping the counter so hard his knuckles were white.

I sighed, wondering what trouble he thought I'd got into. God, did he think I got into some bar fight too?

He swallowed hard and let out a shaky breath. "I take it your old man did that to you?"

I nodded, just barely, relieved he didn't assume it was my fault. "Are you mad at me?"

His eyes went wide and he crossed the floor in three long strides. He pulled me closer to the sink and took a clean tea towel from the bottom drawer. Then he gently wiped down my wet hair, the side of my face, and he softly dabbed at my eye, wiping away the water. His eyes searched mine and he put his other hand to my cheek and lightly traced his thumb near my purple eye. He touched me so gently, so kindly, it felt so good and hurt my heart at the same time.

"Why would I be mad at you?" he whispered.

"Maryanne, the lady who runs the drugs and alcohol meetings, assumed I'd got in a fight. I keep tellin' her I don't take drugs or really even drink, but I can see she don't believe me. She thinks I'm good for nothing. I can see it in the way she looks at me. Same with the people on the bus. They see my beat-up face and assume I'm some trouble-maker. But I don't do nothin' wrong. I try, every day, to be a good person. To help out and take care of Pops, ya know? I don't ask for nothin'. I don't have anything and I don't blame the world for that. I don't think nobody owes me a goddamn thing. I'm just trying to get through each fucking day."

My eyes burned with tears and I had to suck back a breath. I could feel myself about to cry and I forced myself to stop. But then he slid his hand around my neck and pulled me against him. In that safe and warm place I'd only ever known with him.

A hug. A simple fucking hug. His warm arms, gentle and kind touch, that I could feel sewing up the gaping holes in my heart, in my soul.

It was just a hug, but it wasn't. It was so much more.

It was human touch. It was kindness and understanding. It was reassuring and soul-mending.

I clung to him, like a fucking kid. Like if I let go, I'd fall apart. And he held me, just held me without question, without judgement.

"Sorry," I blubbered, finally. "I feel so stupid."

"It's not stupid." He pulled back and ran his hands up to my face. He pulled me in and kissed my sore eye, then pressed his lips to the corner of my split lip, like it would somehow heal my pain.

And my God, it did. It really fucking did.

"Are you okay?" he asked, wiping the towel down my neck where water ran from my hair. "Are you hurt anywhere else?"

I shook my head. Not even my tears bothered him. "No, I'm fine. Better now."

His smile was sad. "What happened?"

"He was drunk and he'd done nothing all day. I got home from spending the day with you and the fire was almost out and Pops was coughing real bad in the kitchen and Dad was sitting in Pops' seat smokin'. So I stoked up the fire and got it going then told him not to smoke in the damn house. I was a bit of a smartarse to him, but I've had a gutful. He doesn't give a shit about Pops bein' sick and all. He does nothing around the house and I lost my shit with him, and he lost his right back at me."

Noah's eyes narrowed. "Don't think for one second you deserved this. You can be a smartarse all you like, nobody deserves to be hit."

"Yeah well, it's done now." I shrugged. "He hasn't apologised or nothin'. Not that I expect him to, I guess. But he won't look at me. He's a piece of shit."

"You want me to report him?" Noah asked. "I can tell Terrell. He's your dad's PO. One charge of assault and his arse is back in jail. It's all it would take to make him gone."

I shook my head. "And what? He does twelve months and gets out knowin' I put him in there?" I snorted. "Because that'll end well."

"There are laws—"

"Laws don't do shit, Noah. You think my old man gives

one fuck about the law?" I shook my head. "Never has. Never will."

"It's not fair. You don't have to live like this."

"It's okay. I've had worse."

Noah's nostrils flared and he inhaled sharply. "That doesn't make it okay."

I sighed heavily and realised I still had hold of his shirt, fisted at his sides. "Thank you. For listening and not thinking bad of me." I doubted he had any clue how much better I felt.

He touched my hair and scanned my eyes. "Anytime." Then he backed away and went into the living room. "I'll drive you back to Ten Mile Creek. The last bus has gone. But do me a favour," he said. I could hear him rummaging through something and so I went in there to find him going through the drawer in the cabinet with the photos on it. He pulled out a phone and what looked like some kind of charger. "It's old. It doesn't do anything fancy, but at least this way we can text and you can call me if you need to talk, or if you need me to come get you."

He gave me a look that said this wasn't negotiable. He was right about one thing. It was old. It wasn't a brick phone by any means, but it wasn't far from it. "Um, okay."

"I had it years ago and then I upgraded. It works just fine, but I'll need to call into a servo and grab one of those charge cards." He grabbed his keys. "Come on. I don't want you to be late. No point in giving him anything else to be mad at you about." He stopped and looked me up and down. "Are you warm enough? You were pretty soaked through."

I smiled at him. "Yeah, I'm fine."

He cocked his head. "What're you smiling at?"

"You." I shrugged. "I never had anyone, I dunno, care, I guess."

He stared at me for the longest second. To the point where I regretted saying anything. But then he walked up to me, looked me right in the eye, and said, "Well, get used to it. Because I care about you. And it's about time the rest of the world saw the real CJ Davis."

CHAPTER THIRTEEN

NOAH

MAYBE I WAS a bit too blunt. Maybe I went in over my head. I told CJ I cared about him because it was the truth, and he needed to hear it.

And because I'd learned the very hardest way that life is just too damn short.

Things shouldn't be left unsaid.

He clearly wasn't used to hearing kind things said to him, and compliments may as well have been in a foreign language. God, I couldn't imagine the life he'd lived. And how he came out of it still trying to find the good in people, I'd never know.

I wasn't lying when I said it was about time the world saw the real CJ Davis. He was a good man. A good-hearted man who'd been dealt a really shitty life. The way he'd clung to me when I'd hugged him hurt my heart, like he was starved for affection. I wanted to hold him and never let him go.

His face . . . the black eye and cut through his lip . . . I hated that he was hurt and I hated that it was his father who did it to him. I hated the fact he was going home to where his father was. But it was CJ's home. The only home he'd ever known. And truthfully, CJ had lived there longer than his father ever had. His father had spent more years in jail than he had in that house.

I hated that CJ felt so unsafe in his own home.

I called into the servo on the way out of town and grabbed a mobile phone SIM card with a twenty-dollar credit. I got back in the car, where I'd left CJ with the heater on full bore, and handed him the SIM card. He looked like he was about to object to me spending money on him, so I quickly added, "Please take this. It will make me feel better knowing you can call me if you have to."

He sat back in his seat with a sigh. "I've got money at home. I can pay you back."

"You can buy pizza on Saturday night," I amended. "Then we'll be even."

He looked at the SIM card package. "I uh, I don't know how this is supposed to work."

"Here," I said. "Let me. I'll show you." I took out the old SIM and put the new one in. "The phone number on the back of the package is your new number." I quickly took out my phone and typed it in. "You'll need to charge it for a while. It's been dead for years, but it should work."

I handed it back to him and he smiled at it, turning it over in his hand. "Thank you."

I drove out onto the highway, and when we were on our way to Ten Mile Creek, I said, "You can text me whenever."

His smile died. "Did you forget?"

"What?"

"That I can't read."

"No, you can't read *well*. But you *can* read." I gave him a grin. "And I'll go easy on you."

"Can you make it silent so my dad doesn't know I have it?"

"Yeah, of course." I wasn't smiling now. "I won't text or call you unless you ask me something or need me to reply. Just charge it, and there's a button on the side; click it over and you'll see a speaker with a line through it on the screen. That means mute."

"Like on the TV."

"Exactly. If you want, you can just bring it to work with you on Thursday and I'll help you set it up then, when I call in for that unscheduled work visit."

He smiled at my joke but seemed happier with the idea of me helping. "Okay, thanks."

I drove through Ten Mile Creek, over the railway lines, and pulled up at the turn-off to Davis Road, and I shut off the engine. "You have my card with my number on it, yeah?"

He nodded. "Yeah."

"If you need, I'll come straight back and get you, okay?"

"I'll be fine. But promise me you won't say anything to Dad's PO."

"Okay."

"I mean it. Believe me, no good'll come from that."

The very last thing I wanted to do was to make things more difficult for him. I said I wouldn't, and I meant it. I took his hand and his gaze shot to mine. I ignored his black eye, wanting him to know I saw the man inside. "You're not alone, okay?"

He stared at me and my heart was screaming at me to lean in and kiss him. But I couldn't. Eventually he nodded, shoved the phone and charger into his jacket pocket, and got out. The rain had eased up but it was freezing cold outside.

He pulled his coat up around his neck and disappeared down the darkening road.

I drove home repeating the words I'd just told him over and over in my head.

You're not alone. You're not alone. You're not alone.

Eighteen months ago, I'd have given anything—anything—for someone to say those words to me.

THE NEXT MORNING AT WORK, I fixed myself a coffee and knocked on Terrell's door. "Got a sec?"

He looked up from his laptop and smiled. "Sure."

I sat opposite him and sipped my coffee. "This is a hypothetical only . . ."

"Yes," he said, drawn out slowly.

"Say, hypothetically, that someone on parole physically assaulted a family member . . ."

His eyes narrowed. "If this is, say for example, not a hypothetical case, you should report it."

"And if this person made you promise not to tell because it would only make things worse?"

He sighed. "Noah."

"It's just a what-if scenario."

"Then you could do a surprise house-call and see if anyone's in danger?"

"Would that just make things worse?"

"Not if the person in question is breaking their parole."

"What if the person who asked me to promise not to tell was the one who got hit. Not the one who did the hitting."

"The guy on parole was the one who got hit?"

"Actually, what if they were both on parole?"

Terrell sat back in his chair and sighed. "Noah."

"It's hypothetical."

"Mm-hm."

"I'm sure if anyone was questioned, all parties would deny it, and then when we were to leave, parolee A would know parolee B had talked and that would put parolee B in further danger. Hypothetically."

"Hypothetically, parolee B could be removed from the house."

"Hypothetically, he won't leave. I've suggested that."

"If they'll both deny it, it can't be proved, and if parolee B refuses to leave the situation, then unfortunately our hands would be tied until the situation becomes more serious."

"So, hypothetically, keeping an eye on the situation is all we can do. For now. Until something else happens. Which I hope it doesn't."

Terrell studied me for a moment and then smiled. "In a completely unrelated matter, I'm scheduled to call in to see Dwayne Davis tomorrow."

"Oh." I acted surprised. "That is a coincidence. I have a scheduled work visit on CJ tomorrow."

"Then we can go up together."

I smiled at him and gave him a nod. "Good idea."

THE NEXT DAY when Terrell and I drove up to Ten Mile Creek, the plan was he would drop me off at Mr Barese's shop and he'd go and see Dwayne on his own. "I've been doing this long enough to know the likes of him," Terrell had said. "If we both turn up, he'll feel threatened and be less inclined to talk. If it's just me, I'll see what I can get out of him."

It was probably for the best too. I didn't think I'd be able to look at CJ's father and not want to haul his arse back to jail.

I walked into the workshop and the smell of grease and oil hit me, making me think of CJ, and I smiled. Mr Barese saw me first and greeted me with his usual wide grin and warm handshake. "So good to see you!" He was such a genuine man and I really liked him. Not just for what he'd done for CJ, but he was an honest, hard-working man, and I admired him. Then he called out, "CJ, visitor!"

"Quiet day?" I asked.

"Yeah. But we have two cars booked in tomorrow."

"That's great!"

Just then, CJ came in from somewhere holding a wide broom. He stopped when he saw me and his lips twisted like he tried not to smile. "Hey," he said coolly.

"Hey," I replied. Then, to distract myself, I turned to Mr Barese. "Can I borrow CJ for a few minutes?"

"Of course," he replied.

"But I have some forms to run past you later, if that's okay?"

He nodded. "Sure thing. You come find me. I'll be here somewhere." He wandered out to the front of his shop, leaving me alone with CJ.

He was wearing old mechanic's overalls, unbuttoned to show a black shirt underneath. It matched his hair and eyes. He looked sexy as hell, and I couldn't even bring myself to care that I just stood there checking him out while he watched.

"You right there?" he asked with a smirk.

"Totally." I met his gaze and didn't look away. "I have to say, I like the uniform."

He leant the broom against the wall and when he

looked at me again, he laughed and shook his head. "Is your visit today work related, or you just here to check out the scenery?"

I shrugged. "Both." I dropped my voice. "Your eye looks better."

He nodded and gave a pointed glance to the back doors, which opened to the creek. When we were outside, he took his phone out of his pocket and handed it to me. "I charged it like you said, but then it wanted to do some set-up thing, so I left it because I didn't want to click on something wrong."

"Oh sure," I said. I powered it up and went through the setting questions with him, and when it was done, I handed it back to him. Then I took my phone out and sent him a quick text.

Hi.

His phone beeped in his hand, startling him. He held it out like it was a bomb, and I showed him how to scroll and find messages, what to click on, and how to read them.

"Is that from you?" he asked, looking at the screen.

"Yep."

So then I showed him how to reply. "Send 'hi' back to me," I said and waited for him to find the letters on the small keyboard onscreen.

"Then I press the little arrow to send it?"

I nodded, and a second later my phone beeped.

Hi

I grinned at him. "Welcome to the age of the iPhone."

He rolled his eyes, but there was an edge of pride there. So then I rang his number, and it rang in his hand, scaring the shit out of him.

"Press the green button on the screen," I told him. "Green is to answer, red is to hang up."

He pressed the green button and I put my phone to my ear. "Hey," I said, looking right at him.

He rolled his eyes. "Hey. Now can you make it not ring?" He held the phone out to me and I showed him again where the little switch was to mute it.

"How's your Dad been?" I asked. "Terrell dropped me off and he's gone out to see your dad. It's just a scheduled house call."

"Yeah, he's been all right. No different." He shrugged, slid his phone into his pocket, pulled out his cigarette, and lit one. "We haven't really spoken since. I'm not backing down to him. Not anymore."

"Good," I answered. "I mean, I don't want you to be unsafe, but I don't want him to treat you like shit either."

He nodded and did that one-eye, squinting-at-the-sky thing he did when he blew out smoke.

"How's Pops?"

"Yeah, good."

"That's good, I'm glad. And Mr Barese said you've got a busy day tomorrow."

He gave me a look and a smile that was like some rare insight into the real CJ Davis. It was as though he didn't have to pretend to be indifferent with me, like me—and only me—got to see the real him. It was a privilege to witness. "Yeah, it'll be good."

"I have an appointment about getting your apprentice fees waivered."

He tried for nonchalant, but I could see underneath the façade. "That'd be, uh, that'd be good."

"It will. But I better go find Mr Barese and give him these forms to look over and sign before Terrell comes back," I said. "And remember, you can text me at any time. Even just to say hi." I winked, then went inside in search of

Mr Barese. He was in his office with a pile of receipts in front of him. I tapped lightly on the door. "Hello there."

"Come in, come in," he said, doing that Italian hand-waving thing. "You done with CJ already?"

"Yeah, didn't take long." I held out the manila folder I was holding. "I've got some forms for you to look at for CJ's apprenticeship."

He brightened. "Ah, yes! Such a good thing you do for him."

"And you too. He's really looking forward to it." Then I whispered, "He might act like it's no big deal, but he's excited about this."

Mr Barese beamed. "I know! I can tell. He's a good boy, he deserves good things." Then he paused to frown. "Not like his father. Did you see his eye? That man doesn't deserve him."

I nodded with a sigh. "Yeah, I saw it. And I told CJ to call me if he needs to."

"Me too." Mr Barese picked up a pen. "Where do I sign?"

"You don't want to take it home and read it?" I mean, it was clearly just an apprenticeship enrolment form, but still.

"No need. I trust you. You want good things for him too."

"I do." I don't think Mr Barese knew just how much that was true. "You just need to sign everywhere I put those sticky 'sign here' tabs."

A moment later, he'd signed everywhere I needed him to and he looked back to the door. "We better not let him hear us talking about him, or he'll be mad." Mr Barese winked at me. "God forbid we say nice things behind his back."

I laughed at that. "God forbid."

Then I heard CJ's familiar footfalls in the workshop. "Hey, CJ?" I called out. "Can you come in here, please?"

He appeared cautiously in the doorway. "Wassup?"

"I forgot," I said, holding my pen out to him. "I need you to sign something."

His brow furrowed but he walked into the office and took the pen. I pointed to the one spot he had left to sign and watched as he scrawled his name. "Done," he said bluntly, giving me back my pen. Then he cocked his head to a sound I didn't hear. "Someone just pulled up. I'll go," he said as he was already walking out.

Then we heard CJ greet someone, the voice I soon recognised to be Terrell's. "Ah, that's my ride," I said.

Mr Barese and I walked out to find CJ and Terrell talking about football or something, both standing there with their feet spread wide and arms crossed. They were aiming for pleasant small talk, but body language spoke volumes; neither one of them wanted to be part of that conversation.

CJ gave me a strange look. "Your Uber is here," he said with a nod to Terrell.

Terrell laughed. "Yeah, thanks."

I didn't know what that was about, but I gave him a look I hoped he understood. "I'll be in touch."

CJ replied with the bit of a grunt as he walked away, swiping the broom from where it stood against the wall on his way. I thanked Mr Barese again, then Terrell and I headed back to town.

"Did you see CJ's eye?" I asked as we got to the highway.

Terrell nodded. "Yeah, his old man pretended he knew nothing about it."

"You mentioned it to him?"

"Yep. Told him I saw CJ when I dropped you off. Dwayne said he must have got it knocking about with the boys playing footy. I mentioned footy to CJ just now and he said he's never played. Just watches it on TV with his Pops."

"So Dwayne lied to you."

"Seems that way. But it's hearsay at the moment. Well, more like he said/he said. Just document in his file with the date, and if any more comes of it, we'll have a record."

I held out the manila folder like it was a trophy. "I got CJ signed up for an apprenticeship.

Terrell gave me a smile that pretty much said I was still a newbie who got excited over paperwork. "You can think I'm an optimistic greenhorn all you like. But this is going to change his life."

Terrell laughed and shook his head. "Damn right it will. And that optimistic greenhorn attitude you got going on there?"

"Yeah?"

"Don't ever lose it."

I sighed happily but then remembered what he said about football. "You didn't look too happy to be talking to CJ back there. You both had your arms crossed."

"Nah." Terrell waved his hand. "I've been doing this long enough that I don't let them bother me too much."

"Bother you? What did CJ do that bothered you?"

"Nothing personally, and he seems like a nice kid. But he still did what he did. He broke the law. I hope he finishes the apprenticeship, and I hope he gets his life on track because if he doesn't, he'll end up just like his old man, down on Davis Row."

I was really beginning to hate that name. "Not all Davises are pieces of shit. His old man yes, and probably his brothers too. But CJ and Pops are good people."

"Did you read his case file?"

"Most of it."

"The legal transcript?"

"No. Not all of it." I'd been so caught up on the past reports on his childhood, I hadn't read every single thing.

Terrell hummed. "Drug addicts are good liars, Noah."

Drug addicts? "CJ's not a drug addict."

"Is that what he said?"

Jesus. It wasn't like I could say that I'd been spending time with him, that I *knew* him better than he thought I did. "He's not."

Terrell nodded slowly and smiled at the highway.

"He got busted breaking into a chemist. The cops caught him inside, stealing bags of drugs."

I knew what he got busted for. And truthfully, I hadn't given CJ's criminal history much thought. I'd been so caught up in reading about his troubled childhood . . . Even now, knowing CJ like I did, I couldn't join the dots. It wasn't like him. The CJ I knew had a kind heart, he worked hard, and he cared for an old man with failing health.

But he did get caught halfway through a B and E, red-handed. There were even surveillance cameras. It was indisputable.

Was Terrell right? Had CJ lied to me? Had he taken me for a fool?

"Read the police report, then read what the lawyers said in court. Then come tell me what you think of CJ Davis."

I DID EXACTLY what Terrell told me to do. I sat in my office, started at the beginning, and read CJ's whole case file through.

My heart sank as I read the police report. He'd broken into a chemist, unknowingly setting off a silent alarm. The police arrived and found CJ alone, standing in a row of shelving with a plastic bag full of prescription drugs.

He didn't try and run. He didn't resist arrest. He didn't say a word.

When they asked him why he did it, he shrugged and said nothing. He was twenty-one years old, no previous record. It was noted by the attending officer that CJ had a black eye at the time of his arrest. It was also noted he was released, pending his court appearance, and was collected by his father, Mr Dwayne Davis. The officer also noted CJ appeared reluctant to leave.

Fast forward twelve months, when his case went to court, the judge acknowledged CJ had maintained an impeccable work attendance record and had remained out of trouble, and it was duly noted that it was first offence. But the police had a strong case against him.

Evidence provided to the court was the contents of the bag found on CJ's person on the night of his arrest: Cold and flu tablets, Vicks nasal spray, Promethazine, Rentamine, and butane.

Oh, Jesus H Christ.

Pseudoephedrine, desoxyephedrine, amphetamine, ephedrine, and lighter fluid.

CJ had ingredients to cook methamphetamine.

The police had a strong case, the judge agreed. CJ's lawyer had pleaded for leniency, as CJ's father had just returned to prison, leaving CJ as the sole carer for his ill and elderly relative, and his ageing employer also relied on him. The judge found CJ guilty and handed down a two-year suspended sentence, with strict parole conditions pertaining to employment and drugs and alcohol meetings.

I could almost hear the slam of the gavel as I read it. Closing the file, I sat back in my seat and ran my hands through my hair. I didn't know what to think. I didn't know how to feel.

How could I have been so blind to truth? Because even if he had the best excuse for doing what he did, I should have known all the facts before I got so close to him. I should have known better. I jeopardised everything for him. To what end? For some stupid chance at happiness? With a meth dealer?

Is that what he was?

I stared at the file on my desk. I wished I'd read it months ago. I wished I'd never read it at all. The CJ I thought I knew wasn't in this file, and I had to ask myself, which CJ was the real one?

I needed to ask him for the truth. But when? He had his rider licence course tomorrow, and the next weekend, then he had to sit for his actual licence. I promised to help him, regardless of how things stood between us. And maybe I didn't know him as well as I thought I did, but I knew him well enough to know if I confronted him and accused him of lying to me and worse, asking about his meth-cooking skills, there was no way he'd let me help him.

He'd shut me out, and not only me, he'd shut out anyone who tried to help him in the future. I knew him well enough to know that. He'd never get qualified as a mechanic, he'd never get his licence, he'd never get off Davis Row.

I couldn't let that happen. I'd promised him.

He was off parole in one week. He only had to get through a week, and we'd have some breathing room at least. Well, that's what the rational part of my mind said. But my heart . . . well, my heart was another matter entirely.

CHAPTER FOURTEEN

CJ

WORK ON FRIDAY was busy as hell. We had two cars booked in for a service. Mr Barese worked on one while I did the other, and we still had to man the petrol bowsers and the phone. But we worked well together; I did the work underneath the engines, Mr Barese did his work from the top. He claimed his body wasn't up for getting on the creeper trolley anymore. Well, he said he could still get down and under 'em. It was the gettin' back up that his body didn't like too much.

But I didn't mind. In fact, I loved it.

Changing oil and checking fuel pumps wasn't exactly high-end stuff, but there was a method of precision, of steps that had to be taken to get each procedure done properly. And it was satisfying doing each job and doing it well.

It was even better to see the happy customers and an even happier Mr Barese. When knock-off time rolled around, we fell into our chairs in his office and sipped our cups of tea. Sure, most people probably sat around at five o'clock on a Friday afternoon with a beer, but not us. Mrs Barese brought over some fresh scones with cream and jam and even some for me to take home to Pops. He would love them, and I was grateful she'd thought of him.

"What's your plans for this evening?" Mr Barese asked.

"Nothin' much. Go home. Cook dinner. Dad'll probably wanna watch the footy."

"Thought you didn't like the footy?" he asked.

"Don't much. But there'll be a movie on after it."

He sipped his tea. "Not heading into town?"

"Nah."

He paused for a second. "That Noah seems like a nice fella."

Well, that came from nowhere. Just what was he getting at? What did he know? I shrugged, trying to act like I didn't care either way. "Yeah. Seems okay."

He thankfully left it alone. "You do your motorbike lesson tomorrow?"

It wasn't really a lesson, more of a class with an instructor, but I didn't see the point in correcting him. "Yep. First one tomorrow, second one next weekend, then I can sit for my licence."

"Good, good," he said, nodding. "Do you need a lift there?"

"Nah, she'll be right. Thanks."

I tried to hide my excitement. Not just at the riding course, but also at seeing Noah again. So I told Mr Barese how the motorbikes were provided for this course and joked that I would probably end up with a postie's two-stroke bike that sounded like a lawnmower. He laughed at that. He took the empty teacups and I closed up roller doors, padlocking them shut. He wished me good luck and said goodbye, and I sat on my motorbike. But before I started it, I pulled out my phone and went to the messages like Noah had showed me.

There were no messages from him, not that I expected any, but I was still disappointed that I hadn't heard from him. He was the tech-savvy one not me, and he could probably type out a long message in just a few seconds, like it was nothing at all. But I also told him that I couldn't have my phone beeping in case my old man heard it. So maybe he was waiting to hear from me.

I looked at his earlier message to me, and it was easy enough to copy. It was just two letters, but even those took me a few seconds to find.

Hi

The cursor blinked at me, waiting for me to write something else or to hit Send. It was so ridiculous that I was nervous, but my palms were sweaty and I had butterflies in my stomach. I shook my head at myself and hit the damn Send button.

I waited for about five seconds but there was no reply. Maybe he was driving home, or maybe he called into a shop on the way home to grab some dinner, I told myself. He would reply when he could.

Jesus, CJ. Desperate, much?

Making sure the phone was still switched to silent, I pocketed it, kick-started my bike, and went home. I rode my bike in the shed, closed it up and went inside to find Pops in his recliner watching his soaps on TV.

"Hey, Pops. How's life with the Forresters today? Oh, Mrs Barese gave me some scones to bring home for you." The fire was going, the house was warm, and there was no sign of my father. "Where's Dad?"

Pops sighed. "CJ, sit down. Got something to tell ya."

Well, that didn't sound good.

I sat on the sofa. "What is it?"

"He's gone to town."

"What? How? I didn't see him catch the bus." The bus stop was close to work, and I'm sure he would have asked me for money because he didn't have any.

"No, he got a lift." Pops frowned. "CJ, he sold your lawnmower."

I blinked. "He what?"

"I told him he had no right. I told him it was yours and you bought it with your own money. But he didn't care. Some guy from Maitland paid a hundred bucks for it, and he got a lift back to town with him."

I couldn't believe it. "He sold my lawnmower?"

Pops nodded. "I tried to stop him."

My hands started to shake; anger and rage flared in my belly and my blood. I clenched my teeth and made fists, trying to breathe calm as I could. "He sold my lawnmower? For a hundred bucks? I paid two hundred for it!"

His frown deepened. "I know."

"One hundred dollars. To him, that's just a packet of smokes and a dozen schooners." It wasn't even five thirty. "He's probably already spent it."

Pops nodded solemnly. "He was in a foul mood all day. Searched the house for money, looking for anything he could hock."

I felt the blood run from my face. "Oh no." I ran to my room and shoved the wardrobe from the wall. I stuck my hand in the hole, and for a moment of panic, I couldn't feel the Weet-Bix box. But then I reached in further, and thankfully, there it was. I carefully pulled it out and took it to my bed just as Pops walked into my room. With a lump of dread in my throat, I opened the lid.

God, I almost didn't want to know.

"Is it all there?" Pops asked.

I let out an almighty breath. There, just as I left it, was my pile of money. "Looks like it."

Pops visibly sagged with relief. "Thank God."

"Can you count it for me?" I asked him. I could do it, but he was quicker at it than me.

He shuffled in and sat on my bed and proceeded to count out loud every note. "One hundred and eighty dollars," he said, looking at me like it was a question.

I nodded. "I had to use sixty dollars the other day to help pay for the rider course I'm doing tomorrow. So that's right, isn't it?"

Pops let out a wheezy sigh. "Oh, thank heavens."

The relief was immediate, but it still didn't fix the fact that the bastard had sold my lawnmower. I packed the money away, hid the box back in the wall, and put the wardrobe back in its place. We went back out to the kitchen, and I made the pot of tea, put the scones in the microwave so they were good and warm, and slathered on some butter. Just how Pops liked it.

"I should report my mower as stolen," I said.

Pops nodded seriously. "You should."

"Don't know where it will get me. He'll just tell the cops I told him he could sell it, and the minute they walked out the door, he'd give me another black eye."

He frowned. "I thought he would've been back in jail by now."

"I did too." Pops patted my hand. "It'll get better, son."

"When?"

He didn't have an answer for that.

AFTER AN EARLY DINNER WITH POPS, I went out to

the shed. I hadn't even realised when I parked my bike that the lawnmower was gone. But yeah, it definitely was. That son of a bitch. I was a lot of things: angry, hurt, betrayed. But I wasn't surprised.

Just when I thought he couldn't sink any lower.

I considered putting a padlock on the shed door but then realised he would only smash it, or break down the doors to get in. And I wondered if I had left my bike at home today, would he have sold it instead?

I was definitely going to say something. I didn't care that it would end up with me copping another black eye, more than likely, but I wouldn't let this go. Because fuck him.

I lit up a cigarette and sat on my bike, wondering what on earth I was going to say to my old man. I couldn't very well ask him to move out. It was his house after all. And I certainly couldn't afford to move. I remembered Noah offering to report him so he would go back to jail, and for a brief moment, I considered it.

Should I? Could I?

As much as I wanted my old man out of my life, I just wasn't sure I could be the one to do it.

Thinking about Noah, I took out my phone to see if he'd replied, and my heart sank when I realised he hadn't. He said he would reply, and I didn't take him to be no liar. He was genuine, wasn't he?

Did I send the message wrong? Did I not send it at all? What if he didn't get it and was still waiting for me to text first?

So I typed out another one, a little quicker this time.

Hi

And I waited. Then I waited some more. Nothing, no reply. Stupid phone.

Stupid hope.

I finished my cigarette and flicked the butt outside, trying not to overthink it. Him, he and me together, the promises he made, the look in his eyes, the way he would hug me and make everything in the world feel right.

And then I got to thinking, what if something was wrong? Is that why he hadn't replied? Maybe he was sick, maybe there'd been some trouble at work. Figuring my dad was gone and Pops wouldn't hear me, I pressed on Noah's name, then on the telephone button to call him.

It rang, and kept ringing. Then it cut off and I got his voicemail. "You've reached Noah Huxley. Please leave a short message. I'll get back to you when I can."

I wasn't prepared to leave a message. Just hearing his voice threw me off and I stammered, "Uh yeah, it's um, me. CJ. Sorry, I didn't mean to . . . fucking hell."

I hit the End Call button as fast as I could. My heart was pounding. I felt like an idiot. God, was there a way to delete a voice message? I let my head fall back and I groaned. I was so, *so* stupid.

Trying to put it out of my mind, I had another ciggie, then went inside. Pops and I watched a movie, though I barely paid attention. I checked my phone every now and then, but there was nothing.

"What's got you so worried, CJ?" Pops asked. God knows how long he was watching me.

"Nothing." I shrugged. "Just this motorbike course tomorrow."

"You've been riding motorbikes since you were a kid. You got nothing to worry about."

I couldn't very well tell him the truth. It wasn't the course so much; it was doing it without Noah that had me worried. He said he would meet me afterwards, but if he wasn't answering his phone . . .

Of course Pops saw through me. "What are you really worried about, CJ? You worried about what your dad will say about the mower?"

I'd forgotten about that, and remembering now made me sigh. "Nah. There's no point in losing sleep over him. Learned that a long time ago." I turned the phone over in my hand and figured I owed Pops the truth. "Noah said he would take me there, and I sent him a text and left a message, but he hasn't replied."

Pops frowned. "Doesn't sound like him to give up on you. Maybe he's busy, or maybe he's out on a date or something."

I shot him a look, not really meaning to, but I couldn't help my reaction. *A date? No, surely not.* "Yeah, maybe." The thought of him with someone else made my stomach turn.

Shit.

This was getting far too complicated. And this, *this,* was the reason I never got attached to anyone in the first place.

"I'm just gonna head out for one last ciggie before bed," I said to Pops, walking out of the house and into the shed. I pulled out my smokes, lit one up, and then took out my phone. There was still nothing from Noah. And before, I had been keen to hear from him, just for the sake of hearing from him. Now, I needed to know if he was still taking me to this stupid rider licence course in the morning or if I should catch a bus. I shouldn't ride my bike because the teacher would see me pull up on it and know I didn't have a licence and would most likely report me. But I also didn't want to leave my bike here in case my arsehole father decided to hock it for a quick buck.

God, I hated being reliant on other people. I *hated* it.

I really needed to speak to him, but if I left another

message for him now, I'd just look desperate. My finger hovered over Noah's number, and my pride decided for me that I'd just make my own bloody way there in the morning. I didn't need Noah. I didn't need anyone. Then, like he somehow knew, my phone buzzed in my hand and Noah's name came up on the screen.

With a hammering heart and ridiculous smile, I hit Answer.

Didn't need him? Yeah, right.

"Hey."

"Hey," he replied. There was a rustling sound like he dropped the phone. "Didn't know if it was okay to call."

He sounded drunk. "Yeah, it's fine. My old man's not here. Have you been drinking?"

"Maybe."

Yeah. He definitely had. "Wondered why you didn't reply earlier. Thought I fucked up the message somehow."

"No, I got it, but I just got home.

He sounded different. Colder, somehow.

"Right. Um, yeah, I was just wondering if you were still picking me up in the morning. If not, I can catch the bus. It's no big deal."

"I said I would. So I'll be there."

I frowned at the lit end of my cigarette. "Um, can you pick me up from Mr Barese's shop? If that's okay. I don't want to leave my bike at home." Then, because his distant replies were confusing, I added, "Or I can just ride to your place. Or I can just catch the bus into town. It's no problem. How about I do that, yeah? I'll get there, it's fine."

He sighed into the phone and it sounded like he ran his hand over his face. "Why?"

"So you don't have to worry about it. I'm not your responsibility. I've been looking after myself long enough—"

"No, why don't you wanna leave your bike at home?"

I took a long drag of my cigarette and blew the smoke out slowly. "My dad sold my lawnmower today. It's why he's not here. He took the money and is pissing it up the wall at some shithole pub in town as I speak."

"Oh, CJ . . ."

"I bought that with my own money. I used to mow Mr Barese's lawn for him . . . Now I can't do that anymore."

"Why would he do that? It wasn't his to sell."

"Because he's an arsehole, and he doesn't give a fuck who he hurts. He just thinks about himself, no one else."

"I'm sorry," he whispered.

"Me too." I drew back on the cigarette and sighed. "I'm so sick of his bullshit."

He didn't say anything for a while and I looked at the phone to see if we were still connected. "So, tomorrow?"

"I said I'll come pick you up." His voice was quiet. "From the shop, at half-past eight, okay?"

"Yeah, okay. Thanks. If it's a pain in the arse—"

"CJ, it's fine. See you then."

The call cut off and I stared at the phone. What the fuck was up with him? This version of Noah was someone I didn't know and was someone I wasn't sure I liked too much. If he was gonna be a dick to me every time he had a bad day, I wasn't sure I wanted to be a part of that. If he had a problem with me, then he could damn well fess up and tell me.

Confused, I pocketed my phone, took a last drag of my cigarette, and flicked the butt into the dirt. I closed the shed up and went inside.

"Get it sorted?" Pops asked. The movie was almost done and he'd made himself a cup of tea. "Want a cup. Kettle just boiled."

"Nah, I'm good. Just gonna have a shower and head to bed. I'll be leaving by eight-ish in the morning. Noah's gonna pick me up from the shop. I'll leave my bike there."

Pops nodded. "Probably for the best."

Yeah, I think so too. "See you in the morning, 'kay?"

"Sure thing, CJ."

I was pretty sure Pops knew something was bothering me, but he knew I wouldn't talk about it if I didn't want to, and he also knew not to push me. And talking about this would probably be a good idea if my issue wasn't about a guy. How could I say I was confused about mixed messages *with a guy*? How could I tell him I thought I had feelings for someone but then lie to him about who it was? I wouldn't lie to him. I couldn't.

So, instead of sitting down and asking for some perspective, I just said, "Night," and left him to it.

DESPITE MY HESITATION about seeing Noah, I couldn't deny the butterflies when his car came into view. I took one last drag of my cigarette and butted it out just as he pulled up. I had no idea what to expect from him, but I'd hoped his weird mood had passed and things were back to normal between us.

Not that I really knew what *normal* was for us. Snark and banter, lingering looks, and anticipation of what might happen when I was off parole.

One more week.

I got into the car and pulled on my seatbelt. The smell of his deodorant washed over me, making me smile. *God, he smelt good.* "Morning."

There was something wrong with his smile. "Morning."

Okay then. "Thanks again for coming to get me."

"Where's your bike?"

"Mr Barese let me lock it in his workshop."

Noah nodded. "Okay, good."

He drove us out of Ten Mile Creek, back out onto the highway, pressing buttons on his stereo, clearly not happy with the radio station's choices of music.

"Wow," I said, nodding to the new estate development. "They're really moving ahead with that." Bulldozers had cleared what looked like a road and housing blocks. There were surveyor pegs everywhere and heavy machinery and trucks. It was just a bare paddock a week ago.

"Yeah, they're not mucking around," Noah mumbled.

And that was about it for conversation.

I had no idea what I'd done or what had happened for the change in him. Had he met someone else? Or did he just realise the truth? That he was starting a career in corrections and I was a Davis.

He pulled up at the high school, where the course was to take place. And there, in the car park, was a guy wearing a high-vis vest with five motorbikes in a neat row. There were traffic cones set out and two other people standing nearby, clearly waiting for class to start.

"Well, this is it," I said.

Noah gripped the steering wheel so tight, his knuckles were white. "Good luck."

I looked at him, trying to figure out what the hell was wrong, but he wouldn't look at me. "Is there something wrong?" I asked.

"Nope." He gave me a tight smile. He couldn't lie for shit. "You better go. Don't want to be late."

I opened the door but didn't get out. I knew when I wasn't wanted, and I sure as hell wasn't waiting around for the insults that usually followed. "Have fun at soccer. You don't have to worry about picking me up. I'll find my own way home. Thanks for the lift."

His eyes shot to mine, full of something that looked like indignation and resentment. "I said I'd pick you up."

"Well, I'm not a fucking obligation." I didn't give a shit if that was abrupt. I'd done nothing to deserve the attitude he was spraying all over me. "Thanks for the lift, but I'll be fine."

I got out and slammed the door—because fuck him too— and as I walked away, I could have sworn I heard him cussing and banging his hands on his steering wheel.

I didn't turn around.

I walked over to the riding instructor and tried to shake off my mood. I needed to get through the next few hours. I could worry about Noah fucking Huxley later.

The instructor's name was Nigel. He was a big burly man with a grey moustache and a wide smile. If I was expecting some high school science teacher, I couldn't have been more wrong. He was just like a guy I'd expect to find at a Harley Motorbike convention. And twenty minutes into our initiation, he quickly recognised that I knew motorbikes better than anyone else there, probably just as well as he did. And he liked me after that. Well, maybe not liked, but he respected me. Or respected that I wasn't some smartarse kid like he might have assumed.

Two others in the class knew the basics of motorbikes, and the other two would have been lucky to know how to put fuel in one, so Nigel probably liked having someone who knew their way around a bike.

After that, the course was easy. When we were having a break, I stood near the school fence and lit up a smoke, and Nigel came over to me. "So, you're a mechanic?"

"Not quite. I'm going to be. I've been working as one for years but just need the piece of paper to prove it."

He nodded but seemed confused. "Why so late? I mean, you're what? Twenty-three?"

"Twenty-four. But yeah, well, me and school didn't exactly get on."

He laughed like something made sense. "I hated school too."

I took a drag of my cigarette and thought now might be a good time to bring this up. "I uh, I have trouble with reading and I don't write so good." I blew out the smoke. "I can read traffic signs and all that, so that's no problem. Just don't give me a book and expect an essay on it."

He rocked back on his heels and nodded slowly, like he was assessing me and what he should say. "There's nothing wrong with that, Clinton."

"CJ," I corrected him. "People call me CJ."

"Well, CJ," he said. "There's nothing wrong with not reading or writing too well. Lots of people can't. Thanks for telling me though."

"Is there a test for this?" I asked. "This course, I mean? I know I have to do the computer test at the RMS, but I mean for this, with you?" I took another drag of my cigarette, trying to quell my nerves. "Because if there is, if you read the questions to me, I'll be able to answer 'em. Anything you ask: road signs, traffic rules, anything mechanical."

He clapped his hand on my shoulder and smiled. "I can do that."

WHEN THE COURSE WAS OVER, I was feeling pretty good. There would be a small test at the end of next week's course, but Nigel said he could read it for me. And I knew, as much as I didn't want to admit it, that if it weren't for Noah, I never would have had the balls to ask Nigel for help.

Let alone done the course at all.

And as we all went out the gates to go our separate ways, Noah was standing, leaning against his car. He was wearing his soccer clothes and he had his arms crossed.

I considered walking in the opposite direction, but then I saw he was wearing his soccer socks and those stupid slides on his feet. "Cool slippers."

He tried not to smile. "Fuck you."

"What are you doing here?" I asked. "I said I could find my own way home."

His jaw ticked, his eyes bore into mine. "We need to talk."

CHAPTER FIFTEEN

NOAH

I WALKED into my kitchen and CJ followed. The tension between us was palpable and heavy in the air. I wanted to fix this, but I needed the truth and I needed to hear it from him. Yesterday afternoon, I was determined to walk away from him until he sent me that damn text message.

Hi

That was all it said.

But I knew how much it would have taken him to write that and then to find the courage to send it. Those two simple, innocent letters were like a red-hot poker to my heart. Then a few hours later, he sent it again, and it almost killed me. I could picture him trying to figure out if he'd somehow fucked up the first one, and even imagining him staring at the phone confused just about broke my heart.

When my phone rang and it was his number, I almost hit Answer. My God, I almost did. I wanted to speak to him so badly. I wanted to hear his voice, to say I was sorry for ignoring his texts, that he didn't mess the text messages up, he did it perfectly, but my heart wouldn't let me.

But then his voice message . . . he sounded so confused

and hurt, and for him to call me when his father might hear or find out he actually had a phone . . . well, I just couldn't stand it anymore. I called him back and his voice was like a song written just for me. Even all the beers I'd had couldn't lessen the pull I felt for him. I'd hoped the alcohol would help numb me, but if anything, it made it worse.

It's funny how alcohol affects your vision. Sometimes things tilt and blur, then other times it strips away all the bullshit and the truth is all that remains.

I was in love with CJ Davis.

That was the truth right there. I was in love with a convicted meth dealer.

And seeing him this morning didn't make it any easier. He was bright-eyed and gorgeous, all smiles and warmth when he saw me. I tried to put up a defensive barrier, but it did more damage than good.

The truth was, CJ was so new to this. He'd never had a relationship before. He'd never trusted anyone enough to give his heart to, and he'd had such a shitty life. He was taking a huge chance on me. The least I owed him was honesty. I just hoped he'd afford me the same.

"What did you want to talk about?" he asked me quietly.

"I read your case file."

CJ blinked in confusion. "So? I thought you read it before."

"Not all of it."

He folded his arms and his eyes hardened. "Which part didn't you like exactly? The fact my old man broke my arm when I was nine because I dropped his cigarettes in a puddle of water? Believe me, breaking my arm wasn't the worst thing he did to me that day. Or was it the fact they found cigarette burns up my arms?"

Oh, God. My heart hurt. "The fact you got caught with all the ingredients to make meth."

He stared at me, like the light had been snuffed out inside him. His voice was whisper quiet. "Do you think for one second I would do that?"

"What am I supposed to believe? Pseudoephedrine, desoxyephedrine, amphetamine, ephedrine, lighter fluid." I counted them off on my fingers. "Jesus, CJ."

"I don't even know what they are!" he cried, throwing his hands up. "Well, I didn't until that night. Fuck, Noah. Do you think I would know the first thing about that shit? I'm too stupid to fucking know!"

His anger, his defiance, his hurt was all too real.

"You're not stupid."

"I ain't no fucking meth dealer either. You, of all people, should know that. You are the only person who knows the real me! How many times have I told you I don't do drugs? I don't touch that shit. Not ever."

"I don't want to believe it. The CJ in that case file is not the CJ I know. But the evidence—"

"Fuck the evidence," he spat. "It don't mean shit."

"So tell me. Tell me what happened that night."

"Just like I told my lawyer back then. It don't matter when they've already made up their minds. Of course I'm guilty, I'm from Davis Row." He took a step back like he was about to turn and run, so I grabbed his arm.

"Tell me what happened that night."

He grabbed my shirt and we ended up pushing and shoving, our frustrations at the boiling point, and he pushed me against the kitchen counter. "Why? You already think I'm guilty!"

"Because I deserve the truth."

"And I deserve the benefit of the doubt! But I didn't get that from you, did I?"

I let my hand fall from his arm, the fight in me breaking with my heart. He was right. I didn't give him the benefit of the doubt. All CJ had ever wanted was for someone to believe in him, and I'd failed. "I'm sorry. I didn't want to believe it. I know you, CJ, and none of it made sense to me."

"Then why did you believe it?" he murmured.

"Because you pleaded guilty."

"I didn't have a choice. Plead guilty and get a suspended sentence. Or plead innocent and let it go to trial where twelve people will see footage of me breaking into the chemist and stealing stuff?" He huffed out. His eyes were glassy. "Yeah, right."

I put my hand to his face. "Then tell me what happened."

He ran his hands down my chest and fisted my shirt. "I had money for Pops' medication put aside, but Dad was out of jail and he found it. We had a massive fight, but he didn't give a shit and he took it anyway. I tried to stop him and he punched the shit outta me." His eyes welled with tears. "It was cold and Pops' breathing was bad. The stress didn't help. Anyway, my old man drank all the money and got into a fight at a bar in town. The cops came and he ended up grabbing one of them in a fight. It was ugly, but they threw his arse back in jail, which was great for me and Pops. But it didn't get him any medication."

"So you broke into the chemist?"

He nodded. "I didn't know what else to do. He couldn't breathe, and I asked the chemist if we could work out some kind of payment plan but she said they couldn't do that. So I went back that night." He frowned and looked down between us. I put my hand through his hair and he sucked back a breath. "So I grabbed what I thought was his medication, but it all looks the same . . ."

Oh God. He couldn't read the labels . . .

"I grabbed some cold and flu tablets and a nose spray thing. I'd seen those ads on TV and I thought that might help him. And I took some packets of tablets. The packaging looked like the ones he normally takes."

"But you couldn't read it," I whispered.

He shook his head and the first of his tears fell. "And I'd bought some lighter fluid from the smoke shop earlier that day. I didn't know all those things together is what methheads use. I had no idea." He looked up at me then, and I could see his broken heart in his eyes.

It all made sense. He'd had a black eye when he'd been caught, and the only reason he'd have that was because of his old man. And of course he couldn't read the labels, especially big words like pseudoephedrine and desoxyephedrine.

I should have known.

I should have trusted him.

I cupped his face and wiped his tears with my thumbs. "I'm sorry I didn't put the pieces together. I'm sorry I didn't trust you. I should have, I should have believed in you, and I'm sorry I didn't. I guess I was too hurt to realise about the reading thing."

He nodded and more tears fell, so I pulled him in for a hug.

"I'm sorry your old man hit you. I'm sorry no one believed you back then, and I'm sorry your Pops is sick. But I'm really sorry I didn't believe in you." I rubbed his back and kissed the side of his head. "I'm sorry I hurt you."

He buried his face in my neck and held on to me like

he'd fall over if he didn't. It was one of those fixes-every-thing hugs that we both needed, him more than me.

"I thought I'd done something wrong," he mumbled. "Or that maybe you found someone else."

I pulled back from him and cupped his face. "No. You've done nothing wrong, and there isn't anyone else."

"And you were drunk last night and I thought maybe you hooked up."

"I don't want anyone else, CJ."

"You didn't want me last night either. On the phone."

"I'm sorry. I was so confused. I thought a few beers would help me see a bit clearer."

"Did it?"

I nodded. "Yep. 'Cause all I could see was you." I looked at his mouth, so close, so perfect. His eyes were smouldering with emotion and need. "I want to kiss you so bad."

He put his hand around my neck and brought our lips closer. "We can't do this. Not for one more week."

"Fuck the rules," I murmured and crushed my lips to his.

He tilted his head and opened his mouth, letting our tongues collide. He tasted of cigarettes and mint, emotion, and everything I wanted. I held his face and he slid his hands down my back and pulled our bodies together, making us both moan.

Fuck.

He pushed me harder against the counter, our bodies melding together, our mouths, our tongues, our hearts.

I dragged my hands down his neck to his chest, letting them find their way lower, lower . . . and he pulled away and stepped back. "We should stop right there."

We were both breathing hard. "I'm not sure I want to."

He barked out a laugh. "I sure as hell don't want to. But we should. You're my parole officer."

"For one more week." I took a few breaths. "Can you wait that long?"

He ran his hand through his hair, looked up to the ceiling, and made a pained groaning sound. "We have to."

"You have more self-control than me." I put my hand to his chest and slid it up to his cheek. "But if we've kissed once . . ."

He smiled. "Then twice won't matter."

I brought our lips together, softer this time with slower, tender kisses. I wanted him to know how sorry I was, how much I never meant to hurt him, how I would never hurt him again.

But then he trailed his hand around my back and lifted my shirt a little. He slid his fingertips along the line of skin above the waistband of my shorts.

It damn near brought me undone.

I smiled into the kiss and gently pushed his hips from mine. My flimsy soccer shorts didn't leave much to the imagination. I was turned on, hard and aching, and it was very obvious.

"Um," he started, looking down at my tented shorts.

I palmed myself. "Shut up. I can't help it. You're just lucky to be wearing jeans."

He laughed and the tension between us settled into something else. I took his hand. "Are we good?" I asked. "I really am sorry. I acted like a jerk."

"Yeah, you did." He held my gaze for a beat. "But we're good."

I sighed in relief. "Okay, can you give me a sec. I need a real quick shower because I'm all sweaty after soccer, and these shorts are not my friend right now."

He raised one eyebrow. "I dunno. I like 'em."

I chuckled and squeezed his hand. "Will you stay? Please?"

He nodded. "Yeah."

"I won't be long."

He gave a pointed glance at my still-tented shorts. "Oh, really?"

"I'll be having a cold shower, thanks."

He laughed. "Let me guess. You won't be opposed to me making you a toasted cheese sandwich while you're gone?"

"Not at all." I grinned at him, then pecked his lips with mine. "Then we can talk, okay?"

CJ nodded. "Go, shower." He palmed himself now. "Before we well and truly break your stupid rules."

I eyed the bulge in his jeans. "Well, if we've broken one rule . . ."

He turned me around and pushed me toward the door. "Go."

I heard him clanging a saucepan and grumbling to himself as I walked into the bathroom. Ten minutes later, I was cold-showered and clean and smelling a whole lot better. He had two toasted sandwiches made and handed me one on a plate as I walked in. "Feel better?"

I bit into my sandwich and spoke with my mouth half-full. "Cold showers suck, just so you know."

He snorted. "How was soccer?"

"We won!"

"You did? That's pretty cool."

"Yeah. How was your riding course?"

"Pretty good. Nigel, the instructor guy, was impressed with me. Well, impressed that I know my way around a bike, anyway. I asked him if there was a quiz at the end if he could read it to me because I don't read too good."

My God, I couldn't believe he'd asked the instructor for help. "You did? What did he say?"

He swallowed down his food. "Said it was no problem. That it's nothing to be ashamed of because lots of people don't read too well." He shrugged. "I told him I had no problem with road signs or nothing like that, just tests and lots of big words."

God, I felt like I could burst. I put my hand on his arm. "I'm really proud of you."

He blushed and tried not to smile. "There are two guys in the class who don't know nothin' about bikes. I'm surprised they could even kick-start one. One turned on with a key, so maybe he didn't know how to kick-start one."

I chuckled. "And you know how to pull one apart, fix it, and put it back together again."

He nodded, this time not even trying to hide his pride. "First time I've ever been the smartest in the class, that's for sure."

Now I laughed. "You'll nail it next weekend. Then you can sit the test after you finish the course. I can drive you straight to the RMS if you like. This time next week, you'll have your rider licence."

He finished his sandwich and smiled. "Sounds good."

"I really am sorry, CJ. I need you to know that I do believe in you. I should never have doubted you, not even for one second. I know what kind of man you are, and I feel like shit that I let you down."

He swallowed hard and he never looked away, even though I bet he probably wanted to. "Thank you. What I did was a stupid mistake. I should have found another way."

"You were only trying to help Pops. I don't blame you. I would have done the same thing."

"No, you wouldn't have."

I shrugged. "Desperate times call for desperate measures. There's no saying what I'd do for someone I loved."

His eyes shot to mine and my heart galloped, overtaken only by the butterflies that flooded my throat. I held his gaze until he looked away. I wanted to kiss him again and figured if I'd done it twice, then three times wouldn't hurt. I took his plate and put it on the counter beside him and stepped in front of him. "What are you doing?" he whispered.

"I'd really like to kiss you again."

He bit his bottom lip. "You know, I never did beg you to kiss me. You said you'd make me beg."

"Is that a problem?"

He smirked. "No, just that you said I'd be begging you for it."

Right, then. I took a step back and let out a breath. I was disappointed at not kissing him right now, but he was right. "Challenge accepted."

He barked out a laugh. "So now you won't do it unless I beg? How is that fair?"

"It's not, but I never said it would be."

He pushed my shoulder playfully and I flicked his arm away and his eyes went wide and he shoved me against the fridge, pressing his body against mine. His grin was full of heat and daring. "What if I make you beg?"

If he wanted to play, I'd play. "You reckon you're good enough?"

He put his hand to my face, almost a little too roughly, then in a contrast of touch, he gently slid his thumb across my lip and dipped the tip into my mouth. I licked it and his nostrils flared, so I sucked it into my mouth before drawing it out with a flick of my tongue and never broke eye contact.

He laughed, a tortured sound. "Fuck." His hips rolled

into mine, our bodies pressed tight, and just when I thought he would cave in and kiss me, he stepped back.

I was breathless and light-headed. "Your self-control is impeccable."

He took a deep breath and shook his head. "Nah. I just don't like to lose."

I snorted. "It's probably just as well one of us is thinking straight anyway."

"Not sure if straight's the right word."

Now I laughed. "Any way you look at it, I think some distance is a good idea."

He flinched. "Distance? Should I go . . . ?"

"No, just to the other side of the kitchen would be a good start." I readjusted myself. "Jesus, I need another cold shower."

He grinned with satisfaction. "So, this time next week . . ."

"This time next week you'll be finished with your rider course and will have sat for your licence already."

"No, I meant"—he motioned between the two of us—"you won't be my parole officer anymore and your rules won't apply."

"Uh, I'm pretty sure the rules went out the window this afternoon."

He smirked. "Will there be any rules this time next week?"

"What exactly are you asking?"

He swallowed hard and shook his head. "Don't make me say it."

"You want to know if we'll end up in bed?"

His eyes shot to mine, and he didn't have to actually answer. It was written on his face.

I waggled my eyebrows at him. "Depends what you beg me for."

He barked out a laugh. "Right. So, nothing then."

I was grinning at him. "Or what I beg you for."

He nodded slowly and let out a steadying breath. "So are we doing this?"

"This?" Now I motioned between us. "As in boyfriends?"

"Like I told ya before, I ain't ever had a boyfriend."

"But you're not opposed to having one?"

CJ stared at me, vulnerable yet defiant. "Is this you asking?"

I stared right back at him. "Yes."

"What about your rules? Shouldn't we wait until next weekend?"

"Probably. So, we could be unofficial boyfriends until then."

"I ain't ever had an unofficial boyfriend either."

"We really should start that list of firsts."

He chuckled and a delicious blush crept along his cheeks, but then he lifted his chin. "I can't promise I'll get it right. And for as long as my old man's outta jail, I can't be around much. And I ain't exactly out and proud either."

"I can live with that. As long as we know from the beginning, there's no miscommunication."

"Miscommunication . . . Like you assuming I'm a meth dealer?" He gave me a pointed look.

I groaned. "I really am sorry. Can you forgive me?"

He smirked. "I already have. But next time, ask me."

"I will. I promise." He still hadn't strictly answered me. "So? Are we doing this?"

He chewed the inside of his lip like he was trying not to smile. "Yeah."

I pushed away from the fridge, where he'd had me pinned earlier, and stepped in front of him. I leaned in as if I was going to kiss him but whispered in his ear instead. "You just made me very happy."

I went to pull back but he had a hold of my shirt. He still had his head down but he pulled me against him and wrapped both arms around me. It wasn't a hug that was leading to something more physical. It was one of those soul-soothing hugs that I didn't reckon he got too often. So I slid my hands over his back, letting him feel my touch as much as I could, and he sighed into me. "You made me pretty happy too."

I smiled into his neck and neither one of us were in any hurry to move. "I never thought I'd like the smell of cigarettes, but on you, it mixes with something else. I dunno what it is, but I like it."

He chuckled, his breath warm on my neck. He still didn't want to let go of me. "I really like how you smell. I've always had a thing for guys who smell nice and it was the first thing I noticed about you."

"Is that so?"

"Mmm." His arms tightened around me. "This is nice. Hugs are good."

I chuckled. "Hugs with you are particularly good."

He rested his forehead on my shoulder. "Are you gonna hound me to quit smoking?"

"Nope."

"Good."

"As your unofficial boyfriend, I accept all your dirty, stinking, cancer-causing habits."

He snorted. "Gee, thanks." He pulled back now, and with his hands on my hips, he met my eyes. "I wish I could stay, but I should probably get home."

I sighed. "Yeah." I cupped his face, and begging be damned, I pressed my lips to his. "I'll drive you."

Then he baulked like he remembered something. "Shit. I was supposed to pick up a few things from the supermarket."

I smiled. "Then let's go shopping."

I'D KINDA FORGOTTEN about CJ's reading levels until we got to Coles. He picked up a basket and I did the same, figuring I may as well grab a few things while I was there. The funny thing was, a lot of products were obvious. Like loaves of bread or cartons of milk or trays of sausages or bags of carrots, for example. It was only the products with non-see-through packaging and ambiguous labels that were difficult, and I noticed CJ avoided those.

I never said a word. I never asked him anything. But I did pretend, just to myself, to recognise products without looking at the words or labels. I wanted to view what the world looked like to CJ, especially in a supermarket where I took the ability to read for granted.

How did he tell the difference between a can of refried beans and a can of whole beans? Sure, most labels had pictures on them, but not all. What happened if they didn't have the kind of toothpaste he was used to buying? Would he know which other one to get?

He only grabbed some sausages, bread, milk, and two packs of cigarettes, so it was hardly a challenge. But it got me thinking . . . what *challenges* did he have? What else did I take for granted that he struggled with? Like the carton of milk in my fridge: it wasn't a bottle, it didn't look like milk, and the writing on the carton was swirly and there was no picture of a cow.

And for personal products, how did he know which condoms or lube to buy? How did he know if he was buying lube or massage oil that affected the latex in condoms? I mean, the list was endless. For household stuff, Pops would soon tell him if he bought the wrong kind of detergent, but he couldn't very well ask his Pops if the lube he bought was self-warming or if that slight burning sensation was something he should go to the clinic for.

I remember hearing a story when I was a kid of a dad who couldn't read, confused the small tube of superglue with his kid's conjunctivitis ointment and didn't realise until he'd glued the poor kid's eyes shut.

Jesus. Getting cow's milk confused with almond milk would be a bit of a shock to the taste buds but it wasn't a serious medical emergency. Just what kind of shit did he have to deal with?

CJ sighed. "Just ask me."

"What?"

"You've been in your own world for five minutes looking at that packet mix like you're trying to solve the world's problems."

"Oh." The packet I was holding was a chilli con carne spices mix. The one next to it was a savoury mince packet. Both pictures on the packets looked similar, but they sure as hell tasted different. "Yeah."

"You wanna know how I know which ones to buy?"

I looked at him and nodded.

He smiled, a little sadly. "Pictures, mostly. You'd be surprised. This one is spicy because of the red powder in a pile behind the meat. And the cut lime, that tells me it's

Mexican or Spanish or something. This one is just like a gravy because, see the vegetables? Potato, carrots, peas. That means Irish or English to me. I mean, not spicy. Sometimes there'll be a little chilli pepper to say how hot it is, but not always. Most cans have pictures. Like baked beans or tinned tomatoes. Washing up detergent has plates on a sink on the bottle. I know what toothpaste looks like, and I can read the word Colgate. It's the fancy words after it that stump me."

"Like fluoride and stuff?"

"No, just that now there are ten different types. Some kind of whitening or antibacterial bullshit, I dunno."

"I never thought of that."

CJ shrugged. "I usually stick to the cheap brands anyway, and sometimes their labels don't have pictures but I look at the ones next to it. And if I have time, I can stand there and sound the word out in my head. It's not as bad as you'd think."

"Actually, you're pretty damn clever."

He laughed. "I dunno about that."

"I do."

"Sometimes I get the wrong thing and Pops helps me read it out loud. It's never a big deal. And sometimes we've had an interesting dinner we wouldn't have had otherwise."

I chuckled at that. "It's still pretty cool though. You're kinda incredible, the way you improvise like that."

"Don't really have a choice."

"Can I ask you about something . . . personal?"

He eyed a woman who was pushing a trolley past us and waited until she was out of earshot. "I don't know. Can you ask me something personal?"

"You don't have to answer, but how do you know which condoms to buy?" Then it occurred to me that he might not practise safe sex. "Ummm, do you buy them? At all? I mean, do you use them? You mentioned the studded ones once, but I think that was a joke . . ." I sorely regretted asking this line of questioning. "You know what, never mind. You don't have to answer that. Actually, you should. Because if that's something we're going to explore together, then I need to know that, I guess. Oh God, this got really awkward."

CJ stared at me for a full three seconds, then burst out laughing. "Come with me." He walked off and I followed, right to the personals aisle. "Here," he pointed to one packet. "It's got a woman on the box in a sexy pose, and I can read the word 'her' there." He pointed to the word. It actually said 'for her pleasure' but he was right. "Then this one here has ribbing on the picture, and this one says 'XL'— don't need an English lesson for that one."

I chuckled. "Okay, okay. It's not as hard as I thought it would be."

He raised one eyebrow and a slow grin spread across his face. "There are pills for that."

I realised what I said and rolled my eyes. "I think we both know that's not an issue. I had to have a cold shower earlier to prove that."

He laughed, took a twelve pack of condoms, and threw them into my basket. I raised my eyebrows and he smiled. "Problem?" he asked.

Jesus. "Nope. Not a one." While we were being brave and forthright, I picked up a bottle of lube and tossed it into my basket as well.

His voice was low and he was standing way too close. "Do you have any other questions?"

"I have so many, but I don't think here is the place."

He snorted. "Got everything you need then?"

I looked at my basket. "Uh, yeah. I do now."

We went through the checkout and when CJ paid with cash, I was reminded that we hadn't gotten him a bank account. Something else to add to my list of things to do this week.

Seven more days.

CHAPTER SIXTEEN

CJ

WHEN NOAH PULLED up at Mr Barese's shop, he turned the engine off. All the roller doors were down, and it seemed all of Ten Mile Creek was quiet. "Thanks for the lift, and um, thanks for today."

"You're welcome. And thank you, for today, as well." One corner of his lip curled up. "For, you know, hearing me out when you had every right to tell me to piss off."

"I probably should have told you to piss off." I smiled when his gaze shot to mine. "But then we wouldn't be doing the unofficial boyfriend thing, right?"

He chuckled. "Right."

"And anyway, you're not all bad."

"Thanks," he said with a snort. Then he sighed. "Did your dad really sell your lawnmower?"

I nodded. "Yep."

"Will you promise me something?"

"Okay."

"If he," Noah frowned. "If he becomes difficult, promise me you'll call me. I'll come get you."

Having someone worry about me was new. It was

different to how Mr Barese cared. Strange, a little restricting even, but nice. "I'll be fine."

"Promise me."

"I promise." Then I said, "So, this is my last week on probation. Do you still need to do your workplace visit? I have my last drugs and alcohol meeting on Thursday. I could call in and see you then?"

"I don't mind seeing you more than once." He smirked. "But I can hold out till Thursday."

I took my bag of groceries and opened the door. "I'll text you later. I ain't real fast at it, so you'll need to be patient."

He smiled warmly. "You'll do great."

I got out, certain I was grinning like a fool. I waved him off and shoved my bag of groceries down the front of my jacket. I let myself into the workshop and wheeled my bike out, locked the workshop up, and went home. I was still in a good mood when I walked inside, and not even my poor excuse for a father could piss me off.

"Hey, boy," he said from Pops' recliner. He tried to sound cheerful, which was his way of assuming all was well. At least the fire was going. "Don't happen to have any smokes on ya?"

I dumped the bag of groceries on the kitchen table, gave Pops a tight smile, and fished one pack of cigarettes out. I walked into him, calmly handed the unopened packet to him, and walked back into the kitchen. Pops patted my arm but didn't say anything. He didn't need to.

I took out the packet of sausages. "I got some snags for dinner. How's that sound?"

"Sounds great," Pops said.

"Sausages again?" my dad replied from the living room. I could smell the cigarette he was smoking. Inside.

I took a breath and tried to channel my inner calm.

"Maybe I'd have more money for steak if I didn't have to save for a new lawnmower."

No reply.

Yeah, that's what I thought.

"And I told you before. Don't smoke in the house."

"You giving me shit, boy?" His tone was louder, angrier.

I didn't have it in me to care, but Pops' shoulders sagged like he knew we were about to fight. So I bit back my attitude and spoke nicely. "Can you please smoke outside while I cook dinner?"

There was a beat of silence, then the recliner creaked and his footsteps stomped past. I held my breath, waiting for him to walk in and for hell to erupt. But it didn't. He walked out the front to have his cigarette outside.

I could suddenly breathe, and Pops sank into a chair at the table. "You okay?" I asked him.

He nodded. "Yeah." Then he brightened some. "How was your course today?"

"Good." I checked over my shoulder to make sure my father was still outside. "Went well. The guy running it said he can help me with the quiz at the end, and then Noah said he can drive me to get my licence right after."

Pops smiled proudly. "I'm proud of you, CJ."

And there it was. Recognition that I would never get from my father. "Thanks, Pops."

"Want me to help?" he asked.

"Nah. You can tell me what you did today while I peel some potatoes."

So even though my father was technically living with us, Pops and I carried on like he wasn't. It made it bearable.

After dinner when Pops and Dad were both in bed, I stoked up the fire, turned off the TV, and got ready for bed. I fished out my phone, plugged it into the charger, and climbed into bed. I opened the messages like Noah had shown me and repeated my lame text.

Hi

My phone vibrated just a few seconds later. *Hi. How was your night?*

I had to read it out slowly.

Good

I felt slow and stupid but I wanted to learn how to do this.

Did you cook the sausages for dinner?

That took me a while to sound out. *Yep.*

Is Pops keeping warm?

I realised then that he was asking me questions that I only had to give short, easy answers to in return. Not in a patronising way but in a helpful way. *Yep. He is good.*

God, I sucked at this. I sounded like I was four years old. *You in bed?*

I blinked. Was he implying something or just asking? *Yep. You?* I tapped my finger, waiting on his reply.

Yep. I didn't sleep much last night.

I sounded each word out. It took a little while but I was adamant to do this. I wanted to type out that he should've spoken to me instead of assuming bad things about me and maybe he would've slept better, but there was no way I could type that out. So I hit the Call button.

"Hey," he answered. "Everything okay?"

"Yeah," I whispered. "Can't talk loud though."

"That's okay. I can hear you just fine. Did you want to talk about something?"

"Well, yeah. I couldn't type everything I wanted to say. It'd take too long and I'd get it wrong. It's just easier to talk."

"What did you want to say?"

"You said you didn't sleep well. I was going to say you should talk to me next time. Ask me instead of assuming the worst."

"I am sorry."

"I know you are."

"Will you ever let me live that down?"

"Dunno. Jury's still out."

He snorted. "I can make it up to you. Next weekend."

"Oh really?" That sounded promising in a sexual way. "How?"

"Pizza. Oh, hey! That reminds me. You were supposed to buy pizza tonight."

I snorted quietly. "You'll have to take a raincheck."

"I will. Until next weekend."

"Deal."

"What are you doing tomorrow?"

"Not mowing the lawn."

He made an unhappy sound. "Did you talk to your dad about it?"

"Not really. Told him to smoke outside, again. Thought he was gonna clip me up the back of the head."

"Did he hit you?" he sounded alarmed.

"Nah. He just never said a word and went outside for his smoke."

"Man, I'm sorry you have to deal with that."

"Me too." I sighed and scrubbed my hand over my face. "What are you doing tomorrow?"

"Groceries. Laundry. Super exciting stuff."

"Yeah, same. Well, laundry. Need to get firewood. Nothing too exciting either."

"When will I see you next?" he asked. "Thursday seems so far away."

I smiled, knowing exactly what he meant. "It's just five days."

"Five days is forever."

"I have to work Monday, Wednesday, and Friday."

"Could you tell your dad you need to come into town on Tuesday for something?"

"I don't actually need to lie to him. I don't have to tell him nothin'. I'll just get home when I get home."

"I don't want to cause you any problems with your father."

"You're the least of my problems when it comes to my father." I scrubbed my hand over my face. "Families, huh? Sometimes I reckon we're better off without 'em."

He didn't answer for a while. "Mmm."

Shit. I'd forgotten about his family. Me and my stupid mouth. "I didn't mean . . . Noah, I didn't . . . I'm sorry."

"It's okay," he murmured.

Shit, shit, shit. "Noah. I didn't think, sorry."

"It's okay, CJ. Honestly."

I didn't know what to say. It clearly wasn't okay because his silence said more than words ever could. "Can I tell you something?"

"Yeah, of course."

"I might not always get things right. But things with me are pretty cut and dry, and I guess I ain't real complicated. I might not have had a boyfriend before, but I like it. I like having you in my life, and I just thought you should know."

"Oh." He hummed quietly. "I like having you in my life too."

"I'm closer to you than I've ever been to anyone in my entire life." I swallowed hard. "And I don't mean to sound sappy or nothin' but I just wanted to say thanks."

"Thank you, too, CJ," he murmured. "For taking a

chance on me. For not bailing when I called you a meth-cooking dealer."

I snorted. "I'd forgotten about that."

"I shouldn't have reminded you."

I smiled at the ceiling. "So I was thinking maybe I could buy pizza on Tuesday night."

He made a happy sound. "Sounds good. I'll be home by five thirty. We can watch a movie and I can drive you home."

That sounded utterly perfect. "See you then."

"Sleep well, CJ." His voice was low and lovely.

"You too."

He ended the call and I made sure the phone was on silent before I put it down the side of my bed. I couldn't deny it; he made me happy. He made my heart skip and stutter. He made my belly tight, full of butterflies and nerves. But he made me smile and feel warm all over, and he made me feel special and wanted. Someone else on the planet actually liked me, knew the wrongs I'd done and things I'd endured, and he shared his past with me. He wanted to know more of me. He wanted *me*. Not just physically, but he wanted me, CJ Davis. I'd never thought, not for one minute, that I'd find that with anyone. I never expected to be with anyone. I was gay in a family, a world, where that wasn't even a consideration. I just assumed I'd never have nothing more than a few quick fucks or hand jobs in the backroom of HQ.

I was never supposed to have dinner dates and movies, and conversations and hand-holding, or those hugs that mended parts of me long broken.

Sleep well, he'd said. I closed my eyes and his voice played through my memory like a warm blanket, like comfort and happiness.

I dreamed of him, of things just out of my reach but close enough to taste. Of a shared heartache, of laughter and kisses, of romance and other absurd things I never knew I wanted.

Longed for.

Craved.

I KNOCKED on Noah's back door at five thirty-two. Not that I was counting. Except I really was. I'd spent Sunday doing chores around the house. Monday was busy at work. I had to service the Burkes' Ford Territory and Mr Barese finished up the monthly accounts. I texted Noah every night when I was alone in my room. Always starting with my usual *Hi* and he would answer with questions I could answer with short replies.

By Tuesday, I was itching to see him. I shoved a casserole in the oven for Pops and Dad to be ready by the time they'd want dinner. I drove my bike to the shop and caught the last bus to town. It really would have been easier if I'd ridden my bike, but with just a few days of probation to go, I couldn't risk getting caught by the cops.

There was a shuffling behind the door before it opened, then Noah was there, pulling his jeans up. I caught a glimpse of black briefs, but his otherwise naked torso was kind of distracting. He grinned. If he was happy to see me or laughing at my expression, I wasn't sure. He snatched up a folded shirt off the top of the dryer and pulled it over his head. "I just got in," he said as I stepped inside.

By the time I'd gathered my wits enough to speak, he had his shirt on. "Answer the door naked all the time?"

He laughed. "I can't wait to get out of my work clothes every day."

"I'm not complaining."

His smile turned smug. He stepped in close, his face just an inch from mine, and his damn scent of deodorant or aftershave washed over me. His blue eyes were full of spark and daring. "Ready to beg for a kiss yet?"

"Are you?" I slid my hands along his waist and pulled us together. His nostrils flared and his eyes darkened. "God, you smell good."

Now he smiled. "I should kiss you for that."

"I won't beg you."

"Not yet. But you will." He ghosted his lips over mine but it wasn't a real kiss.

My heart was hammering and I wanted him to kiss me, but this game of who would break first and who would beg was too much fun. "I don't think so." I pushed him against the washing machine, pressing our hips together, and ran my nose along his ear. "You will beg me."

He made a bitten back groan sound that lit something inside me, and I was powerless to fight it. I crushed my mouth to his and he raked his hands through my hair, pouring gasoline on a fire I could barely contain. He held my mouth to his; our tongues tasted and teased until we were both breathless and panting for air.

"Holy shit," he whispered, his chest heaving.

I moved back a step. "For the record, I didn't beg. But you made that sound." I waved my hand toward his throat and chest.

"What sound?"

"That groany-growl sound." I took another step back. I needed to palm myself but didn't want to do it in front of him.

"I didn't make a groany-growl sound."

"Oh yes you did."

He tilted his head. "You liked it." It wasn't a question, so I didn't answer. I didn't have to. He smirked at me. "I'll have to remember that."

"Shut up."

He laughed, took my hand, and led me into the kitchen. "Can I get you a drink?"

"Ah, sure." The distraction was welcome, but it meant he had to let go of my hand. He passed me a bottle of water, and after we'd both had a drink and a minute to clear our heads, he held his hand out back out.

I took it, not knowing why he was offering, and not caring. I just wanted to touch some part of him. He threaded our fingers and gave me a smile that made me blush. "Never thought I'd like this," I admitted quietly.

"Holding hands?"

I nodded. I'd told him before it wasn't something I'd done much of—or any of, to be honest. "Yeah."

He squeezed my hand. "I like it too."

"I want to say it's nice, but it's more than that."

"It's human touch and comfort. And reassurance."

My gaze shot to his. He knew exactly what I meant. "Yeah." Then I looked to our joined hands between us. "I'm glad you're good with words because I'm not."

"You don't need to be. I get you."

My eyes found his again, and my heart squeezed. "You do. I dunno how, but you do."

"We're not that different," he murmured, bringing our hands up to his lips. He looked at my grease-and-oil ingrained fingernails and smiled.

"Thank you for telling me about your family and about your life," I said. I was probably ruining the mood between us but I needed him to know . . . "It means a lot that you shared that part of you with me. I mean, you know all the horrible shit about me and I'm glad you told me. I know I'm not good at this whole being-with-someone thing and this probably just made you feel like shit for bringing this up—"

He smirked. "Thank you for listening. It's not something I tell a lot of people, but I'm glad you know. I told you we're not that different. And you know what?"

"What?"

"You're cute when you rant."

I baulked and blushed, though I pretended I couldn't feel my cheeks heat. "Well, I'm not very good at talking about this kind of thing. You're the one that's good with words, not me."

He ran his thumb over the back of my hand and smiled. His voice was soft and smooth, and it made my belly flip. "You're doing just fine."

I chuckled, trying to laugh off my embarrassment. Or his compliment—if that's what that was. He took pity on me and changed the subject. "So, I was thinking, this Thursday before your last ever drugs and alcohol meeting, we could get you a bank account set up."

"Uh, sure. Maybe."

"I just figured it's my last chance to spend time with you on company time. Well, government department time."

"Are you trying to rort the system?" I raised an eyebrow and smirked at him.

"Only for personal gain."

I chuckled. "Then I guess I can't argue." Truthfully, spending more time with him wasn't exactly a hardship.

"How about we order that pizza. I'm starving."

"That depends. Do you like olives?"

He looked horrified. "Good Lord, no. They're little black circles of nastiness."

Now I laughed. "Thank God. For a second there, I thought I was going to have to call this whole unofficial-boyfriend thing off."

"Olives are a deal breaker. Duly noted." Noah led me into the lounge room and pulled me onto the sofa with him. "Now, about movies." He eyed me cautiously. "How do you feel about Arnold Schwarzenegger?"

"This is a test, isn't it?"

He fought a smile. "Yes."

"Loved *Predator* and *The Expendables*. *Twins* was embarrassing, but *Kindergarten Cop* was okay."

He cracked up and planted a sound kiss on my lips. "Correct answer. I was thinking *Predator*. How does that sound?"

Pizza, a movie, and hand-holding. "Perfect."

MY DAD never said much when I got home, but he gave me a strange look, which I ignored. I was pretty fucking happy when I walked through the door, and if he thought my smile was suspect, he never said. I just stoked up the fire, said goodnight, and went to bed.

Wednesday was quiet at work, but I helped Mrs Barese in her yard and she needed a few things at the store so I walked up and grabbed them for her. I swept out the shop, cleaned tools, did a stocktake on engine and transmission oils, and made the whole place as tidy as a mechanic workshop could be. Quiet, but productive. It felt good.

I was still buzzing on cloud nine when I got home. I couldn't deny it; Noah made me happy. I wanted to tell everyone, I wanted to scream it through the street, but I couldn't tell a soul. Not even Pops. I wanted him to know I was happy, that things were finally looking good for me, but I couldn't. I wasn't ready to come out. Especially with my old man in the house.

"Thought I'd make some burgers for dinner," I announced. Dad was in Pops' recliner, again, and Pops followed me into the kitchen. "We've got bread, rissoles, and beetroot, cheese and eggs. How's that sound?"

"Sounds good, CJ," Pops said with a smile.

Dad didn't answer. I didn't really expect him to, and I didn't really care if he wanted it or not. That's what I was making. He could eat it or make himself something else.

"Work was good today?" Pops asked. He must have assumed my smile and good mood was because I'd had a good day.

"Yep. Got lots done."

"When are you going to town next?" he asked.

"Tomorrow. Got my last meeting tomorrow arvo." I got the rissoles out of the fridge and put them on the counter. "Why? Wassup?"

"Need more of my tablets, that's all."

"No problem. If you give me your script, I can pick them up." Then I whispered, "I need a phone bill or electricity bill or something. Have you seen the last one we got?"

He nodded. "I'll get it for ya later," he mouthed the words so my dad wouldn't hear.

"Thanks." He didn't ask what I needed it for, and I loved that he was all for me trying to improve the way I did things. I checked that Dad was still watching the TV, then whispered to Pops, "Noah reckons I should get a bank account. Helps with ID and stuff. He reckons I might be able to apply for some government assistance." I rubbed my thumb against my fingers, the universal sign for 'money.'

"Worth looking into," he whispered.

Then my dad was in the doorway. "What are you two whisperin' about?"

He startled me. "Oh, nothing."

He stared right at me. "You got yourself a girlfriend or something? Walkin' around smiling like the cat that got the cream. You gettin' some action, boy?"

I rolled my eyes. "Nuh."

"You can't lie for shit."

I expected him to smile, but he didn't. He had that mean look about him, like his anger was just waiting for one wrong word, one wrong look. He had an energy rolling off him, black and seething, bristling and strained, just waiting to snap.

It was an aura I knew all too well.

"I'm making burgers for dinner," I said, aiming for cheerful though probably missing the mark.

He walked in, bumping my shoulder as he stalked in, then opened the fridge door with so much oomph everything in the fridge rattled. He grabbed out a beer and stomped out of the kitchen. He did it to intimidate and to remind us all of the pecking order in the house. I hated it, and I hated it more because it worked.

I glared after him, then mouthed to Pops, "I hate him."

Pops nodded sympathetically. "I know."

He drank another beer as I cooked dinner, then another while he ate, then another as I cleaned up. Then after dinner, because the mood in the house was so tense, Pops went in for a shower so I mumbled something about working on my bike and went out to the shed. Despite the cold and drizzling rain, it was still better than being cooped up with him. The house was too damn small for the kind of energy he was putting off.

Anyways, I'd seen how nights like this ended. He'd drink until there was nothing left, and then he'd cuss and stomp, maybe throw a few things, because it was someone else's fault he'd run out of beer.

Usually mine.

But apparently steering clear of him wasn't enough. When I heard the back door slam, I knew he was coming. I was crouching down beside my bike and I sighed. *Fuck.*

"Hey, boy!" he barked.

I didn't even have to look up. He sounded drunk and pissed off. I didn't need to see him to confirm it.

"Said, hey, boy!" he slurred. "Answer when I'm talkin' to you."

I never stood up. I kept wiping down the cylinder head. "What do you want?"

"Some fuckin' respect's what I want, boy. You gettin' too big for ya boots."

I rose to my full height. If this is how it was gonna be, then I wouldn't let him tower over me. If he wanted dominance, he could fuck off. "My boots fit me just fine."

"You wanna be a smartarse?" His jaw bulged. His eyes were flat, dulled by beer and self-loathing. "You think you're too good for your old man?"

I threw the dirty rag onto my banged-up toolbox. "I don't think anything. Just tryin' to get by, ya know?"

He lifted his chin and clenched his fist. I could have placated him or tried to make a joke, but I was done with that bullshit. I was done with him. I took my cigarettes out of my pocket, put one between my lips, and he watched as I lit it up. I didn't look at him. I certainly wasn't offering him one.

"Gimme one."

I looked at him then. "What?"

"I said, give me a fuckin' cigarette."

"Please." I took a drag. "Or how about, 'Hey, CJ, can I have a smoke please?'"

His glare narrowed. "You want a smack in the mouth?"

I took another drag of my cigarette and stared at him. I knew he was about to snap, but I didn't give a shit. My blood ran hot and my skin felt cold, and I knew this was about to get physical. I blew the smoke out at him and never said a word.

He grabbed my shirt and I shoved his hand away. He was drunk and unsteady on his feet, and I was fucking done with his shit. I wasn't backing down. He stumbled back, then came at me again, swinging his fist at my face. I ducked back but he caught the corner of my eye. It wasn't hard enough to knock me down, but it was gonna leave a mark.

While he was off-balance, I shoved him with both hands, hard.

He fell back, tripped over his own feet and fell on his arse in the driveway. He snarled at me and scrambled to his feet, still unsteady, and it took him a second too long because, before he could charge at me again, he wobbled and I shoved him again, sending him sprawling backwards. I stood over him, my fist shaking. I ain't ever hit anyone, but I'd happily make him my first. "Stay the fuck down," I spat at him.

He groaned, drunk, but he knew when he was beat. I was pretty sure he'd get even with me at some point, but I'd take my chances then too.

"I'm done with your shit," I said, pointing at him. "You can't come back here and just expect to sit around doin' nothing. Get a fucking job. Buy me a new goddamn lawn mower to replace the one you stole from me. You want cigarettes? Fucking have them." I took my cigarettes out of my pocket and threw them at him, hitting him in the chest. "And stop smoking in the fucking house."

I stormed off and half expected him to get up and tackle me to the ground. But he never did. I thought he might wait till I was asleep and come into my room and smack me around, but he didn't. And it was probably worse that he didn't. Because it meant another eruption was waiting, a worse one, more than likely, and I was pretty sure I didn't want to be around for that.

"I'M HERE TO SEE NOAH," I said to the lady behind the reception desk. I'm pretty sure her name was Sheryl. I'd come here often enough over the last two years to hear her say it when she answered the phone.

"CJ?" she asked.

I nodded and gave her a smile, but she kept looking at the bruise on my cheekbone. *Great.* Someone else that assumed the worst of me.

She walked off down a hallway and I waited in a chair in reception. She came back out a minute later with Noah behind her, and he stopped when he saw me. His eyes grew tight, and he waved his hand back down the hall. "This way."

I followed him, and as soon as we were in his office, he shut the door. "What happened?"

"My old man wanted a cigarette."

He flinched. "Just say the word, CJ, and I'll have Terrell throw his arse back in jail."

I shook my head. "Don't worry about him." I looked at

the door, and not knowing just how soundproof his office was, I whispered, "It's real good to see you."

He finally smiled. "You too. Real good." Then he frowned at my cheekbone. "Does it hurt?"

"Nope. He caught me with his knuckle. He was drunk and falling over, so I pushed him on his arse and told him to get a fucking job."

Noah's eyes went wide. "Holy shit."

I sighed. "Yeah, well, I'm not expecting him to let me get away with it, but at least he knows how I feel."

"You don't have to stay there," he said quietly, seriously. "You have options, CJ. You never have to stay where you don't feel safe."

"I won't leave Pops."

"You don't have to. Bring him."

"Where to?"

"My place."

Now it was my eyes that went wide, but I quickly shook it off. "Noah."

"I'm being serious. It doesn't have to be permanent. Just somewhere safe and he won't know where you are."

I ignored his offer, not ready for the meaning behind it. I reached into the inside pocket of my jacket. "I brought a phone bill and my birth certificate. I wasn't sure what you needed for a bank account."

Noah nodded slowly, resigned that any talk about my father was finished with. "Then let's go get it sorted."

Half an hour later, we were sitting in the bank, and after I scribbled my signature where I was told to, the lady handed me an ATM card. "All done. You just need to activate your card and pick a PIN."

I looked at Noah, and he smiled. "A four-digit number for when you want to use your card or take money out."

The lady looked at me like I was seven kinds of stupid. I'd never had a bank account before. How would I know how these things worked? I inserted it into the machine like she showed me and had to pick four numbers I'd remember. Then I saw the little letters under the numbers. No, I weren't too good with spelling but I could spell that.

I smiled and slowly punched in the numbers 6624.

N-O-A-H

I sat back, still smiling proudly.

"Will you remember it?" Noah asked.

"I won't ever forget it." He gave me a confused look, so I explained. "It spells Noah."

He barked out a laugh. "You're not supposed to tell people." Then he realised what I'd said and a slow, gorgeous smile spread across his face. "Really?"

I nodded, and my God, I thought he was going to kiss me in the middle of the bank. But the lady handed me a bunch of papers I'd never read. "All done!"

We walked out without speaking, and by the time we got to his car, he was grinning. "Really? Did you really pick my name?"

I nodded. "Yep."

He paused and looked right at me. "You know, that just might be the most romantic thing anyone's ever done for me."

That made something wonderful bloom in my chest. "Really?"

"Yep." But then he ruined the moment by checking his watch. "We need to get to your drug and alcohol meeting." And just like that, my heart sank.

He drove me there and pulled the key from the ignition. "What are you doing?" I asked.

"I'm coming with you."

"What for?"

"I want to support you. It's your last one."

"Are you even allowed to do that?" I asked.

"As your boyfriend, probably not. But as your parole officer, I sure can." I was about to object, but then he said, "I'm really proud of you, CJ. You've never missed a meeting. Even though you've never done drugs, you keep doing the right thing by showing up."

"Didn't really have much choice, did I?"

He shrugged. "Still. You should be proud. I'll even buy you dinner afterwards. How does that sound?"

"Dinner and a movie on your couch?"

He grinned. "Hell yes."

"Deal."

THE MEETING WAS as they always were. A group of eight people sat around with Maryanne leading conversation and discussions. Noah had introduced himself to her before we got started and he stood to the back of the room, leaning against a desk, just watching and listening. No one seemed to even notice him, much less care that he was there. And I wasn't gonna say anything—I mean, I hadn't in two years, so why start now? But then near the end of the meeting, Maryanne singled me out. "It's CJ's last meeting with us today," she announced. "He's been coming for two years, never missed a meeting." She glanced quickly at Noah before smiling back at me. "He's been a quiet member of our group."

Which was her way of saying 'he's never contributed or joined in.' Which was true, but I'd told her from the very beginning, I ain't ever did no drugs. She just chose not to believe me. And given she'd brought me to the centre of attention, I figured why the hell not finally say something.

I sat up straighter in my seat and cleared my throat. "Well, I ain't ever said anything before because I don't really have much to say. You guys come here to talk about your problems and that's great and all, and I can really see some improvements and you all should be proud. But I ain't ever taken drugs, and I rarely drink. I've been made to come to these meetings because I got busted stealing prescription meds from a chemist. I didn't know, but what I took was the ingredients for cookin' up meth or something." I shrugged. "But I didn't know because I don't read too good and I was trying to get my Pops' medication because he don't breathe too well without it, and normally I pay for it, but my old man stole my money." I looked right at Maryanne and pointed to the bruise on my cheekbone. "He's the one who gave me this, so before you just assume I'm a meth-head gettin' in bar fights, you might wanna ask if everything's okay at home. Because sometimes it's not."

Okay, so saying something turned into word vomit. I stood up and wiped my hands down my thighs. Maryanne sat there, stunned and hopefully thinking about how she'd treated me over the last two years. "Are we done? Because I'm done."

Maryanne blinked and nodded. "Uh, yes, of course."

I looked around at the others, who were all staring at me. "Good luck." And with that, I turned and walked towards the door. Noah was standing there, not leaning on the desk anymore, with wide, disbelieving eyes and a smile that squeezed my already thumping heart.

I pushed open the door and gulped back fresh air as I walked outside. God, my hands were shaking, and I had no idea what the hell made me say all that.

"CJ! Wait up!" Noah called out behind me. I stopped walking and turned and he ran to catch up but he didn't stop when he got to me. He almost tackled me in a hug. "Holy shit," he murmured into my ear. Then he pulled back, keeping his hands on my shoulder. "I can't believe you just said all that."

"Neither can I."

He was grinning. "How does it feel?"

"I don't know. Good, I think." I held up my hands. "I'm shaking."

He laughed and pulled me against him again. I didn't even care that it was in public because it felt so damn good—I was starting to think his hugs were magical. I could literally feel the weight of my troubles get lighter every time he did it.

I slid my arms around him and hugged him back, and to any passers-by, they'd know this wasn't a man-hug. There was no back-slapping, no awkwardness; it wasn't brief. We were joined from thigh to head with our arms wound tight around each other. This wasn't really a hug. It was an embrace, a moment between two men. My first-ever public display of affection, with anyone, let alone a guy. It was getting kinda late but it wasn't dark, and yet I just couldn't bring myself to care.

I needed him and he was there. That's all that mattered.

"I'm so proud of you," he said softly. Then he pulled back and gave me a smile. "You ready for our date?"

"Date?"

"Well, yeah. Dinner and a movie, maybe a little making out. Pretty sure that's a date."

I took a deep breath and tried not to smile too hard. "Something else to add to my list of firsts."

CHAPTER SEVENTEEN

NOAH

IT WAS hard to believe that CJ had yet to do so many firsts. Not the big stuff like sex, but the little stuff like holding hands, watching movies while lying about on a sofa, kissing and hugging. And one thing I learned about CJ was that he really liked to hug.

It was kinda heartbreaking.

He was so devoid of human touch. His entire life was a hardship, growing up in a house where emotions were something you just didn't show. Sure, he had his Pops and he loved him fiercely, but I got the feeling they weren't exactly touchy-feely kind of people.

Every time I hugged him, he held on for dear life. I loved it, truly I did, but it tugged at my heartstrings, reminding me of all the things he'd missed. Of all the things he'd been deprived of.

When we walked into my kitchen, I threw my keys and wallet onto the kitchen counter, turned, and pulled him close. I wrapped my arms around him and buried my face into his neck. Yeah, the hug in the car park after his drug and alcohol meeting was nice, but this was nicer. Slower, more tender. More intimate.

He breathed in deep and sighed on the exhale, like it was exactly what he needed. I loved how my arms fit under his leather jacket, feeling the shirt on his back, skin warm and firm. He was kinda lean but strong. I guess he worked hard and didn't eat a lot of junk food or takeaway, and it showed. Maybe I should do the same.

"Did you want Chinese food or want me to cook something? I can rustle up a salad or something."

He sighed again and rolled his shoulders like my hug was a warm blanket. He pulled back a bit but kept his hands at my waist. "Can't say I eat a lot of salad."

"Do you like Chinese food?"

He tried to play it down, I think, but there was something in his eyes. Something told me ordering Chinese food was a luxury. "Don't get to eat it much. Being out of town and all."

"Chinese, it is." It was then I noticed the mark on his cheek—a red line and faint purple bruising—and now we were alone, I could get a closer look. It wasn't big and it didn't look particularly sore, but his father hit him, and that had to hurt. I traced my finger lightly along his cheek. "I'm sorry he did that to you. I wish . . ."

"You wish what?"

That his father would go back to jail? That he never got out? That CJ didn't have to live with him, that he didn't have to deal with him. The fact he simply shrugged off domestic violence like it was normal hurt my heart. "I wish things were different for you. I wish I could help in some way."

"You are helping," he whispered. "More than you know."

I slid my hand from his cheek to his neck and brought him in for a kiss. It started soft, warm, and tender, but with the touch of tongues, like a match to gunpowder, passion ignited and he pushed me against the kitchen counter. He ran his hands all over my back, down over my arse, and ground his hips into mine.

He was turned on. I could feel it.

And it was too much and too hot, too soon, because he shuddered and gasped before pulling back. "Shit." He was breathing hard and statue-still, and I realised in my desire-addled brain that he was trying to calm himself down.

I wasn't having any of that.

I walked him backwards until he was pressed against the sink, and I slid my hands down the front of his jeans, under the elastic of his briefs, and wrapped my fingers around his hot and hard shaft.

His eyes went wide, his mouth fell open, so I crushed my lips to his as I pumped and squeezed. And because I knew he liked it, I groaned into his mouth, and the sound set off a chain reaction. He bucked into my fist and throbbed, crying out into my kiss as he came. He shuddered and writhed as he spilt over my hand, his eyes rolled back and his forehead fell onto my shoulder.

Fuck.

That went from tender to hot to climax in minutes. He groaned into my neck like he couldn't function.

I let go of his still-hard cock and he slumped into me, breathing hard. "Shit. I'm sorry."

I leaned back and lifted his chin with my clean hand. "Sorry? What for?"

"That was embarrassing."

"Uh, no. That was hot as hell. That was the hottest thing I've ever seen."

He blushed and almost smiled, but he was clearly embarrassed. So I leaned against him and kissed him, soft and sweet, languid, and if he wouldn't believe my words, then maybe he'd believe my actions. I pulled his bottom lip between mine before kissing him again.

When he was smiling against my lips, I finally pulled away. "I'll grab you some pants and we'll get yours washed and dried before you need to go home." I went into the bathroom first to wash my hand, then quickly stripped out of my work clothes and threw on some track pants and a hoodie. I grabbed some trackies for him and found him, unmoved in the kitchen. I handed him the grey trackies. "You get changed and cleaned up and I'll find the takeaway menu. How does that sound?"

He nodded, still a little embarrassed. It was the last thing I wanted for him . . . God, I was the one who brought him undone, so it was more my fault than his. "Was me touching you okay? I mean, jerking you off? I should have asked first, sorry."

He sobered. "Oh, um, yeah it was fine. More than fine, really. I mean, Jesus. I normally last a lot longer than that."

I barked out a laugh. "I'll take that as a compliment."

He tried not to smile. "I still didn't beg. Just so you know."

I put my forehead to his. "You will." Then I spoke against his lips. "I promise."

He growled at me and went into the bathroom. When he came back out, we set his jeans and briefs for a quick wash and ordered dinner. By the time that was delivered, we'd settled on watching *Commando*, because it was CJ's next favourite Schwarzenegger film and because I hadn't given him any clean undies to wear with the trackies and he was, in fact, going commando.

When the movie was about halfway through, and with our empty takeaway containers on the coffee table and the lights off, I shoved a cushion against the armrest and stuck my feet over his thighs.

"You right there?" he asked.

"Nope." I wriggled down a bit and pulled him over so he was lying between my legs, his back to my chest. He was stiff at first, reluctant or unsure, but when I shoved another cushion under his head, he relaxed and settled back. "That's much better."

I didn't have to ask: this was another first. Last time we'd watched a movie, we'd just sat with our feet on the coffee table and our bodies touching, shoulder to thigh. It was nice and a comfortable first for CJ, given he was so new to it all. But this was better.

"This okay?" I asked, gently stroking the hair at his temple.

He lifted his head, pulled the cushion out, and tossed it to the floor, then laid his head back on my chest. "That's better."

Yes, yes it is.

We watched the rest of the movie like that, both of us laughing at the corny one-liners and *ewwww*ing at the same gruesome carnage Arnie inflicted onscreen. The fact we had the same sense of humour and weak stomach for blood and guts made me happy. On the surface, CJ and I appeared worlds apart, but really, we weren't that different at all.

I stroked his hair again, and as the credits signalled the end of the movie, neither one of us seemed too keen to move. I certainly didn't want to ever move.

"That feels really good," he murmured. "If you keep doing that, I'll fall asleep."

I didn't stop. "I wouldn't mind."

He took a few seconds to answer. "I wish I could, but . . ."

"But you should be going home?"

He sighed. "Yeah."

"Clinton?"

He lifted his head and looked at me. "What?"

"Two more days."

He rolled his eyes. "I think we've broken your stupid rule, well and truly. Not sure it matters at this point."

"I don't regret what we did this afternoon in the kitchen." I looked him square in the eyes. "Not one bit."

"Me either. Though I do owe you one. You didn't . . ." He made an embarrassed face.

"Come in my pants?" I asked with a grin. "I'll take a raincheck on that."

His mouth fell open. "I couldn't help it. It was your fault anyway. If you hadn't stuck your hands down there."

"I do apologise." I tried for sincere but he could tell I wasn't sorry at all.

He stared at me for a long while. "Why do you call me Clinton?"

"Because it's your name."

He repositioned himself so his chin now rested on my chest, and he looked right at me. His dark eyes were like galaxies. He opened his mouth to speak but said nothing instead.

"Do you not like it?" I asked. "Would you prefer I call you CJ?"

"I always hated being called Clinton. The teachers at school would call me that and the other kids would laugh, so I've always shied away from it, and I've been CJ forever. It's what most people know me as. But you . . . When you call me that . . . well, I like it. You say it different. Like it's not a curse or something."

"It's not a curse," I whispered, touching the hair at his forehead. "You're not a curse."

He closed his eyes and leaned into my touch. "Well, maybe not to you."

"You're a good man. An honourable man. And I can't wait to get to know you better."

He laid his head down on my chest, looking at the TV. "You already know me better than anyone else."

I ran my fingers through his hair and let the silence between us linger, enjoying the moment.

"Can I ask you something?" he murmured.

"Of course."

"It's personal."

"That's okay."

"Do you . . . ? Are you . . . ? Um, ugh." He leaned up off me a little so he could scrub his hand over his face. "Sorry."

I put my hand to his cheek. "Clinton, just ask me."

His gaze shot to mine. "Do you top or bottom? Because in two days, if we're . . ." He blushed and groaned out a painful sound. "This is so embarrassing."

"Don't be embarrassed," I said gently. "I've been wondering the same about you, so I'm glad you asked. I usually top, but I'm all for bottoming with the right guy."

His smile was pure relief. "Okay, that's good."

"So you're a bottom?"

He mumbled something and looked away, so I put my fingers to his chin and made him look at me. He met my gaze but his eyebrows furrowed.

"CJ, talk to me, please."

"So now I'm CJ?"

I smiled. "Sorry, Clinton James Davis."

He rolled his eyes. "Noah . . ."

"My middle name is Robert."

"Noah Robert Huxley."

"You can tell me anything. I won't judge you. Or laugh at you. Or think any less of you." He still didn't want to repeat what he'd mumbled earlier, and he still hadn't answered my question. "You know, there's nothing wrong with being a bottom."

He pulled away and sat up, so I did too. My legs were still kinda folded up on the couch between us, and when I offered him my hand, he took it.

He stared at our joined fingers when he spoke. "Can you imagine my old man finding out I was gay? And not that I just liked guys, but in the whole sex thing, I was the one taking it?" He scoffed. "It's like the worst kind."

"That's not true."

"I know it's not, but it would be to him. That's exactly what he'd think. That I'd be the 'woman.'" CJ's eyes were glassy. "Fuck knows he hates women as much as gay men. Well, maybe not quite as much."

I covered our joined hands with my other one. "Don't ever be ashamed of who you are. You're perfect, just the way you are. And you know what? Fuck him. He's a piece of shit whose opinion doesn't matter."

But that was the problem. Because as much as CJ hated his father, his opinions, his words of hate and disgust still hurt like hell.

"Sorry," I continued. "I know he's your dad, but he hurts you, physically, emotionally, psychologically. And I can't respect that. I won't."

CJ tried to smile but couldn't quite make it work. "It's okay. I get it. I wish he were gone. I wish he was back inside, and I wish he'd never got out. I thought when he first got out that he wouldn't be out for long, but I'm not sure this time. Normally he'd be at the pubs and bars making an arse of himself. But now he don't leave the house like he used to, so chances of him gettin' into trouble are slim. He just stays at home and makes it miserable for me and Pops."

I threaded our fingers and leaned in so I could kiss his shoulder. "He doesn't ever have to know about us or about you being gay. It wouldn't be worth it, and I can't trust him not to physically hurt you." No, it wasn't worth it at all.

He sighed. "He's already pissed with me from our last fight. He's gonna get me back. I know he will."

"Then don't go back there."

"I have to. It's my home. And Pops is there."

I sighed heavily and, this time rested my forehead on his shoulder. "I wish it was different for you. I hate that you deal with that every day."

His answer was a quiet but resounding, "Me too."

CJ HAD to work on Friday, and I spent the morning doing house calls and my afternoon was dedicated to paperwork. But this wasn't all bad because it was the day I signed off on CJ's case. His probation wasn't technically up until midnight Saturday, but given I couldn't write the report on Sunday, I figured I'd get it all finalised and leave it on my desk to sign off on first thing Monday morning.

He literally just had to get through one more day.

I waited for his text on Friday night, and the longer the night went on, the more worried I became. He'd said when I'd dropped him home last night that he'd text me when he went to bed. But had something happened? Did he have a fight with his father?

God, I hated his old man.

But when my phone beeped at half past ten, I almost dropped it. But then I could have hugged my phone when his usual message showed onscreen.

Hi

Relief and a sense of peace settled in my chest and I was helpless to stop the smile. I knew how much effort it was for him to text with me, but he was willing, and no matter how long it took for him to read and reply, I would be patient and wait.

Hey. I was getting worried. Everything okay?

His reply took a few minutes. *Yes. Good.*

I'm glad. As long as you're okay.

Can call?

Yes.

My phone rang straight after and his voice was a whisper. "Sorry. Easier for me to speak."

"No worries. I like hearing your voice so I don't mind. You're getting better with the texting though."

He scoffed. "I'm so slow at it."

"No, you're fine. How was your dad?"

"All right. Bit like the calm before the storm. Things look okay, but you know the shit'll hit the fan soon."

"Just try and stay away from him."

"Bit hard in this house."

God I hated that he lived like that. Like living with a ticking time bomb.

"Are you looking forward to tomorrow?"

His tone brightened. "Yeah, for sure. You reckon I can get my licence tomorrow?"

"Yep. You pass the rider course, then I can take you straight to the RMS. Don't forget the ninety bucks to pay for it."

"Yeah, that's fine. I got paid today."

"Want me to pick you up from your work in the morning?" I asked.

"I can bus it. Save you the trip."

"I don't mind."

"I know you don't. Thanks anyway, but one last trip on the bus won't kill me."

"I'll pick you up after your course is finished then and go to the RMS."

"Yeah okay, sounds good. What time do you play soccer? Will you be done in time?"

"Yeah, I just might be a little sweaty and smelly but I'll be there."

"Thank you," he said reverently. "It means a lot."

His words warmed my heart. "I know. And I'm just glad to help."

"Noah?" It sounded like he was smiling. "Guess what?"

"What's that?"

"One more day."

I groaned out a laugh. "Believe me, I know and I cannot wait."

I SPENT Saturday morning getting all my chores done: laundry, groceries, cleaning. I had hopes for today, or tonight, rather. It was CJ's last day on probation, our last day as parole officer and parolee. I wasn't expecting all-out sex, but I was hoping for a lot of making out, possibly some nakedness, and I was really hoping he'd stay the night.

I wasn't joking when I said I wanted him to beg; I wanted him writhing in pleasure, so close to climax, desperate for release. I wanted him to know how good it could be, how perfect. I wanted to watch him unravel. I wanted him in my bed. I wanted to know his body, and I wanted him to know mine.

But not just physically. I wanted to know him. All of him.

If he said no, then that was that. I'd be gutted, devastated. But I'd understand. And I'd make good on my promise. I'd still help him.

Tonight was going to be interesting, that was for sure. I was a bit disappointed that he didn't want me to pick him up and drive him to his rider course, but he didn't like relying on other people. And he was too proud—a trait I didn't mind in him, given what he'd been through. I mean, the chip on his shoulder was pretty big, but the fact he'd survived growing up in that house with any kind of self-respect was a testament to the kind of guy he was. And he really was kinda great. Every moment I spent with him, I fell a little bit harder.

Yeah, I was in trouble. I'd pinned all my hopes on us moving forward tonight. I just had to get through soccer first.

I dropped my bag alongside everyone else's and sat on the damp ground to put my shin pads on. It was cold, winter was well and truly here, but at least it wasn't raining.

"Here he is," Gallan said, bending over and stretching his quads. "How's things with Bad-Boy-Motorbike guy?"

I tried not to smile as I got to my feet. "Good. I'm picking him up after the game. How's things with uh, the blond, wall-sex guy. I don't know his name."

Gallan laughed loudly. "Things with *Anthony*—" He gave me a pointed stare. "—are going well. He'll be here soon. He wants to watch me play."

"So should we line up some game-plays, you know, make you look good. Score a few goals?"

He grinned. "I don't need help looking good."

I snorted. "Don't need help with your ego either."

"Don't worry. Anthony knows how good I am," he added, his grin somehow widening.

"You're terrible."

"Don't tell me your Bad Boy's holding out on ya?"

"Not exactly. It's complicated."

He snorted. "It's been complicated for weeks. You need to *un*complicate things." Then he leaned in and whispered, "Take him home and fuck his brains out. Always uncomplicates things for me."

"Some things are worth the wait, Gallan."

He shook his head. "Holy shit. You really like this guy."

"Yeah, I do."

Just then, the pretty blond guy from HQ—Anthony—made his way over. He wore skinny jeans, a long coat and scarf, his platinum hair styled just so, and his eyes were trained on Gallan. When I looked up at Gallan, he was staring at Anthony with hearts in his eyes. He could joke all he liked about CJ and me but a blind man could see he was smitten. I snorted loudly. "Jesus, Gallan. You oughtta talk. You look like one of those cartoons where the hearts literally beat out of your eyes."

He shoved my shoulder and laughed, but he never denied it.

We took to the field and the game began. We played well, though Gallan was distracted, watching the sidelines more than the game. He missed one easy mark because he was too busy looking for Anthony, making me laugh. He shot me a glare. "The more you try to impress him," I told him. "The stupider you look."

After halftime, which he'd spent talking to Anthony instead of talking with the team, he ran back over to us. I tried not to smile. "Shut up," he said flatly. "I recall you spending halftime with Mr Complicated the other weekend."

Mr Complicated. I snorted. "I wasn't gonna say a word."

The second half was better than the first and we ended up winning the game. Even with Gallan distracted and my mind on this afternoon. We were playing better as a team and it spilt over to after the match.

"Come for a drink?" Tony asked.

"Oh, I can't today," I explained. "I have um, plans."

Gallan chuckled. "It's complicated."

I wiped my face down with my towel to hide my smile. "Yes, it is."

When the others were chatting, Gallan nudged my elbow. "Bring him next weekend. For drinks after the game. Anthony'll come too. We'll have dinner or something."

Next week . . . I had no idea where we'd be, relationship-wise, next week. I hoped though. I hoped we'd moved from unofficial boyfriends to the very official kind. "I'll ask. But it sounds good, thanks." I checked my watch. CJ's course would almost be over. "I better get going."

Gallan gave me a warm smile. "Have fun . . . uncomplicating things."

"I plan to."

I drove straight to the high school, parked the car, and waited. I knew he'd do well, and he said the guy who ran the course was happy with what he knew. The question would be whether CJ trusted in his own abilities.

Soon two of the guys I'd seen last week walked out, then another one. I got out of the car and leaned against my door just as someone else walked out, then one more. But there was no sign of CJ. Did he leave already? Did he get frustrated and bail out? I pulled out my phone but had no messages from him. God, did he even turn up? Had something happened at home?

A feeling of unease crept over me, and I started walking toward the gate just as CJ came walking out. He was with the instructor, both of them smiling. They stopped walking, shook hands, and CJ walked toward me.

Relief didn't quite cover what I felt. He grinned when he saw me, and I had to stop myself from throwing my arms around him or even just touching him when he was close enough.

"Hey," I said, aiming for cool. "Was worried something had happened."

He grinned. "Just busy passing my first test."

I smiled at him. "You passed?"

He nodded and held up a piece of paper I hadn't even noticed he was holding. "Sure did!"

"I really wanna hug you right now," I said.

He looked around, seeing if we were alone, most probably. "Tell ya what? If I pass my actual licence test, you can hug me." He gave a nervous shrug. "In public."

I grinned at him. "Deal." I nodded back toward my car. "Come on. Let's get it done."

Once we were driving, I asked him, "How did the test go?"

"Yeah, good. He read the questions to me, exactly as they were written, and I just told him the answers."

His smile crinkled his eyes and he genuinely looked proud. It warmed my heart.

"Did you want to go through the booklet again?" I asked. "Before you go in, I can help you."

"Do ya reckon we'll have time? What time does it close?"

"I think the last tests run at three o'clock because it's Saturday. It's a quarter past two now. How about we go book you in then spend a few minutes going through the booklet until it's time?"

He nodded, and his happy smile from before was gone. He wiped his hand down his thigh so I reached over and slid my hand over his. "Don't worry, CJ. You've got this. You can do this."

"And if I fail?"

"Then we rebook another appointment and we go home this afternoon and re-read the rule book. No big deal. Lots of people fail the first time." That wasn't probably the best thing to say right now. "But you won't. You'll nail it."

He mumbled something, but his confidence was now replaced with nerves and, subsequently, self-doubt.

"What did the instructor say today?" I asked. "Did he tell you what percentage you got?"

He turned the piece of paper over. "Don't think it says."

From what I could see, the certificate just said his name with the word 'competence.'

CJ shrugged. "He said I did well. Never said I got any wrong."

"So you got them all right," I urged. I pulled the car into the car park at the RMS, shut off the engine, and turned in my seat to face him. "You will do just fine. There'll be a reader for you, just like the instructor today. You don't have to get one hundred per cent; they allow a few incorrect answers, so if you get one wrong, don't worry and just keep going. You'll be fine."

"You don't know that."

"But I know you. And I know you know all there is to

know about riding motorbikes. How long have you been riding your bike around town and on the road?"

"Six years."

"And how many times have you got it wrong?"

"Got what wrong?"

"Road rules or safety, or been pulled over for negligent driving?"

He frowned at me. "Never."

"See? You know the answers, CJ. You'll be fine."

He still didn't look too convinced, but he followed me into the RMS. We filled in the application, booked in, and the lady gave us a ticket and told us we'd have to wait ten or so minutes. I took a road rules handbook and we sat away from any other people and I read questions to him, all of which he answered correctly. If he would just believe in himself. I closed the book. "She's going to read the questions to you exactly as they're written. Just like the mock tests we've done online, they'll be multiple choice answers, so you have to choose A, B, C, or D."

"I know what multiple choice is."

"Two answers will be obviously wrong, one close to right, but only one is the right answer. Just take your time. You'll be fine. And just remember, if it doesn't work out this time, you'll know what to expect next time."

"You practise this speech?"

"Kinda."

He rolled his eyes, but when the number before his was called, I could see the nerves and agitation.

"Clinton, look at me."

His proper name caught his attention and his gaze shot to mine.

"You've got this. Okay?"

His number was called, and as much as I wanted to go

with him, I knew I couldn't. A lady met him at the computers assigned to licencing, and so CJ wouldn't keep looking for me, I went outside.

I tried to sit and wait, then I tried pacing. I got a few weird looks from people leaving, but I couldn't help it. I was nervous on CJ's behalf. He knew the answers, but what if he panicked, or what if the lady was rude, or what if his mind just went blank?

How much time should it take? How long was too long? How long had it been already? Should I go back in? Would that be too clingy?

After what felt like an eternity, the automatic doors opened and I turned. CJ stood there, looking all kinds of dejected.

Oh no.

I went to him and put my hand on his arm. "Clinton, it's okay. We'll come back next weekend."

"Why?" he asked. Then a slow-spreading grin crossed his face, and he produced a small plastic rider's learner licence and some L-plates. "When I passed already."

"You passed?"

He laughed and nodded, and I kept true to my end of the deal. He said if he passed, I could hug him right there in front of everyone. So that's exactly what I did.

CHAPTER EIGHTEEN

CJ

THE WOMAN who read for my test was nice enough. I told her I could read some, just not full pages of words and not tests that had time limits on answering questions. I even swallowed my pride and showed her how I could read the beginning of the test.

"You . . . have . . . forty . . . s-s-seconds . . . for . . . each?" She nodded. "Each . . . question." It was embarrassing, but I could read. I just wasn't great at it. Then she showed me a bunch of road sign images and asked me to identify them, even the ones with writing on them, but they were so much easier. "Stop. Give way. Bus stop. No parking. Transit lane. That one means Clearway. One-hour parking. Police cars only."

She smiled after that and we started the actual test. I was nervous as hell and had to ask her to repeat the questions a couple of times but got through the computer part of the test pretty quick. Then she did the eye test, where I had to say each letter out loud on whichever line she asked for, and well, she didn't say I got any wrong, she just smiled and told me to take a seat.

A minute or two later, she called me over and said, "Congratulations."

I couldn't believe it! I'd done it! A month ago, I would have said it was impossible. Hell, a month ago, it *was* impossible. But Noah . . . well, Noah helped me more than I could ever explain.

Sure, he helped with the mock tests and organising it all for me and helping me read through the booklet, but he also believed in me.

Another thing for my first list.

I had my photo taken, and two minutes later, I walked out of the RMS as a legitimate licenced motorbike rider. Well, a learner rider, and I'd have to use those lame-arse L-plates, but I didn't even care.

I'd achieved something. And man, it felt good.

When Noah saw me, he was watching, waiting for me to say if I'd passed or failed, so I had to play with him a bit. I frowned and acted all sad, and his face fell, but his first reaction was to tell me it was okay, we'd just try again next weekend. He didn't mock me, he didn't tell me I was stupid, he didn't laugh.

I could get used to that.

I pulled out my licence and his whole face changed, like he beamed pride for me or something. Then he hugged me. Right in front of the RMS, in front of whoever was there, he just threw his arms around me and almost lifted me off my feet.

"I'm so proud of you," he whispered in my ear.

And if I had any reservations about him touching me in public, I didn't after that. He was proud of me. Me, CJ Davis.

"Thank you. I couldn't have done this without you. I wouldn't have even known how."

He pulled away but kept his hands on my shoulders. "You did it. Not me."

I took out my wallet and put my new licence in the card slot next to my ID card and my new bank card. God, he had no idea what he'd done for me. Before Noah, I was a nobody. A no-hoper with no paper proof I was even alive, except for the bills I had to pay. But now I had things, material proof with my name and photo, and responsible adult things that most people probably didn't think twice about, but they were important to me.

"We should celebrate," I said.

"What do you wanna do?" he asked brightly, starting to walk to his car. "Order food? Go out for dinner? To the movies? Shopping? How do you wanna celebrate?"

I grinned at him. "How about we go back to your place and decide there?"

He stopped walking. "Oh. That kind of celebrating?"

Now I laughed. "Well, no, I wasn't thinking of that kind of celebrating. I was thinking you might wanna have a shower and get out of your stinky soccer clothes."

He smelt his armpit, then narrowed his eyes at me. "Shut up. I'll have you know, we won our match today."

"Then we really do need to celebrate."

"Yes. Yes, we do."

AS SOON AS we'd walked into Noah's kitchen, he asked to see my licence. I handed it over and he smiled, nodding as he looked at it. "Great photo."

"No it's not. It's crap."

He took his licence from his wallet and showed it to me. "*This* is a crap photo."

I took it and inspected it, trying not to smile, then trying not to laugh. "Jesus, did you pay the homeless man to stand in for you?"

He busted up laughing and snatched his licence back. "Well, it's not that bad. But yours is a good photo."

I took my licence back and looked over it again. "Still can't believe it's real. That I have a licence!"

Noah was smiling so hard his eyes were crinkled at the sides. "You deserve good things, CJ."

I shrugged, trying to play it cool. "What happened to Clinton?"

He stepped right in close and pulled my chin between his finger and thumb. "Clinton."

Jesus. Just hearing him say my name like that made my heart feel too big for my chest. Then he licked his bottom lip and I couldn't help myself. I kissed him, hard. I could never get enough of him, and when he opened his mouth and slid his tongue against mine, it almost buckled my knees.

If he was fire, I was gasoline. As soon as we touched, we became something else. I couldn't explain it—I didn't know the words—but there were sparks, heat, fire; consuming, raging fire. I wanted him like I'd never wanted anyone, or anything, ever.

And from the way he held me and kissed me back, I was pretty sure he felt exactly the same. He pushed away from me and gasped for air. "God, CJ." He was breathless, his chest heaving, his lips red and swollen.

"It's not just me, is it?" I asked, putting my hand to my heart. "You feel it too."

He barked out a strained laugh. "Oh yeah." Then he thought about what I'd said. "You feel the same?"

The same . . . Was he asking me if I felt the passion

between us? Or if I felt the same things that I hoped to God he felt about me? I guessed it didn't matter. My answer was one and the same.

"Um, yeah."

He grinned then. "I'm glad. I really like you, Clinton. Maybe it's more than that, I don't know. But I want to see where this thing between us can go."

"I really like you too." Then I added what he did. "Or maybe it's more than that, I don't know."

His smile went all shy-like and I'm sure I blushed a dozen shades of red, but he pulled me in for another hug. It wasn't a passionate embrace, it was a bone-deep comfort thing. Well, it was for me, anyway. He stepped away and cleared his throat, then readjusted himself. "These damn soccer shorts. I'm going to go grab that shower." He took another step backwards. I had to will myself not to look at his shorts. "Make yourself at home."

"Is that your way of asking me to make you a toasted cheese sandwich?"

He laughed from the hallway. "I wouldn't say no."

I stood in his kitchen smiling. What a crazy-wonderful day. I couldn't remember being this happy. I doubted I ever had been. First, I passed my rider course, then I got my rider licence, then got to make out with a super-hot, nicest-ever guy who, for reasons I'll never understand, just told me he liked me.

Maybe it's more than that.

That's what he'd said. Could it be more than that? Did I, CJ Davis, get a shot at love? A month ago, I'd have laughed at the idea. Now, after Noah, I was hoping like all hell that's what this was.

After Noah.

Maybe my list of firsts should be really be a Before Noah/After Noah list. It was one and the same thing to me.

Was I falling in love with him?

I didn't need to answer that. I knew the answer already. So I went about making him a toasted cheese sandwich instead.

By the time Noah was showered and changed and we'd eaten our sandwiches, we found ourselves on his couch not really watching the footy. "What's your idea of a celebration night?" he asked. "Is there something you've always wanted to do but thought it was too out of reach?"

"Well," I shrugged. "You'll probably laugh."

"No I won't." His eyes bored into mine, and he was so sincere I couldn't doubt him.

"Well, this."

He looked around us. "What about this?"

"This. Like I told you before, bein' here with you like this is something I never thought I'd ever have. People like me don't get happy ever afters, Noah. So this, layin' about on the sofa, wearing sweatpants in front of the heater, watching crap on TV, holding hands and making out, it's like perfection for me."

He took a second to answer, blinked a few times. "Oh."

"I get that it's not very exciting and you'll probably get bored of it. If you want to do something adventurous like hiking or even just going out for dinner, I guess we could. I'm up for that too. But you asked what I thought was perfect or something I never thought I'd have—"

"Clinton," he murmured, stopping my rant. He slid closer, and there was something in his eyes that I couldn't place. "This is kinda perfect for me too. I wasn't joking when I told you the other weekend that I'm a homebody. I like just being at home, hanging out. And I especially like doing it with you." He smirked. "But you're wrong about one thing."

"What's that?"

"You said that sitting here watching crap on TV, holding hands, and making out is your favourite thing."

"So?"

"We're not holding hands. Or making out."

He put his hand, palm facing upwards, on my knee. I slid my hand over his and he was quick to thread our fingers.

"And the making out part?" he asked. He was being playful but there was a serious look to his eyes.

So I leaned back and pulled him down so he was on top of me. It wasn't graceful, but from his smile and heated gaze, he didn't seem to mind. I manoeuvred my legs and wriggled down a bit so I was more comfortable, then he kissed me, slow and deep. The fire was there, but it burned differently this time. It wasn't a raging bushfire, consuming and sure to burn itself out. No, this was a smouldering, long burn. Still intense, still everything I never dreamed possible. Tender and loving, with slow mouths, slow hands, and gentle rocking hips.

He was everything I never knew I needed. He was everything I wanted, longed for, dreamed of, and never thought I could have.

Maybe it's something more than that.

There was no maybe about it. There was no doubt in my mind.

I was in love with him.

That thing I'd seen in movies that made smart people do stupid things, that kind of love. The kind where they risk everything they've ever known, the kind that changes lives, that changes souls.

He kissed down my neck and I turned my head to give him more room. I pulled on the neck of his T-shirt so I could kiss his shoulder, and he hummed in the most delicious way. He liked that. I wanted to learn more.

"I want to know everything about you," I whispered. "Your body. I want to know every part I have to kiss to make you make that sound."

I felt his lips at my neck turn into a smile. "And you. What drives you crazy?"

I stilled. "I don't know. No one's ever tried. No one's ever wanted to know before."

He pulled back and looked down at me, his lips red and swollen, his pupils blown out. "Then I promise you, Clinton, I will find every single one. I will map out every inch of your body."

Holy shit.

His words just about set my blood on fire.

He smiled. "Okay, so it's safe for me to assume you like a little bit of dirty talk?"

Before I could answer, a phone rang, and it took a second for me to realise it was my phone.

Oh no.

Noah got up off me and I scrambled to sit up, reaching for my phone on the coffee table. "You and Pops are the only ones who have my number." *And Pops had said he'd only ever call if it was an emergency.* I heard his breathing first. A sound I'd know anywhere. "Hello?"

"Pops?"

"Yeah, CJ. Sorry." He sounded like he was trying to whisper, but he also sounded worse than normal.

"What's wrong?"

"It's your dad. He's gone off the rails and he was going through your room, looking for money. He reckons you're holding out on him. He's gone out to the shed looking for it, so I thought I best call you. You'd better come home. I tried to stop him . . ."

"I'm on my way."

I didn't even have to ask. Noah was already up, grabbing his wallet and keys. "I'll drive you. What happened? Is Pops okay?"

"I dunno. He sounded worse but said my old man's in a mood and he's going through everything looking for my money."

"Your money?"

I put my jacket on. "The money hidden in my room—it's just a hundred and eighty bucks but I keep it in case Pops needs extra pills—but I didn't think he knew about it. Maybe he's guessing, I dunno. He's just pissed off because I'm not there. Probably out of smokes and beer and that'll be my fault."

Noah fumed, his jaw clenched and he shook his head. "You know what? Fuck him."

I snorted and walked to the back door. "Oh yeah. I'm so fucking done with his shit."

I HADN'T REALISED it'd gotten so late. It was getting dark, the clouds were low and looked set in, the wind had turned cold. I'd bet any money Dad had let the fire go out and God only knows what damage he'd done to the shed so far.

Noah and I didn't say much on the drive to Ten Mile Creek. I guess there wasn't much to say. "Not how I wanted to celebrate tonight, sorry."

"It's fine," he said quickly. "Don't apologise because

of him."

God, I hated my old man. "I wish he'd go back to jail."

Noah reached over and squeezed my hand. "I know."

When we got to Davis Road, he turned down instead of stopping. "You can just drop me here," I said.

"I'll come in with you."

"No," I said quickly. "It'll just make everything worse."

He slowed to a stop, maybe a hundred metres from my house but out of sight, thanks to the long grass and overgrown trees. "CJ, you don't have to go in there alone. I can help you."

"You already help me, more than you know," I whispered.

His face fell but he squeezed my hand. "You promise you'll call me if you need anything. I can be back here in ten minutes."

I nodded and went to get out of the car.

"Clinton," he said, stopping me. He waited for me to look at him. "Be careful."

"Always am."

I got out of the car and jogged down the rest of the dirt road to my house. By the time I came to the fence, Noah had turned around and was heading away, thankfully. As much as I would've liked him by my side, there was no need for him to go through this.

From the outside, the house looked quiet, peaceful. But the storm clouds that rolled above it were a pretty good indication of what was going on inside. I could hear my old man banging and cursing at the shed at the side of the house, so I went in the front door to check on Pops first.

"Oh CJ," he said, wheezing. "Sorry I called you, son. But I didn't want your dad to take your bike. Not after how hard you worked for it."

"How are you?" I asked, walking over to his recliner. The fire was out, like I knew it would be. "Let me get this fire going first, huh?"

He nodded and frowned, worry and apology ingrained in every line on his face.

I threw some kindling on the almost-out embers, added some old newspaper, and flipped the lid on my zippo to restart the fire. The orange flames took hold and I closed the door, and knowing I had to go out and face my father, I stood up.

Only I didn't go looking for him. He came looking for me. The front door banged loud enough to sound like a gun, and he stomped into the living room. If the clouds outside looked like a storm, it had nothing on him. His eyes were dark, his face a tempest: rage and fury, uncontained.

I'd seen that look before.

I knew what was coming.

I was even happier now that Noah wasn't here.

Except all the times before, I'd borne the brunt of his anger. Well, not anymore and never again.

"Where the fuck've you been?" he spat, glowering and shaking with rage. He'd also been drinking. I could smell bourbon from across the room.

"I told you I'd be out all day. What's your problem?"

"My problem?" His eyes sparked with disbelief that I'd speak to him like that. "My problem is you. I'm stuck here all fuckin' day, no money, no smokes, and you just fuck off for the day."

"I'm an adult. If I need to go to town for the day, I don't need no one's permission," I said, trying to keep my tone neutral. His knuckles were white, his fists clenched. "If you need cigarettes or more alcohol, you could try asking."

He took a step closer, his jaw ticked, and he spoke

through his teeth. "Or you could try showin' me some respect, boy."

I glared right back at him. "You could try earning it."

He rushed at me, drunkenly, but still, there wasn't much room. He came in swinging his fist but I shouldered him and shoved him off me into the wall. By the time he righted himself, I was ready. I didn't want to hit him, but I would.

"Please don't fight," Pops said weakly from the kitchen door.

Dad never took his eyes off me. "Shut up, old man." He charged at me again, this time tackling me into the recliner, head-butting me on the way down. Well, it was more of a clash of heads, but he got me on my left temple.

I saw stars.

He seemed unaffected; alcohol gave him an injury buffer. He wouldn't feel any pain tonight. He reared back and came back at me with his full strength behind his fist, connecting with my eye.

More stars.

There was yelling and more shuffling and his weight was gone while the room around me spun to a slow stop. I got to my feet and turned around. That's when I saw him.

Dad had Pops pinned against the wall.

And my never-hit, never-resort-to-violence, don't-be-like-him policy dissolved. I saw red. I tasted blood, and I wanted to kill him.

No one hurt Pops.

I ran to him, and with strength I didn't know I had, I pulled Dad around and he let go of Pops. He was off balance for a moment and I took my chance; I closed my fist, and with all the rage I could summon, I hit him.

He sprawled backward and fell through the front screen

door, landing on his arse half out the threshold. I stood over him, my fists shaking. "Stay the fuck down, arsehole. Touch him again, and I will knock you on your arse every time."

He gripped the doorframe and tried to get up, stumbling and struggling. I turned to Pops. "Are you okay?"

He nodded, but he looked scared and pale. He was breathing hard, too hard for my liking. "I'm fine."

My father somehow managed to get to his feet, fuelled by rage alone, and half-staggered, half-fell forward, aiming his clumsy weight at me. But this time he gripped my jacket in one hand, my face in his other, and we fell. I fell heavy on my shoulder, but my father's fingers tightened on my face, in my eye and scratching down my cheek.

I kneed him as hard as I could, and his breath left him in a harsh woof. So I kneed him again, the last time I connected with his balls and it was all over.

He groaned and recoiled, a dead weight, and I shoved him off me. I clambered to my feet and looked down at him writhing, holding his junk, groaning on the floor. My adrenaline was pumping, fuelled by my anger at the piece of shit on the ground. I wanted to kick him again.

I *wanted* to.

For the time he broke my arm, for when he put a cigarette out on my just-a-kid body. For every time he hit me, yelled at me, laughed at me. Stole from me, told me I was a worthless son of a whore, refused to feed me. For every time he failed me.

Pops stood beside me and put his hand on my arm. He looked down at my father, and with a look of total disgust— or maybe for every reason I just named—Pops spat at him. His frail voice shook with anger but he spoke loud and clear. "You never deserved him."

My father groaned. "Get the fuck out of my house." He

rolled over and got to all fours, and bellowed, "I said, get the fuck out of my house!"

I had two choices: I could pick this piece of shit up by the scruff of his shirt, throw him outside and lock the door behind him, and he'd no doubt break the door down or smash windows to get back inside. Or Pops and I could leave. We didn't exactly have anywhere to go, but we could walk out right now because we deserved better.

I turned to Pops. "Grab your things. We're leaving."

My father slowly got to his feet, standing to his full height, though still in obvious pain. Part of me smiled in satisfaction. He glowered at me, pure disgust on his face. "You're not taking a damn thing. Get out now."

"He will grab his medication," I said, gritting my teeth. I didn't care about anything of my own, but Pops needed his pills. I took a step toward my old man, fists clenched and ready. Pops disappeared into the hall while my father and I stared each other down. I despised this man. Loathed everything about him.

Then Pops was behind me with a black rucksack in his hand. He looked between us, scared of the hatred that crackled in the air. "Come on, CJ. Let's go."

I walked to the front door and stopped, turning to take in one last look. The room was wrecked; the recliner was on its side, cushions on the floor. There was a dent in the wall, the TV was pushed back, and there was my father, standing in the middle of it.

I wondered what to say. What could I possibly say to mark this night or for any of the shit he'd given me over the last twenty-four years? I could tell him he was a failure, a good-for-nothing, piece-of-shit father. I could tell him I hated him. But I was done. I was done expending energy on him. In the end, he simply wasn't worth it.

So without a word, I followed Pops out the front door, and together we walked away.

CHAPTER NINETEEN

I WOKE to the sound of banging, and it took me a minute to realise it was someone knocking on my laundry door. At first it scared the shit outta me, but then there was only one person who would come to back door instead of the front. My first thought went to CJ, but I wasn't awake enough to wonder why he was banging on my door at one o'clock in the morning.

"Hang on, I'm coming," I called out, my voice croaking with sleep.

I unlocked the deadbolt and pulled the door open, just a crack. I'd expected as much, but it was still a shock to see him. CJ and a smaller figure, hunched over, covered in a coat, standing under the stoop trying to get out of the rain.

Then I heard the rattled breathing.

Pops.

"Jesus Christ. Quick, come in." I opened the door wide and ushered them both inside. I hit the light switch and my heart sank. They were both dripping wet. Pops had CJ's jacket on, CJ was shivering, and his shirt was soaked and clinging to his body. His eye was red and swollen; he had what looked like red, angry finger-gouge marks down one side of his face, and Pops . . . he had a red mark across one cheekbone.

"S-s-sorry," CJ said, shivering. "Didn't know where else to go."

"Come in by the heater," I said, pulling CJ by the arm. I cranked the heater up full bore, and taking a closer look at Pops, I knew it wouldn't be enough. "Pops, how about you have a hot shower. It'll warm you up good and proper, and I'll find you some dry clothes."

Still shivering and every breath raspy, he nodded. "Th-thanks."

I grabbed a clean towel from the linen cupboard and an old pair of tracksuit pants and a sweater. "Here," I said, handing them to him. "They'll be miles too big, but at least they're warm and dry."

He gave me a nod. His wheezing was bad, but he looked so damn sad, it almost broke my heart. "Thanks, son."

I left him to it and found CJ trying to get warm by the heater. I pulled him into my room. "Take your clothes off," I said, pulling out a pair of jogger pants and a long-sleeve shirt. "Put these on, and tell me what happened."

While he stripped, I went and grabbed another towel. He was pulling up the sweatpants when I walked back in. He looked at me and sagged. "Thank you," he murmured quietly. "I didn't know where else to go."

I wiped the towel over his chest, gently patted his face, and dried his hair. "Why didn't you call?"

"Must've lost my phone in the fight, sorry."

"It's okay. What happened?"

"Dad went off, like really bad. And maybe I should have backed down, but I stood up to him. I'm so sick of his shit."

I scanned his face: the shiner, the red lines from the

corner of his eye down his cheek. "He hit you." It wasn't a question.

He sighed and looked down between us. "I hit him back tonight. I ain't ever hit anyone before, and I never wanted to be like him, but if I hadn't defended myself, I dunno what he would've done."

I put my fingers to his chin and lifted his face so he could see my eyes. "You're nothing like him. And for what it's worth, I'm glad you did. You defended yourself."

"He hit me so hard the room spun, and when I could see straight, he had Pops pinned to the wall." CJ's eyes welled with tears. "I hate him so much."

"I know you do. And it's justified, CJ. Just because you're related to someone doesn't mean you have to like them."

"He told us to leave. Pops spat at him." He snorted through his tears. "Told my old man he never deserved me."

"Pops is a smart man."

"He's not breathing too well. We had to walk to the workshop. I'd left my bike at Mr Barese's when I'd caught the bus to town yesterday. Then I rode us to town. And it was raining and freezing cold. I could feel him shaking behind me, but we couldn't stay there. I didn't want to wake up Mr Barese, and that's the first place Dad'll look for me. At least here, like you said, he won't know where we are."

"I'm glad you did."

We heard the water shut off, and I knew it wouldn't be long until Pops came out. "I'll go put the kettle on, and if his breathing isn't any better, we'll take him to hospital, okay?"

"He won't go."

"He will if I tell him." I put my hand to his injured cheek and kissed him softly. "I'm sorry you had a horrible night, but I'm glad you're here."

He smiled sadly, and I went into the kitchen. I filled the kettle and got cups ready for tea. "You weren't wrong when you said they'd be too big for me," Pops said behind me. He pulled at the waistband of the sweatpants, smiling. "But thanks. Where's CJ?"

CJ walked in behind him and put his hand on his shoulder. "I'm here, Pops."

The first thing I noticed about Pops was that he was breathing better. Maybe the steam helped with that or maybe now because he was warmer; I didn't know.

"You feeling okay?" I asked him.

He nodded and I noticed the red hand mark on his neck. Jesus Christ. I had to swallow down my anger. "Want to go to the hospital and get checked over?"

"Nah. Cuppa tea'll fix me right up." He still wheezed but he seemed much brighter.

"I'll make it," CJ said, taking over. "You hungry, Pops? Want me to fix you a sandwich or something?"

Pops looked straight at me, as if CJ offering him food in my house was out of line. "It's fine," I said. "Anything you want."

"Maybe some toast," Pops said.

CJ took the bread from the breadbox and added two slices to the toaster, then he went to the fridge and collected the butter. It was then I realised what Pops found so strange; CJ knew his way around my kitchen.

"Come and sit in by the heater," I suggested. "I'll grab you a blanket."

Pops gave me a tired smile. "Thanks, son. You've been real generous."

"It's no trouble."

I pulled the doona off the spare bed and wrapped it around Pops' shoulders, and before he could ask any questions about me and CJ I wasn't ready to answer, CJ came in with a plate of toast and a cup of tea and sat down next to Pops on the sofa.

"I'll grab ours," I said, darting into the kitchen. I came back out with the two other cups of tea and handed one to CJ, and Pops was already eating his toast. "How about you, CJ? Hungry?"

He shook his head. "No, thanks." He was clearly worried but seemed happier now that Pops was eating. "Bit of a cold ride to town, huh?"

Pops nodded. "Been a while since I've been on a motorbike." He sipped his tea and sighed with the first taste of the warm drink. "This is good tea. CJ, my bag . . ." He pointed to the black bag near the door.

CJ grabbed it. "Here you go."

Pops opened it, pulled out an old Weet-Bix box, and handed it to CJ. "I saved it. When your dad had ransacked your room he didn't find it, so when he went out to look in the shed, I took it and hid it in my room."

CJ smiled sadly. "Thanks, Pops." He opened the box and took out a small wad of money. He looked at me. "My life savings. He'd have thought he struck gold if he found it."

Pops sipped his tea. "And he'd drink every cent in one night."

CJ nodded in agreement and put the money back in the box. "But then maybe he would've left you alone."

Pops frowned. "No, CJ. We both know that ain't true." Noah conceded a nod and Pops took out some pills and washed one down with his tea.

The elephant in the room was huge, almost overbearing. I had to say something. "You're both welcome to stay here as long as you need."

CJ's eyes met mine and I stared right back at him, hoping he'd see my sincerity. "Um, thanks."

"That's mighty nice of you to offer," Pops added.

"But we talked on the walk to the workshop," CJ said. "We'll just give my dad a few days to calm down." He shrugged. "I don't work till Tuesday, so if it's okay with you that we maybe stay here until then . . ."

I gave him a smile. "Of course."

"He'll be so desperate for one of us to get him more booze and smokes by then, he'll be happy to see us."

I wanted to argue that they shouldn't ever go back, but it wasn't my place. They'd been through enough for one night.

Pops finished his toast and drained his tea. He was clearly exhausted. "Pops, you can have the spare room," I said. "Get some sleep, I'll make us a big breakfast when you wake up, and we'll deal with tomorrow in the morning."

He glanced at CJ before nodding. "Yeah," he said with a groan as he got to his feet. "Better put this weary bag o' bones to bed. Night, CJ."

"Goodnight, Pops." He swallowed hard. "And thanks for sticking up for me back at the house."

Pops put his hand on CJ's shoulder and gave it a squeeze as he walked past. I showed him to the spare room and put the doona back on the bed. "He's a good boy," Pops said quietly.

"He is."

"Thank you for having us."

"Anytime."

I closed the door and found CJ on the sofa with his head in his hands. I sat side-on and pulled him into my arms, my fingers in his hair and rubbing his back. I kissed the side of his head. "My God, Clinton," I whispered. "Tell me what to do."

"Just this." He sounded so tired, so defeated. "Just this, right here."

I squeezed him and kissed his head again. My heart ached for him. I wanted to fix everything that was broken. I wanted to take away his pain. I ran my hand over his back and up to his neck, cupping his face and bringing his lips to mine. I wanted him to feel connected, to feel loved. I wanted him to know everything was going to be okay.

The kiss was soft and sweet to begin with, but he opened his mouth, deepening it, and his grip on me became desperate. He dug his fingers into my skin, frantic and clinging for human touch. Then he began to pull at my shirt, trying to take it off.

I pulled my mouth from his and the look of rejection flashed in his eyes. I squeezed his hand. "I think we should go to my bedroom."

"Oh." He exhaled in a rush. "Good idea."

Still holding his hand, I led us to my room and closed the door behind him. "There's no pressure here," I whispered. "You've had an emotional day. We don't have to do anything if you don't want."

He put one hand around my neck and pulled me in for a harsh kiss. Passion bloomed, desire sparked somewhere inside him, and he kissed me, held me, gripped me harder than I'd ever known.

I guess that answered that.

He wanted this.

I pulled the hem of his shirt and lifted it over his head, quickly running my hands over his chest. Maybe it was the silver lighting of the night, but I noticed a small round scar on his bicep and on the inside of his forearm. It looked like a cigarette burn, and my heart twinged with an ache for everything he'd been through.

I knew then that I would show him what it means to love.

I kissed the scars, then kissed up his neck to his jaw, and his ear. "I want to take my time with you. Make this so good for you," I whispered before sucking his earlobe between my lips. His fingers dug into my hips and he frantically tried to rip off my shirt. "Slow down," I murmured. "I'm not going anywhere, Clinton."

His gaze struck mine, vulnerable, open, and raw.

"I'm not going anywhere," I repeated. "There's no rush."

"I've never . . ."

I paused. "Never what?"

He shook his head. "No, I mean, I've had sex. I'm not a virgin." He frowned. "I've just only ever done things in the backroom at HQ or in a park somewhere. Always fast and not much else, if you know what I mean. It was always for their pleasure."

Oh, would my heart ever not hurt to hear his stories?

I put my hand to his face and searched his eyes. "I will take all the time you need. I will make this good for you. I want to adore every inch of your body."

His nostrils flared and he kissed me again, though this time I could feel him trying to rein in his desire. I slid my fingers under the waistband of his pants and slid them down over his arse, and he stepped out of them.

"Lie down on your back for me," I murmured.

He quickly complied and the sight of him naked on my bed took my breath away. I stripped out of my pyjamas and took the lube and condoms he'd selected at the supermarket out of the top drawer of my bedside table. I threw them on the bed next to him. "Best purchase, ever."

He chuckled nervously. I could see his eyes scanning

my body, lingering on my cock. I was already hard and so I gave myself a stroke for him. "Like what you see?"

He nodded. "God, yes."

"You're gorgeous, Clinton," I said, kneeling on the bed. I crawled up his legs, between them, kissing as I went. His knees, his thigh, his hipbone. His cock lay up to his navel almost and I nuzzled him, breathing him in, then licked him from base to tip.

He gripped the bedcover. "Shit."

I took him in my hand and licked his cockhead, feeling him pulse and jerk in response. He was so sensitive and I had to wonder if this could be added to his list of firsts. I fondled his balls and skimmed his perineum, making his whole body twitch. God, this wasn't going to take either of us very long.

I grabbed the lube and slicked my fingers, rubbing over his hole. He sucked back a breath, then bit back a groan. I slid a fingertip inside him, in and out, a little further with each pass. "Fuck, you're beautiful," I whispered.

"Noah," he said, his voice clipped and tight. He looked up at me. "What are you . . . what . . . ?"

"I'm getting you ready, stretching you so you're ready for me. I want my cock inside you and I need it to be good for you."

His head fell back on the bed and he whined, but he spread his legs and lifted his arse a little. Jesus.

I added another finger, marvelling at the beauty of his body accepting mine. He was freaking loving this and I had barely even got started. I curled my fingers, pushing in harder and searching, searching . . .

"Holy shit!"

I pulled back a little, not wanting to overwhelm him. I

knew how intense a prostate orgasm could be. "You like that?"

"Fuck." He panted. "Do it again."

I chuckled and did as he asked. He bent his legs, feet flat on the bed, and raised his hips, giving me better access. Fuck, he wasn't kidding when he said he liked to bottom. I found his prostate again and he gasped, so I rubbed, back and forth. "Fuck, Noah. Stop."

I stopped, slowly pulling my fingers out. He was ready and I was far too turned on. "Can you open a condom for me?" I asked. With my slippery fingers, it would take too long.

He fumbled and fiddled, but eventually got one open. "Want me to . . . ?"

"No. If you touch my cock right now, it'll be all over."

He chuckled. "Good to know I'm not the only one."

I rolled the condom on, giving myself a squeeze to try and quell the pleasure, and knelt between his thighs. I lifted his legs up toward his chest and he gripped the backs of his knees, keeping himself spread. I gripped the base of my cock at his hole and leaned over him so I could kiss him as I entered him.

He gasped, quick short breaths, and I pushed in as slow as I was able. He was tight and hot, and his swollen eye tightened when I was only halfway in. "Are you okay?"

He nodded. "Please, Noah. Please."

I kissed him with smiling lips. "Told you you'd beg me."

He groaned and arched his back, his neck corded as I pushed all the way in. He let go of his legs and gripped my shoulders, my back, digging blunt fingers into my skin. "Too slow," he grunted.

I took his wrists and pinned them to the mattress near his head. His eyes went wide and his mouth opened as I thrust up into him. I kissed him, his mouth, his banged-up eye, his jaw, rocking slowly, tenderly. There was no mistaking this. There was no room for doubt. It was in every squeeze of our joined hands, in every kiss, in every moan.

We were making love.

Then he jerked underneath me and cried out into my mouth. "Fuck. I'm gonna come."

Letting go of his hands, I leaned back and slid my fingers around his cock. I pumped him and he swelled and throbbed, his body pulsed around me, and with a strangled cry, he came.

I thrust into him, over and over, prolonging his orgasm as I succumbed to my own. Every nerve in my body caught alight, crashing pleasure and ecstasy through my veins, and I came, filling the condom deep inside him.

We rocked back and forth, kissing, always touching, until his body had had enough. He writhed and chuckled. "Bit sensitive," he mumbled.

I slowly slid out of him and took care of the condom, then quickly pulled him into my arms, not caring about the mess between us. "You are amazing, Clinton." I kissed the side of his head. "That was amazing."

He hummed. "Yeah."

"Was it too slow for you?"

He laughed. "Are we really gonna talk about it?"

"Uh, yeah. That's what boyfriends do. Talk about things."

"I thought we were unofficial boyfriends."

"Well, it's after midnight. You're no longer on proba-tion. So, if you want, we can move to official boyfriends."

He squeezed me. "Official sounds good."

"Is your eye okay? Not too sore?"

"It's fine. All of me is fine right now."

"So, was it too slow?"

He chuckled again. "Ah, no. Kinda perfect, actually."

"I can go slower."

"I think slower could border on torture."

I kissed the side of his head with smiling lips. "You must be exhausted. Let me grab a towel to get you cleaned up."

I took care of him, with slow and soft hands, and we were soon back in bed in each other's arms. "I could get used to this," I murmured.

He mumbled sleepily, "Me too."

I WOKE when CJ sat up in bed. I'd slept alone for so long, the movement startled me. "What's wrong?"

"Nothing," he whispered. "Pops will be up soon."

Oh, right.

I sat up as well. "I promised him a cooked breakfast."

CJ pulled on the jogger pants left on the floor from last night, and without a word, he walked out of my room. His reaction confused me. Was he pushing me away, or was he just not a morning person. Was he sore? Did he not like what we'd done last night? Was he embarrassed?

I heard the toilet flush and got out of bed. I pulled on my sleep pants and went to the bathroom, took a piss, washed my hands and my face, and found CJ in the kitchen alone. He was at the sink filling the kettle with water.

"Everything okay?"

"Sure." He flicked the kettle on but didn't turn around.

"Did I do something wrong last night?" I asked quietly.

He spun then to look at me, and I saw his face. His black eye was almost swollen shut, puffy and purple, his cheekbone was pink, the scratch marks down the other side of his face were still there.

"Oh, God." I went to him and put my hands to his face. How could I have forgotten? In bed last night it didn't seem so bad, but it looked sore as hell in the morning light.

He pulled his head back a little, not wanting me to touch his injuries. "I'm okay."

"No, you're not. And it's okay to admit it. Let me get you something for that." I took a bag of frozen peas from the freezer and gently applied it to the corner of his eye. "I should've thought to do this last night, sorry."

"'S okay. I've had worse."

I frowned at him. "I'm sorry for that too. I wish it weren't so."

He leaned against the kitchen counter and closed his eyes. I guessed the weight of what happened last night with his father had finally settled in.

"If you want to go home and see him today, I'll go with you," I offered quietly.

He shook his head and put the bag of peas on the sink. "And you didn't do anything wrong last night. Everything you did was perfect." He gripped the kitchen countertop behind him. "I'm not used to . . . I've never had . . . What we did . . ."

He was struggling with the emotion of yesterday, such anger and violence with his father and such tenderness between us. Talk about extreme lows and highs.

I put my hand to his neck and caressed his jaw with my thumb. "What we did was perfect. What we have could be perfect, CJ. No matter what your old man said to you, you're safe here with me. And you deserve to be happy."

His eyes met mine, dark wells of insecurity. "It scares the hell outta me."

I pulled us together and he did that holding-tight hug thing again, and I might have held him just as hard.

Then someone cleared their throat behind us.

CJ pushed me away, startled with jarring speed, and darted through the kitchen to the laundry, heading for the back door. I tried to grab for his arm, but he was too fast.

"CJ, wait," Pops called out.

CJ was fumbling with the deadbolt on the back door, trying to escape. I dashed after him and put my hand on the door. "It's okay," I whispered.

He was agitated and scared to death; his shaking fingers couldn't get the lock open.

"Clinton," I murmured. "It's okay."

He shot me a look, and he was so close but somehow so distant.

"CJ," Pops said from the kitchen doorway. "'S okay, son. I've always known. Since you were fourteen, anyways." He took a few rattled breaths. "I'm sorry I never said nothing before now. I shouldn't have let you carry the weight of it for so long."

All the fight, the struggle, left CJ's body like the air from a balloon, and he sagged. He leaned his head against the back door, his hands still on the lock, and swallowed hard, but when he tried to breathe, it came out as a sob.

Then Pops was there and CJ turned and fell into his arms, and Pops held him as he cried. "I'm sorry," he mumbled, over and over.

"No need to be sorry," Pops reassured gently. He pulled back, his gnarled hands on CJ's arms. "There's no apologies, and there's no shame. You like this boy, and I'm pretty sure he likes you, so you grab it with both hands and don't let go, you hear me?"

CJ started to cry again, his banged-up face a crumpled mess. "Nobody can know."

Pops frowned. "Come sit with me. Let's talk."

CJ went willingly and I stood there, my heart in my mouth. "I'll make breakfast," I said, to no one in particular, but making myself busy so they had some privacy seemed like a good idea.

I tried not to listen, and mostly all I could hear was the gentle murmur of their voices. It helped that I boiled the kettle a few times so it would whistle loudly and I couldn't hear, and the bacon sizzled and the microwave helped in drowning out their conversation. By the time I'd plated up bacon, eggs, toast, and cups of tea, they must have talked for twenty minutes.

I carried the laden tray in and slid it on the dining table. They both sat on the sofa. CJ still looked sad but Pops gave me a reassuring smile. "Something smells good."

"Breakfast, if you're ready," I said. "I'll just grab the milk."

I took the milk from the fridge, and when I went back to the table, CJ was standing near one of the dining chairs. He still looked ready to bolt or like he was about to collapse in a heap. Maybe both. I gave him a reassuring smile and put the milk in the middle of the table. "For your tea, Pops." I put a cup of hot tea in front of him, and when I looked up, CJ was staring at me.

His words were choked up. "Thank you."

I met his gaze, unwavering. "Anytime."

We ate in silence, and I tried not to keep watching CJ. But with his banged-up face, and his so-sad expression, it was hard not to. But he was hungrier than he'd probably realised, because he cleaned up everything I cooked. "Want something else?" I asked. "I can make more toast."

He leaned back and sighed. "Nah. I'm good, thanks."

Pops sipped his tea and smiled. "It was very good, thank you, chef."

I chuckled. "Dunno about chef. And breakfast is about all I'm good for cooking, I'm afraid."

"Well, I'm very grateful," Pops said. He then looked between CJ and me. "So, how long've you been seeing each other?"

CJ blanched. "Pops, I . . ."

"You're not ready to talk about it, I get it," Pops said. "Like I said, CJ, it don't bother me none. But I seen the way you look at him, and you'd smile every time you talked of him, which was often." Pops gave me a smile and CJ blushed. "You'd spent more time in town recently, then when you knew your way around his kitchen last night, I figured you'd been here a time or two."

CJ let his head fall down. "I tried to keep it a secret."

"So, it's been a little while then?" Pops asked again.

CJ didn't answer, so I did. "Unofficially, a few weeks. Officially, since last night. Clinton's now no longer on probation, so . . ."

Pops looked to CJ. "You're not?"

"Ended midnight last night," he mumbled.

"Well, that is good news!" Pops smiled widely. "And Clinton? Didn't think you liked being called Clinton?"

"I don't," he shot back quickly.

"Only from me," I added, trying not to smile.

CJ shot to his feet, a mortified look on his face. "I'm gonna grab a shower. Leave breakfast and I'll wash up after." He made a quick escape to the bathroom.

A second later, we heard the shower start and Pops sighed and tried to smile but it was watery at best. "Did I push him too hard? I just want him to know it's okay."

"What you said was perfect. Just give him time. In twenty-four hours, he's passed his rider course, got his rider's licence, had a terrible fight with his father, got kicked out of his home, and came out of the closet to you." I blew a breath out through puffed cheeks. "It's no wonder he's a bit lost right now. But he has you, and your support will mean everything to him. When he's processed everything and gets his head around it all, he'll appreciate you even more."

Pops turned his empty teacup by the handle. "He's a good boy. Always has been. He never was like the rest of 'em."

"Because he was raised by you, not his father."

He shrugged. "Maybe." Then he looked at me. "I'm glad he has you."

That made me smile. "I hope he is too. I mean, I hope he wants to be with me too. He has a lot going on right now and I don't want him to feel pressured, you know? Because you're more than welcome to stay here, even if he decides he doesn't want to be with me. I don't want him to think he's obligated."

"I don't think so," he replied kindly. "CJ never stood for anyone who did the wrong thing by him."

"I won't hurt him."

He met my gaze. "No, I don't think you would."

It made me smile. "But he'd be really pissed if he knew we were talking about him."

Pops chuckled, a throaty rasp. "Oh boy, would he ever."

We were silent for a moment. I wondered how I could say this without showing my cards, but I needed him to know. "He really is kinda great," I said, ignoring how my cheeks heated.

Pops knew exactly what I was saying without directly saying it. I was head over heels for CJ. I couldn't deny it anymore. He smiled widely, patted my hand, and took his plate to the kitchen.

"Leave these, I'll take care of them," I said, loading up the tray. "How about we have another cup of tea, then we can get your clothes you wore last night into the washing machine and dryer. If those clothes you're wearing were any bigger on you, we'd have to send out a search party for you."

He gave me a warm, kind smile. "That sounds real good."

I looked over his face. "How are you feeling? Anything hurt? Your neck looked a little red last night."

He waved me off. "Don't worry about me. I'm fine. I actually breathe better without a wood fire. I mean, the warmth of our old fire was good, but the dust and smoke did me no favours." But then he sighed and leaned against the kitchen counter. "I was scared for CJ last night. They fought pretty hard. I mean, they've fought before, but not like that. It was scary as hell. I thought he was gonna kill him."

I don't know who he meant by *he* or *him*. I didn't want to find out. "For what it's worth, I'm glad you both left."

"Me too."

I fixed us another cup of tea each and we'd just taken our first sips when CJ stood in the doorway. He was wearing the jogger pants I'd loaned him and the shirt he'd been wearing last night. He looked brighter, his hair neatly combed, but his eye was still swollen. He gave a bit of a smile. "What's going on?"

"Tea. Want one?" I asked.

He nodded and walked in. "I can get it." He poured himself another cup, turned to face us, and sipped it.

"How's your eye?" I asked.

"Bit sore."

"Want a Panadol?"

He made a face. "Maybe later."

Pops took a long mouthful of his tea and swallowed it, then put his cup on the bench. "I'll just use the bathroom," he said, rushing out of the kitchen as fast as he could in a not-so-subtle move to leave us alone.

CJ sighed. "Not obvious at all, Pops," he called out.

I smiled behind my tea. "He's the sweetest man."

"He is." We stared at each other for a moment. "Noah—"

"CJ, look . . ." We spoke at the same time. "Please, let me say this first."

He nodded for me to continue.

"I need you to know you and Pops are welcome to stay here, regardless of what happens between us."

He opened his mouth but closed it again and put his cup down. He had that scared look about him again that, quite frankly, gutted me.

"Clinton," I whispered, putting my hand to his face. "I want there to be an us, but if you feel overwhelmed right now and need some space, I'll understand."

He leaned into my palm, his eyes closed. "I am overwhelmed. Can't lie. It's been a shit twenty-four hours." He looked at me then, and I could see the white of his eye was red under the swelling. "But it's been pretty damn good too. Noah, I don't think I can do this without you."

My heart surged and I leaned in and kissed him softly. The touch of his lips against mine felt like heaven.

He smiled, though it was twinged with sadness. "And I know we can stay here for a day or two, no matter what happens between us, because you've told me ten times."

I gently touched the red mark on his cheekbone. "I needed you to know."

"I want there to be an us too," he whispered. "Noah, last night was . . ." He bit his bottom lip and blushed.

"Last night was what?" I prompted.

His eyes shot to mine. "The best night of my life. What we did, what you did to me, I've never experienced anything like that."

I leaned against him, pressing him against the sink, and slid my arms around his lower back. "Me either. Not with anyone but you."

This seemed to please him; his smile was genuine. I thought he was going to kiss me, but he put his forehead on my shoulder and slowly but surely buried his face in my neck. He breathed in deep and tightened his arms around me. God, he just loved being held. It was as heart-wrenching as it was beautiful.

"Your Pops knows about us," I whispered.

"I know."

"And he still loves you."

His hold on me tightened. "I know." He let out a shuddered breath. "I never thought that'd happen. I never thought any of this could happen."

I pulled back a little and kissed him softly on the lips, then on his swollen eye. "You deserve good things."

Pops shuffled into the room and CJ froze and pushed me away, his instincts kicking in. "Here's my clothes that—" He stopped. "Oh, sorry." Then he looked at the distance now between CJ and me, tucked his laundry under one arm, and took CJ's arm with his free hand and dragged CJ toward me until we were touching. "As you were, soldier."

I barked out a laugh and slid my arm around CJ. He blushed a thousand shades of embarrassed and ducked his head, and I pulled him in for a proper hug, the kind he couldn't resist. He mumbled something into my chest and

Pops chuckled as he walked into the laundry. "Want me to set this going?" he asked. "Oh. Your machine's a lot newer than ours."

"I can do it. Just throw them in the machine and I'll sort it out." I kissed the side of CJ's head. "Wanna grab your clothes and we'll get 'em washed and dried."

He pulled back, somewhat reluctantly. "It's just my jeans and underclothes, really. Oh, and this shirt."

"Take it off and I'll wash it," I suggested.

CJ shot a horrified look to Pops, who was walking back through the kitchen. "Oh, CJ," Pops said. "I'm gonna presume it ain't nothing he hasn't seen before, since you didn't sleep on the couch last night."

CJ's shoulders sagged. "Can we just go back to you not knowing?"

Pops just laughed and continued walking through, back to the lounge room.

"It'll be okay," I said softly. It might be fine to joke about it one day, but it was probably all still a bit too new and real. "You'll get used to it."

He grumbled and, lifting from the hem first, pulled his shirt off. He held it out for me, so I took it but not before I looked him over. I hadn't seen him shirtless in the daylight before. I ran my hand over his chest up to his neck and sighed. "You're really hot," I whispered.

He snorted like it was a ridiculous notion.

Then I noticed those small circular scars on his arm. I traced one with my finger, and CJ frowned. "My dad . . ."

I nodded slowly. "I figured."

"I was eight when he did this one," he whispered, pointing to one scar. "Twelve when he did this one."

My heart fell to my stomach, and I lifted his arm and

pressed my lips to the scar, then another on his lips. "You're beautiful."

He looked at me, a dozen conflicting emotions in his eyes, but before he could disagree, I went to the laundry. "Grab me your jeans and I'll set the wash going."

We started the laundry and I tossed him a clean shirt and a hoodie from my wardrobe, then we cleaned up the kitchen while Pops watched some telly. Then I had an idea. "How about we head down to the supermarket. We'll cook up a feast for dinner."

"Yeah, I need to buy us a toothbrush each," CJ said. "We literally left with nothing. Pops, do you need anything else?"

"Some decent daytime TV on a Sunday," he replied.

I remembered CJ telling me Pops liked his soaps. "Do you watch *Young and the Restless?*"

Pops eyed me cautiously. "Yeah?"

I picked up the remote. "I have cable. And there are dedicated channels for American soap shows. *Young and the Restless* marathons, every weekend."

Pops whole face lit up. "All day?"

I laughed and found the channel for him, then handed him the remote. "Oh God," CJ mumbled. "You'll never get control of your TV again."

As it turned out, after CJ and I made a trip to the supermarket, we spent the afternoon lazing about watching episode after episode of *Young and the Restless* with Pops. CJ sat on the sofa next to him and I sat on the floor, resting between CJ's legs, and we laughed and ate snacks, and the show was as addictive as it was silly. Later, we cooked a huge stew for dinner, and Pops went to bed early, claiming he was tired, but it was pretty obvious just a ruse to give us some alone time.

"I ain't seen Pops smile so much," CJ said quietly. "And he's breathing a bit better. Must look at getting a gas heater when we go home."

I pulled him against me so he was lying back on me while we watched Arnie's *Conan the Barbarian*. I'd kiss his temple every so often, and he'd squeeze my hand in his. When I finally took him to bed, I kissed down every inch of his body, bringing him to climax with a pleasure he'd never known. Another first for his list of many. And when he settled into sleep, he held me so tight like he was scared I'd disappear.

I kissed him and told I wasn't going anywhere. Not now, not ever.

———

THE NEXT MORNING, when I walked into the kitchen ready for work, I was met with a smiling Pops and CJ and a cup of tea and plate of toast. CJ was talking of helping out by mowing the lawn this morning and what we could have for dinner when I got home, and it was strangely domestic and equally wonderful, and I drove to work with a smile plastered on my face.

Until I walked into my office and was met with Terrell and two uniformed police officers, and everything came to a screeching halt. They didn't even have to speak; somehow I already knew.

"They're looking for Clinton Davis," Terrell said.

I could feel the blood drain from my face. "Why?"

"There's been an incident," one of the officers said. "And we can't find him."

"What kind of incident?"

The other cop tilted his head and narrowed his eyes.

"Do you know where Mr Davis is? He was one of your parolees up until this weekend, correct?"

"Yes, that's correct. His probation period ended midnight Saturday." I swallowed hard. "And yes, I know where he is. And Pops—I mean, Ronnie Davis. I know where they both are." The three of them stared at me and I knew I couldn't leave it at that. "If his father wants to know where they went, I'd rather he not find out. He has a long history of violence and abuse and—"

"Mr Huxley," the first officer said. "Dwayne Davis is dead. His son, Clinton Davis, is a person of interest."

CHAPTER TWENTY

CJ

AFTER THE WEEKEND we'd had, doing something normal like mowing the lawn felt good. I still couldn't really get my head around everything, and Noah said it would probably take some time.

I didn't doubt that. Not one bit.

I wondered if I would ever get used to the fact Pops knew I was gay, let alone hanging out with him and my boyfriend like we'd done yesterday. If this is my new normal, I wouldn't complain, but it was going to take some getting used to.

I wasn't looking forward to facing my father tomorrow. He'd probably just go back to how things used to be. No apologies, no acknowledgement, and just expect me to do the same.

I didn't want to. I didn't want to go back to walking on eggs shells, wondering how bad his next outburst would be. I didn't want to live like that anymore. I didn't want him to hurt Pops anymore.

As I mowed neat lines into Noah's front lawn, I made a decision: if he wanted us back under his roof, things would need to be different. There would be rules, manners, and he could pay me back for the mower he stole. And if he told me tomorrow that we ain't welcome back, then Pops and I would figure something else out. We would find somewhere else; we'd get by. We always did.

When I was almost finished, Noah's car pulled into the driveway. I cut the engine, wondering what on earth he was doing home so early, wondering what he forgot to take with him, when a cop car pulled up behind him. And then I saw Noah's face and I knew something was really wrong.

I stared at him, trying to calm my heart, trying not to run. "Noah, what is it?"

By now, two cops stood beside him. "CJ, we should go inside," Noah said.

I nodded numbly—I knew this had to be bad—but somehow my feet wouldn't move. Noah walked over to me with one hand out, like I was a frightened horse, like he could tell I was about to turn and run. He put his hand on my arm. "Come inside with me." He led me inside. "Pops?" he called out.

When Pops saw me and Noah come into the kitchen and the two cops behind us, he slowly got to his feet. I'd imagine the look on his face mirrored mine.

"We have some bad news for you," one cop said. "You might want to sit down."

We sat woodenly, mechanically, and stared up at the two cops in front of us. Noah sat beside me and held my hand.

"There was a fire," the cop said. "It was called in by a neighbouring property, but by the time the fire brigade arrived, it was too late. The house couldn't be saved. They found a body. Dental records confirm the deceased was your father."

I blinked.

Everything went hot and cold and Noah's hand in mine was the only thing that kept me from losing the plot.

"Where were you on Saturday night?" the other cop asked.

I looked at Noah. He squeezed my hand. "It's okay. Tell them the truth. I've already told them what I know."

I swallowed hard. "I was here in the afternoon. With Noah. Then Pops called me, saying my dad was out of control. Noah drove me home."

One cop wrote in his notepad, the other asked, "What time?"

I shrugged. "Dunno. It was getting dark. Maybe five or six."

"What happened when you arrived at the house?"

"I fought with him, my father," I said weakly. I waved my hand to my black eye. "He did this. We fought for a while. He got a few good shots on me, and I was a bit dazed." I looked at Pops. "He held Pops against the wall by his neck and I ran at him and knocked him on his arse. I punched him and we fought some more. I kneed him in the balls. I didn't mean to, but it was the only thing that stopped him." My mouth was so dry, I couldn't even swallow. "He told us to get out of his house, so we did. Pops grabbed his medication and we walked out. With nothing else. We walked to my work, where my motorbike was, then rode here to Noah's."

"Where is your work?"

"Mr Barese's mechanic shop, in Ten Mile Creek." I shot Noah a look. "Oh God, Mr Barese. He must be worried sick."

The cop looked at me like something didn't make sense. "What time did you arrive here, at Mr Huxley's?"

I shrugged. "Not sure. After midnight, maybe one o'clock."

"How long did it take you to walk?" the cop pressed. "That's a lot of time in between."

"Took a while," Pops answered defensively. "It was raining, pitch black, and I can't walk too fast."

"Pops don't breathe too good when he's cold. I wanted to take him to hospital but he wouldn't let me." I took a second to try and make sense of what they were saying. "Is the house really gone?"

"I'm afraid so. I don't think anything will be salvageable."

I did some deep breathing, trying not to freak out, and Noah kept squeezing my hand. I looked up at the cops. "Do you think I had something to do with it?"

"You don't seem too upset at the news of your father," the first cop said.

"I hate him," I replied. "Wished every day he'd go back to jail, but I never wished him dead."

"If he did this to you," the cop with the notepad said, indicating to my face, "why didn't you report him? He would've been picked up and put away."

"And what?" I asked rhetorically. "Make him so mad that the next time he sees me, he belts the ever-loving shit outta me? Or kills me? You've never lived with a violent alcoholic, have you?"

The cop didn't answer. I didn't expect him to.

I glared at him. "Don't blame the victim for just tryin' to survive." My eyes burned, and as much as I didn't want to cry, I didn't seem able to stop it. I turned to Pops. "We'll be okay, won't we?"

His chin wobbled and his teary eyes met mine. "Course we will. You and me, we've always been okay."

His breathing was rougher than normal. "Need your medication?"

He shook his head, but Noah was already on his feet. "I'll get it." He came back a second later with his pills and a glass of water while the cops just stood and watched.

I looked up at them. "Can we go to the house?"

"It'll be cordoned off as a crime scene until cause of death is determined." The cop put his notepad away. "You can go look from the road, but you won't be allowed to touch anything."

"Mr Barese'll be so worried. I should call him."

"We spoke to Mr Barese earlier. He was concerned when we said we weren't able to contact you. He spoke very highly of you, Clinton," the cop said. "But he didn't have much time for your father."

I almost snorted. "Because my father wasn't a nice person."

The first cop nodded slowly. "Will you be willing to come to the police station to make an official statement?"

"Yeah, of course."

He turned to Pops. "You as well, Mr Davis?"

"Yes. Anything you need."

Then it was Noah's turn. "Mr Huxley?"

"Yes, no problem. We'll follow you directly, yes?"

They nodded and left, and the three of us sat there and stared at each other, not knowing what to say. Noah eventually took out his phone and handed it to me. "Call Mr Barese. He'll want to hear from you."

I nodded and robotically dialled the number. "Hello?"

"Mr Barese—"

"CJ? Oh my God, son, where are you? Are you okay? And Pops? We've been so worried!"

"I'm okay."

His voice turned soft. "Have you heard the news?"

"Yeah, I heard." I swallowed hard. "Not sure I'll be in tomorrow, but I'll come see you sometime soon, okay? Just wanted to let you know me and Pops are okay."

"Yes, yes. You take as much time as you need. Thank you for calling me. Mrs Barese will be so relieved."

It made my heart ache even more. "Thank you."

NUMB. Shock. Disbelief.

Words that hadn't meant much to me until that moment. I had no idea, no idea at all, at the weight they would carry.

I was also sorry. Sorry my father was dead. I never wished death on anyone, and I was sorry the last time I'd seen him had been a fight. I was sorry things would be forever unresolved.

I was sorry that part of me, deep down, unbidden and without mercy, was glad that he was gone.

We each had to go into separate rooms, and each of us was questioned. Noah had told me to tell the truth, so I did.

They asked me what my relationship to Noah was, and I knew that he was in trouble at work. But I wouldn't lie; he'd told me not to. "He's my boyfriend."

"How long have you been together?"

So I told the truth. "Officially, since midnight Saturday. When I weren't on parole no more. It was his stupid rule."

The cop nodded and wrote something down, then kept asking more questions about timelines and what happened, and I told them that my father and I fought many times since he got out of jail. Mostly over him smoking in the house and selling my things for cash to buy alcohol with, and how I was done taking shit from him. I'd taken it my whole life, and I refused to take one more hit.

When he was done, he asked me to sign the bottom of the statement I'd just given. I looked at the pages of words and put the pen down. Now, before Noah, I'd never known to do this, I'd never had the courage to ask. I would have just signed it blindly. "I can't read too good, so could you please have someone else read it to me?"

The cop nodded, disappeared, and came back with a woman who read it, word for word, back to me. I thanked her, she gave me a smile, and I signed the bottom of each page. I was told, basically, not to leave town and was shown back to the waiting room.

Pops and Noah were already there, and Noah stood when he saw me. "How'd you go?" he asked me sadly.

I nodded. "Okay. You?"

"Yeah, okay." He rubbed my arm. "I asked them if you wanted to see the house, if they could take us. They said we can follow them up, but only if you want."

I nodded. "Yeah. I want to see it."

So, that's what we did. Noah drove, following the cop car up to Ten Mile Creek. No one spoke, but Noah held my hand over the centre console. Pops was quiet in the backseat. It was as though it wasn't real. Like everything the police had said was a joke and we'd drive down Davis Road and the house'd still be there, and my father'd have his arse planted in Pops' recliner and yelling about getting his dinner ready.

Only when we did turn down Davis Road, it became very real.

There was a fire truck and a white police van and police 'do not cross' tape across the front fence. And blackened, smouldering remains of what used to be our house.

"Crime Scene Investigation," Noah said, nodding to the writing on the van.

I assumed the two people in white overalls belonged with that. There were also two firemen with clipboards standing near the shed, talking and pointing to the fire-damaged wall closest to the house. I was surprised it was still standing, but maybe from the way they were looking and pointing at it, making angle gestures with their hands, it wouldn't be there for long.

"Someone should tell 'em the shed's leaned like that forever," I said quietly.

Noah gave me a sad smile but turned to look back at what was left of the house. "Jesus Christ."

Pops opened his door and climbed out, so I joined him. We watched the uniform cops walk over to their colleagues in the white overalls. One of them spared us a look and I shook my head. "Can you believe they think I did this?" I asked. "Guilty before proven innocent."

Noah was now beside me. "We have nothing to hide. You had nothing to do with this."

"Yeah well, to them I'm just a Davis. From this house, down this fucking road. Davis Row. Don't think we don't know what the cops call it. It's been Davis Row since before I was born, and I'm just another piece of shit on their shoe."

Pops frowned at me. "We had some good times in this house, didn't we? You and me? It wasn't all bad was it?"

Oh God, he thought I was insulting him. The look on his face was devastated, and I couldn't bear it. I put my arms around him. "Of course we did. You and me did real good. Had the best times here. You did a real good job looking after me. I wouldn't be alive if it weren't for you, Pops. And that's the truth."

"We've got nothing," he said, waving his hand at the cordoned-off, burned-down house. "We left with nothing."

"We'll be okay, Pops. You and me, we've always been okay. We'll find a way."

Pops sniffled, his breathing a little laboured. "And Noah."

I looked at Noah then, who was watching us. He shrugged one shoulder. "If you'll have me."

If I'll have him? "If I'll have you? I already said I can't do this without you. Noah . . ."

He walked over and put his arm around me, pulling me in for a side-on hug. "You have a home with me for as long as you want it. My house's kinda small, but it's yours. And we'll work out getting some clothes and personal belongings. You'll both be okay. I promise."

The three of us stood there, staring at the charcoal remains of the house for I don't know how long. It was so hard to get my head around. "My father died in there," I whispered.

Noah rubbed my back. "It's hard to believe, isn't it?"

"Yeah."

Pops frowned. "Death ain't ever easy. I'm sorry he went that way."

I nodded because I understood exactly. Sorry he went this way, but not all too sorry he was gone. "I am too."

Noah was patient and never asked if we were done or ready to leave; he never hurried us along. He just waited and offered a kind smile every time I looked at him. There was something in his eyes, though, something that told me he understood.

Another car came down the road and my heart squeezed when I saw that it was Mr Barese's car. He pulled up, got out, and walked straight over. He never even paused, not even for a second. He just opened his arms and hugged me. "Oh, my boy, I'm so sorry." His voice was gruff and warm. "The police came to see me. I didn't know where you were. Maria and I have been so worried. I saw you drive past, so I locked the shop up to come see you."

I pulled back and wiped my face, careful of my eye. "Sorry. We've been staying with Noah."

Mr Barese turned to him, then hugged him too. "Thank you for looking out for him."

Noah just smiled and watched on fondly as Mr Barese then hugged Pops. Only after he made sure we were okay— he fussed over my beat-up face a bit—did he then stare at the charred remains of the house in disbelief. He invited us for dinner any time we wanted, and he told me to take as much time as I needed. Funnily enough, I'd reckon keeping busy at work was probably what I needed more than not. He put his big hand on my shoulder like he knew exactly what I'd say.

Eventually, Mr Barese left us to it, and we made the quiet trip back to Noah's. Home, I guess. For now or for how long, I didn't know. When Pops was settled on the sofa in front of the heater and TV with a cup of tea, Noah followed me into the kitchen and took me in a crushing embrace.

Fierce, strong, safe, and everything—*everything*—I needed. I melted against him and could literally feel him mending the broken pieces of my heart, putting me back together again.

I didn't ever want to let him go.

"I'm so sorry," he whispered.

"I don't know how to feel," I admitted quietly.

"You don't have to. It'll change. From every hour to every day, how you feel will be different. Anger, disappointment, betrayal, loss, relief. There's no right or wrong way to grieve, Clinton."

My God, he got it. Described it better than I ever could. I nodded against his neck. "He was such a mean bastard, but he was my dad, ya know?"

He kissed the side of my head. "Yeah, I know."

I still wasn't ready to let him go. "This feels so good," I murmured into his shirt. "Thank you."

He held me just that little bit tighter. "Anytime."

"Do you think the police will know I didn't do it?"

"They'll have to. Their forensic people will work out when and how he died, and you'll be cleared."

"You believe that?"

"I have to. I can't imagine anything else." He sighed. "I just found you. I can't lose you. And you're a *good* man, CJ. They'll see that. Everyone who knows you says it." He pulled back so he could look me in the face. "They'll see that the whole Davis Row stereotype is wrong. They'll see *they* were wrong."

"And if they don't?" I couldn't shake the feeling. "I've put up with it all my life."

He cupped his hand to my cheek. "I'll make them see." He kissed me softly. "I'm sorry about your dad."

I sighed, and my heart felt too heavy for my chest. "You get it, don't you? You know what this feels like?"

He nodded once and his face fell. "Yeah, I do. It won't be easy, CJ. But we'll get through this."

He just included himself right along with me, no questions asked, like a buoy in my turbulent sea.

With his hands still to my face, he kissed my forehead. "Six months after we buried my parents, I buried my sister. So I get it, Clinton. I get what you're feeling. You can tell me anything. There'll be days where you'll want to punch something and days you'll want to cry, I get that. And some days you'll need to be around people and days when you'll need some space, and I'll understand that too." He put his hands to my jaw, cupping my face. "But you're not alone."

Tears burned my eyes and one escaped. "Thank you."

He kissed me sweetly, then hugged me like he knew it was what I needed. "Anytime."

We stayed like that, just standing in his kitchen with the hideous lino, with our arms around each other, until Pops started to snore from the living room. I felt Noah's quiet chuckle through his chest, and even then I didn't want to pull away. "He's had a tiring day," I murmured, giving him a squeeze.

Noah rubbed my back. "So have you."

"You missed work today," I said.

"I told them I was taking a day's leave. I'll need to go in tomorrow."

"Will you get into trouble?" I asked. "You know, because of me. Because of us."

He took a second to answer. I almost pulled out of his arms but he held me close. "I don't think so. I might have to explain, but you're no longer one of my cases and we weren't technically official before then."

"Well, we kinda were. I told the cops we weren't together until midnight when your rules ran out. Dunno if they believed me."

He kissed my forehead with smiling lips. "I said the same. Look, Clinton," he said, pulling back this time and looking me right in the eyes. "If they have a problem with it, I'll find something else."

I blinked. "You'd do that?"

"For you, yes, I would." He kissed me again and Pops snored so loud he woke himself up with a snort and a cough.

I almost smiled. It had been such a long, exhausting day, I'd lost track of time. "Want some dinner, Pops?" I called out.

"Mm. Hmph." He coughed again. "Yeah, I'm awake."

Noah chuckled. "How about toasted cheese sandwiches and tomato soup?"

I was reluctant to let him go, but I did. "Sounds perfect."

"You're on toastie duty. I'm on soup." Then he added, quietly, just for me, "And we can have an early night, yeah?"

I nodded. "Yes, please."

He kissed my forehead and busied himself with making tomato soup so I started on the toasted sandwiches, and a minute later, Pops came into the kitchen. He would quite often sit in the kitchen and chat with me while I made dinner, and I was glad today was no different.

The normalcy, especially now it included Noah, felt really good.

Things were so different now. Everything was different now.

It still didn't feel real.

I had so much to think about, so much to get in order. So much I had no clue about.

"You okay, CJ?" Pops asked. We'd finished dinner and I must have got lost in my head.

"Yeah, just thinking." I pushed my plate away. "What do you reckon'll happen? To me, to the house, to Dad . . . I mean, his body?"

Pops frowned, and it was Noah who answered. "The coroner will give their findings to the police and we can probably expect to hear from them in a day or two. They might contact you tomorrow, just to check in on you both.

Or they might not. They can't do anything to you without evidence, so you'll have a day or two, at least, before they'll process all that." His gaze intensified. "CJ, you did nothing wrong."

I sighed. "We fought beforehand, and I told the cops I hated him. Doesn't look good for me." I scrubbed my hand over my face and my shiner smarted. "Shit."

"Clinton," Noah said gently. "You did nothing wrong. You have witnesses to him hitting you before, so the fight is explainable. It's a tragedy that your father died. A horrible, tragic accident. You're not to blame."

Pops nodded. "Listen to him, CJ. He's a smart one."

I looked at Pops then. "Did he have a will?"

Pops shook his head. "I don't know. I doubt it."

I sighed. "Figured as much. Just means more legal fees, don't it? I can't afford legal fees. Don't even know how we'll pay for the funeral. Oh God, the funeral . . ."

Noah reached over and took my hand. "Don't worry about any of that yet. We'll cross that bridge when we get to it."

My eyes met his. "We'll?"

"Yes, *we* will." He nodded and squeezed my hand, then without another word, he collected the plates off the table.

God, yesterday my biggest concern was showing affection in front of Pops, and now, after the day we'd had, that seemed irrelevant.

Pops stood up and put his hand on my shoulder. "Thank you, both, for dinner. And for being so good today. It hasn't been easy." Noah stood in the doorway wiping his hands on a tea towel. "And Noah, thank you for being so good to my boy."

"Oh." Noah blushed. "You're welcome."

Pops squeezed my shoulder. "But I have to turn in, if

that's okay. I'm beat. I promise I'll be on dish duty after breakfast."

I gave him a smile. "Night, Pops."

"Sleep well, CJ," Pops said. "We'll deal with tomorrow when it comes, okay?"

I watched him walk slowly to his room, and when his door latched closed, Noah walked over and tilted my head back so he could kiss me. "Did you want to watch a movie? Or did you want to just go to bed?"

I hummed. That was a no contest. "Bed."

He smiled. "I'll wash up. You get ready for bed."

"You sure?"

He leaned down and kissed me. "Absolutely."

It was remarkable to me how he knew when to push and when to pull back. Like he somehow knew when I would freak out or when I needed to lean on him. Right now, I was in a headspace where I needed time to think but I wanted those goddamn hugs and hands that healed me from the inside out.

I needed both and he knew it.

I took my time in the bathroom and I crawled into Noah's bed, breathing in the smell of him, of us. It was comforting and made my heart swell in a way that was new and wonderful. Noah wasn't far behind me. He shut the door, turned the light off, stripped right there, and slid in beside me. Without hesitating, he wrapped me up in his arms and I snuggled right in. I buried my face in his neck and settled flush against him.

He stroked my hair and kissed the top of my head. "Tell me what you need," he murmured.

"This. You." He could obviously feel my body's reaction; I was getting hard. "I don't know."

He rubbed my back. "Whatever you want."

"What you did the other night," I mumbled, embarrassed, but desperate for it all the same. "I've never felt that before and I need to feel it again, but I'm not sure if my heart can take it today."

"Oh, Clinton." Noah rolled me over so I was on my back and he was lying on top of me. I spread my legs for him, he settled between my thighs, and he crushed his mouth to mine.

Later, after he got me ready for him and he was inside me, he held me, he rocked me, stared into my eyes, kissing me, adoring me . . . loving me.

I couldn't doubt it. My heart felt like it would burst. After a day of loss and drifting, he anchored me. With my body strung tight, he drew my orgasm from me with every thrust, every kiss, begging for me to come until I gave him what he wanted. As my cock spilt between us, he stilled inside me, crying out as he came. He held me so damn tight and murmured in my ear, "I want to make love to you forever."

And my emotional dam burst, my heart couldn't take anymore, and I cried.

Noah rolled us onto our sides and held me. He never questioned me; he never told me I was being stupid. He just pulled the blankets up over us, rubbed my back, and kissed my forehead, and never, not once, let me go.

When I'd cried myself out, I took a few shuddering breaths, trying to get some control. "Sorry. Don't know what came over me," I whispered, wiping my nose on the back of my hand. "I ain't ever cried like that before. Not that I remember, anyhow."

"Oh, Clinton," he murmured, kissing the top of my head. "Don't ever apologise. You've been through a lot."

"You get it though, don't you?"

He nodded. "Yeah." Then after a stretch of silence, he said, "Can I tell you something?"

"Yeah."

"I wasn't going to. I wasn't sure if it was the right time, you've probably had enough dumped on you for one day. But maybe it's the perfect time. If I'd had someone in my life when my family died, I would have done anything in the world to hear it . . ."

I pulled back so I could see his face. "What is it?"

"I love you." He said it so softly, I'd wondered if I'd heard him right. He put his hand to the side of my face and stared into my eyes. "I love you, Clinton Davis. I know it's only been a few weeks, but it's true. What I feel for you is"—he smiled—"amazing and I want you to know that you're loved. You should know that, today of all days. You're an incredible guy, and I'm so lucky to have met you."

My heart stopped beating. Then it thundered, roared, and took flight. My eyes burned with tears, and I didn't even try to stop them. I nodded because it was all I could do. He was right. I needed to hear that, I needed to know that, and my God, I needed to feel it. He smiled again and pulled me back into his neck and held me, just fucking held me.

It was a minute or two before I could speak. "I ain't ever loved anyone before, so I don't know if that's what this is." I swallowed so I could finish. "But I think I'm in love with you too."

He put his hands to my face and kissed me, and I swear I could taste emotion on his tongue. Then he kissed my cheek, my closed, swollen eyelid, my sore cheek, my forehead, before he tucked me into his neck. And that's right where I stayed until morning.

CHAPTER TWENTY-ONE

NOAH

Four years later

I WAS RUNNING LATE for work. I made a mad dash through the kitchen, grabbed my wallet and keys, and was met by Pops, who stood there with a piece of toast in one hand and a travel mug of tea in the other. "Have a good day," he said with a smile.

His breathing had improved with a change of medication. His general health was stable, and the smile he wore every day now was worth every fight I had with the government to subsidise his medical costs and get better care. And his pension. And CJ's carer's allowance.

"Is CJ at work already?" I asked with a mouthful of toast.

Pops nodded. "Can't keep him away."

I grinned and backed out, pushing the door open with my butt. "See you tonight." He waved me off and I shoved more toast in and headed next door. The roller door was up, and I could hear CJ talking on the phone as I walked in.

I stood at his office door, smiling as he wrote down a name in the appointment book. Yes, he *wrote*. It hadn't been easy, and there had been many *Writing and Reading* workbooks thrown in frustration, but we were getting there. Spending a lazy evening lying on the sofa with him reading to me was one of my favourite ways to unwind. CJ was now at high school level reading and writing, and I couldn't have been prouder.

I looked down at the appointment book, to where he'd written the name *Franklin*, along with *Ford Explorer* and *8 am*. He'd spelt it all perfectly and I could have just about burst. He hung up the phone. "Full service tomorrow." He beamed. "And you'll be late for work if you don't hurry. Sheryl will bust your arse."

"It's your fault. Keeping me busy this morning." I smirked at him, not complaining at all. "I don't get to live next door to my work, unlike some."

It was uncanny how one of the worst things to happen to CJ could turn into the best things. His father dying was a difficult time for him; reconciling the grief and loss he felt for a man he hated and loved in equal measure was a lot to deal with.

The police report had ruled his death as an accident. From where the fire had started and the blood alcohol levels in the autopsy, they believe he fell asleep or passed out with a lit cigarette.

Ironic, CJ had said, that they'd fought so often about him smoking in the house. And CJ quit smoking the day after the funeral. In true CJ form, he did it cold turkey, just made up his mind and stuck to it.

Of course his father had no will and testament, and

after two years of legal to-ing and fro-ing, the land on Davis Road was sold to a local developer. After legal expenses, CJ requested the money be split equally amongst all brothers— true to his nature, CJ was nothing if not fair. He wanted no more or no less than anyone else, even if they were all incarcerated and would probably never see a cent of it.

The town of Ten Mile Creek was thriving again, with the new estate built and plans for more housing, and new plans for two estates down Davis Road. The shop got a facelift, the butcher's reopened, and even a café started up. Mr Barese's mechanics shop got busier and busier, and claiming he was getting too old for it, he offered to sell it to CJ, adjoining house and all.

So, CJ and I joined finances, took out a business loan, and had been the proud owner-operators of a house *and* Davis Mechanical for over a year. CJ had passed his apprenticeship in record time and was a fully qualified mechanic. Even had his car licence now as well. Pops helped out, keeping the office tidy and washing windscreens for the people who got fuel. He loved a chat, and they kept that old-fashioned service that Mr Barese had built the business on.

I kept my job as a parole officer. I got a reprimand after they discovered I had officially begun a relationship with a parolee the day he was no longer a parolee. I was pretty sure they knew, unofficially it began before that, but our stories had matched and there wasn't much else they could do.

And anyway, I was bloody good at my job. I had a one hundred per cent positive strike rate with my case files; not one went back to prison. I went above and beyond, getting them extra qualifications, pushing the envelope in getting them scholarships and bursaries for courses, and not taking no for an answer when it came to bureaucrats who tried to dodge responsibility. I'd even had my colleagues follow suit. I knew they only did it just so they didn't look bad compared to me when it came to our employment appraisals, but I didn't care. Our cases were getting a better deal. Last year, our office had the best ratio statistics in the state.

I'd even got a young street kid, who got busted for stealing a car, an apprenticeship with CJ. Her name was Stevie. She was a good, smart kid, who just got dealt a really shitty hand in life. Her parents didn't give a shit, and her teachers were happiest when she skipped school.

Her story was almost identical to CJ's, except whereas he had Pops, she had no one.

Until her case landed on my desk, and I got a sense of déjà vu reading her file. She was alone and scared, angry, and had a chip on her shoulder the size of a small country. Just like CJ used to be. And apparently, with little more than a hammer and a socket wrench, she could break down an engine in less than a day. I made some calls, introduced her to CJ, and watched him become a mentor and she a student in a heartbeat.

"Stevie'll be here soon," CJ said. "And you better get to work."

I nodded. "I'll be home before *The Bold and the Beautiful*."

CJ laughed. "You and Pops, I swear."

"You watch it too, don't lie."

He rolled his eyes but smiled. "Have a good day."

"You too." Then I remembered. "Oh, Gallan and Anthony invited us around for a BBQ this weekend. Told him I'd ask you."

He smiled. "Sure. Sunday's good." Then he pretended to scold me. "Go. To. Work."

"I'm going, I'm going." I grinned like a fool the whole way there. And work was busy but productive. I made house calls and work placement calls to clients and a hundred phone calls for them. I got one guy signed up for his forklift licence, another guy a house-painting gig, and one lady a place in a Retail Baking course at TAFE.

All in all, it was a bloody good day.

But I was keen to get home. I always was. CJ, Pops, and me made an awesome team, and we just worked. I told them they could live with me when their house burned down, for as long or as little as they needed. But we got on so well, them moving out never happened.

I walked inside and found Pops stirring something on the stove that smelt good. "Hey," I greeted him.

"Oh, hi Noah," he said warmly. "CJ's in taking a shower. He was all weird about something, but he wouldn't say so I quit asking."

I frowned. "Was he okay?"

He gave me a smile. "Oh yes. Nothing to be worried about, I'm sure." He looked at the clock. "Time for our soaps soon."

Yep, at five thirty, like religion, we watched *The Bold and the Beautiful*. It was Pops' favourite show, and CJ knew enough about it by association, so I started to catch bits and pieces and that shit is addictive.

I fell into the sofa and Pops sat in his new recliner, and when CJ came out, he was freshly showered, his hair all brushed neat, and he'd shaven like he was going somewhere. "Have you got a hot date tonight?" I joked.

He rolled his eyes and sat next to me, then leaned against me. I put my arm over his chest and he linked our hands. But he was fidgety and distracted. "You okay?" I asked him quietly.

He nodded. Then after a moment, he shook his head. "No." He sat up off me and stood up, then he paced.

He was starting to scare me. "CJ, what is it?"

He stopped and stared at me, then like he made some decision in his head, he said, "I didn't know how to do this, and Stevie suggested I do something fancy. Like a dinner? Or maybe take a drive somewhere pretty." He swallowed hard. "But then I thought, this is us. Right here, this is us, here watching TV with Pops, this is what we do. We don't need nothin' fancy. This is our family right here, right?"

I was confused. "Clinton, baby. What are you talking about?"

"I was tellin' Stevie that family is who you make it. Blood don't always make someone family, and I was telling her how we're a family. Even though we're not really. Not officially anyway. And she said we should be, like make it real. And at first I laughed and asked her if she wanted me to adopt you and she cracked up and said, 'No, silly. Marry him.'"

Oh.

Oh, holy shit.

He went to one knee in front of me. "Noah Huxley. You are the most incredible man I know." He looked like he might very well vomit and he swallowed hard, and my heart skidded to a stop. "When I think of family, I think of Pops, and I think of you. But we're not really a family, and I want us to be. A legal one. So, will you make us into a real family? Will you marry me?"

I stared at him.

He blinked rapidly and looked down at the floor. "Or adopt me. Either works."

I grabbed hold of his face and kissed him, standing up and bringing him to his feet with me. I was laughing and in complete and utter shock, kissing him and laughing some more.

"So is that a yes?" he asked.

I had to wipe my eyes. "Hell yes, that's a yes."

Then I noticed Pops was on his feet next to us. He was grinning and teary, and CJ hugged him too. "Pops, will you be my best man?"

Pops had to sit down, and he cried for an hour straight. We missed *The Bold and The Beautiful* and dinner was ruined, but we didn't care.

Unofficially, we were already a family, in our own way. But now we were going to be a real family. Officially, and forever.

The End

ABOUT THE AUTHOR

N.R. Walker is an Australian author, who loves her genre of gay romance.
She loves writing and spends far too much time doing it, but wouldn't have it any other way.

She is many things: a mother, a wife, a sister, a writer. She has pretty, pretty boys who live in her head, who don't let her sleep at night unless she gives them life with words.

She likes it when they do dirty, dirty things... but likes it even more when they fall in love.

She used to think having people in her head talking to her was weird, until one day she happened across other writers who told her it was normal.

She's been writing ever since...

Contact the author:
nrwalker.net
nrwalker@nrwalker.net

Evolved

Sixty Five Hours

Learning to Feel

His Grandfather's Watch (And The Story of Billy and Hale)

The Twelfth of Never (Blind Faith 3.5)

Twelve Days of Christmas (Sixty Five Hours Christmas)

Best of Both Worlds

Translated Titles:

Fiducia Cieca (Italian translation of Blind Faith)

Attraverso Questi Occhi (Italian translation of Through These Eyes)

Preso alla Sprovvista (Italian translation of Blindside)

Il giorno del Mai (Italian translation of Blind Faith 3.5)

Cuore di Terra Rossa (Italian translation of Red Dirt Heart)

Cuore di Terra Rossa 2 (Italian translation of Red Dirt Heart 2)

Cuore di Terra Rossa 3 (Italian translation of Red Dirt Heart 3)

Cuore di Terra Rossa 4 (Italian translation of Red Dirt Heart 4)

Confiance Aveugle (French translation of Blind Faith)